Praise for Cheryl Mendelson

Love, Work, Children

"Told elegantly, and with great grace and insight."
—Kingston, Massachusetts, *Observer*

"Mendelson returns to the old-fashioned neighborhood on Manhattan's Upper West Side that she depicted so marvelously in *Morningside Heights;* while some familiar characters reappear, they play minor roles, so this can be read as a stand-alone. . . . Readers will empathize with Peter and his family's dilemmas and wonder what's next for the residents of Morningside Heights."   —*Library Journal*

"A deeply satisfying story, told in fluid, elegant prose."   —*Booklist*

"[A] loving inquiry into generational fissures and the bonds that ultimately carry families . . . A deeply intelligent book."
—*Milwaukee Journal Sentinel*

"Mendelson proves she has staying power with this subtly drawn second novel. . . . She has polished an elegant, omniscient prose style modeled on the finest English novelists."   —*Kirkus Reviews*

"Totally satisfying . . . Mendelson has an unsparing but all-forgiving attitude toward her characters, so that they are wonderfully detailed and three-dimensional."   —Nancy Pearl, *The Beat*

Morningside Heights

"[A] rich, romantic novel . . . peopled with emotionally intriguing characters. Mendelson [creates] a stage akin to those of Jane Austen and George Eliot."   —*O: The Oprah Magazine*

LOVE, WORK, CHILDREN

Also by Cheryl Mendelson

Home Comforts

Morningside Heights

LOVE, WORK, CHILDREN

A Novel

Cheryl Mendelson

Random House Trade Paperbacks
New York

2006 Random House Trade Paperback Edition

Copyright © 2005 by Cheryl Mendelson
Reading group guide copyright © 2006 by Random House, Inc.

Published in the United States by Random House Trade Paperbacks,
an imprint of The Random House Publishing Group,
a division of Random House, Inc., New York.

RANDOM HOUSE TRADE PAPERBACKS and colophon are trademarks
of Random House, Inc.
READER'S CIRCLE and colophon are trademarks of Random House, Inc.

Originally published in hardcover in the United States by Random House,
an imprint of The Random House Publishing Group,
a division of Random House, Inc., in 2005.

Library of Congress Cataloging-in-Publication Data
Mendelson, Cheryl.
Love, work, children: a novel / Cheryl Mendelson.
p. cm.
ISBN 978-0-375-76069-3
1. Morningside Heights (New York, N.Y.)—Fiction.   2. Middle-aged men—
Fiction.   3. Midlife crisis—Fiction.   I. Title.
PS3613.E48L68 2005
813'.6—dc22   2004061457

www.thereaderscircle.com

Book design by Mercedes Everett

146119709

For Blanche Neel

PART ONE

CHAPTER 1

Four Forty-four Riverside Drive, a fine old residential building in Morningside Heights, was filled with aging couples whose grown children remained unmarried. The phenomenon was so general that it had begun to be openly talked of. Not so long ago, the Frankls and the Holmeses, whose daughters had been best friends all their lives, had been congratulating themselves on how successfully they had taught their children not to rush into marriage and how this augured well for their ultimate happiness. But now that the children were all around thirty, their restraint began to look like indifference and their unmarried state like a permanent one.

Until now, their sixtyish parents had led placid lives. Peter Frankl was a lawyer who, with his wife, Lesley, lived in one of the building's two penthouses, with forty feet of windows framing sunsets over the Hudson. The Holmeses, Herbert and Ingrid, were both psychotherapists. They had a pleasant corner apartment on the fourth floor, from which, in winter when the trees were bare, they could see a few gleaming inches of the river. Neither the Frankls nor the Holmeses had money worries or health problems; all of them had significant careers except Lesley, who, however, painted contentedly in a home studio and now and then sold a canvas.

Peter Frankl's marriage wasn't all he would have liked. But he had put the children first, ensuring that they grew up in the calm of civil and secure family life, and deemed his marital problems tolerable. The Holmeses, by contrast, had one of those extraordinarily close, warm marriages that succeed through an unlikely amalgam of egoism and altruism, which, although rare and peculiar, is inevitably regarded as ordinary—perhaps because such unions are as boring and offputting to others as they are satisfying to the married pair itself.

The tenderly reared offspring of these couples had grown up to be everything their fathers and mothers could wish for. The children's happiness and safety was the sweetest part of their parents' lives and the rock on which the rest was built. This was true of all of them, but of Peter Frankl especially.

Peter, who had been orphaned when he was twenty, was terrified of loneliness. Loneliness, he knew, was fierce, with claws and fangs, not at all the tame, mild, forlorn thing people pretended it was. His wish for the children to find love was urgent and fearful, therefore, but he saw ominous evidence that, for them, love was not going to come easy.

True, his son, Louis, now in his early thirties, always had girls running after him, but he never seemed to get serious about any of them—not that Peter had ever really liked any that he had seen. Peter shifted from theory to theory about this: maybe there weren't many nice girls out there nowadays, or maybe nice girls didn't like Louis. Sometimes he even wondered how much Louis liked girls. His daughter Susan's problem was even worse. Boys had always ignored her; a real boyfriend had appeared only once or twice in her life, the last time in college. Nonetheless, Peter had felt serious concern about her only when she passed her twenty-sixth birthday with no attachment, and his anxiety increased on each subsequent birthday until, on her twenty-ninth, when Susan had not had a real date for years, it sharpened into something more painful. Peter then became unequivocally unhappy about Susan. Right around then, Louis, too, had been wounded by someone he had been seeing briefly, a serious girl who was studying history. She went out with Louis three or four times, then told him that he was just not her type. Peter was delighted that Louis had pursued someone like her and was not surprised that she did not pursue Louis. Whatever the reasons, both his children now seemed to him lonely and troubled, settling permanently into a scattered, dry existence devoid of the intimate comforts of family life. Peter could no longer say to himself, as he always had before, that he didn't really mind his own disappointments—not as long as the children were happy. There were now times when, adding their disappointments to his own, he felt that life had mistreated him.

Both Susan and Louis were good-looking, and Louis was tall, incomprehensibly so, given the merely average height of his parents; but in temperament and tastes the two were startlingly different. Louis, in his father's opinion, was his sister's inferior in the personal qualities that favored love—empathy, warmth, loyalty, altruism—despite the fact that he had so many girlfriends and Susan had no boyfriends. Susan had all those virtues, but only a few intimates ever saw much of them. With strangers, she often had a grave manner that made her come across as somewhat older than she was, and her conversation got stilted and bookish. Sometimes even her adoring father felt that something was a little off in Susan. As she got older, he more and more often wondered whether she hadn't turned into a bit of a nebbish.

Susan was working for her PhD in musicology at Columbia, and her conversation was obscure with Renaissance musical arcana. Peter admired and encouraged her plans for a scholarly career and thought her brilliant, sure of professional, if not personal, success. She spent hours practicing her piano, pursuing her studies, and playing endless games of solitaire in the little apartment Peter had bought her on 114th Street a couple of years ago, when, at twenty-six, she insisted that she was too old to live at home.

Louis had had his own place on the East Side until he gave it up to return to school, but he had no scholarly tastes. He never read a book and never spent a minute indoors if he could avoid it. He had dates and played sports and went to parties with friends who were as unthinking as he and generally even richer. He was finishing an MBA at Harvard, where he had made a respectable record with surprisingly little effort, considering that the program was famously geared to grinds; he would undoubtedly line up a high-paying job in finance when he graduated—a plan his mother approved and his father did not. Louis had brains, Peter thought, if he'd only use them. Why would a boy with all his options, all his privileges and connections, go into finance? Peter, who admired scholars, artists, and philosophers, and regretted having settled for the law, which was at least better than finance, found it baffling.

The senior members of the Frankl family never socialized with those of the Holmes family, but the two sets of parents had plenty of opportunities on the elevator and at the mailboxes to comment on their girls' situations, and each knew the other's daughter well. The Holmeses' Mallory had played beside Susan Frankl in the sandbox at the playground on the Riverside Promenade and attended nursery school with her, and afterward they had gone to the same exclusive school, where both were outstanding students, although Mallory, unlike Susan, was neither bookish nor musical, and was what has always been called "popular." From the time she turned thirteen, Mallory had never been without a boyfriend for more than seven nanoseconds, as she put it—at least not until now. There were always a host of girls and boys with whom she went places and did things casually, whereas

Susan's connections with people were either intimate or distant, nothing in between. For the most part, Mallory was truly close only with Susan or, occasionally, with some friend of Susan's, and with her own parents, whose love was so rich and wise that she felt little need for anyone else's. Possibly there had been too many boyfriends, but none of the breakups seemed to have much effect on Mallory's high spirits and friendly cheerfulness. The Holmeses had only recently begun to worry that something was wrong in this pattern, when Mallory broke up with the young man with whom she had been living for two years. To her parents, this felt awfully like a divorce, and they were upset. But Mallory did not appear to feel it as much as her parents. She was quiet, perhaps a bit low-key, perhaps worked a little too much, and that was about the extent of it. Mallory had picked up an MA in journalism at Columbia a couple of years ago and had recently got a job in the Features section of the *New York Gazette.* With her salary and a little help from her parents, she was just able to afford the small apartment near Columbia where she had lived while finishing her degree.

Susan and Mallory, now settled blocks apart in the neighborhood where they had grown up, had recently begun to discuss a shared sense that the shape of the future was vague. Mallory, for once, had no one new waiting in the wings and had begun to falter in her confidence about finding the sort of man who would suit her, and Susan had begun saying right out that she thought she would stay single. She questioned the institution of marriage and doubted, in any event, that she was suited for it. Also, she saw that remaining single was commonly the fate of women like herself, despite their privileges and advantages, even among those who believed in and sought marriage, and she had a hard time imagining the man who might fall in love with her. After all, no one had felt that way about her yet. Why should it happen now, when she was almost thirty?

"Of course I wish I had someone," Susan said to her father shyly, "not necessarily a husband—just someone to be with, but it's not in the cards, as far as I can tell. I don't seem to send the right message or something." Peter Frankl grieved when she said this, and afterward he brooded more intensely than ever about how he might help her.

Susan said much the same to Mallory in an intimate late-night talk on her sofa. "That's not true!" Mallory protested. She was always protective and affectionately loyal with Susan. "You just need to find someone who's a little quirky, like you, and sooner or later you will. You have to be patient." This was simple-minded encouragement, but Susan wanted it badly enough that it succeeded in making her look a little happier. Mallory, though, wished to give more substantial aid, and she thought and thought about how she might shorten her friend's wait. Despite her malaise, Mallory herself, never having waited very long, didn't expect to this time.

In the meantime, Peter Frankl was so distressed by his sad conversation with Susan that, after worrying for several days, he decided to talk the situation over with his wife, even though Susan's remarks had been, implicitly, confidential. Susan and Lesley weren't as close as some mothers and daughters, and she wouldn't have said such things to her mother. But still, he thought, it was worth a try. Weren't mothers supposed to help daughters with problems like these? Didn't they know how it all worked?

"I told you so, Peter," Lesley responded when Peter described his conversation with Susan, "years and years ago. I washed my hands years ago." Her husband's unaccustomed soliciting of her opinion provoked anxiety, which in turn made her feel spiteful toward him.

"Refresh my memory," he said with a peculiarly mild, tolerant sarcasm in which the secure assumption of being undetected would have been clear to an observer but, apparently, was not to his wife, with whom he often adopted this attitude.

"Don't be silly."

"Lesley, you never said anything of the kind."

"I told you she should've gone on Teen Tour in her senior year."

"You can't send a girl who's reading Henry James and playing Scriabin on Teen Tour. She wouldn't have fit in. She would never have spoken to us again."

"We should have made her go and made her fit in. The kind of kids who go on Teen Tour get married. They know how to have fun and talk to people and get along with each other. Look at Louis. He doesn't have these problems."

"I'm sorry I brought it up. And, Lesley, I'm beginning to think that Louis isn't doing any better than Susan, no matter how it looks."

"Don't be silly. When Louis decides he's ready to get married, he'll find someone right away—not that you'd care if *he* had problems. And with Susan, the damage was done years ago. She's not a normal girl. You never wanted her to be normal. You wanted this fancy intellectual, and now you're paying the price. I washed my hands."

"You're making it up. But, okay, have it your way. Louis is perfect, and I personally, all by myself, ruined Susan, whatever. Still, you could take a little interest in what could be done to help her now." Peter's real opinion, of course, was that Susan, whatever her problems, had become a daughter to be proud of, while Louis's character was flimsy; Susan's intellectuality, and Louis's lack of it, in Peter's opinion, went far to explain why.

"There's nothing you can do for her now," Lesley said. "She wouldn't let you anyway. She wants to be *independent*. And you're all for it—even though buying her that apartment was maybe not such a good idea, which I told you at the time, because she'll just hole up there and never meet anyone. She should have roommates."

"All right, Lesley. We'll let it go. Susan and Louis can take care of themselves." This was only what he wished were true, not what he believed. But, in the Frankl family, Peter was the designated worrier, and when his appeal for wifely help proved futile, he felt obliged to restore his wife to peace of mind and reassume the burden of concern. Lesley immediately sensed her liberation and relaxed.

"Peter, you're on your own Saturday night, darling. I'm going to the fund-raiser, that legal aid thing in New Jersey, with the Rostovs."

"I can't see why you have any interest in doing that, but I'll be fine. Maybe I'll take Susan to dinner."

"No. She's going to Mallory's party. Mallory's having thirty or forty people in that tiny place."

"Good. Maybe Susan'll meet someone."

"Not with Mallory around—and all those girls who know enough to smile and talk."

"Your daughter is not the loser you think she is, Lesley."

"I washed my hands."

CHAPTER 2

———————

L ate on a clear, cold Sunday morning in mid-March, Mallory Holmes's party was under discussion in several neighborhood apartments that smelled of coffee and were strewn with newspapers and clothes. The night before, despite a spring storm so violent that Mallory had worried that people would stay home, her two small rooms, even the half closet that held her desk and chair, had been crowded with people. And from the first moments it had been clear that the party was a success, notwithstanding a brief quarrel that was snarling enough to shock into silence the dozen or so guests who heard it. Everyone except Mallory herself came away with the transformed inner landscape, the altered perspective, that good parties always give.

One skeptic insisted to her roommate that it was all a matter of timing. The best times for parties were the second and third weeks of December or the first two weeks of spring, because that's when people were trying hardest to hook up. Last night, the sap was flowing. Someone else, however, pointed out how skilled Mallory was at mixing people—all kinds, all ages—and how totally unsnobby she was. Last night's guests had included an assortment of Mallory's colleagues from work, a middle-aged divorcée on her hall who claimed she acted but who mostly waitressed, a former English professor and his wife, Mallory's computer man, and a few downtown theater and film people, along with the expectable cohort of age-mates and old friends who operated socially more or less in a circle of which Mallory was the hub.

"It has nothing to do with social savvy," Alcott Adams had remarked at dawn over blueberry pancakes in Tom's a few blocks away, "or loosening inhibitions, or anything like that. It's all obligation."

"Exactly. Mallory finds people who do what they're supposed to do," Sylvie Kimura replied. "They do the right thing and in exchange they get to belong to the host household and be taken care of. Everybody gives up their freedom and gets a secure identity. I don't mind. It's a nice feeling, that party feeling."

"Huh," said Alcott after a second's thought, and his face showed a suggestion of increased attention. He hadn't been expecting her to contribute anything—to be able to contribute anything—to his little riff. On social occasions, he expected that only he himself, or perhaps one of his good buddies, would have anything to say worth listening to.

"Do you go to lots of downtown parties?" Sylvie asked.

This, however, was more the sort of thing that Alcott expected women to ask, and his attention drifted away from her and back to his own thoughts. "No, they don't invite me."

"Why not?"

"Who knows?" he said.

Sylvie had asked only to see what Alcott would say, because she thought it obvious that few people would really enjoy having him around. He was aloof, critical, and self-involved. Nonetheless, for her own part, she was finding it difficult to avoid liking him almost excessively. Later, she intended to call Mallory and get the story on Alcott.

It had taken Susan and Louis Frankl's mysteriously abrupt departure at nearly 4:00 A.M. to induce the last guests to leave. Mallory, after seeing out the stragglers, had turned to discover Alexei Mikhailov on the sofa, fast asleep. The sofa was narrow, and his arms and legs dangled from it awkwardly. She covered him with a blanket and went to bed. At 9:30 A.M., when she got up, he was still asleep. She made coffee, trusting to the clatter and aroma to waken him. Alexei's unwanted presence underlined what a failure the party had been from her own point of view. She had invited two men in whom she was interested, but they had been interested instead in her two best friends! Never, until now, had Mallory had the experience of seeing other women preferred when she was present and available.

Louis Frankl was partly responsible for this. He had followed her around, wisecracking, half the night, effectively preventing her from getting into real conversation with anyone else, making a game of a display of aggressive devotion. She hadn't invited Louis at all, let alone as a romantic possibility; Susan had called at the last minute to say that her brother was in town for a job interview and had nothing to do that night. Mallory could hardly insist that he stay away, although she had never much liked him and had scarcely seen him since he had gone to college more than a dozen years ago.

Mallory had been interested in Chris Wylie, a playwright who had already had an off-off-Broadway production that got a good review in the *Gazette*. She had thought of Chris within twenty-four hours of her breakup with Paul. Chris was taciturn and not handsome, but appealing-looking, and was said to be rich. Very downtown, but that didn't put Mallory off. She had met Chris and Paul years back at Yale, when she was a senior, they were graduate students, and all of them were in a school production in which Chris's talent outshone everyone else's. Or if not Chris, then possibly Alcott Adams, a supposedly talented filmmaker whom she didn't know well. But last night Alcott had liked Sylvie, and in an extraordinary development, Chris had immediately been taken with Susan Frankl.

Susan was standing in the doorway, sipping wine and wearing an expression of artificial delight, affectedly open and wide-eyed, gratuitously polite. She appeared awkward and overly smiling in the way parents do when they intrude on gatherings of college students. Mallory thought Susan looked simple-minded. Why on earth does she do this? Why doesn't she at least get out of the doorway? Mallory resolved to rescue her just as soon as she had laid out the platters of food now stacked precariously in the nook that functioned as her kitchen. But, as it happened, rescue was by then unnecessary.

Susan, after looking about her from the doorway, walked over to Mallory's coffee table to pick up a book that someone had left lying there—*Effie Briest*, which she'd been meaning to read forever. She felt confident that the book was not Mallory's, knowing Mallory's tastes as well as she did; and there were little scraps of paper in it with someone else's handwriting. "Is this yours?" she asked no one in particular in the general vicinity of the book, and, as no one answered, she sat cross-legged on the floor beside the table, among the forest of legs, and began reading. Before she had gotten through one paragraph, the foolish expression on her face transformed into a knowing one. At the same time, a habitual melancholy, which she usually hid, became detectable. She became so engrossed in the book that she did not respond until the third time Chris Wylie spoke to her.

Chris had seen Susan pick up the book and sit down to read it, and, curious about this, he had watched her. Otherwise he would have overlooked her attractiveness. You had to look twice to see it, for she lacked that air that pretty girls usually have, of knowing that their looks entitle them to privileges and attention. At a gathering like this, Susan was capable of being taken, at first glance, as thirty-five-ish, almost frumpy, and not very interesting, even though the plainness of her dress, which was cleverly figure enhancing, was ironic and her unkempt hair was artful. But Chris, whose sensibilities were especially keen, noticed. He looked away, then looked back and saw that she was peculiarly pretty, with a narrow face that was mostly eyes, nose, and mouth—"all features," he told someone who couldn't tell him who she was. She was clearly odd, but Chris liked that. He walked to the table and stood there silently while people jostled around them, rocking on his heels, looking up, then down at Susan, then around, and glanced several more times down at Susan, waiting for her to look up and smile an invitation. When she did not, he finally spoke first.

"How long have you known Mallory?" he asked, three times. Susan looked up from her book into Chris's face with a vague expression and took a moment to get her bearings.

"Since birth," she answered at length, and a first, small twitch at the corner of her lips suggested she knew things of the infant Mallory that might interest him. "She's my lifelong best friend."

Chris appeared to think this an encouraging fact. It raised Susan's value in his eyes. She was not just anyone, but best friends with Mallory Holmes, whom she had known all her life; and he had known Mallory since Yale, years ago. It was safe to proceed.

"And how do you know Mallory?" Susan asked, her voice unexpectedly gentle and kind in a maternal way. Susan, having been pulled out of her book into conversation, was unusually unguarded and natural, and Chris detected complicated depths in her.

"I don't," he said, observing Susan with narrowed eyes. He was not particularly interested in her question, it seemed.

"So whose friend are you, then?" Susan asked. His studying her so obviously and intently aroused her own interest in return. She was actually a little disappointed to think that he was with someone.

"No, I mean, I met her at Yale."

"Oh. You just don't know her well."

Chris said nothing, which Susan interpreted as assent. He was certainly not forthcoming. Nor was he shy or insecure, though. He was just awfully downtown—no polite filling in the blanks, no willingness to go through a little bland small talk just to oil the social mechanisms. It made the conversation seem so dramatic.

Chris soon made an awkward excuse and, leaving Susan on the floor, went to seek out Mallory.

"Yes, she really is my lifelong best friend," Mallory told him, pleased that he was interested in Susan, and like the true affectionate friend she was, she added, "and the best and most wonderful person I have ever known—and smart. She's writing a thesis here in musicology, but undergrad was Harvard."

"She has an unusual air," he said. "You feel . . . held up, buoyant . . . or anchored. . . ."

"Susan must like you, Chris," said Mallory, restraining a smile at his incoherence. Mallory looked across the room at Susan, who at that moment stood frowning into the face of a tall, gangly young man with a professorial demeanor who, apparently, was making numbered points that he was ticking off on his fingers. Chris looked, too, although he pretended not to.

"Or he likes *her*," said Alcott Adams when Chris wandered off. "I never heard anyone say the word *buoyant* out loud before."

"Yes. He's avoiding her," said Mallory, watching Chris pretend to listen to a conversation at the side of the room opposite from Susan.

Mallory, holding an uncorked bottle of wine, maneuvered her way to Susan's side and, as she filled glasses, whispered about Chris in her ear—playwright, Yale drama, rich. The moment Mallory had caught on to Chris's attraction to Susan, she had given up thoughts of him for herself. If Chris liked Susan's style and off-kilter good looks, Mallory's cheery girl-next-door prettiness would never attract him, and there was no point in being annoyed with Susan, even though that gangly young man, a graduate student in English, was the one she had actually invited as a possibility for Susan or, maybe, for Sylvie Kimura. But he had dropped too many names and talked too much literary theory. As for Sylvie, a bristly would-be writer who rarely liked anyone, when Alcott Adams started talking to her, she had looked right through that graduate student.

Mallory kept an eye on Chris and watched him feign indifference to Susan for almost an hour before reapproaching her. Susan smiled unaffectedly at him then, and from that point on the two of them had stuck together. Mallory had rarely known Susan to behave so naturally with a stranger or to accept anyone so quickly, and she had so often been pained by Susan's being overlooked and undervalued that her pleasure now in seeing her appreciated was correspondingly intense. And to have Susan singled out by someone with Chris's brains and perception—it almost proved the world was rational. However, just as it had begun to look as though Chris and Susan would leave the party together, Susan had received a call on her cell phone, and she had run out with Louis instead, not saying a word to Mallory, leaving Chris looking after her, bewildered. Mallory hoped that things had gotten far enough along that this abrupt interruption wouldn't cut them off permanently.

Alcott, by this time, had already left with Sylvie, which was almost as astonishing as Susan and Chris linking up, for he had not been with any woman except on a strictly friends basis for at least three years—not since he had been abandoned by his last girlfriend—and Sylvie, too, rarely found anyone to be interested in. Alcott had spent the evening meandering through Mallory's rooms looking distant, except to behave with fraternal warmth toward Mallory, until he got into a long discussion with Sylvie. Tough and touchy as she was, Sylvie may have been the only woman there as smart as Alcott. Mallory wouldn't have thought that would matter so much, but maybe it did. Mallory had never had much hope that Alcott could be interested in her, and the fact was that she usually chose good-looking men. Alcott was discouragingly plain and badly dressed. Nonetheless, knowing his work, she admired him so greatly that, watching him leave with Sylvie, she yearned painfully for whatever qualities in Sylvie had succeeded in attracting someone like him.

Taking stock the next morning over her coffee, while Alexei slept on her sofa, Mallory thought that at least two pairings had occurred at her party—more, for all she knew. Perhaps it meant that thirty was the new mating age. But the majority of Mallory's friends were probably going to remain single. Everyone said that it was because they'd grown up with divorce, which had made them fearful, suspicious, and cool. It was true that many of them liked stories about two cold, hard, soured people eventually warming, softening, and sweetening up and forming an unsentimental union. And they liked playing at love—making a big deal of Valentine's Day and reading Heathcliff's passionate speeches to Cathy. But this was all amusing pretense, both childish and deeply cynical; not for a minute did they think that they themselves could speak any authentic language of love or romance. And when it came to sizing up potential sweethearts, their ambition made them as ruthless on their own behalf as any medieval father dickering over a dowry. Mallory thought that what had changed was the psychological economy of emotion; her generation just didn't need love the way people used to and didn't value it the same way. They saw it for what it was: a source of pleasure, but nothing you planned on.

People still wanted to be with someone, though, and Mallory had a reputation for being good at "fixing up." She never consciously did so; it was simply that she somehow conferred legitimacy on people's connections, a legitimacy the absence of which, nine times out of ten, was precisely what inhibited connections in the social world of urban singles. What Mallory offered, therefore, was an antidote to something that everyone in the mating market feared: what Sylvie Kimura called "ghost encounters," at the office or in cafés or at gyms, where you talked and traded bios and sometimes even went to bed together but remained without ectoplasm, insubstantial, in each other's eyes. Inevitably, the person vanished from your life, leaving behind half a name or a half-remembered face and a bad feeling. Mallory herself had never had this common experience. Whatever good office she performed for her friends, she performed for herself as well.

Seeing Louis Frankl last night, and how his long black lashes curled, Mallory had wondered for a while whether he was not the sort of conventional man who would marry as soon as he finished his degree and took a good job. She herself was bored with living like a student, in her student apartment; her life as a journalist was not even particularly different from her student life. But, perhaps, in order to graduate into a co-op, a marriage, and a kid or two, you needed someone preparing for one of those quintessentially adult, meaningless jobs, in banking or business or law, with an office and mortgage-worthy salary. That sort of man, no doubt, often made a good husband, whereas the Alcott Adamses and Chris Wylies of the world were tricky to get along with, and either did not marry at all or frequently divorced their wives. "Next time, don't pick anybody interesting," her mother had said when informed of the breakup with Paul. "Why do you always go for the interesting ones?" Paul, an actor, had been sweet but flaky, at least according to Mallory's parents.

Mallory sat for a few more moments in a chair opposite the sleeping figure on her sofa, then called, "Alex!"

At first, he was disoriented and looked around uncomprehendingly. But he did not apologize for falling asleep on her sofa and soon stood drinking coffee at her counter, acting quite at home, which, however, emphasized a foreignness detectable not only in the slightly strange shape of his excellent English, but in his lounging posture, even in the characteristic tensions of his facial muscles—it all had something painfully Russian about it. When Mallory's telephone rang, he reached past her and answered it before she could get to it and politely asked who was calling. It happened to be her mother, and Mallory felt mildly discomfited. Her mother would think that he was a new boyfriend. Then it dawned on her that this was what he intended. He was making a mischievous sort of play, a little Russian joke. He handed her the telephone with a satisfied, bright smile. She felt sorry for him, but this was overreaching on his part, obnoxiously aggressive. Mallory was not one to have an affair with her computer service person, no matter how attractive. She had found Alex's home-printed flyer, with its fringe of phone number tabs at the bottom, taped to a bus shelter on Broadway across from the Columbia campus:

WINDOWS BROKEN?

All Computer Services in Your Home—PC or Mac
Lessons—Word, Excel, WP, and More
Lockups unlocked
Software installed
Fonts adjusted
Spam rerouted
Total messes unscrambled
Call day or night:
Alex (212) 555-1234

She had called him at least four times in the past three months, and he had rescued her twice when she had a deadline. Once he had come over at 1:00 A.M. and worked for two hours while Paul slept in the next room, and scolded her in a voice with a shadow of a Russian accent. "I can't believe you stuck a floppy disk in the zip drive. Next time you do something like that, you can take the machine apart yourself. Don't call me." He made her laugh until her face ached.

He had been surprised to learn that she was four years older than him.

"I feel so much older," he said once. "It feels to me as though you're just a girl, and I'm a man. Don't you think so?"

Mallory had firmly, authoritatively, denied it, while thinking to herself that it was remarkably true. It was rare to encounter someone of her own generation who already had the older generation's weightiness. It was sad, too, because she knew that people lower down the social ladder, like Alexei, were forced to take on that burden far younger than people from her own world.

Mallory was a good-hearted young woman who had everything—job, looks, friends, family, even an apartment. Alexei had never finished college and was one of scores of twenty- and thirty-somethings who hovered on the fringes of Morningside Heights, waiting on tables, word processing for $15 per hour, starting short-lived services and businesses—dog walking, personal shopping, editing, teaching foreign languages or aerobics, tutoring, giving lessons on the cello or the guitar—yearning for the bit of freedom that they thought might be held on to here, searching for any escape from the cramped, constrained, transient lives, the paid serfdoms, that were all the world had to offer most little people. Like all of them, Alexei wanted work that used his talents and expressed his own will. He was studying voice—which was depressing even to think about. That made him one of the thousands of New York aspirants who pushed meager talents to their limits and ended with derailed lives. He was such a type, and he wasn't even American enough to recognize the trap he was in. He was so good-looking, too, with dark hair and eyes and arched black brows, thin rosy lips, that it somehow accentuated his deficiencies in Mallory's mind.

Mallory knew that in addition to his computer services, he sometimes worked as a personal trainer at a local health club, waited on tables, even baby-sat. She tried to steer work his way whenever she could. God knew where he lived or how he paid rent. He was the sort of person who might just disappear, just socially disintegrate and leave you with nothing but a queasy memory. She couldn't talk to him, really, and he didn't even realize that, probably because, on the surface, they were so chatty and giggly together.

Still, nothing should have given him the idea that she would welcome an approach on his part. Last night, she'd left him to sink or swim and didn't speak to him, even when he and Chris Wylie got into a big argument, of which she had heard only the loudest part. There he was, the most marginal guest at the party, making himself the center of attention being pushy about things he knew nothing of.

"They don't belong in colleges and universities. That always kills arts—poetry, painting, music, plays and films, and acting—none of them are any good anymore when universities take over. Is obvious," Alexei had said far too vehemently, but Mallory, standing outside the group involved in the discussion, could not see whom he was talking to. Of course, Alexei didn't understand that he was talking to several products of university drama, film, arts, music, and writing programs, and the whole thing was embarrassing. She noticed that he was dropping his articles and his *its*. Stress, apparently.

Then she heard Chris Wylie say sarcastically, "You seem to know all about it, whoever you are."

"Wait a minute, wait a minute, Chris," Alcott had cut in in a way that made clear he regarded Chris as having transgressed. The rest of Alcott's speech was drowned out by a loud conversation behind her, but it was followed by a burst of laughter. Alexei laughed, too, and she was relieved.

Now she shook her head no at Alexei without awkwardness, good-naturedly, when he tried to put his arm around her. Mallory felt that she had a right to refuse any man's attentions and never equivocated out of fear of hurting someone's feelings. In high school, she had rejected an Arab prince with as little embarrassment as she now turned away Alexei.

"See you Wednesday—and we'll do the anti-spam thing?" he asked on his way out.

"Six-thirty—yes," she replied. No reason to cancel. Who would have thought he would be so brash? Then she remembered: last week she had told him about her breakup. He thought she was available. She probably shouldn't have let him sleep on the sofa.

Alexei and Louis instead of Chris or Alcott—good God! Louis was less out of place among her friends than Alexei, but Mallory's party was not really home territory for an investment banker. Mallory knew from the first that she should gently, tactfully, tell him to back off. But she had found, oddly enough, that she was tempted by the very fact that he seemed alien. He was not at all interesting, she noticed, and her heartbeat accelerated. Mallory sometimes wished to cease striving and to learn to be content with the prosaic. She dreamed of peace, order, and safety in a world like Louis's. Last night, for a short time, she had felt attracted to him.

Louis had talked a lot. "I graduate in May," he had said, "and I just got a job at Hartley Stanton Thornwick."

"Are you going to live at home?"

"Are you crazy? I'm in the market for a place. I'll be down in April for a few days to start looking. You can help me. You want to share a place?"

Mallory laughed and shook her head.

"I like you so much. You know that?"

Mallory shrugged. "Why?" she asked. "I don't think I'm your type at all."

Louis scoffed at this. "You should be more open-minded. I like all kinds of people. Most women are more interested in me than you are. Don't you know I'm a great catch?"

"That depends on what kind of game we're playing, I think."

"I'm good-looking, I'm smart. Good sense of humor. Warm. I've just been offered an incredible job. My start-up bonus is huge. What are you waiting for? Take my advice—grab me. You'll never have a chance like this again."

"We'd have nothing to say to each other after about fifteen minutes."

"What's the big deal about talking? We won't be talking that much. Look, don't be so serious. This is not serious. Let's have fun."

But Mallory shook her head. What did he mean, "not serious"?

"So," he said. "This is going to be harder than I thought. All right. Actually I like talking. You first. What's your latest exciting assignment?"

"A little thing about . . . facial hair." She had to smile.

"On women, you mean?" he asked, his eyes widening. "Like how to remove it?"

"What causes it, how to deal with it."

"And you probably think *I'm* selling my soul for a living."

"I have to be patient. Later I'll get to write about things that matter. Right now I'm lucky to have any job in journalism at all."

Louis, weighing his tactics, chose to be silent for a few moments while he stared at her, ostentatiously pretending to suppress skepticism and dismay. Mallory took advantage of the pause to excuse herself.

"I see someone I need to talk to," she said, pointing across the room toward a shy-looking young man sitting on the sofa. But Louis maneuvered his way through the crowd behind her, carrying her drink, and was soon dominating the conversation, as she actually had nothing to say to the young man, who soon felt so uncomfortable that he got up and left. Mallory dropped into his place on the sofa, grateful both for a little rest and what seemed the perfect way to evade Louis, as the sofa now held three. But Louis squeezed himself in beside her and handed her the drink.

"Just what is it you're going to write later on when you've paid your dues?"

Mallory hesitated. "I want to get into political reporting."

"I don't think the road from facial hair leads to political reporting."

"For now, I'm doing medical stories, and I get only the unimportant ones. But I have a big project in the works. If it succeeds, then . . ."

"What's the project?"

"A series of pieces on pharmaceutical company lobbies. There's an enormous amount of research to do for it."

"Mm, I see. Sort of transitional. Maybe it'll work, but that's long-range thinking. I'm a long-range thinker, too. We have a lot in common."

"Tell me *your* dreams."

"I don't have dreams. I have plans. I'm going to get rich, sit on boards, have fun, and in about a dozen years get married and have four point six kids."

"You're going to get married when you're over forty?"

"Well, no one ever knows, right? But I'm going to be working eighty hours a week for a long time. Then, when I'm rich enough to cut back on hours and ready to settle down—whenever that happens—I'll be a dedicated, hands-on, middle-aged dad." He smiled.

Mallory undeniably felt some slight disappointment on learning that Louis was not currently looking for a wife, which left her in little doubt as to her own precipitate wishes. A feeling of giddy enticement, along with the interesting sensations that she had had looking up into his eyes, vanished.

"We're perfect for each other. You know that?" said Louis.

"I can't see why. Just what are you proposing?"

"I'm not proposing anything. I'm just stating facts. I'll call you in April."

Shaking her head no, she got up and walked away, but Louis did not stop pursuing her. He had made up his mind that he *would* call her when he got back. He wasn't going to fall madly in love with her, of course. But it would be nice to have someone for a while, someone to go places with, especially when everyone else was with someone. She was kind of interesting, an appealing person. She was the same type as Giuliana, who had wounded him last semester by refusing to see him anymore—the kind of girl his father would probably approve of, nice person, serious, sort of deep. Besides, he found her attractive, although that didn't jump out at you. Mallory was not a major beauty, but she was certainly pretty enough, blond, with a good figure. And she was energetic, easy to talk to, good-natured. No matter what Mallory said, he did not believe that she was indifferent to him. Louis did not fail to perceive that she lost interest only when he ruled out marriage. They were all like that, but sooner or later they came around. They were just like him. They needed someone for the time being.

An affair with Louis was not tempting, Mallory thought as she closed the door behind Alexei.

The telephone began ringing early that afternoon. Sylvie Kimura called first and said that she had spent the rest of the night in Tom's diner with Alcott Adams.

"I'm so glad you're home," she said. "Your party was amazing. Tell me about Alcott."

Mallory did away with Sylvie's doubts. Indeed, the sorts of doubts Mallory had about him were irrelevant to someone like Sylvie, who had few conventional urges. Despite her reservations, Mallory herself would gladly have welcomed Alcott's attentions and readily told Sylvie so; she was always straightforward. Now Sylvie felt it was safe to perceive his ambiguous qualities as good, to tolerate quirks, to permit herself fantasies.

As the day wore on, Mallory sank into a low, blue-tinged mood. She finished clearing away the party detritus, then found the thought of settling down to finish the facial hair story too repugnant. She decided to turn it in late and instead went for a long run in Riverside Park, where the air was cool and clear after the storm. After that she went to her parents' apartment in 444 Riverside, hoping to find a meal and a little shoring up. But they greeted her with traitorously grave expressions of the sort she had disliked from childhood, expressions that put something other than Mallory herself at the center of their lives.

CHAPTER 3

The Henry Hudson Parkway runs along the Hudson River from 72nd Street to the northern edge of Manhattan and, en route, hugs the stretch of Riverside Park, from 110th through 122nd streets, that forms the western edge of the neighborhood of Morningside Heights. Traffic on the Henry Hudson is always wild and dense with commuters making their way in and out of the city as fast as they can, and the park lies under the highway's constant blanketing roar of traffic. In the day, the din muffles the shouts of children playing baseball and soccer in the park's fields. At night, its shrieking brakes, sirens, and horns accompany the nervous duets of lovers and drug dealers huddling on its benches.

Years ago, in summers, all those residents of Morningside Heights who could, would take the Henry Hudson to get to the country. But by the new millennium they were less interested in escaping heat and bad air; they had air-conditioning now, and city air and country air were not so different. And where once they admired the quiet civility of the suburbs, even while insisting on the superiority of "urban energy," and where suburbanites once protected themselves against the hatred and anarchy that the city spewed forth, all that had been reversed. Now city people viewed the suburbs as places that incubated hatred and the lust for destruction. Surely terrorists' schemes of death were plotted in two-story, Colonial-style coverts with three bedrooms, two baths, and a concrete driveway. And now it was the city that was forced to defend its humane ways against the predations of outsiders who, inspired by resentment, fear, and envy of its goods and goodnesses, attacked it with homicidal fury.

You could see all this on the Henry Hudson. You take your life in your hands, complained the sedate drivers of Morningside Heights after a terrifying excursion to Westchester or the Catskills or Long Island. Aggressive suburbanites in massive vehicles, insisting on their right to be first and fastest, cut you off, hemmed you in, refused to accept a position at the end of any string of cars, and had actually been known to nudge bumpers or swipe fenders to force someone to move, or as punishment for going too slowly. They failed to perceive the intricate web of cooperation in the massive high-speed urban traffic flow, or responded as moral solipsists, treating courtesy as weakness and substituting insane speeds for the polite hurry that made it all work. The days were long gone when gentle out-of-towners thought New York drivers were the ones who were impatient, tough, and aggressive.

On the stormy Saturday night in March 2002 when Mallory had her party, everyone in Morningside Heights who lacked strong reasons to face the weather kept indoors, and neither dealers nor lovers were searching for quiet seclusion in the park. In a dense cold rain, manic winds whipped the trees, shimmied the cars skimming along the rain-slick highway, and blinded their drivers. By 3:00 A.M., there had been two accidents on the Henry Hudson, although neither was as bad as it might have been, and an ambulance from St. Luke's had already been out to one of them and brought back three bloodied young men who had crawled alive from a rolled-over car. The second call came when that trio were still in the emergency room at St. Luke's, and the same team of paramedics that had brought them in went back, along with another team, because this time it was immediately clear that things were serious.

When the medics arrived minutes later, and seconds ahead of the police, their lights disclosed two wrecks. A woman was attempting CPR on a man who lay beside a smashed-up sedan, while the rain washed away blood that continued to flow from a gash on his forehead. In a single motion, one medic deftly wrapped the woman in a blanket and lifted her away from the body, while another slipped into her place and continued the CPR and a third began to insert an intravenous line into the man's arm. Although the scarlet flow from the wound looked alive and vital, one medic muttered to the other, "He's gone." The woman heard and let out a terrible wail. A policeman determined that the only person in the other vehicle, a station wagon, was alive and stood by to let the medics get to him.

"There's another one in here," called a policeman, who was shining a flashlight into the sedan, "but the back doors are jammed."

"She said, 'Help me,' " the woman told the medic. She was lying on her back in an ambulance, water dripping to the floor from her hair. "I couldn't help her. Henry was there on the ground. I said, 'Wait.' Then she never said another word. Now maybe she's dead."

"You couldn't have gotten to her. Didn't you hear the man? The back doors are jammed. Hope for the best now," said the medic. "Were there just three of you?"

She nodded. "My bag—I want my cell phone. I want to call—"

"We'll get it for you. You just hang on. You related to the man out there?"

She nodded.

"Your husband? I'm sorry, ma'am."

They carried the man on a backboard into the ambulance with her while continuing the IV and CPR, and she heard someone shout over the wind and rain, "This one's breathing."

"Lesley," said the woman, not looking up. Then she leaned over and took the motionless hand of the man lying beside her. "Henry, don't die," she said. "Henry, honey." The CPR, the IV, and the haste, even the fresh blood—all convinced her that it wasn't over.

"We're going to St. Luke's," said the same medic, patting her shoulder. The ambulance motor revved aggressively and they moved out fast, the siren shrilly demanding death's right-of-way.

At St. Luke's, a kindly young resident held her hand, looked directly into her eyes, and affirmed that Henry—his name was Henry Rostov, she had told them, and he was sixty-three—had died instantly and that nothing could have been done to help him at any time. She, Judy Rostov, stared back into the young doctor's eyes, apparently uncomprehending, and said nothing. Then, when she had been examined and found to have nothing more than scratches and bruises, they left her alone for a while to recover herself.

"What about her family?" the resident asked the nurse.

"Two daughters," said the nurse, "and her best friend is the one in there," nodding her head to the cubicle where a team was working frantically on the woman Mrs. Rostov had said was Lesley Frankl. "She doesn't want to call anyone yet."

"She needs a little time to accept it," said the resident. "It would make it too real if she had to tell her daughters their father's dead."

A policeman appeared at the opening of the curtain around Judy Rostov's bed sometime later. Did she feel up to describing how the accident had happened? She was sitting up, staring, a cell phone lying in her lap.

"I didn't really see," she said. "I was listening to Lesley, who was in the backseat, looking back at her, mostly. I just swung around at the last second, because Henry said a four-letter word, which he never does."

"Do you know your rate of speed at the time of the accident?"

"No, I wasn't paying any attention. I think it was slow because of the storm. You couldn't see anything. Maybe we should have pulled over, but we were almost home."

The police officers said nothing to her about the driver of the station wagon. Among themselves, they agreed that Rostov, the driver of the sedan, probably had been going slowly and then had got knocked pretty hard, and for some reason had accelerated and then skidded and struck the station wagon when it tried to pass him; and then he just ran his car into the post. Maybe he got rattled, hit the accelerator when he meant to hit the brake—something like that. That was all they could say. There was an indentation, with green paint, on the driver's side of his silver sedan. They were not surprised that whoever was driving it had not stopped to help. One of the policemen had noticed an SUV, dark green, he thought, drive by the site slowly while the wreckage crew was still working, but he didn't get its Jersey plate number. "Should I try to follow that guy?" he asked his comrades. They thought, then shook their heads. After all, this happened maybe fifteen or twenty minutes after the crash. The chances were zilch that someone had circled back to see what happened and even worse that anyone could actually find the guy again.

"I want to call my daughter," said Judy Rostov.

"Where is your daughter, ma'am?" asked the nurse. "Do you want me to call her for you?"

Mrs. Rostov tried to call but found that her fingers didn't work. The nurse held her hand and said, "Tell me the number, and I'll do it for you."

"I don't feel a thing," said Mrs. Rostov. "I don't even feel like crying. I was talking too much when he was trying to concentrate on driving. I probably killed both of them."

The nurse shook her head. "It wasn't you, dear," she said. "And your friend has a chance. Don't give up on her."

This, however, was not comforting to Mrs. Rostov, who, on learning that Lesley was still alive, found herself resenting it. In fact, although she hardly grasped her own thoughts, she would have preferred that both Henry and Lesley die than that Lesley survive when Henry had to die. Or all three die. Or she and Henry die together. Anything but this grotesque substitution, as she couldn't help thinking of it, of Lesley for Henry.

Peter Frankl, his face unshaven and livid, arrived while these thoughts were forming and concealing themselves in the back of Judy's brain; and his son and daughter, Louis and Susan, ran in not long after him.

"She's this way, Mr. Frankl," said the senior nurse on duty, her face a kindly, composed mask, leading him. "The resident is with her, and Dr. Baird is on the way."

Standing around Lesley's unconscious form, they listened to the doctors give a long, ominously noncommittal explanation, in low voices, of Lesley's injuries. Then the doctors asked them to step out. Louis took a chair outside her cubicle, and Peter Frankl, with Susan, went to Judy, who told them what she had told the police.

"I shouldn't have been talking so much," she said, still sitting up on the bed, with Peter Frankl's arm around her, and she wept for the first time since out there in the rain.

Both Susan and her father, whose thoughts had the floating, disjointed quality that comes with sudden horror, nonetheless noticed that this statement was peculiar. Susan could not help detecting resentment behind it, for, as Susan well knew, it was her own mother who never stopped talking. Susan suspected that Judy was tempted to blame her mother for the accident. Peter, not as psychologically adept as his daughter, saw only that Judy irrationally feared that she had caused her husband's death.

"That's crazy," he said. "You can't think like that, Judy."

This attempt at comfort only made Judy more insistent on her guilt, which Peter found distasteful and unaccountable. But the circumstances called for forbearance, and as his intimates knew, he was a man with an outsized capacity to put up with things.

Susan put her hand on her father's arm and shook her head almost imperceptibly.

"I'm going back to Lesley," he told Judy, still holding her. "You need anything, anything at all, we're here. Understand me? Look, here, I'm writing down my cell phone number for you. Night or day. I mean anything you need. And I'll be checking on you. You called the girls?"

"I have to call Riverside Chapel and make the arrangements."

"No, I don't think you should. You're too shaken up. We'll get your brother to come take you home. You need someone to help you with everything. I'll talk to your brother."

Susan observed how Judy responded to her father's kindness. The note of reproach fading out of her voice, she agreed to this, and Peter and Susan soon went back to Lesley. Judy never asked after Lesley. Of course, she was preoccupied with her own loss. This was forgivable, and Susan did forgive her. Then she examined the idea that Judy had covertly been blaming the accident on Lesley's garrulity, and she forgave that, too. Her father's conventional kindness and obliviousness, she saw, served better here than insight. It was often unkind to see these little things that Susan saw.

Susan also suspected that her father did not understand how pessimistic the doctors were, but she was mistaken. Like Susan, Peter had arrived at St. Luke's with the conviction that his wife's life was in danger but somehow had lost it in the meantime and was struggling to recover it. He felt an irrational confidence that she would wake up, feeling and acting herself. He tried to take seriously the doctors' warning that there was a likelihood of brain damage, that even if she awoke, she might be unable to speak, think, walk. This, too, he simply could not believe. Why? he wondered, beginning to feel uneasy, as his incredulity felt disturbingly like indifference. He looked at Louis, who reminded him of a puzzled child, his round eyes moving searchingly, pleadingly, from one face to another; Louis was old enough to know that no one could fix this for him. Annoyed with his son, he turned to Susan, whose face was pale and tear streaked and whose hands were trembling as she pushed her hair out of her eyes and awkwardly clipped it back with some contraption. Louis and Susan, he saw, did believe that their mother might be dying and were afraid. Susan was dressed up and, unaccustomedly, wearing mascara, which had smeared from her crying. Then Peter remembered that Susan had gone to Mallory's party and Louis had gone along. Poor kids, leaving a party to confront this. He could not bear his children's grief and fear, and his own eyes filled.

"Daddy," Susan said, misunderstanding her father's tears, "what's going to happen?"

Louis looked from his father to his sister, still unable to think the thoughts that would let him grasp the dimensions of the danger.

"I believe she'll be all right," said Peter. "I don't know why, I just think she will."

"Dr. Romano doesn't," said Susan.

"He's just trying to avoid giving out false hope, although I don't know why they hate false hope so much. Hope is hope. What could be false about it?"

At Lesley's bedside, they bent over and whispered encouraging nonsense; then they held her hands and watched the electronic medical monitors. In a few minutes, the Frankls' own Dr. Baird arrived; having already had a long cell phone conference with Dr. Romano on the ride over, he was almost immediately prepared to offer advice that sidestepped the issue of prognosis and distracted them.

"I see no reason to move her uptown," he said, referring to his own hospital, Columbia Presbyterian, fifty blocks north, "at least not just yet. Right now, we can't do anything up there that they're not doing here. She's closer to home here, easier for you to visit, and for the time being I think that matters as much as anything else. I'll be in to check on her, and Dr. Romano is good. I know him. I'll work with him here."

Peter inferred from this that Dr. Baird thought it very likely that Lesley would not survive, or would survive with serious brain damage; still, he himself could not believe any of it. When he, Susan, and Louis finally left on Monday evening, Lesley was still unconscious and had been moved into intensive care.

CHAPTER 4

Peter Frankl had his virtues and his talents, but basically he was ordinary, and for such an ordinary man, he was much loved—if not by his law partners, then by many: friends, clients, judges, clerks, waiters, the doormen, the housekeeper, his internist. Yet there was nothing obvious that he did to inspire such feelings. Certainly, people talked about his kindness and warmth or his generosity or his good humor or his brains, but those things didn't really explain it. Lots of men were nice, smart guys who weren't remarkable for it, the way Peter Frankl was. Peter Frankl was a *really* nice guy, was how people tended to put it, and no doubt he was all the more lovable because his faults and his problems were so apparent to anyone who knew him.

At sixty, he looked sixty, with glasses, the start of a double chin, and folds of flesh at the sides of his mouth. He had gray hair that receded in the shape of a shallow W, a slight paunch, a ruddy complexion, and a closet full of suits, ties, and shirts handsome enough to create the illusion that he was an attractive man, a misimpression furthered by the strong appeal of his air of shrewd intelligence and goodwill. Despite the deficiencies of his relationship with his wife, he was exceedingly married in the way that almost all people of sixty, and few younger people, are—except, perhaps, in places like Morningside Heights, where a divorce or an affair, at any age, still shocked.

Peter thought this was because the residents of the neighborhood combined moral keenness with skill in choosing compatible spouses. Likewise, there was a near universal ability to profit from psychotherapy, with the result that ordinary marital logjams and irritations were diminished and marital satisfactions amplified. People married late, too, and were skeptical about the potential benefits of partner hopping. Whatever the reasons, the neighborhood was home to a high percentage of stable and contented unions, and people always asked, horrified, "What happened?" when they heard of a breakup. How, Peter asked himself, did we all manage to raise kids who are no more fond of marriage than children of tortured unions and anguished divorces?

A lawyer with a thoughtful sociolegal policy bent, partner in a prominent New York firm, Peter always argued that no-fault divorce was good law for people who had a high level of self-governance but bad law for people who hadn't. For most people, therefore, it was a good idea, even though divorce, of course, was usually wrong. Why was that so hard to understand? Neither the conservatives nor the California libertines who divorced and married half a dozen times really understood that no-fault divorce laws did not establish a moral standard. Decent men and women did not divorce, except in extremis, and certainly not because they decided they were "incompatible." After all, he and Lesley weren't all that compatible, yet they had managed to live peacefully together and raise their children well.

The Frankls had lived their entire marriage in their penthouse on Riverside Drive. Lesley had pushed Peter hard to move out of the neighborhood in the seventies, when they had become prosperous and Morningside Heights was doing even worse than the rest of the near bankrupt city. But Peter, who rarely opposed his wife, had been unbending on this issue. Move to Park Avenue he would not. So Lesley redecorated, first in the seventies and for the second time in the millennium year. Their friends said that she did it wonderfully, but as far as Peter was concerned it hadn't worked out, especially this last time. The rooms had a "done" feel, almost as though Lesley and Peter had committed the crime—by local standards—of calling in decorators, an impression reinforced by Lesley's having hung certain canvasses that she had painted with her decorating scheme in mind. These were typical of her work—highly abstract, but in colors that were suspiciously effective with the upholstery and rugs.

Peter especially disliked the den Lesley had created for him out of the children's old playroom, insisting that he should spend more of his insufficient leisure there, "enjoying himself," rather than hiding in his library reading, as he had been doing for most of the thirty-odd years of their marriage. She had dedicated one of its walls to photographs of his ancestors going back to the 1880s, even though she knew that his ancestors and those pho-

tographs were something of a sore point. Peter's father, Leonard Frankl, had
been a Jew, a rabbi who, when his Jewish first wife died, fell in love with a
young gentile girl whom he met at a poetry reading at Cooper Union in
1939. Despite the fury of his family, especially his grown children, who
thought he had gone mad, Leonard had married that girl, Della, when he
was not far from the age that Peter was now and retired from his rabbinical
duties and, for all practical purposes, from Judaism.

When she first met Leonard, Della knew nothing at all about what
being Jewish meant or what it felt like, how deep it went, or even that, psychologically, it was not on a par with being Methodist or Presbyterian or
Catholic. She was a lapsed Catholic who called herself an agnostic and had
recently come to the city from a small town in Ohio as free of agnostics as
Jews. She certainly could never have guessed that Leonard went so crazy for
her possibly for just that reason. He could not resist her uninformed perception of him, which, being innocent of ideas about what a Jew was or
should be, allowed her to see everything about him, even what was pre-
shaped in Jewish molds and laden with weighty Jewish demands, as individual traits—as him, not them. It made him feel light and free, even, for some
reason, exhilarated with himself—a frame of mind conducive to falling in
love.

Although Leonard Frankl was with half his soul a deeply religious Jew
who willingly undertook the responsibility of preserving these forms that
lived through him and others like him, with the other half he wanted to run
away and try life out on a different set of terms. The chief result of his succumbing to this temptation was the birth of Peter, his non-Jewish son, when
Leonard was sixty-two. After this, Leonard rarely saw the children of his
first marriage, and Peter, until his teens, never met his half-siblings, who
wanted nothing to do with him. Peter's mother, Della, told him in whispers
that there were grandchildren, too, some not far from Peter's age, and that
the first wife had been a termagant. Della and Leonard were isolated in their
marriage; her friends were too young for Leonard, and his wanted nothing
to do with either of them. Leonard continued to play viola in his Wednesday night chamber group, and the cellist in this group, a tolerant and gentle
younger rabbi named Eli Friedman, became their only close friend.

The senior Frankl, who was Orthodox, taught Peter that he was not
Jewish because his mother was not and encouraged him to avoid any religious affiliation. "Don't bother with converting," he had told Peter. "It
doesn't really make you Jewish as far as I'm concerned, no matter what they
tell you, and take my word for it, it's all nonsense—Jewish, Christian, whatever. Just be a good boy and a good man. That's all there is to any of it."

When he was about fifteen, Peter, perceiving his elderly father's doubleness, called him on it. Leonard confessed that he had always found being Jewish a great burden and that if he were not duty-bound to support the Jews, "I would certainly be an atheist."

"But then you are an atheist," Peter had insisted nervously. "You don't really believe in God. You just think you should."

"No. I have to believe in God, so I do," Leonard had said. "But you don't have to."

"That's double-talk!"

"Someday you'll understand. Listen to me, Peter, I raised you right. Just stay clear of the whole thing, and be good—be a good father and husband and friend and citizen." From this time on, Peter was quietly enraged with his gentle, affectionate father. His mother understood, but Leonard did not.

Della had died not long after this, and Peter fell into a sink of loneliness. Indeed, he still missed her now, at sixty. Son and father had been no help to each other when she was gone. Leonard Frankl was inconsolable, so consumed with longing for his sweet young wife that he could pay little attention to his son's sufferings. Not long after Della died, members of Leonard's first family began to show up at their apartment now and then. Peter would come home from school and one of them would be there, ignoring the boy or glancing sideways at him without speaking, and when Peter went to college in 1960, they took his father back.

Peter came home one night and the old man had gone, leaving behind a cryptic note. Panicked, Peter called numbers in his parents' address book and finally talked to a nice-sounding girl—his own niece, he learned later, who was about the same age he was. She told him that his father had gotten sick and had gone to stay at his daughter's apartment, where Peter wouldn't be allowed to visit. "You have to understand," said the pleasant-voiced girl, "how betrayed and abandoned his first kids felt. They know none of it is your fault, but they don't want to deal with you." For a while, his father was strong enough to come out to the park near his daughter's apartment, and Peter would meet him there. Then, one day he was too sick to go out, and the next day he was dead.

Peter went to the funeral and showed up to sit shiva because Eli Friedman told him to, but the other family felt his presence—as he overheard his elderly aunt muttering to someone—like a curse, a black shadow over them all. Still, at first they were not unkind. Then a quarrel erupted when they learned that Peter was his father's sole heir.

It was not a question of money. The problem was that Peter got photographs and other memorabilia—of Leonard's parents and grandparents and people who died in the camps. They couldn't see what business Peter had with those things. When his aunt, Leonard's sister, suggested politely enough that he give those pictures to them, he had balked, and that was the last he'd seen of his father's family.

It was those photographs that Lesley had dug out of his desk and framed and hung on the wall in the den. Peter had not scolded, but he couldn't bear looking at them and being reminded of that time when, still just a boy, he found himself so friendless, frightened, and miserable that night after night, alone in his dead parents' apartment, he huddled in his father's worn old chair, unable to stop shaking. The mere thought that Susan or Louis might ever experience such dreadful feelings put Peter in a state just short of outright panic.

Peter, Susan, and Louis stayed at the hospital until late Monday evening, when the doctors insisted they go home for a few hours' sleep. Lesley's condition was critical but had not changed for the last twenty-four hours. Peter and Louis walked Susan to the door of the row house on 114th Street where she had her apartment and then made their way to Riverside Drive in silence. Louis disappeared immediately into his room. Would he cry now, Peter wondered, amid all the infantile paraphernalia that Lesley had enshrined there—childish books, trophies, toys, posters, pennants, and the rest?

Peter switched on the answering machine and listened to a dozen worried messages that for the most part were painful to hear. In cases of death and illness, people knew reliably comforting formulas to recite, but for this situation, when no one had died and the value of life was open to question, they were forced to find their own words. Some offered coarsely aggressive empathy: "It must be *torture* not knowing. I don't know how you *stand* it." Others were timid: "Just heard the bad news, Peter. So . . . wanted to let you know . . . uh, so talk to you later." To Peter's astonishment, several messages sounded hip; he wouldn't have guessed that so many of his sedate friends would choose such a downtown way of expressing themselves at a time like this: "Hey, man, look . . . this sucks. What can I say? Hang in." To Peter, it sounded as though they had taken a lesson from the movies, where you often saw such cool, hard-hitting approaches to sympathy.

Peter returned a few calls, then checked back on Louis and found him lying awkwardly crosswise on his bed, asleep, fully clothed. He pulled off Louis's shoes, covered him up, and switched off the light. Then he worried about Susan, home alone, and called to make sure she was not going to pieces. "Do you have any wine? Try just a half glass and read in bed for a while—it'll help you relax." An exceedingly maternal man, Peter mothered his children, his wife, his friends—even his business associates, a fact that went far to explain his legal success. He was a good lawyer even among the top tier of good lawyers, but he gained and kept his enviable set of clients as much because of his talent at hand-holding and comforting anxiety as because of his admirable legal mind. Like many such people, he himself had no one to lean on when trouble came.

Peter stepped into the den to read the morning paper but found himself warding off the habitual thought that he hated what Lesley had done in there. He went to read in the living room instead, but the sight of his bathrobe lying on the coffee table, where he had flung it Saturday night when the phone call came, drove him out. Finally, he went to the library and read until a sudden sense that it was very late broke his concentration. He half expected to hear Lesley call him to come to bed, then recalled with a start that he had left her in the hospital and, taken unawares, he experienced a sweet moment of relief. He was horrified by his own hardness of heart.

Lesley deserved better than this. Whatever her flaws, they were forgivable, and she was his wife forever, no matter how imperfect. He was not perfect himself; marriage was never perfect. Reasoning in this way in defense of Lesley and his marriage, Peter had for most of his married life been able to ignore his frustrations and maintain an ironic smile. Yet now, two days after the accident, he was tormented by growing fantasies of life without Lesley.

To Peter, such thoughts were the moral equivalent of murder and a betrayal of his children, who loved their mother, as all children do. The last reflection helped somewhat. Peter was able to wish for the preservation of his children's mother for their sake. This wish, however, quickly embroidered itself into a fantasy that Lesley got well and decided that for the sake of her health she would spend several months each year without him in Santa Fe, near her younger sister and a friend who also painted. Alas, the reality was that Lesley was determined to persuade him to retire and go there with her as soon as possible. She envisaged for Peter a life of taking care of Lesley, with lots of traveling, shopping, visiting; then he would read and she would paint, and he would use his connections to organize some shows for her. Judging others' feelings by her own wishes, she did not understand that this was a program for wrecking Peter, but then, that was Lesley. Peter, no masochist, didn't intend to let her destroy both of them with her blindness.

Lesley never opposed him when he really put his foot down. It was remarkable, in fact, how little conflict there was in their marriage given how different they were. After some initial squabbling about discipline and nursery schools, they had hit on the happy plan of dividing the children and, even more happily, hardly noticed they had done it. Now, however, Peter feared that this had sacrificed the children to his cowardly wish to avoid fights with Lesley. Maybe it even had something to do with why Susan was withdrawn and odd and Louis shallow, immature, and sneaky. But, telling himself that he shouldn't judge his own children so harshly, Peter pushed such thoughts out of his mind. They gave him that same near panicky feeling, for he knew that there was nothing he could do to save his children from suffering the lonely consequences of their own flaws.

Just as they had each taken one of the children, Lesley and Peter had settled on turn-taking as the answer to their conflicting tastes in dinner guests, music, and movies. Lesley, like Peter, had a Jewish father and a gentile mother, they were both from the Bronx, and they each had a little sixties' nonconformism. She was artistic; he was idealistic and radical. In Peter's mind, this similarity in their backgrounds lent propriety to their marriage despite his knowledge that Leonard Frankl would greatly have disapproved of his marrying a girl who never read anything and was, mainly, sexy. Peter had married her, he now thought, partly to spite his dead father and partly because he had been so lonely, poor, and frightened when he met her, not six months after his father died. She was fun, dressed well, and willingly shared his bed. She thought she should marry him. Her mother shrewdly sized Peter up and pushed for the whole thing.

Peter had always hoped to give up his law practice and seek more satisfying but less remunerative work, on the bench, say, or in the academy, but Lesley considered this a betrayal. They had a deal, and his end of the deal was to meet her wishes to have things and to go places—to Europe in the spring, mostly for shopping, country resorts in the summer, and the islands in the winter. In exchange, Peter got not just a wife and babies, but, early in their marriage, a great deal of money from Lesley's father—law school tuition, a huge down payment on their co-op, and periodic presents of cash that made a fairly luxurious life possible even back when Peter wasn't earning so much. All three of them understood that accepting the money indebted Peter to Lesley's father and, therefore, that his first obligation was to support his family at the level of luxury that conformed to Lesley's sense of her deserts. Did Peter want his father-in-law to take responsibility for his children, she asked him, because she would not deprive them of the kind of life they should have. Something sinister relating to his children, not exactly in these words, but hovering in their penumbra, decided Peter to stay on with his firm. But he suffered.

He clung to Morningside Heights, although he felt himself an outsider, because he derived satisfaction simply from being near a world that seemed to him to be dedicated to knowledge and virtue—like a richer Jude Fawley at Christminster, he told himself. He maintained his state of ironic marital cheer in the face of painful frustrations, tormented by constant yearnings for transcendent things—for ideas, for music that took you out of yourself, into ecstatic contemplation of brotherhood, justice, and love, for knowledge of the deep, the right, the good. He never succeeded in freeing himself of his dream of being, like his father, a learned man who helped others and was indifferent to wealth. Leonard Frankl would have looked, not disapprovingly but incomprehendingly, on Peter's decision to become a mainstream lawyer representing multinationals and the super-rich. That one should do such grim things for the sake of a larger income would have seemed to him laughable, unreal—something you might read about in a novel but certainly never encounter in real life. Peter could just hear his father's voice: "But why would you want to do that, Peter? What do you get out of it? That will be a bit boring." Peter's work had indeed been a bit boring—and worse—and his dissatisfactions seeped into his life, like water into a rotting boat, from a dozen different leaks. His marriage and his job stayed afloat thanks only to silent, arduous bailing.

The children had helped, for until recently he had been able to channel his yearnings into self-sacrificing hopes for them. There had also been occasional professional enthusiasms that bore him along, but it seemed that each of these eventually ran into opposition from his partners, legal and marital. Two or three times he had taught seminars at Columbia Law School on one of the obscure historical subjects in which he read obsessively: the concept of judgment in early English law, and marriage and divorce in Saxon law. A couple of eccentric students, sometimes a law professor, would attend, and Peter would for a time find himself in the heaven he sought. But then a big case would come along at his firm, or Lesley would throw a fit because he was never home or spent all his time holed up reading moldy books.

Then there was the Devereaux Foundation, a wealthy, not-for-profit, do-gooder operation run by a collection of well-meaning and unbusinesslike eccentrics. Its mission was philanthropy: searching for virtue and talent and giving it a boost, granting money to artists, theologians, musicians, dramatists. Peter got deeply involved there. He never had as much fun on any vacation as he did spending long hours at work on behalf of the foundation. Despite angry opposition from Lesley and his firm, where his caseload and billable hours dropped markedly, he had prolonged this holiday from the hungers of his ordinary life until, finally, five or six years ago, their pressure became intolerable. Even now, he continued to attend the foundation's quarterly meetings and review its annual statement, but, deprived of the sense of sharing in its daily work, his life went flat.

So Peter was a frustrated man, but he had managed to keep faith with Lesley. She spent most of what he made, but she had had her costly clothes, jewelry, furnishings, and trips, with her much admired husband at her side, and the children had had everything that children on Park Avenue have. Basically, she was contented, and she had a right to feel that he was contented, too, so he had made himself feel that way. If he couldn't offer Lesley his highest level of interest or engagement, she didn't seem to mind.

It was almost midnight, and Peter gave up trying to find equilibrium in this unsteady new situation. He remembered that he had thought unkindly about Louis and went to his door, turned the knob quietly, and peered in. Louis was asleep, still lying diagonally on the bed. Peter hoped Susan, too, was sleeping. Then he remembered how Lesley had looked, unconscious in the hospital bed, when they had left, and he broke into sobs. Lying on his bed, he called the hospital and heard that Lesley's condition was unchanged. When he hung up the phone, he fell at once into a sleep so deep that his dreams came from somewhere below the mental threshold at which they were dominated by Lesley and her fate.

Peter was wakened at 8:00 A.M. by a sober call from Lesley's sister, who was about to board a plane for LaGuardia. He called the hospital and heard once more that there was no change in his wife's condition. Louis was still sleeping when Peter, having showered and dressed, tiptoed past his door and, after leaving a note in the kitchen, set out for the hospital. He decided not to call Susan, who should get all the sleep she could, but he wished they had made plans to breakfast together or something. In front of his building, he ran into Edmond Lockhart, his neighbor, who went out for his newspaper every morning with his dog, Burke. Lockhart's head was bent, and he seemed to be staring at the ground, seeing nothing. Yet he noticed Peter walking his way, and when he looked up, Peter saw that his complexion was sallow and his skin had an unwholesome, repugnant texture, like dumplings or clay. His features were frozen until the moment he spied Peter.

"Peter," said Lockhart, adjusting his face into an expression of meaningful gravity in place of the empty look the preceding moment, "the doorman told me about Lesley. I can't tell you how sorry I am. If there's anything I can do . . ."

Peter shook his head and held up his hand to stave off inquiries or further condolences. From Lockhart, with whom he had a history of unpleasant neighborly relations, they were not welcome. Peter was not softened by the perception that Lockhart had some misery of his own that had laid him lower even than Peter, or by the knowledge that it was Lockhart who, shortly after moving in across the hall from the Frankls, had first put him in contact with the Devereaux Foundation, which was headed by his elderly aunt. Peter controlled his dislike well enough to mutter "Thank you," and he strode off toward St. Luke's.

Lockhart, looking after him, forgave his rudeness; obviously the man was stressed. And whatever their quarrels, Frankl was a very likable man, although Lockhart couldn't put his finger on just what it was about him that was so likable.

CHAPTER 5

The Morningside Heights branch of the New York Public Library was housed in the ground floor of a newly built Columbia University dormitory on Broadway. Despite the building's gestures toward conformity with the turn-of-the-century style of the neighborhood, its interiors were bright, modern, and open, and the library was popular with neighborhood children, the unemployed, the elderly and retired, and university students looking for a change of scenery. At opening time, the line stretched down the block.

One of the library's regular visitors was Victor Marx, a shabby elderly man who wrote on political and historical subjects. He worked there almost daily, despite the relative noisiness and lack of antiquated charm, supplementing the library's limited collection with interlibrary loans and fortnightly trips to the main branch on Forty-second Street. He much preferred staying in the neighborhood and going home for lunch with his partner. Vic was always near the front of the line at opening time and sat at the same table on the second floor by the window, where the light was particularly good.

When Alexei came in, he generally took the table that neighbored Victor's, and the two had seen each other there so often that they had become friends. In good weather, they sometimes took sandwiches down to the promenade on Riverside Drive and ate together on a bench. Vic was aware of all Alexei's doings and sympathized with his strivings.

Occasionally, they were joined by a slightly stout young woman, Cora

Bledsoe, who was a violist always looking for gigs. Like Alexei, she had studied at the Manhattan School of Music and took odd jobs as a word processor or research assistant to earn rent money. Alexei more than once helped her with her computer, free of charge, and shared sandwiches with her. She practiced hard for no reward that Alexei ever saw, yet she was happy for no reason—happy was her default setting, he thought—and sweet-natured, living in Morningside Heights by small-town social rules she had learned out west somewhere.

Alexei had recently added chess lessons to his job repertoire and, until he discovered the library, had been hard up for a place to teach. In good weather, he used the stone chess tables down on the promenade until, for obscure reasons, the parks people had removed them, reducing the regulars to playing on overturned plastic cartons. Sometimes he had to go to the children's homes, but this was a last resort because he disliked parental supervision. For months, he'd been trying unsuccessfully to link up with some after-school chess program. They probably just didn't want anyone without a degree, he thought, for he considered himself a far better coach, with better chess credentials, than most of the people they hired.

Alexei's instructional games in the library were played in whispers, and he and his student wrote down all the moves for later discussion. Library patrons occasionally came and stood mute, watching, now and then smiling at the intensity of it, at the ingenuity of the young players, or at how patiently Alexei set out the openings and methods of responding to them. Alexei and his student often borrowed chess books as they left and analyzed games walking home. Alexei now had seven regular students, plus a few others whom he saw occasionally. With these earnings, together with his income from computer services and some regular personal-training clients, he had money enough to rent a decrepit studio on Tiemann Place, at the border between Morningside Heights and Harlem, to give his parents a little money every week, and to pay something to his voice teacher, who had reduced his usual rate in exchange for chess lessons for two of his children. But at twenty-five, Alexei was still far from able to afford a decent place of his own and felt past the age of tolerating roommates.

On this Wednesday afternoon, Mallory Holmes came to the library, hoping to fill in some gaps in her story about facial hair. All she needed was a good medical dictionary and a little material on side effects of treatments. She was surprised to see Alexei sitting at a table near the windows on the second floor, concentrating deeply a chess game with a boy so small that his feet swung freely several inches above the floor; the two of them were observed by a shrewd-faced elderly man wearing a shapeless cardigan. Alexei barely nodded when Mallory came smiling to watch, and he put his fingers to his lips when she began, "Alex, I . . ." The boy looked up curiously, but Alexei tapped the board impatiently with his forefinger, and the child again concentrated on the game. She watched for another minute, until the boy made a move and relaxed, then she began again. "Alex, I didn't know you were a man of so many talents. You . . ." But the old man glared and shushed her in a loud whisper. Cora observed the scene thoughtfully from a nearby table. Mallory was blond and slender, maybe too sleek altogether by local standards. Her hair was straight, and she wore lipstick—pink lipstick.

Mallory was offended by Vic's interference. Gay, she thought, perceiving his sexual indifference and attributing to this his readiness to be annoyed. Age never made a difference. Alexei himself, however, also paid her no attention. She had probably hurt his feelings Sunday morning, but that was no excuse for his behaving so oafishly. Mallory walked away a bit too briskly. When she had finished her research, Alexei and the boy were still bent over the board, watched by the old man, who was leaning thoughtfully on one skinny arm, ignoring a notebook in his lap. She left without speaking. A few minutes later, Alexei glanced at his watch. Then, after three quick moves, he whispered, "Checkmate," and stuck out his hand to the little boy, who shook hands but looked sullen.

Alexei packed up the game in a tote bag, which he offered to the child, who put his hands behind his back.

"Stuart, here, carry your game," Alexei said softly, hoisting his own heavy backpack to his shoulder. Victor Marx, too, gathered his notebook and pens and prepared to walk out with the two of them.

"You carry it," Stuart answered defiantly.

"You think maybe you're just mad because you lost?" asked Alexei in a wheedling voice.

"You were tricking me. You could have checkmated a long time ago."

"He was just giving you a chance to see you were cornered and do something about it," Vic said. But the little boy was not ready to forgive.

"Anyway, you played well. You're coming along," said Alexei. He looked appraisingly down at the boy, who made a show of unfriendliness by refusing Alexei's hand and stuffing his into his pockets.

"Do you think you might like to play in a tournament?" Alexei asked, smiling coaxingly at him after they had trudged along in silence for a couple of blocks. He looked into Alexei's face, his big eyes wide for a moment, then shook his head, no, no, he didn't think that sounded very good. Alexei and Vic smiled slightly at each other over his head.

"Okay, if it's not for you. But you'd probably like to go watch a tournament." The child did not oppose this suggestion, and Alexei knew that he had found a way to get him to a tournament without confessing a desire to win one.

When he had brought the boy home and parted from Victor Marx, Alexei strode south down Broadway to the gym, his bag of workout clothes, shoes, and towel slung over his shoulder. He hadn't meant to snub Mallory, he argued to himself, but with a young child you had to be careful to follow the rules you wanted him to follow and not to break his fragile concentration. Besides, it annoyed him that she just assumed he would interrupt whatever he was doing; it had been perfectly obvious that he was busy. She was so arrogant and condescending! He hadn't liked her tone at all or that imperious little smile. She wasn't *that* pretty or that brilliant, either, and he suspected she was no better educated than he was—whatever her degrees. Her tastes were limited. She missed allusions to Pushkin and Ravel, which were not exactly obscure names. But he had very much liked getting her into giggling fits. Reminiscing wistfully about those nights he had spent working at her neat little desk, making her laugh, Alexei actually found disappointed tears filling his eyes—no matter that he wasn't even sure he liked Mallory very much. It was painful, thinking of all those people at Mallory's party with their ease and easy satisfactions, their confident expectations and lordliness, and comparing this with his own scrambles for work and money and the discouragement with which people repeatedly subdued his hopes. Mallory's friends were so sure that what they thought was true and that what they had was nothing more than what they were entitled to. And they thought people like himself merited their deprivations and could be looked down on. Oh, yes, they probably even thought they had rich, indulgent parents because they deserved to. People like that drove him crazy.

Today, one chess lesson finished, he had two appointments at the gym. Alexei was done with them by 6:30, when he trotted home to Tiemann Place for a quick supper, then ran back to the library for his last chess appointment of the day, with a pair of Columbia students. When he left the library at a little past 9:00 to walk home, Alexei was tired but in better spirits.

Wednesdays, Alexei taught. Thursdays, Alexei got taught. He looked forward to Thursdays and his voice lesson.

CHAPTER 6

Two weeks after Lesley Frankl's accident, while she still lay in a coma at St. Luke's Hospital, Peter went back to work. Until this calamity, nothing kept Peter away from his clients; after it, he missed his job no more than he missed his wife. And when he returned to the office, everything felt familiar and bizarre at the same time.

For one thing, he became aware that the simple act of arriving at the office every morning produced in him a familiar emotional sludge no matter how much he struggled against it. He would open the door to the lobby and strain against its carpeted muteness, the denatured odor of the place, and the costly, cool paintings on the wall, as though he were starved for sensory input, for any crumb of libidinal interest. Then these seemingly minor feelings would silently coalesce into a dark, massy sensation of—of . . . And it came to him that it was his longtime sensation of life at the firm. It had always felt just this way.

Years ago, he fought this feeling so hard that he pushed it permanently out of awareness. But now Lesley's accident had created such an upheaval in his mind that he didn't know the way around his own thoughts anymore. Here he was, bumping into out-of-place ideas and feelings that he'd moth-balled thirty years back. His antipathy for the office, no doubt, had been obvious to at least seventy of his seventy-five partners, even though he had managed to conceal it from himself. It was why they tended to be mistrust-ful of him, although they didn't actively dislike him. They tolerated his eccentricities, even boasted about him to outsiders, with bogus affection, for this proved how humane and bighearted they were.

Peter's poor fit into the mold of the firm had at times inspired worshipfulness and desperate clinging on the part of junior associates struggling to survive its pressures—Orwellian pressures, one young lawyer called them just before he left for lunch and never returned. Peter wished he had gotten to know that young fellow, but he rarely worked with low-level associates; as often as not, Peter's secretary, or a paralegal, or Peter himself did his dreck work. It amazed him that with all these people gathering here every day by the hundreds, friendship and love were so rare—aside from the dismal office affairs that never seemed to achieve either. Where else in the world were warmth and affection so thoroughly squelched? In prison, you might think, but actually, Peter thought, prisons were usually more favorable to love than his law firm. In prisons, yes, you had the guards against the prisoners, but within both groups friendships frequently took hold.

Law firms, unlike prisons, had intricate hierarchies: senior partners, junior partners, permanent associates, senior associates, junior associates—all ranked by year, with juniors bound to follow orders from anyone senior. Under the lawyers were the paralegals, then administrative staff with its own hierarchy, management at the top, computer experts, maintenance people, secretaries, word processors, with a motley collection of true servants at the bottom: messengers, mailroom workers, food service workers, and cleaners. And the entire nonlegal staff were slaves, servile in fact and feeling, inferior in wealth, privilege, status, and power, swiftly dismissed for failures in obedience. Peter avoided eye contact with these people—the same way he didn't look at dead furry things on the roadside. With three or four of the staff he had forged a tenuous equality and something like mutual regard, but usually, if they were worth knowing, they were too hostile to respond to Peter's gestures with anything but suspicion.

On his fifth day back, as he came out of the elevator, Peter's thoughts were full of treason—just as they had been when he was fresh out of school and openly argued to his young colleagues that their firm was a monstrous, amoral society, deforming to the human spirit, that the precondition for working there was to refuse to see this or to disconnect these ideas from feeling and action—and to end up being monstrous and amoral oneself. Although several of them had been persuaded to leave by Peter's youthful eloquence, he himself had gotten trapped there and, gradually, had come to regard such ideas as immature and extreme. I lost the truth of it, he thought today. And this loss of the truth of things was what let the firm grow and prosper, nourished by an ichor of misery. Misery was the all-purpose fuel and lubricant of every serious moneymaking operation that Peter had ever seen. Unless some people were whipping other people, no one got rich, Peter's father had told him—matter-of-factly, as part of what you could take for granted in life.

The release of these disloyal thoughts freed up some reserve of energy and momentarily buoyed Peter against the firm's downward drag. But he faltered at the long-familiar sight of Laurie McIntyre, the receptionist. Laurie had been a beautiful young redhead when he started at the firm more than thirty years ago. Now the silken strawberry locks were dyed an unconvincing auburn. She was past middle age, past affairs with lawyers of the firm, and past hopes for love and children. She had turned into an old girl, with the permanent chirpy demeanor of a twenty-two-year-old. She was the firm's reservoir of history and gossip. It had taken her over from the inside—her prides, shames, fears, and comforts were the firm's: the cases it won, the charities it supported, the important clients it served. And her private life, Peter reflected, was now mostly plumbing—showers, cups of coffee in the morning, and drinks before bed. She had meals at her desk or at a restaurant with someone from the office. Nothing left of her own insides at all, thought Peter as he called out, almost shouted, "Morning, Laurie." Her life so appalled him, and he felt so guilty for seeing her failures and deprivations so clearly, for never having done anything to save her in all those years, that his volume rose involuntarily in tension—although he was aware that she was not his responsibility.

"What am I, deaf?" she said, self-righteously snippy, because she didn't have to put up with being shouted at all day long.

Peter pushed on toward his office, past the inner corridors where the lowest-ranked associates labored in windowless offices and on to the cubicles where the secretaries and paralegals sat, the partial walls providing a fig leaf of dignity, like inadequate little towels in public showers. But they adjusted, finding security in the cubicles, like puppies in their crates. The cubicle people worked long hours. They were forced to, but they usually wanted to anyway because they always needed the overtime. They lived far away, on Long Island or in New Jersey, and commuted in and out on trains at hours it made you tired to think about. You could hear them talking low on the phone with their kids at 8:00 or 9:00 P.M. on those many nights when someone had ordered them to stay to type a brief or a contract.

"Just put it in the oven at three hundred and fifty degrees—that's all. Tell Danny either give it to you or get on the phone. Yes, he will. You tell him . . ."

Cubicles were better than the old typing pools anyway, Peter thought, where a few dozen girls sat in one big room with a supervisor, but it wasn't at all as good as the anterooms secretaries used to have—like the one Milton Steinberg still had at the Devereaux Foundation. And at least you no longer saw the shoeshine boy, who was in fact an aged black man, kneeling at the partners' feet and brushing away. That seemed to have ended when the women lawyers arrived, in the eighties, maybe partly *because* the women arrived. Somehow it seemed worse in front of women to have some poor shabby guy down on his knees in front of a rich man in a fancy suit who was too high and mighty even to pay any attention, who'd keep talking on the phone or reading his newspaper or court documents. The first time Peter saw that, he had to go into his office, shut the door, and breathe deeply.

Peter silently saluted a slight man of about forty, gray at the temples, whose cubicle was so laden with files that only a sliver of his face was visible from behind stacks on his desk; a nameplate on the counter said JON ABERNATHY. "I need to talk to you, Mr. Frankl," the man called after him, and he followed Peter down the aisle, to the outer corridor where the offices of higher-rank lawyers, senior associates, and partners were located. These were proper rooms with windows and doors that closed and locked to allow you to keep secrets, make private calls, and let down for a minute. They were gorgeously furnished and filled with books and mementos of deals and cases and photos of friends in high places. Peter had such an office—not the corner office that his successes deserved, but the ambiguously superior office that his ambiguous status called for; it had the very best views and was located in a quiet cul-de-sac near the library. A corner office would be a comedown, yet a corner office would also be a step up. Lawyers were experts at creating situations like that.

Peter's secretary, Mary, was typing in her cubicle outside his office, having already collected a pile of mail and telephone messages on her counter for him to retrieve on his way in. She was an Englishwoman in her fifties, smart, cool, efficient, and loyal, and she had been with him for twenty years. When she had breast cancer, Peter had paid her uninsured medical expenses and refused to let her repay him. They thought well of each other but in all their years together had had only two intimate conversations. The first was in the eighties when he had detected her teary anxiety about the cancer and unpaid medical bills. He called her into his office and demanded to know what was wrong. Her disclosure and his offer of help, behind the closed door, created a nuclear burst of mutual warmth, understanding, tears. But it was the damnedest thing. The minute she walked out the door again, it was all gone. They had nothing like it again for nearly fifteen years—not even when she got her five-year all-clear and had a big lunch celebration with the other secretaries—not until he had to tell her, again behind the closed door, about Lesley's accident. Then it happened again, just the same way. What gives with this? Peter had wondered. They didn't love each other—not even platonically. It felt like intimacy, but it was something different—maybe just the unexpected secret chance to be human and equal, free, in this place of coercion, masters and slaves, rulers and subjects. It created an emotional riptide.

He offered Mary a brief, dry "Morning" as he picked up the stack of papers and entered his office. She responded with a nod, and the arid quality of this interchange made a disconcerting contrast with the emotion of that second scene with her, on the first day he had returned to work after Lesley's accident.

Jon Abernathy followed Peter into the office.

"Look, you have to do something," he said. His voice was a thin, Alabama-accented tenor, but just now it was so fortified by conviction that it sounded almost robust. "Because they're taking advantage of you."

Peter knew that Jon, a paralegal, was right. He was talking about a group of three other paralegals who were responsible for keeping the case files of two big, complicated cases in working order. They had been sloppy and caused problems in and out of the courtroom. Probably they should be fired, or at least get final warnings, because Peter had spoken to them about it twice already. They ignored him because they knew that Peter wouldn't rage or write bad reports to Human Resources. In fact, he had an inkling that they messed him up just because he tried to be decent. They were real underlings, unable to perform up to snuff unless the whip cracked. Totally unlike Jon, a would-be poet—quite a bad one, in Peter's opinion—who regarded his work at the firm as a mere day job. Peter and Jon had an understanding; they had worked together for many years. Jon was decent. He would never take advantage of Peter, and oddly enough, it angered him that others did. Peter and Jon had had several philosophical discussions about it. They talked about everything.

"You're so nice to them," said Jon, "like they care. They don't care. They have no respect for you because you respect them. Equality is good and all that. I mean, my politics, I'm a social democrat, if you want to know. But these people are nazis. They respect meanness and power, that's all. What do you think they'd be like if they were on top?"

Jon was a good sort, Peter thought when, after asking about Lesley in a feeling and unintrusive way, he had gone. Peter knew Jon was trying to protect him. When he thought about that, it got to him. Jon, who was so weak and unimportant and, really, helpless, didn't think he was thereby absolved from trying to help Peter, who was strong and important. Jon thought Peter should be treated right no matter if he had the advantage. This gave Peter a peculiar mixture of feelings—shy and exposed, along with some melting sensation in his gut; he almost wanted to cry. No doubt the situation with Lesley was making him . . . labile, as the shrinks said.

A strikingly thin, handsome but haggard-looking man suddenly stood in Peter's doorway. He was wearing a sleek suit and an intimidatingly bright, fashionable tie. He appeared just in time to see the vulnerable expression on Peter's face.

"Jon's trying to teach you jungle survival skills, eh," said the man. "You know, I question whether you should let him talk to you that way. He's more out of line than the other three. You'll have no authority with him. You know that? Even if he's right." The man laughed. "Especially if he's right— you shouldn't let him say it to you. How's Lesley?"

"Walter, if I listened to you, I'd be a big success in life, wouldn't I," Peter said with collegial warmth.

Walter laughed a little again and was gone. He was Walter Bramford, who had the corner office across from Peter's, one of a handful of partners Peter counted as friends. He was only forty, although he looked older, and he was already a superstar at the firm thanks to a string of courtroom successes. He was a real lawyer's lawyer, not one of these guys who gets on top by golfing with the right people. Peter suspected that he was thin and worn from too many women and too much cocaine. According to Jon, in fact, Bramford actually bought the cocaine right here at the firm, from a couple of guys in the mailroom who never did much of anything. Bramford took care of them, kept Human Resources off their backs. None of this did Peter hold against Bramford. In fact, without quite knowing why, he admired this part of Bramford's character as much as his talent. He felt at home with him, and he liked his refined, dissipated air, that beyond-good-and-evil savoir faire—so unlike Peter himself, who was, and always would be, something of a Boy Scout.

Peter, still going through his papers, smiled at one message as he called after Bramford, "Free for lunch?"

"He said no," came Mary's voice on the speakerphone.

"Mary," Peter said into his own speaker, suddenly chipper, "make sure the Devereaux board meeting is on my calendar for tomorrow."

The Devereaux Foundation's secretary had called to remind him of the regular quarterly meeting to be held Friday—tomorrow. He really shouldn't go; he had a backlog of calls and correspondence. But with no more struggle than the registering of this doubt, he decided that nonetheless he would go. They needed him. He often managed to stop them from taking some ruinous or mad or prodigally futile step. They were fruitcakes, all of them—aged, nutty fruitcakes. He had better just go up there and do his best to keep them in line. In fact, he thought, his mood rising further, perhaps he wouldn't come into the office at all tomorrow. The Devereaux Foundation was only a few blocks from home, walking distance from the hospital. Tomorrow morning after he visited Lesley, he would walk over to the meeting. He'd just call Mary and say he'd be in . . . Monday. And he became so cheerful at the prospect of a Devereaux meeting, followed by three days out of the office, that in the next moment he was hit with boomeranging guilt: how could he be so indifferent to his wife, his children's mother? And then his eyes rested on an envelope still lying on his desk, addressed by hand in block print to "Peter Frankl—personal."

"Mary, it's another one." This time Peter got to his feet and called to her through the doorway.

"Another what?" she said, coming to the door because she heard dismay in his voice.

"Another one of those notes, the anonymous critic notes."

"Oh, good heavens," Mary said.

With his lawyerly memory for evidence, Peter knew when all the notes had come. The first was in 1992. It accused him, in venomous terms, of hypocrisy and moral weakness, for patting himself on the back for his political and environmental ideals while failing to act on them. At the time, Peter had been lead defense lawyer for a utility that ran nuclear power plants. The litigation had little to do with nuclear power issues (and, in general, Peter disapproved of nuclear plants). He had thought that some disgruntled junior associate, disappointed in him, had probably written the note.

He got a similar note in 1996, when he had almost forgotten the first one. This one attacked him for defending corporate misconduct so that CEOs got off while poor people went to jail for little more than making rich ones feel nervous. A third came in 1998, a fourth and fifth in 2000 and 2001. This was his second in 2002, and it was only April. Both Peter and Mary were sure that the phenomenon was escalating—the notes were both more frequent and more nasty. They read this one together, their heads almost touching.

"To say such things to you of all people," Mary gasped, shaking her head. "I think you'd better tell someone. This person might be dangerous."

"What, a dangerous moral critic? Nonsense. Anyway, what could anyone do about it?" said Peter. "No, best just to ignore it. Keep it under your hat." But the notes were hard to ignore, and this one especially.

The worried husband act is not very convincing, Frankl, and I was already sick of having you around. Why don't you do everyone a favor and clear out permanently? Who do you love anyway?

The author of the note, obviously, was psychotic. But despite this, the accusations in the new note, like those in the others, felt to Peter as if he had thought them up himself.

CHAPTER 7

On Friday morning, buttoning up his fresh shirt and fastening bright links in his cuffs, Peter was full of hope. For a short while, he attempted to convince himself that this was hope for Lesley's recovery. Her doctors had begun saying it was conceivable, if unlikely; despite a continuing danger of stroke. They had decided to keep her at St. Luke's. Therapists visited her daily, and she was subjected to a variety of stimulating treatments intended to help her wake. She had muttered words a couple of times, and that was an encouraging sign. But Peter soon confessed to himself that his sanguine mood was not about Lesley. No, it arose entirely from the prospect of staying home from the office, going to the Devereaux Foundation, and, happiest of all, soon seeing his daughter, a daily pleasure since Lesley's accident.

Peter and Susan visited Lesley every morning and, usually, each evening as well, and Louis came on the weekend. It had all become routine. After the first two weeks, Peter had insisted that Louis go back to Boston and finish his degree. Graduation wasn't far off, and Louis couldn't do anything here but grow more depressed. But he had flown back last Friday evening and gone to sit by Lesley's bedside, and he was coming back this Friday, too. Peter worried about the way his son sat at his mother's side, staring. She propped him up; without her, his deficiencies were more obvious. Even at the hospital you could see how the staff respected Susan but only tolerated Louis. Susan herself, where Louis was concerned, seemed to step into her mother's shoes; she was willing to baby him, shore him up. She was younger by a few years, but she was a grown-up, and he was a kid.

The air was cold for April and the sidewalk still wet with dew when Peter set out for the hospital. His mood rose even higher at the morning's new tokens of spring. The flower beds across Riverside Drive along the promenade were bright with tulips, and the trees were tipped with yellow-green leaves. His cheerfulness was checked, however, by the sight of Lockhart returning home with his dog, Burke, as he always did at this hour.

"Off to the hospital?" he asked Peter, who nodded and waved but didn't slow his vigorous pace.

"Wait—Peter, got a second? I'll walk you up the block," said Lockhart as Peter did not conceal his impatience at being stopped. Years ago, Peter and Lesley had hoped to be friends with Lockhart and Ivy Hurst, the Columbia professor whom Lockhart called his "partner." But they had felt condescended to, and Lockhart had been interfering where his aunt and the Devereaux Foundation were concerned. As a result, things had long been cool among the four of them, although none of them acknowledged this. Indeed, they had accomplished that invaluable social magic trick: regression to a state of having never been acquainted. Their two dinners together were erased from memory, forgetfulness doing its effective second best for forgiveness. Peter had learned only recently, in fact, that Susan, on the suggestion of her thesis adviser and knowing little of her parents' past relations with the Lockhart-Hurst household, had asked Ivy Hurst to sit as outside reader on her dissertation committee. Ivy had agreed, and Peter was uncertain whether or not Ivy even realized that Susan was her neighbors' daughter.

"Ivy and I want you to come to dinner," Lockhart said, breathless from trying to match Peter's stride. "We're having a few friends over—two weeks from Friday. Very informal. We hope you can come."

Lockhart, Peter thought, was determined to do the good neighbor thing. "Thanks," he replied, "but Louis is coming in, and I've got plans to take Susan and Louis to dinner."

"Bring them," said Lockhart. "All of you come."

Peter thought about it and hesitated. Lockhart and Ivy had been much nicer lately. He knew that it was less he himself than Lesley who had inspired their condescending behavior in the past, although he had always blamed them. Lesley didn't know how to deal with their sort. What the hell, he thought. When did he ever get a chance to have dinner with intellectual types? There'd have to be some decent conversation even though Lockhart was a little too right-wing for Peter's taste.

"Well, if you're sure two extra won't be a lot of trouble . . ."

"Not at all! We'll see all three of you at eight-thirty?"

Peter had misgivings as soon as they parted. He had momentarily forgotten the uncomfortable issue of the Devereaux Foundation in the background. He owed his position there to Lockhart, and Lockhart, at first, had
tried to keep tabs on his aunt by questioning Peter incessantly about her ad-
ministration of the foundation. Peter had angrily refused to answer, as a
matter of professional ethics, and Lockhart had finally backed off, feeling
betrayed—which only further incensed Peter. Now, however, Peter was willing to overlook these offenses and hope that just possibly, without Lesley
around, there would be some good talk.

Peter stopped in at the hardware store on Broadway, and the young men
who worked there greeted him warmly.

"Mr. Frankl!" and "How you doin'?" they said.

They all knew about Mrs. Frankl. They had heard about it from the
444 Riverside doorman, but they were too well mannered to mention it.
They were even careful not to scurry any faster than they usually did when
Peter, with a hopeful expression, held up a burned-out bulb in one hand and
a dead battery in the other. Peter tucked the new bulb and battery into his
pockets, paid, and made a good-bye gesture with his forefinger to the nice
young fellows. Then he stepped out into the bright light of Broadway, where
the first face he saw, looking vacant and lost, was Susan's.

"Morning, Susie," he said. He looked and sounded calm, but the unexpected sight of her, even in her melancholy distraction, gave him an emotional spike of wild, warm joy.

Susan, who was very nearsighted, squinted and stared at him with de-
fensively hunched shoulders. "Daddy," she said, pleasure and recognition
filling in her blank expression. "I don't have my lenses in—I didn't see it was
you."

"Don't tell me you ran out of those damned disposable things again.
Where are your glasses?"

"I couldn't find them."

"You have to put them in your nightstand drawer," Peter told her, guid-
ing her through the morning rush-hour throng on Broadway, "so you always
know where they are—especially if you have to find them in the night. Watch
the broken pavement there. Don't trip. And don't walk on the grate if you
don't have to. You don't hear about it, but in fact you wouldn't believe how
many people fall through those. Here's the coffee place. Want some, sweetie?"

She said yes, just to let him do something for her. She used to say,
"Please, Daddy, don't fuss over me," but now she let him.

At the hospital, at least five people had said "Good morning, Mr. Frankl" and "Hi, Susan" by the time Peter and Susan reached Lesley's room. Peter stood in the corridor speaking with the doctors while Susan went in. When he joined her at Lesley's bedside, Susan was holding her mother's hand and staring hard at her face.

"She said it again, Daddy," said Susan.

"Just 'top drawer'?"

"Yes. I gave her a kiss and said, 'Good morning, Mother,' and she said, very unmistakably, 'top drawer.' "

They both sighed and sat on opposite sides of the bed, each holding one of Lesley's hands.

"What in heaven's name could it mean?" he said. "Is she trying to tell us something?"

Susan shook her head.

"Top drawer," muttered Lesley in a low, hoarse voice, her eyes shut.

"My God," said Peter, shocked. He had never before been present during one of these episodes.

"Dr. Baird said he didn't have a clue. He said it probably meant nothing."

"They have no clue about anything—if she's getting worse, healing. They have no idea," said Peter.

They sat silently for several minutes. " 'Top drawer' means 'excellent,' 'the best,' " said Peter.

"I thought that maybe she was talking about her dresser or nightstand," said Susan. "But I looked, and there's nothing special in the top drawers."

"Whatever," said Peter. "I think it's just random synapses firing."

"Not random. It's the same synapse, about five times now."

"Whatever," said Peter. "Honey, I have to go. There's a board meeting today." He kissed Lesley's cheek, and Susan followed him out into the hallway.

"Daddy, try not to worry."

"Thank you, sweetie. Oh, I hope you won't mind. Edmond and Ivy, next door, want me to come to dinner, so I accepted for all of us for two weeks from this Friday—instead of going out after we visit your mother. All right? Sooner or later I have to go, and it'll be easier with you kids there. They're not my favorite people, but it could be interesting."

"Good. I'd like to get to know her better. But I don't know about Louis." Susan was as pleased for her father's sake as for her own. She knew how he craved serious, literate talk. She even knew that her father had turned to her for satisfaction of such frustrated cravings. But of course he didn't know that, and she didn't tell him.

"He'll be bored, but he can make up some excuse and leave early. It's just across the hall."

"Fine, Daddy. See you here tonight?"

"Sweetie, I want you to take a night off. I'll sit with her. Go see some friends. Have a little fun. Your mother would want you to. You need some fresh air in your life."

"Well . . ." Susan hesitated. "I might leave class and come a little early, then, and be gone before you get here, because Chris wants me to have dinner with him."

"Chris Wylie?" Peter was aware that this name had been mentioned several times. However, it would be premature to ask questions about Chris Wylie, and he tiptoed considerately away from the subject. In a couple of weeks, perhaps, he might indicate that he knew that this name was important. Peter tried to conceal from Susan his anxieties about her. He wished urgently that she have what he had missed in love and in work—this very urgency a measure of what he himself had suffered in the lack. And she must have children, too, but in a more balanced marriage than his own, so that her children's happiness, and her own, would be assured. He kept himself from asking about Chris, but he read worrying things about him on her face.

When her father had gone, Susan stood at Lesley's bedside and held her mother's hand. "Wake up, Mother," she said.

The Devereaux Foundation was just a few doors away from the Nicholas Roerich Museum and only a block or two from the Buddhist temple on Riverside Drive—forming one of a collection of oddball institutions at the southern edge of Morningside Heights that Peter had always found intriguing. Peter greatly admired the foundation's work and had always insisted on donating his services despite the fact that it was richly endowed. Over the years, through a haphazard grant system, it had funded any number of worthwhile scholarly endeavors and fascinating projects in the arts as well as a number of absurd and crackpot ones. When Peter worked for the foundation, he served noble causes, not corporate wealth. Of course, there were other good works that he devoted himself to—fund-raising, legal aid, bar association committees—but none of these provided the same zest in his life or felt like anything but more or less tiresome obligations.

Miss Devereaux, elderly even when she and Peter first met, was still a judge of character and ability. She took to him and soon relied heavily on him. He was honest and straightforward, she thought, and his mind was so quick that he had always reached the correct conclusion when everyone else was still trying to understand the problem; yet he was flexible and tolerant, patient in explaining and making sure that everyone else understood, and without even a trace of arrogance. He knew the city, the arts, personalities, the laws, and their pitfalls. Although there were plenty of people he didn't like, there was no one he hated. Of course, he had no imagination at all and no tolerance for risks, but they didn't need him for those things. Gradually, she ceded to him considerable authority over every aspect of the foundation's functioning.

Peter managed to carry so much responsibility at the foundation only by reducing his caseload and, even then, working most evenings and weekends. Of course, Lesley, who always demanded plenty of attention, began to complain that Peter was neglecting her and "endangering our marriage." For a while, he had tried to conceal his involvement—as though it were an affair—but she always knew anyway, with a wife's uncanny perception, when he had been sneaking over there.

Peter walked to the familiar row house on 107th and was buzzed in to the ground floor, where visitors had their first encounter with the foundation's eccentricities in a small gallery of contemporary works of art. Among these, on this day, were realistic paintings of various saints, in dark serious colors awash with Renaissance overtones and abristle with symbols that Peter could not decipher. There was also a collection of stone sculptures of flowers—Peter saw lilies, roses, pansies—undertaken with no irony at all. These were rather fetching, he had to admit, but then, what was one to do with the experience of sincere, fetching stone flowers? Peter hadn't time to contemplate the artworks further. He took the tiny elevator to, as he always imagined, not the fifth floor but the nineteenth century. The furniture of the dark, wood-paneled reception room was from that era, and it was easy to believe that so was the elderly secretary and receptionist, Milton Steinberg, who had been hired in the days when Miss Devereaux's father still ran things. He was somewhat deaf and never knew that you had come in until you approached his desk and he caught a glimpse of you from the side. Then he turned to you with a welcoming smile, gracious in a 1930s sort of way, cheerful and suave in a debonair tailored suit and shirt that even Peter envied. There was no computer at his desk; he worked at a manual typewriter, going at an impressive, clacky speed, flinging the carriage back at the end of every line—it always stopped just short of his teacup—and he regarded his dial phone as sufficiently up-to-date. Every hour or so, he smoked a cigarette—most elegantly, Peter thought, like Noel Coward or Leslie Howard, although unlike them, he was troubled by no excess of intellect.

"Oh, Mr. Frankl," said Milton, who was just then pausing for a graceful drag. "So good to see you. Miss Devereaux has just gone in. Won't you . . ." He blew smoke and motioned to the familiar heavy door that stood ajar.

Peter found all the others already assembled at the massive old mahogany conference table. Coffee was being poured from a silver pot, and pastries that had been sent up fresh that morning from Bouley Bakery were set out on a sideboard. None of them knew anything about Lesley's accident. Peter kept quiet about it whenever he could, so as to avoid the endless questions and expressions of sympathy to which he was otherwise exposed.

Miss Devereaux, fragile and innocent, sat benignly at the head of the table. Orazio Cromwell, the foundation's secretary-treasurer, was on her right, an unlit cigar clenched in his stained teeth, and Hilda Hughes, the program officer, was on her left. Orazio's face was cheerfully devious, as though his plans to abscond with the foundation's millions were well in hand. When Peter first met him, he had worried about whether the man was honest and went through the books personally to be sure all was well. Finally he concluded that Orazio's shifty expression reflected only his sense that he deserved all decent people's suspicion because of his given name, the explanation of which was that his mother was an Italophile whose maiden name was Horace. The things parents do to children, Peter thought. Children should have names like Jane or Susan or Paul.

Hilda Hughes, as always, sat with eyes averted and nervously tapped and wiggled her trembling fingers and rolled the corners of her papers until they shredded. Next to Hilda was Wendell Bradstreet Ellery IV, who tilted back in his chair, wearing what he intended to be an astute expression. Poor Ellery was slow-witted and afraid that people would notice; therefore, on occasions such as this one, where his acumen might be tested, he adopted a special expression, with one slightly raised eyebrow, that he imagined a powerfully smart and witty man would wear. Peter thought it came across as the expression of someone finding something suspicious in his soup. Miss Devereaux had appointed Ellery to the board because he was the grandson of an old family friend who had begged her to find something for him to do, and she had convinced herself that a man of his simplicity would bring straightforwardness to their deliberations. When Milton Steinberg came in and sat beside Ellery, across from Peter, to make a shorthand record of the meeting, Miss Devereaux tapped the table with a teaspoon.

"Let's get started," she said. "Coffee, Mr. Frankl? Are you sick? You look pale, not well. Or is it just the thought of dealing with us?"

Everyone laughed heartily, Ellery five seconds later and longer than the others.

"Now, uh, you've all read my memorandum, I hope," she continued, looking around graciously, "and I want to hear your reactions. I confess I've sent it already to . . . to, uh . . . oh. Well, I sent it . . . I . . ."

"Oh . . . I think . . . I vote yes," said Hilda in soft little bursts, so embarrassed by this fumbling for the name that she spoke without being spoken to.

"Not so fast," said Peter. Ordinarily the gentlest of men, he regularly found himself roused to protosadism against Hilda because of her timid, tiny voice, which irked him in its assumption that the rest of humanity, other than herself, were all malignant brutes. "There's no motion on the table. Nothing to vote for yet."

Hilda shrank into her chair. "Oh, of course, sorry. . . ."

"What did you think of the project, Wendell?" Peter asked.

"I, uh . . ." Ellery was terrified to give his opinion first. If only Hilda hadn't made a mistake and voted! He looked shrewd, but actually he hadn't been able to figure out the memorandum except that it seemed to have something to do with terrorism and September 11.

"As far as I'm concerned," he said, "we shouldn't get involved in our own business and stay clear of—"

"Janet Millbrook at Columbia," said Miss Devereaux, "and she was very positive. She said she thought they could find a room, and plenty of faculty interest, but she was, shall we say, thoughtful about the idea of non-faculty members. However, she was quite delighted to hear of our connection with Mr. Frankl because she remembered him from . . . from . . ."

"Are you going to invite Arif Ahmed?" asked Orazio Cromwell, looking furtively around the table. "That would make it interesting."

"Hilda has a list," said Miss Devereaux. "Have you got copies of that list, Hilda—a list of names of possible outside members?"

Hilda tried to pass around copies of the list of names, but her hands shook so conspicuously that instead she shoved the stack into the middle of the table where everyone could reach one. She acted as though this were a good idea and gave a shy little chuckle. Peter knew that the woman wasn't stupid and basically kept the whole foundation running, but she was completely, annoyingly, neurotic. He scanned the list, to which she had given a three-line title, "Possible Outside Members for a Two-Year Seminar on Terrorism and Its Causes and Cures, to Be Funded by the Harmon R. Devereaux Foundation and held at Columbia University, Academic Years 2003–04, 2004–05." She had drawn up a very good list, in Peter's opinion, with politicians, scientists, theologians, and Middle East experts, among others whose names he did not recognize, but at the top of the list, she had listed, as chair, Peter Frankl.

"Oh, no, you can't do that," said Peter. "No, no. Columbia would never agree to an outsider as chair. You'll have to have an academic do that, a Columbia person or some renowned visiting someone or other. You can't put me in there, and I can't imagine why you'd want to anyway. Out of the question."

"Hilda thought it would be a good idea to pick someone who is not academic and who isn't tied to one narrow discipline," said Miss Devereaux. "You're so well-read, Mr. Frankl. We all think you're so intelligent and down-to-earth—just the man to keep the group sensible and focused. Besides, most of the people will probably lean left or right, and your opinions are always moderate and well-balanced. We need that if people are going to be forced to think about their most basic premises. And I don't know why Columbia wouldn't agree to it. After all, you taught a course at the law school once, didn't you?"

"Twice," said Peter, "but long ago. Look, I appreciate the compliment, but it's impossible." He found this very bad idea quite tempting, though, and briefly fantasized making the occasional well-appreciated trenchant remark to an attentive circle of leading lights.

"And suppose they do say no," said Miss Devereaux. "How does it hurt to ask?"

"It doesn't hurt to ask, I guess," said Peter. He sighed, thinking of the vow he had made, years ago, to his now perilously ill wife to cut back on his involvement with the Devereaux Foundation so that they would have more time for "enjoying themselves before they got too old." And before he could stop it, the ghastly thought again raced through his mind: maybe Lesley would never wake up. He so thoroughly banished it that he immediately forgot he had thought it at all, however, and was aware only of a trifling hope that something might come of Hilda's little scheme.

Hilda, examining his face surreptitiously, correctly guessed that he was pleased and would accept the job if Columbia permitted. She was exceedingly gratified. She had had an idea that inviting Peter Frankl to lead this seminar would be a good way to repay him for some of the trouble he had been taking over them for all these years. She looked away to avoid the danger of catching his eye accidentally; but Peter knew she was trying to do him a big favor, and he was both touched and humiliated that even Hilda

Hughes saw through him. Poor silly, sweet woman—one of those damaged people. Surely, Peter thought, another terrifying idea breaking loose in his mind, surely there was no chance that someday Susan would end up like Hilda—a strange, lonely lady living hand to mouth in some drab little room somewhere, with some artsy little job. Hilda had no high-earning, devoted father to protect her.

CHAPTER 8

The following evening, Susan kissed her father good-bye at her mother's bedside, then walked home to meet Chris, but he didn't come. When he was almost two hours late, she considered giving him a call. She didn't want to; it would come across as nagging. But when it was nearly 11:00 P.M., she called anyway, first trying his apartment, then, repeatedly, his cell phone, which he finally answered at midnight.

"I'm tied up. Not for another hour at least," Chris said. He sounded tolerant, not at all apologetic. In fact, he sounded as though Susan had called with an unexpected and not very welcome invitation instead of questions about a broken date. This was the third time Chris had done this sort of thing.

Last week for his birthday, Susan, who was an excellent cook, had made a special dinner and given him two tickets to a Yankees game, which she tucked into a card with a note that made it clear she herself did not expect to accompany him. She knew he'd rather go with someone who really understood baseball and rooted for the Yankees. But Chris had not shown up for his birthday dinner, and Susan, Sylvie, and Alcott had had to eat it without him. Susan's humiliation on this occasion was amplified by each compliment Sylvie and Alcott paid to one of the many tokens of special trouble, expense, and skill that appeared on Susan's table, even though their appreciation was offered sensitively, in a cool, understated style. It pained Susan almost as much as their unfriendly opinion of Chris. She herself found it impossible to take what had happened at face value and refused to judge him harshly. Chris's behavior was so appalling that she had to assume some mitigating circumstance—psychological or physical.

"This is just Chris being Chris," she finally told Sylvie and Alcott, to forestall any expression of their almost tender sympathy, which she couldn't help seeing despite their attempts to hide it. But this little speech—so nerdy and dumb, so gauche—made it only harder for them all to hang on to a civilized realism. For the rest of the evening, Susan laughed too much, smiled too politely, and never lost that horrible, wide-eyed, goofy-intellectual expression. By the time they left, Sylvie and Alcott were exhausted with the strain of pretending not to see through her.

When Susan saw Chris the following day, he didn't apologize and showed no interest in the tickets—although she knew he was a fanatical fan and she had consulted experts who told her that this was an important game. On Sunday, he didn't go to the game. He felt too lazy to go, he said on the phone, or to come uptown to see Susan.

"This sort of behavior," she said, stiffly neutral, when several days later they sat down for an awkward talk, "is calculated to alienate. Wouldn't it be more efficient just to tell me what you're thinking? Why bother playing out all these scenes, these set pieces, and make me guess?"

That comment roused Chris from a resentful torpor. "Scenes? You mean like from a play, literally dramatizing? Instead of just telling you . . . That's interesting. That's what I like about you, Susan. You say things like that." He had been exceptionally pleased with her, admiring even, and the threatening breach was healed. But now he'd done it again.

"Let's cancel, then, Chris," Susan said. "It's late. I have an early class, and I want to visit my mother before that."

"All right," he said. "Whatever. I'm starting—" He clicked off in the middle of some final phrase that she couldn't make out. She had noticed that people often did that at the end of cell phone conversations.

After they met in March, Chris pursued Susan for weeks. He invited her to dinners, movies, plays, and parties, but she often turned him down to spend time with her mother instead. Susan had had doubts about Chris. She was attracted to him but mistrustful, and she held something back even after they became lovers. Perceiving this and feeling frustrated and vulnerable, Chris courted her more urgently than ever—marveling that sexual intimacy hadn't ended his interest, as it always had before. He inferred from his own behavior that he was more serious about her than he had ever been about a woman before. When he wasn't with her, he called constantly, looking for reassurances that, finally, just before his birthday, she shyly offered and he eagerly received. But that very night, within half an hour of her confession of love, Chris began to back off. She knew that his indifference when she set up the birthday dinner had augured bad things.

Her father might be right that she shouldn't be mixed up with someone as ambivalent as Chris. Susan had been shocked when she realized that he was interested only in chasing her, not in catching her. How could someone as original as Chris engage in such clichéd behavior? But she had told him that she loved him. Those were words that an adult could not go back on; they were a promise, binding even though he hadn't yet said he loved her. You couldn't base love on a quid pro quo.

Susan had never told any man but Chris that she loved him, although she had said it to two boys: the first when she was nine and the second when she was nineteen. Apparently it was a ten-year cycle. She had little doubt that without Chris she'd be alone for another ten years, perhaps forever. She'd probably never have children—with or without Chris, who sounded unenthusiastic about both kids and marriage. That was all right, because Susan had her own doubts about all that. For one thing, she would surely make any child of hers miserable. She couldn't even make herself happy. And all marriages were dangerously prone to make everyone miserable. To be unambivalent about marriage, you needed to be one of those bland, oblivious people who never expect trouble and never think anything is their fault—like her mother, a great believer in marriage. Or at least you needed to be less like Susan and more like Mallory, who always assumed she made her boyfriends happy, whereas Susan always assumed the contrary.

Susan thought, on the whole, balancing the reality of Chris against the unknowns, that she could be content with Chris, whatever the problems, if she could only be sure of him. After all, she and Chris, with their shared commitments to the arts and their similar educations, were far better suited to each other than her father and mother had been. What a mismatched pair *they* were, with opposed tastes, values, and temperaments. But her father had never left her mother or quarreled with her perfect right to live out her life with him at her side, doing his best to make her happy. Susan concluded her reverie by deciding to let Chris rely on her and see what happened. This, at least, was a course of action that didn't make her feel guilty.

Susan went to bed and awoke at 1:00 a.m. with a sense of foreboding, her heart beating haphazardly with accelerated riffs. It was hours before she could fall asleep again, and when the alarm sounded at 7:00, she woke feeling doomed and resigned. She walked to St. Luke's, gathering herself so as to be able to appear harmless and happy before her father, her unconscious mother, and the nurses. She resolved to talk to Chris despite her fear of exposing the undercurrents of their present situation.

But when she called him after visiting the hospital and going to class, he seemed surprised to hear from her.

"Of course we can talk," said Chris after a disconcerting pause. It was terrible the way his voice, when he finally spoke, was affably intimate and nonplussed. It made her yearn with love for him. She perceived her own emotions as wacky, off. Yet he *was* behaving differently. Susan was now desperate for him to acknowledge the reality of this—if it was a reality. It was more painful losing him this way, with his tolerant distance and decent, mannerly denial, she thought, than if he'd announced openly that he didn't love her or if he'd actually died.

When he finally showed up at her apartment the following night, in high spirits, full of quips and anecdotes and affection, she found it impossible to tell him any of her doubts. They seemed lunatic and distorted. Susan told herself that she had to accept the reality that with no man of her own generation was she going to have the kind of merger of lives that their parents had had. That was all dead. My whole mentality, thought Susan, is an anachronism. If I'm not careful, I'll end up with no one just because I insist on leading the kind of life that made my parents miserable.

CHAPTER 9

"Ms. Braithwaite, Alex coming up," the doorman of 635 West 117th Street said genially into the house phone, and Alexei took the elevator to the ninth floor. As he walked to apartment 9E, the small boy with whom he had been playing chess in the library on Wednesdays opened the door and stood there jumping in excitement. "I beat an eight hundred," he shouted down the hallway.

"Good, Stuart. Why don't you print out the game, and we'll go over it later."

The boy was open to this suggestion. "But I don't know how to print out."

"Ellen knows how. Ask Ellen."

And the boy ran down a long hallway, screaming for Ellen, pursued by a dirty-faced two-year-old in T-shirt and diapers who had appeared behind him and peeked shyly at Alexei.

A tall, good-looking man in his forties was walking toward the far end of the hall. A small fortyish woman, with dark curls beginning to show gray, leaned out of a doorway at the near end.

"Go right in, Alexei," said the man, looking over his shoulder. "I'll be there in a minute."

"It's all yours," said the woman. "I'm just piling up my music and I'm out. How are you? How is it coming?"

"Great."

"Really?"

"Well, I mean, it's . . . it's coming," Alexei said, regretting his immodest first reply. He had a tendency to boast, although he tried to restrain himself, recognizing how it put people off. A friend had once told him that this meant he was insecure, but Alexei did not believe he was insecure. In Alexei's opinion, he simply found it easy—and pleasant—to admire his own accomplishments.

"Of course it is," said the woman. "I could play for you today, if Charles wants to do that. Charles, do you want me to accompany today?"

"Oh, yes, good," said Charles Braithwaite, who had returned with a pair of eyeglasses through which he was now studying a page of music. Alexei was amused by how they dramatically transformed the effect of Charles's handsomeness. Now he came across like an actor playing a professor, whereas a moment ago he had been more of a romantic lead. "If you can. Let us get warmed up first and see how it's going. In about half an hour?"

The woman, Anne Braithwaite, bent over and picked up the toddler, who had run up to her. From this position of safety, he now stared brazenly at Alexei. When they had gone, Charles closed the door of the studio, and outside, only faint sounds evidenced the progress of Alexei's lesson from warm-up through to Donizetti.

"Yes, you're getting that," said Charles, and although he tried to sound neutral, Alexei's face showed that he believed he had been praised. "But you've got to make it bigger," Charles went on. "Three times—five—ten times bigger. If you were at the Met, no one would hear you past the twentieth row. And if you sang in the sextet at that volume, it would be a quintet. Now what about those classes—acting and movement and . . . ?" Charles resisted telling Alexei how greatly he had improved. With Alexei, he felt that his job was always to depress his hopes.

"I can't afford it right now. Maybe I'll sign up for the next term, if I can get some cash together in the meantime."

"You can't afford not to. Look, Alexei, do you want to sing or don't you? I can't recommend you for an audition unless I can say something more substantial about your background. This is two years now I've been on your back about this. You want to do it soon, do you hear me? If you want me to take you seriously—if you want anyone to take you seriously . . ."

"I don't really need any classes, although I understand what you say— that people want you to have them. Anyway, Mr. Braithwaite, you don't understand how impossible it is for me to come up with that much money."

"Apply for a scholarship again."

"They'll only turn me down again. Look, I don't need the classes. You can tell. I'm a natural."

The last remark infuriated Charles, even though he suspected it was true. "I can't sell a natural, Alexei, and I'm sick of your attitude. We live in an unnatural age. They want degrees, certificates. In a couple of years, I'm sure they'll want your PSATs."

Alexei was shaken by Charles's anger, but try as he might, he couldn't feel quite as terrible about it as Charles obviously thought he should; he was still too pleased with his own singing. He reddened slightly and resisted the impulse to ask what PSATs were, but he could think of nothing else to say. Charles, meanwhile, regretted his outburst.

"Look, I'm sorry," he began.

"It's all right," Alexei responded, too cheerfully, too readily. But Charles swallowed his annoyance this time.

"Okay, let's do the duet and then we'll ask Anne to come in. No, wait." Charles opened the door of the studio and shouted, "Jane! Janie!"

In a moment, a tall girl of about sixteen in jeans and bare feet, who strongly resembled Charles, appeared in the doorway of the studio. "What?" She looked unsmilingly at Alexei but briefly raised her fingers in greeting.

"I want you to sing Lucia in this duet, with Edgardo here."

"I don't know it," Jane said. "What are you so mad about?"

"I'm not mad. Of course you know it. Just read through it with him. No big deal. We need to hear something."

Jane shrugged, but she put real effort into her performance, which was obvious to her father. And Alexei said appreciatively to Charles when they had finished, "She even *sounds* like your daughter."

"Very well done, sweetheart," Charles called to her as she ran out, her lips pursed to resist a smile. "Will you ask Mommy to come in now?" His mood was improved by the success of the duet and his daughter's talent.

"You too," he said to Alexei only slightly grudgingly. "That's getting there. That was useful. I have two points for you. When Lucia says this— here, you need to be more responsive. And many tenors miss this little conversation here. You didn't miss it, but you could make more of it."

Anne appeared a few moments later with the toddler in her arms and Jane at her side. "Gillie, Mummy's going to play piano for Daddy for a minute while you play with Janie."

"No," said the child, but he didn't resist being passed to Jane, who was whispering something in his ear.

After his lesson with Charles, Alexei went to the kitchen to find Anne, who was obviously expecting him. A plate of food waited for him on the table, and she placed another on a high chair for the toddler, Gilbert. Alexei sat and ate while studying the computer printout of Stuart's Internet chess game.

"Here, Stuart, why did you use your queen and not your rook? You're just lucky the other guy was asleep or you would have lost right there."

"I don't like the queen. I like rooks better."

Alexei was amused, but Anne, offering a bowl of cut fruit to Gilbert, perked up at hearing this.

"Put your napkin in your lap, Alexei," she said, "and tear the bread before you eat it and take smaller bites. What's wrong with the queen, Stuart?" Alexei did as he was told, apparently unembarrassed.

"The queen always gets you in trouble," Stuart said, and he was serious.

"What!" Alexei exclaimed, but, following Anne's lead, he suppressed a laugh. "But the queen can do everything the rook can do, and more besides. The queen is better at staying out of trouble."

Stuart was not swayed.

"You have to remember," Anne told Alexei when Stuart had gone, "at his age sometimes logic is still controlled by emotion."

"At my age, too," Alexei said.

This was too obvious an invitation for Anne to ignore. Sometimes Alexei liked to talk things over with Anne.

"So you and Stuart are both having girl troubles?"

Alexei laughed self-consciously and twisted his face into some expression that Anne did not know how to read—possibly trying to look tough, she thought.

"It's just that I might be getting interested," he said, "kind of, anyway, sort of, in someone who thinks she's . . . a big deal. Or maybe I'm not that interested, but I just want to make her stop feeling so superior."

"Forget that, Alexei," said Anne. "Who is this person?"

"She's one of my computer clients. She writes for the *Gazette*—Mallory Holmes."

"Oh, I've seen her things. She just had this absurd piece on facial hair. Alexei, really! How could you worry about what someone like that thinks?"

"Don't get the wrong idea. She's actually smart and very ambitious—two degrees, and both are ivy leaves."

"Ivy League," said Anne, straight-faced.

"She only writes that silly stuff because they make her, but she's got plans to do more important things."

"I think you should leave her alone and look for someone who can appreciate you."

"It's true she's kind of ignorant. But she's cute and nice, and she laughs."

Alexei was openly wistful and woebegone now, and Anne suffered for him. He was such a dear—she couldn't bear his being lonely and having some silly girl turn him away because he had no ivy leaves.

"He's driving me out of my mind," Charles fumed at dinner hours later.

"But I'm making a little progress on the table manners," Anne said. They no longer bothered to censor these discussions before the children, who had had all too many opportunities to observe their parents chide, pressure, and correct Alexei.

"The problem is, he's so arrogant," Charles said. "You can't tell the kid anything."

"But that's purely defensive," Anne said. "If he didn't keep telling himself that he's wonderful and that the things he lacks don't matter, he wouldn't have the guts to keep trying. And he really is trying. It's painful to see how hard, and how little chance he has of achieving anything he'll be remotely satisfied with."

The children looked worried.

"It's not defensive," Charles said. "It's egomaniacal."

"No way," Anne insisted. "That doesn't fit with the rest of him."

"Alexei," Charles continued, "reminds me of myself at that age. Everyone thought I was stubborn and unaccommodating, too. But compared to him, I was perfectly reasonable. With him, it's almost a kind of insanity—I mean that he won't take those courses when he so desperately wants to be in opera and his chances are already so poor."

"I know. He's completely irrational about it," said Anne. "You can't imagine what's going to happen to him. Sometimes I wish you'd never agreed to teach him." Such words from Anne, who tended to be excessively sanguine, were ominous.

"I've thought of stopping his lessons. I feel as though I'm encouraging him to self-destruct," said Charles.

"No, don't do that!" said Jane, who had listened to this exchange anxiously. "I like Alexei's singing."

"Don't, Daddy," said Ellen tearfully. She was almost ten and, like Stuart, took chess lessons with Alexei once a week. "Don't be mad at Alexei."

"I'm not mad at him, sweetie. But I have to have a serious talk with him."

"Anyway, I don't think he's going to ruin his life," Jane said with conviction.

"Why?" asked both her parents.

"Because he's right. All that stuff you want him to do would be a waste of time. It wouldn't get him anywhere."

Charles and Anne looked at each other. Jane herself had always been in rebellion against formal schooling, and, yes, a genius here and there could avoid jumping the hoops, but Jane did not see that it was already too late for Alexei to aim at anything he or Jane would regard as success. Alexei had already, utterly and certainly, failed, although he wouldn't admit it. Charles and Anne hoped only to help him find and accept a place at the lower levels of the hierarchies of the professional music world, although he deserved better. But even this would elude him if he continued to be so stubborn and to refuse to lower his sights.

Walking down Broadway after leaving the Braithwaites, Alexei was in high spirits. He stopped into the library and picked up a book he had reserved, then continued walking south on Broadway to the subway stop at 110th Street. The spring evening was pleasant. His singing had earned Charles Braithwaite's approval, and Charles Braithwaite's good opinion was the one most worth having in the whole world. All his scolding, cautions, and pessimisms, therefore, meant nothing. Alexei had arrived at the pinnacle of success, as he privately defined it. In fact, he was so happy with his deserts that he was indifferent to his rewards. To be able to feel that he belonged on the opera stage, whether or not he ever got there, was exhilarating.

Two years ago, when Charles Braithwaite had first agreed to teach him, Alexei had been a dropout from the Manhattan School of Music in Morningside Heights, where he had not done very well. He had failed to take required courses; he had attended others and then never taken the exams. He had impressed a couple of people on the voice faculty, but in the end he was just too much trouble, with his constant money problems and his refusal to meet the very unobjectionable requirements for earning a degree. Alexei was a frustrating mix of egoism, stubbornness, and genuine modesty; his enormous faith in himself never translated into disdain for anyone else or into inflated ideas of his rights—sweetest kid in the world, the professors at MSM had said in each of the several anguished discussions of his case that they had been forced to have before throwing him out. He went to MSM simply to learn certain things he wanted to know with a minimum of fuss. The college, however, had its own goals; it wanted to be able to certify his broad professional competence to do any number of jobs in the musical world and therefore had insisted that he learn a lot of other things in which he had no interest and take exams so that strangers could be assured of his usefulness to them. This was a waste of his time.

Alexei rode the local to Times Square and changed to the Q, which took him to Brighton Beach in Brooklyn. There he got off and walked a few blocks to a shabby building whose door stood ajar and unattended. He walked through a lobby in which the air was tainted by an unpleasant mixture of organic smells and took the stairs to the fourth floor, where he entered a tiny railroad flat that consisted of a foyer and two other rooms, each opening into the other. In the foyer, there was a narrow daybed made up with a coverlet pulled neatly over its pillow next to a computer that sat on a broad wall shelf, for which the daybed evidently served as chair. In the first room, an unshaven man in his sixties with a stained shirtfront sat at a table spread with newspapers. A full ashtray sat in front of him. He held a smoking cigarette between stubby fingers and was reading a Russian-language newspaper. From behind the closed door of the other room came the sounds of a violin playing Bach.

"Did you bring it?" the man said, scarcely glancing at Alexei. Alexei put the library book before him on the table. The man grasped it eagerly and immediately began riffling the pages.

"Here it is," he said, looking Alexei full in the face for the first time and then tapping a diagram on the page with his forefinger. "Look here. What you did in '95, against that fellow Bonham, it's just what Kasparov did against Karpov, in 1986, in London, game five. Make us some tea, will you?"

Alexei would not look but went to put a kettle on a small stove that stood in an alcove near the table.

"And so where have you been?" asked the man, slamming the book on the table. "You didn't show up last week, and you didn't call."

Alexei responded coolly, "Nowhere special. Anyway, I did call. Where's Mama?"

"That haircut—it looks ridiculous. I can see your scalp. And what makes it stand up like that? Absurd." His own untidy gray hair made a long, greasy plume over his forehead and was tucked efficiently behind his ears. In the back, it covered his collar. "Were you spending our last dollar for singing? Pursuing your great career as fitness oaf?"

"It's cheaper to get it short," said Alexei, ignoring the other comments. "The cut lasts longer. Besides, Dad, this is the style now. I like it."

Alexei's father turned and called to the closed door, "Papa! Come have some tea. Alexei is home."

"When's Mama coming?"

"Maybe an hour. The old lady wasn't well today. She's sitting late with her."

"Then I'll cook something. She'll be tired," said Alexei.

A stooped old man appeared in the doorway to the other room. He was frail, with scant snow white hair, dressed in a worn seersucker sports coat over a white shirt buttoned up to the neck. "Alyosha," he said affectionately, and held out his arms to the young man, who came and embraced him.

"Were you at your lesson?" asked the old man. "Did you see the little fellow who plays the violin?"

"Yes, but he didn't play today. I gave him a chess lesson."

"Someday you bring him home and let me hear him. *I'll* give him a lesson, too."

"I will, Grandpa. He'd like that."

The three sat together around the table and lifted mugs of strong tea. Nicolai was unshaven, his fingernails were dirty, and he hunched greedily over his tea and slurped. Alexei had to quell an irritable urge to tell him to stop it. At this moment, his father turned to him angrily.

"Did you send off an application?"

"I've decided not to. The application fee alone is fifty dollars, plus a thirty-dollar late fee, and I couldn't possibly pay the tuition. Anyway, I'm not interested in finishing a degree. I don't need it."

"You're spoiled. You're spoiled, selfish, and stupid. Because of you, your mother is out lifting invalid old ladies all day, which she doesn't have the strength for. And you can't be bothered to study so you can get a decent job. You can't be bothered to play a chess tournament. No, not you."

The old man looked unhappy at this. "Too harsh, Nikolai! How can you speak to him that way? A boy like Alyosha doesn't need to take those silly courses, I promise you. Leave him alone and he'll—"

"Shut up! You've ruined this kid, you and his mother, with that nonsense."

Alexei pushed away from the table and abruptly stood, his face livid. "I'll have to leave if you keep it up. I can't stand it. I'll have to leave."

"So leave. Do you think anyone here wants you to stay?"

"Nikolai—"

"What's all this?" demanded a woman who appeared in the doorway, in a sharp voice. She was stout, with short gray hair, and she wore a loose cotton dress in a summer print. In each plump arm, she held a bag of groceries. Alexei went to her, kissed her, and took the bags.

"Mama," he began.

"Sophia," said Nikolai.

"Sophia, dearest," said the old man.

"If you're going to squabble, I'm going back out again."

"We're not," said Alexei. "You sit. I'll cook tonight." She didn't argue, because she was tired and hungry, and fell into a straight-backed chair from which she called out instructions now and then while Alexei made a supper of eggs and lox scraps. Again, Alexei observed his family's table manners with a critical eye, becoming aware that everyone ate too fast, taking large bites, bending over their plates, and never breaking their bread before eating it.

"So did you finish it?" Sophia asked Nikolai.

"Not yet. I need to retype and then get it copied."

"I keep telling you, you've got to use a computer, Dad. You just put the résumé on and then update it whenever you need to, print out as many copies as . . ." Alexei spoke partly to take his mind off his irritation and partly because he knew his father would dislike this suggestion.

"And I've told you over and over I don't want one and I don't need one."

"Why can't you just try mine?"

"So you sang a duet?" said Sophia in a too obvious attempt to change the subject, which only increased Alexei's determination to needle his father.

"You're being ridiculous, Dad. With a computer—"

"If I am, that's better than selfish, lazy, and arrogant, the way you are—allowing your mother to kill herself with work when you could make everything easy for her."

"Why is it I and not you who does that? I give her money almost every week. What about your job? You've taken a month to write up a résumé."

"There is no work in this country for someone my age, with no degree."

"There are lots of things you could do, but you can't hold the job once you get it."

"Stop, Alexei," said Sophia.

"Are you going to Philadelphia?" asked Nikolai.

"What—to play in the tournament?" replied Alexei. "No way. Don't tell me—let me guess why you want to know. Is the reason legal or illegal?"

"I've never done anything illegal," Nikolai shouted.

"You have lots of times. You even got me thrown out of a game, trying to signal me."

"What's this?" Sophia asked, looking alarmed. "No one told me about getting thrown out of anything. Nikolai, when—"

"Years ago! He was a child and didn't understand. I was just protecting him. But I won't stay here to hear all this lying and disrespect. Alexei, give me five dollars."

And his father got up and left, the rolled-up newspaper under his arm. The racing form, Alexei thought, but he said nothing and put his wallet back in his pocket. He could tell that his mother was shaken by what he had just said, and he had broken a vow to himself not to let her know about some things that she could not help. He hated himself for this and cast around for a convincing way to take back his words.

"I was exaggerating," said Alexei, "because he gets me so mad. It was really nothing. You see, I was—"

"Don't tell me any more. I'm going to forget all about it. Whatever happened, it was long ago, and I have enough problems now. Don't worry, darling."

Alexei felt a little better. She could, he knew, push things out of her mind that way. The two of them cleared the table and washed up the dishes. Alexei donned headphones and sat cross-legged on the daybed listening to CDs for nearly an hour, oblivious to anything said about him or to him. He knew it would make his mother and grandfather happy just to have him in the room. Then he went to his computer and began playing chess online, logging on as "#19." The game was played through an apparently exclusive club in which strict anonymity was required. Alexei had been invited to join only recently, in a pseudonymous e-mail, and had played just one game so far. On that occasion, the other player, #3, had been very skilled, and Alexei had almost lost. It had been really exciting. To his pleased surprise, this night's competitor, #11, was also superb. Alexei almost lost again, in an intriguing game. He was most curious as to who selected the club members and how many of them there were.

When the game was over it was past 9:00, and they all turned in, because Alexei and Sophia had to leave so early in the morning—before 6:00 A.M.—he to return to Morningside Heights and she to the old woman she tended. Late that night, Alexei, cramped in the little daybed, was woken when his father pushed past him into the middle room in which he slept with Sophia on the sofa bed.

CHAPTER 10

One evening, Peter and Susan took their regular seats at Lesley's bedside, he on Lesley's left and she on her right. Lesley's complexion was pasty, and her once glamorous nails were clipped close for easy care. Her hair was combed back off her face in utilitarian style, and the roots were showing two inches of pure white. Peter and Susan talked quietly about the dawning optimism of the doctors and therapists as Lesley showed small signs of arousal and reaction. On the other hand, the longer the coma lasted, the worse the prognosis.

"Her lips just moved, honey," Peter said to Susan, "like she was trying to talk."

Susan studied her mother's face for a moment, then resumed staring out the window, holding her mother's hand. She was pale and a little thin, Peter thought. The more he became aware of how his wife had neglected their daughter, the more oppressed he was by her grieving and devotion. And Susan surely perceived and suffered from his own lack of grief, to which he was now so accustomed that he had been forgetting to berate himself for it.

"What about this guy you're seeing," Peter said after a long silence during which he read the newspaper. Lesley's face twitched, but that, surely, was just coincidence.

"Oh, nothing's going to come of it," Susan said. She stared off again and turned her hands up, helplessly, as though this were exasperating but not tragic. What, Peter wondered, looking at her, is that expression about?

Susan was a cynic in the lower half of her face and an amused intellectual ingénue in the upper half, with wide eyes and raised brows. It was a face that announced its own falseness and subtly demeaned itself, a face that could put off even a loving father.

"But in the meantime it looks like it's getting you down," Peter said.

"It's not Chris," Susan replied. Her father obviously disliked what he heard of Chris. "I'm just down lately."

"Sweetheart, come home, then. Let me take care of you for a while. You spend too much time alone." Peter stood up on the other side of Lesley's bed and gestured over her unconscious form.

But Susan knew that going home wouldn't help. At home, there was the onerous business of not letting her father detect her melancholy. It had been such a relief to move out a couple of years ago and have so many more hours in the day when she could drop the slightly goofy mask, cheerful and accommodating, that helped her family and friends bear her existence. Nonetheless, Susan did something on this occasion that in her adult life she had never done before. She walked around the bed, leaned on her father's chest, and sobbed as noiselessly as she could. Unexpectedly, this seemed to make him feel better. She had thought he would fall apart.

"Well, Susie," he said, patting her back, "of course you're unhappy. Life hasn't been good to you lately, has it. But, honey, I think she's going to be all right, and you too. Isn't that right, Lesley? Everyone's going to be fine."

Susan pulled his handkerchief out of his pocket, blew her nose, and wiped the tears from her face. "But I'm not sure it's about . . . it's about a lot of things," she said.

"Tell me, honey."

She shook her head sorrowfully.

"You're not going to tell me about Chris Wylie, eh?" Peter dropped his voice as though Lesley could hear and Susan would wish to speak privately.

She shook her head again. "There's nothing to tell. He's quite wonderful. I don't think he's in love with me, but I'm in love with him."

"Susie, that's not smart. Why would you love someone who's not in love with you? And what's so wonderful about him, anyway? He would have to be a jerk if he doesn't love you."

Later that evening, Peter described this conversation, with all its complex background, to Hilda Hughes, the shy program officer from the Devereaux Foundation, whom he happened to encounter in a checkout line at University Food Market. Hilda was pushing a shopping cart in which were gathered three varieties of imported chocolate-covered cookies, two pints of ice cream, a head of lettuce, and tea. Peter was buying a can of shaving cream. He was unaccustomed to doing his own shopping. Lesley used to make lists for the housekeeper, who didn't do a very good job without direction; so now he had to keep track of everything. He was only just getting the hang of it.

He was astonished when he saw Hilda.

"What are you doing here?" he asked.

"I live nearby," she said after two attempts to speak in which her mouth moved and no voice emerged, "on 114th."

"My daughter lives on 114th—690 West 114th."

"In my building?" Hilda asked, bewildered.

"*Your* building? No kidding! That's New York for you. I've lived on Riverside near 116th for nearly forty years. I came here for law school and never left. I'm amazed we've never run into each other before this." Six Ninety West 114th was only a couple of blocks from his own large apartment building with its grand entrance on Riverside Drive.

"Well . . . yes, it is strange, isn't it. I always shop here." She recollected a young woman in her building who might be Mr. Frankl's daughter. "Does your daughter have long black hair, curly?"

"Yes. Very strange I never ran into you at your building, except, I guess, I don't often go to Susan's. She moved in the year before last. She comes home, of course. I haven't been in here, either," he said, looking around the crowded market, "for ages."

"Where do you go?"

"What do you mean? Oh, to market! My wife or the housekeeper takes care of shopping. But my wife's in the hospital now, St. Luke's. I was just visiting her with Susan."

"Oh, I'm so sorry."

Peter avoided explanations that might inspire any further sympathy. Sympathy still raised intense guilt.

"Used to be the Ta-Kome here, before this place," he said.

"Salter's Books was next door," said Hilda, stifling an excessive joy at being able to share recollections of the tawdry old places.

"My daughter's upset. Boyfriend troubles," said Peter.

Hilda stared at the thick roll of bills Peter took out of his pocket. He peeled off a crisp fifty to pay for his shaving cream. Then he stood by as the cashier rang up Hilda's purchases. Hilda observed carefully, making sure the charges were correct. She grew uncomfortable when Peter did not walk away. He was waiting for her. He wanted to walk out together, but she had nothing to say to him—nothing at all. She strove vainly to think of small talk. Peter picked up her grocery bag while she paid, and the phrase *sealed her doom* came into her mind.

They walked south on Broadway, slowly, and Hilda's anxiety began to subside, for Peter did all the talking. He told her all about Susan and Chris Wylie, as though her living in the same building gave her some sort of stake in knowing about Susan. Peter knew little about Hilda except that she had worked at the Devereaux Foundation forever and that she was the real brains of the outfit, even though she came across as such an odd duck. He shouldn't be telling her about Susan's boyfriend troubles, but on this particular evening, Peter felt acutely the absence of a confidante. So he told everything to Hilda Hughes, and in such detail that he kept her standing for fifteen minutes on her stoop. Maybe he was becoming just as eccentric as she was.

Hilda Hughes looked interested enough, but the longer he talked, the tenser she grew; and when he finally paused, she could think of nothing to say. She was sorry that he was so unhappy but, with the acute perception of the neurotic, saw that he wanted no sympathy. They both stood silently for too long a time after he had finished. It was her turn to speak, but she knew she had better shut up, or she would come out with a string of inanities and non sequiturs.

"What is the origin of the expression *seal her doom?*" she essayed finally, in a slightly panicked attempt at chitchat.

But she realized immediately what a stupid thing this was to say, and in fact, Peter was confused by it for a moment. Then he gave a small laugh and said, "Hilda, you're a master of tact. Or maybe you're a tactician. I don't know, but I'd say the origin of the phrase is legal. Just guessing, but in Old English law the doom was a punishment or a judgment against someone, and maybe, once they wrote it down and sealed it—you know, with hot wax, or whatever—that was it, no going back. That's what I would guess."

She was astonished to hear this. "Imagine your knowing about things like that!" she exclaimed, and had the rare, blissful experience of feeling her words and her meaning coincide. After this, however, she went silent again, afraid of undoing the good effect of her normal utterance, and tried to think of a way to escape this man and his ghastly, fascinating chatter, so that she could withdraw into her little room and her solitary evening comforts, out of all danger of saying strange things to anyone. She glanced furtively at her door and then faced Peter, summoning the strength not to bolt and fly up the steps of the stoop into safety. At last he waved and walked off toward Riverside Drive.

Once locked securely inside her studio, she browbeat herself for hours with her many failures in this conversation with Peter before she wondered why he had told all this to her, with whom he never discussed his personal affairs. Then she also remembered that, finally, he had laughed. Was it possible that she had been witty? Or tactful?

Peter was surprised at himself, buttonholing eccentric ladies, scaring them, talking their ears off. The strain of everything was getting to him. He had actually walked out of his way so he could tell Susan's intimate secrets to Hilda Hughes from the Devereaux Foundation, who, it turned out, lived in the same row house as Susan. Peter only now recognized Hilda as a type, one of those Morningside Heights semireclusives. She had a dismal, girlish, willowy look, with her skinny calves showing between the hem of the pleated skirt and her flat shoes. Hilda wore her wavy graying hair long, gathered into a tortoiseshell clip at the back of her neck, off her face. No makeup, dry cheeks covered with fine down, but rosy. She was younger than he had realized, maybe late forties, judging from the amount of brown still showing in the long hair. Girls, the baby boom girls, had all started wearing that long hair after he'd graduated and married in the mid-sixties, and he'd always looked wistfully at the Barnard students in the streets in Morningside Heights, feeling a bit cheated. Lesley had a cute figure—still did—but she had always worn one of those short pixie haircuts.

The following morning, at St. Luke's with Lesley, Peter wished that he had not encouraged Susan to sleep late. He paced in and out of Lesley's room, hardly glancing at his wife's motionless body, and tried to think of someone to call, someone he wanted to talk to. Lesley's condition had so distracted him that until this moment he had hardly realized that Henry Rostov, supposedly his best friend, was dead. The realization, however, only proved to him that Henry was a friend the way Lesley was a wife. There had always been some underlying resentment on Henry's part, he supposed. Henry, a legal aid lawyer who was always broke, had resented Peter's money, while Peter, although he respected Henry's dedication to helping poor people, didn't envy Henry anything—his job, his wife, his life.

Peter was not much good to Judy Rostov, either. They traded calls. She checked in on Susan—very sweet of her. Of course, she missed Henry. Henry Rostov had had a more or less friendly, stable marriage, but Peter felt sure that Judy had bored Henry. She certainly bored Peter.

The question arose in Peter's mind whether Henry had run into the post on purpose, but he knew immediately that this was nonsense. Henry, like himself, was well-meaning and protective and only mildly, not bitterly, dissatisfied with his life. Henry certainly would not attempt to murder both their wives even if he had wanted to do himself in. Besides, the police said he'd taken a hit from someone. Strange how that part of it all got dropped. Although it was entirely possible that Henry was actually murdered that night, we don't ask who or why or how, Peter thought, because it's just too pointless. It's impossible to find out what happened. Maybe something, maybe nothing.

CHAPTER 11

Louis grumbled about going to Edmond and Ivy's dinner. He despised family social events and usually managed to avoid them. This one would be particularly painful. Edmond Lockhart and Ivy Hurst were aged bores, and Edmond always acted as though you had thoughtlessly interrupted him when he had been just about to step into the next room and put a bullet through his head. Peter had to admit that this characterization of Edmond was fair. From casual encounters with Edmond, Peter knew that he came out of his chronic gloom for as long as a month or two at a time, but this was no improvement. When the man was up, he was even more unpleasant, snide, and cold.

Edmond Lockhart was an art critic, poet, and social-cultural commentator who fit no obvious mold. He wrote something for the *Times* every now and then, but more often for the *Gazette*—a book review, an op-ed, occasionally a piece for the Arts front page—and he wrote for both *The New York Review of Books* and *The New Criterion.* His politics leaned right, but everybody read and published Edmond Lockhart. He had three volumes of obscure, melancholy poetry out, too, and a collection of critical and political essays. He had something to say about almost everything. Edmond was famously nasty as a critic, and a mean gossip.

On the other hand, Ivy Hurst, a professor in classics and arts, a Columbia interdisciplinary program, perfectly fit the academic mold. Ivy published only in academic journals and socialized only with her fellow scholars. She rarely saw even her own family, finding their middlebrow tastes and opinions harder to take as she got older. Ivy and Edmond were both in their fifties, almost as old as Peter and Lesley, but they seemed somehow comparatively youthful, even though Ivy had a malproportioned figure, undersized above and oversized below. She continued to wear the supershort, stubbly boy haircut that had been daring and popular among academic women in the 1980s, when her youth ended, and, having in her forties gradually lost the habit of studying hairdressing trends, failed to notice that it had become a conventionally middle-aged do; it still made her look young to herself and to people like the Frankls, and her sister and mother still disapproved of it.

Periodically Ivy and Edmond broke up, then got back together; they were not married and had not wanted children. Edmond, however, had been married before he met Ivy and had a son whom the Frankls had never seen. The Frankls inferred that contact between father and son was limited as a result of the ex-wife's hostility.

Peter had last had dinner at Edmond and Ivy's nine years earlier, just after Edmond had introduced Peter to his aunt Emma. At that dinner, Peter perceived that Edmond and Ivy thought the Frankls unintellectual, half-educated, and beneath them. Lesley thought they were boring; Peter saw that they found Lesley vulgar. After that dinner, when he perceived their scorn for him and his wife, he scorned them in return, reducing communication to a fraction of a nod at the corner or a muttered "Good morning" in the lobby. Edmond began to like Peter more at this point, for a time even becoming something of a pest—following him down the block, dragging Burke, his unwilling black Labrador, on a leash behind him, and gabbing away about this or that, while Peter didn't even pretend to listen.

Peter and his children arrived at Edmond and Ivy's door late, having been kept by Lesley's doctors, who took longer and longer to give opinions that were artfully noncommittal as Lesley continued to show occasional small signs of arousal. Edmond and Ivy had three guests besides the Frankls: Ivy's sister and brother-in-law, Debbie and Rich Hart, from Leominster, Massachusetts, and a woman from Morningside Heights named Wanda—information that Peter gleaned for himself from her conversation, as no one introduced her. Ivy, however, dutifully confessed her relation to her sister and brother-in-law and even divulged that they were high school math and science teachers.

It was obvious as soon as the Frankls walked in that Ivy had never before realized that Susan, one of her new dissertation advisees, was Peter and

Lesley's daughter. Small talk, therefore, centered on this coincidence during the first ten minutes after the Frankls' arrival, which was fortunate, for the company found little other common ground.

"Edmond," said Rich when that topic had been explored far beyond any point of interest, "have you really read all these books? Be honest!" Looking ill at ease, Rich was walking around his hosts' book-lined rooms with a glass of wine in his hand.

Edmond did not bother to answer, and Debbie, to fill the silence and end her husband's discomfort, put in, "Edmond has read half, and Ivy has read half," but this remark, too, was met with silence. Debbie knew that her sister and Edmond would find Rich's remark gauche, but she was loyal and ready to defend him.

"How are the kids, Debbie?" said Ivy, although she had already asked and received her answer when Debbie and Rich had arrived some hours earlier. Debbie, for that reason, was hard put to think of a reasonable and polite reply.

"Well, I think I told you all the latest. Lisa's getting ready to apply to college next fall. Actually she's—she . . ." But Debbie was defeated as much by her own lack of interest in telling as by the company's lack of interest in hearing. "Susan," she began, and Susan, who had been sitting on a sofa feeling grateful at being overlooked, started at hearing her name. "How do you like Columbia? Lisa's thinking of applying."

"Uh, fine. But I didn't do undergraduate work here. Graduate school is so different."

"More work, less sex, eh?" asked Rich with a nervous chuckle that was intended to be knowing, and Debbie, suddenly enraged with him, vowed to herself that if he said one more stupid thing, she would go over to the enemy and join the rest of the company in destroying him. "Where did you do undergraduate?" he asked.

"Harvard," Susan replied, turning to pretend to listen to something that Ivy was saying.

"Good for you!" Rich said. He was obviously trying to sound blasé and beneficent, but something unctuous in his voice betrayed that he was overimpressed. Someone who had grown up in Boston's South End and attended U Mass Boston could hardly help that. "Where'd you go, Louis?"

"Columbia," said Louis.

"So—you let your sister beat you!"

Louis looked awkward and pained, since this was all too true, and Debbie now recognized that Rich was so uncomfortable that he had lost all social judgment and was likely to say any horrible thing that came into his head. Her fury turned into despair and, once again, compassion for her suffering mate.

Peter stood by silently during this bloodletting. He had already begun to suspect that Edmond and Ivy had asked him and his children to dinner not out of neighborly concern for their troubles, as he had thought, but to serve as a wedge between them and these despised relations, with whom they had nothing in common. Edmond no doubt regarded Frankl and his family as the same kind of people as Debbie and Rich. And, of course, he probably had thought it would be efficient to take care of his obligations to both sets of philistines with a single horrible dinner. They could all entertain one another while he stood back and looked on with amused contempt. Peter, though, was not much in the mood to allow his children to be made unhappy in this nasty little social experiment. He grew more and more irritable and didn't trust himself to speak. He understood Rich and forgave his gaucherie. He understood exactly.

Edmond seemed more depressed than usual after this interchange and said hardly another word until it was time for dinner.

"How's George, Wanda?" he asked when Ivy finally gave up her mechanical attempts to get people talking and they were sitting at the table with plates of risotto before them.

"I don't really know, Edmond," said Wanda, "I haven't seen him since breakfast." Peter took satisfaction in the unfriendly tone of this but wondered if it was intended as a joke.

"What's he doing with himself lately?"

"I've never known the answer to that question before. Why should I know it now?"

To Peter and the other guests, it was clear that Wanda disliked being asked about George, whoever he was. Peter was more curious about who Wanda herself was, which was still unexplained, and he was as bored as his children. Despite his hopes, he still found nothing interesting or likable about Ivy, or Edmond, who just now was persisting in questioning Wanda.

"Is he planning to go to—"

"Who cares about George?" Peter interrupted in a bland but tight voice drawn from his courtroom repertoire of vocal weaponry. "I don't even know who he is." It had just dawned on him that Edmond hadn't bothered to introduce Wanda to anyone because he considered her above his other visitors. She was his guest, his real guest; they weren't.

"No one does," said Wanda with a grateful look at Peter.

Susan was startled by her father's rudeness and looked at Ivy Hurst, hoping that she, at least, was not offended; but the look on Ivy's face was not reassuring. Louis, however, perked up and for the first time attended to the conversation.

Edmond turned from Wanda to Peter. "I see your firm is representing our city's most notorious corporate criminals. Must be odd—getting paid with loot. Have you ever represented mafiosi? That would be so . . . liberal of you."

Peter was genuinely surprised that Edmond could not come up with a more original insult than this and stared at his host disdainfully without responding. But this was not sufficient to relieve his feelings. He asked himself: Was he really going to sit through the rest of this evening? Walking out was a real possibility. But walking out under a pretext or walking out in open anger? Peter was debating which of these he would do, when Wanda spoke again.

"Read any good books lately?" she asked Louis. Since Peter had come to her rescue, she would come to his.

Louis's "Not really" sounded excruciatingly illiterate at Edmond Lockhart's dinner table, and when he spoke, his eyes did not meet Wanda's. He looked shifty, Peter noticed. What was it about his son that always looked so devious?

"He hasn't read any books," said Peter. "Just case studies."

"Louis and I have both been reading the Harry Potter books," said Susan, who wished to rehabilitate her family in Ivy's eyes but was incapable of deceit. "We were curious."

"Oh!" said Wanda. "That's all right. They're okay—not great, but okay."

"Wanda!" Edmond scoffed. "You don't really read that trash! Trying to be with it and trendy, hm? Why can't you just age gracefully?"

"I like Harry Potter," Wanda said. "Don't be such a snob, Edmond, or I'll tell everyone about your watching Shirley Temple movies."

Louis laughed boyishly, and Peter felt a rare, pleasant concordance of feeling with his son. Edmond, however, looked black.

"That's absurd, Wanda," Edmond said, and Ivy declared: "It isn't true."

Wanda stared at Ivy. "Yes, it is," she said with an air of certainty.

"I would guess . . . ," Peter began, stifling a laugh at her juvenile behavior—his first impulse to laugh in weeks. "Well, never mind." He had been going to offer a guess about which Shirley Temple movies Edmond favored. Wanda looked at him hopefully, but Peter decided to let the truce stand. It was fun having Wanda side so obviously with him against Edmond and Ivy.

"Graham Greene thought Shirley Temple movies were pornographic," Wanda said.

"Wanda, this infantilism isn't all that entertaining," Edmond replied with unmistakable venom this time. "Why don't you tell our guests something *really* interesting? Don't you try to pick up students at the West End? Had any luck?"

Peter flinched at this. It had to hurt, even if she was tough. He loathed Edmond, who was taking an oily satisfaction in having seriously wounded Wanda. There is a time, thought Peter, to be patient and tolerant and a time not to be.

"Lockhart," he said, "you two may have some kind of understanding, but to an outsider that sounds unbelievably rude—what you just said. It's a kind of shock to the digestion."

Louis looked on with good-humored fascination now, but Susan was horrified and aghast.

"So I'm leaving," Peter said, laying his napkin on the table and rising. "Kids, stay if you want. . . ." But Susan and Louis were immediately on their feet.

Ivy looked confused and said, "Peter, what on earth . . . ?"

"Thank you for all your trouble, Ivy. But I don't think the experiment bears repeating," Peter told her. He meant it seriously, and she understood him. She was most unhappy, but Peter could not tell whether she thought he himself or Edmond was the villain. Clearly Wanda, whose face now shone with amused pleasure, was in no doubt about that.

Peter, Susan, and Louis walked quickly to the door. Susan looked imploringly at Ivy but said nothing.

"Cheer up," Peter said to Edmond as they left. To his astonishment, Edmond responded to Peter's transparent contempt with signs of life. What a wretch. Wanda called a cheery "Good night" as the door closed behind them.

"You have to allow for his upset," said Edmond to Ivy, who was still irate long after the dinner was over, Wanda had left, and Debbie and Rich Hart were in bed. Ivy had felt particularly humiliated in front of her sister and brother-in-law, to whom she was accustomed to feeling calmly superior. The Harts had hardly been able to conceal their joy when the Frankls had walked out.

"You can't take this personally," Edmond said. "Obviously he's terribly disturbed by his wife's situation." Nonetheless, even before the Frankls' angry departure, Edmond was convinced by the dullness of the evening that people like the Frankls and Harts were not dull just around him, but never had anything to say among themselves, either. Wanda had been making up to Frankl just to annoy him, Edmond. Yet there was something he liked in

Frankl. You always knew where you stood with him. In any event, he and Ivy had done their duty and could not be accused of snobbery, wearing themselves out for people like that.

Edmond failed to instill any tolerance for the Frankls in Ivy, who grew more and more offended as she thought the whole thing over. She should never have invited people like that, illiterate and socially crude. Yes, she had tried to be kind and neighborly, but there were people who were beneath such attentions. To think that the Music Department had accepted someone like Susan Frankl into a PhD program! Peter and Lesley Frankl's daughter was about as likely to have any intellectual capacity as . . . as Burke.

Susan, meanwhile, was making an omelet in the Frankls' kitchen, and the three of them were joking about the dreary nastiness of the Lockhart-Hurst household. She, too, had been horrified by Edmond's attempts at publicly humiliating Wanda and couldn't blame her father, not really, for what he had done. But it was so astonishingly unlike her usually mild, endlessly forebearing parent, and things now would be so awkward for her with Ivy Hurst. When Peter had retired into his library to read, she told Louis that their father's volatility concerned her.

"Of course, it's because of Mom," she said.

"I think it's because Lockhart is such an ass," Louis said.

Susan didn't tell Louis that she was also worried about her future dealings with Ivy Hurst. She comforted herself that Ivy was just an outside reader, and outside readers were never a problem. Besides, Susan had played no role in the quarrel at all. Later, she thought, I'll send her a friendly e-mail and tell her that Daddy is just overwrought lately because of Mother.

Louis was not worried about his father or his sister and laughed again as he remembered the evening's incidents. He had rather admired his father's performance.

CHAPTER 12

One soft, fresh morning in May, Hilda Hughes, newspaper tucked under her arm, stepped onto Broadway outside Samad's Deli with her usual bagel and coffee in a white paper bag and heard someone far behind her call her name. She walked faster and didn't turn around, although she heard, "Hilda! Hi-i-l-da-a-a!" When she reached Citibank, she ducked in. She stood in the bank lobby for some seconds, heart pounding, breathing hard, before she got her bearings and felt safe from whoever had been so insistent on talking to her.

As long as I'm here, she thought, I may as well open an account. She had been meaning to for years, ever since the local Chase branch office moved from the corner of Broadway and 113th, leaving behind only a few ATMs. Hilda disliked ATMs. She preferred to carry on impersonal transactions with persons and personal transactions with machines. She was an enthusiastic e-mail correspondent and spent hours in anonymous online chats.

The woman at customer service asked her questions and fed the answers to a computer—name, address, telephone number.

"Employer and employer's address?"

"The Devereaux Foundation," said Hilda, and spelled it out. "Four Twenty-seven West 107th Street, 10025, 212-555-7922, but I work mostly from home so you should put that number in, too."

"Married?" asked the clerk.

Hilda felt a familiar swimming sensation, then surprised and dismayed herself by replying "Yes."

"Would you like your husband's name on the account?"

Below the counter, Hilda stealthily moved a ring from her right hand to the wedding finger of her left hand. "Well, let me see. I've never done that before, but—it would be easier."

"By now he knows it's your money, right?" said the clerk, who wore a wedding ring herself and spoke to Hilda familiarly, as one member of the exclusive club of married people to another.

Hilda greatly enjoyed the feeling of being a married woman, making jokes about husbands. She laughed tolerantly at the foibles of men. "Oh no, not mine. He still believes in coverture and curtesy rights." The bank lady did not understand these archaic historical allusions, which Hilda, inspired by Peter Frankl's comments on Old English law, had recently been reading about in a book of English legal history; but she caught the general idea about old-fashioned notions and showed no puzzlement. Hilda realized that this was a close call and felt relieved and happy, so near outright exhilaration, in fact, that she was hardly embarrassed about having used terms so inappropriate in a business conversation with a bank clerk.

"Are those your children?" Hilda asked, pointing at pictures on the woman's desk.

"Yes, and that's my first grandchild."

"I can't wait for that," said Hilda. "I'm always pushing them. I have two kids. The oldest is twenty-five now, but he says 'No way.' "

"Oh, grandchildren, yes," said the woman, implying mutually understood things with her unfinished sentence. "Boys take a while. How old's your other one?"

"She's just fourteen," said Hilda, smiling with shy pride, as she had seen so many mothers do when asked that question.

"Oh, my. Still a real baby," said the woman, typing, politely entering into Hilda's imagined maternal pleasures, and Hilda began mentally reformulating Susan Frankl's difficulties into a narrative about a fourteen-year-old while the clerk continued matter-of-factly, "Okay, your signature—here, and here. Oh, I forgot to get your husband's name for the joint account."

"Hughes, Phoebus—P-h-o-e-b-u-s—A. Hughes."

"And his work address and telephone number."

Hilda froze momentarily, then said brightly, "The same as mine—we work together." But the clerk had observed the brief look of anxiety on Hilda's face, and her own immediately showed uneasiness. The jig is up, thought Hilda; the undertones have registered. Sure enough, the woman turned quiet and more cool, and Hilda began to feel increasingly tense and awkward. She began to feel that her behavior was a bit mad. The polite small talk ceased, and the woman typed silently.

"You're all set," said the clerk. "Here's your card. Remember your password?" The clerk was courteous but avoided eye contact.

Hilda nodded yes, although she had already forgotten the password. She knew she would never use it. She would never use the account at all.

"Good-bye," said the clerk, looking at papers on her desk.

"You're welcome," said Hilda. No sooner had she turned her back on the clerk than full-fledged, stomach-churning mortification at her charade overtook her. She burned with the humiliating fear that the clerk had caught on, although rationally she knew the woman had only some inchoate misgivings. No doubt she had decided that something was wrong with Hilda. Something *was* wrong with Hilda.

Hilda left the bank, stuffing brochures and forms the clerk had handed her into her leather case, and immediately outside the doors came face-to-face with Peter Frankl, who was carrying a cup of coffee like her own from Samad's Deli and a briefcase from which protruded a bundle of magazines and papers freshly purchased from the Global Ink magazine store. She started, shrank back, and gasped, and Peter felt brutish.

"Good God!" he said. "What's the matter?"

"Nothing. Nothing!" said Hilda with a weak smile. "It's just that you surprised me."

"I thought that was you," he said, "from back there. I called and called, but you ignored me. I just wanted to tell you something. I ran into a friend the other day who was telling me that they're going to start building extra floors on the building next door to you. That's going to cut off light on the east side of the building. He says it's all but certain. He was letting me know so we could sell Susan's place if we wanted, before the price falls, but Susan's place is on the west side, which won't be affected. If you're on the east side of the building, you should think about selling and moving. I just wanted you to know." Peter backed off, his hands up in the air to prove to Hilda that he would trouble her with his company no longer.

She was shaking her head, bewildered. "My goodness," she said.

Peter, walking away, ignored this. "I have to hurry," he called back peremptorily. "I have to see my wife in the hospital."

"She's still in the hospital?" Hilda asked in a faint voice. But Peter was already too far off to hear, and she proceeded to 107th Street, where Miss Devereaux was probably already waiting for her.

Despite the nearness of the foundation to her home, Hilda avoided going there. She usually dropped off her reports on weekends, when no one was there, and went in during business hours not more than two or three times a month, although Miss Devereaux would have liked her to come more often. At these times she would pick up her paycheck, discuss her reports, and receive new assignments. For nearly twenty years, Hilda had been the sole in-house reviewer of grant proposals submitted to the foundation, and often, when she and Miss Devereaux felt quite sure of themselves, they didn't bother to get the opinion of an outside expert in the field.

Miss Devereaux herself was interested only in antiquarian and traditionalist projects. She had paid for several girls to come to New York and train for the ballet. She gave music scholarships to talented students, but they'd better play nothing later than nineteenth century in their auditions with her. In fact, Miss Devereaux's greatest enthusiasm in all of more than twenty years that Hilda had worked for her had been early music, in which she had provided Baroque instruments for at least a dozen different performers and helped set up a shop for repairing and refurbishing such instruments. She had also sponsored two early-music festivals, one in Belgium and one upstate.

Hilda could not say that Miss Devereaux was wrong. Even though she herself found much in the twentieth century to admire, and looked forward to the inventions of the twenty-first, Miss Devereaux had a perfect right to devote herself to preserving the Western heritage with her family's money if that's what she wanted to do. Hilda herself occasionally tended to favor the unconventional application and had talked Miss Devereaux into funding a number of wild ideas that now and then had panned out—for example, in the case of the Grandma Moses of musical composition, who had written a really lovely string quartet, or that of the amateur archeologist whose dig had produced some of the finest Anasazi artifacts ever found. "Success in even one project out of twenty," Miss Devereaux told the board, "is an excellent rate. Hilda has an exceptional eye."

"You're smarter than I am—just like your mother," Miss Devereaux told Hilda back in the seventies. "I don't trust all these professional experts, and I don't like what their people do with the money. You're more understanding. If *you* think something is worthwhile, that's good enough for me. The money will be well spent."

Hilda, at the time, was supposed to be finishing a thesis on French poetry at Columbia. She was looking for a job, too, and had begun to panic, thinking that no one would ever hire her because she showed so badly in job interviews. Then Emma Devereaux, a college friend of her mother's, had stepped in. She hired Hilda more to help the girl than to get her help. But as things had turned out, Hilda made extraordinary contributions to the foundation's work. Despite her awkwardness, she had uncanny judgment. Eventually, Miss Devereaux put her in charge of all the key funding decisions, let her interview the candidates, choose the mix of traditional and untraditional projects, and the rest. She was well pleased with the way it had all gone. If only the poor thing hadn't led such a miserable life, but what could she do? Miss Devereaux had long ago accepted the impossibility of doing anything more for Hilda. She couldn't even persuade her to come to dinner—not once in all these years. A very, very willful woman was Hilda, in her opinion.

CHAPTER 13

When Peter arrived at Lesley's hospital room soon after leaving Hilda, the therapist was there, manipulating Lesley's fingers. "I've worked with comatose patients so long, I've developed a sixth sense," she said. "I think I felt her fingers twitch a little when you came in and said 'Hello.' "

Peter nodded but had nothing to say. After watching the therapy for half an hour, he kissed Lesley's cheek and set out for his office. The possibility of Lesley's awakening made him despair. He no longer tried to conceal from himself how contented he was with Lesley's absence. It was appalling and hideous, but true. If she recovered, he thought—he hoped—he would be able to resume behaving like a dutiful husband, but he could not bring himself to want her back. And if her return to life made him unhappy, he would utterly condemn himself. But how could he live under a self-imposed moral death sentence? Misery was certain, whether or not Lesley revived.

Peter was aware that his self-condemnation would seem extreme, even downright anachronistic, to some of his acquaintances. After all, he hadn't actually done anything; he'd only had feelings. But the feelings were both adulterous and murderous. He had no lover, but he wanted to break faith with his wife by undertaking to love, think, and act in ways that precluded a life with her. He had not harmed her, but he preferred that she remain in a state approximating death. He wanted to put her away, in the biblical phrase that so perfectly expressed his wishes. Despite the current tolerant climate of opinion, adultery was a ghastly crime, and Peter had a hard time under-standing why its horrors escaped the modern imagination.

Yet he also wondered just how terrible a sin he was guilty of. His mother, who had been Catholic, told him that the nuns said sinful thoughts were just as bad as sinful actions. This meant that even if Peter stayed with Lesley and tried his damnedest to be a good husband, he'd still be a very bad guy. And although this seemed intuitively right to Peter, it also seemed obvious that it would be worse actually to leave his wife than just to want to—especially if she was desperately ill.

Ruminating on these themes, Peter arrived at work and nodded distracted greetings right and left as he made his way down the outer corridor to his office. Jon was there, talking softly and animatedly to Mary, with his elbows on her counter. Peter knew them both so well that he could tell from their expressions that Jon was favoring Mary with some hot gossip. They both glanced up guiltily at Peter and fell silent, which annoyed him—two middle-aged, grown-up human beings, acting like kids with their hands in the cookie jar when Dad shows up. Jon handed Peter his mail and messages.

"I put the CarGo file on your desk," he said innocently, sounding more southern than usual, a sure sign that he was trying to con someone.

"Jon, what religion were you raised in?" Peter asked him. He knew that Jon wouldn't show surprise at anything Peter talked about, no matter how bizarre or malapropos; they were in the habit of having odd conversations.

"Southern Baptist, of course," he said, and smiled. "But I've left all that behind in Alabama."

"None, really—I mean, Anglican, of course, for weddings and such," Mary volunteered, although no one had asked.

They both looked expectantly at Peter.

"They tried to raise me atheist," Peter said, "but somehow I ended up a Catholic atheist, with a mind like my mother's—although she always insisted she was an agnostic."

"Hm. I would've thought you were more . . . Jewish," Jon said, as though the thought had just occurred to him. He smiled politely.

"No, religious ideas are transmitted through the mother. Take my word for it. Jews know this—that's why they say you're Jewish if your mother is, and not otherwise. You can convert, but they don't think converts are really Jewish."

"Now that's so interesting," said Jon, again with his unconvincing smile and drawl. "Christians are just the opposite. They think converts are the most Christian. In fact, some of them think *only* converts are Christian."

"So I've heard," said Peter. "So you're an atheist, eh?"

"Well, I don't put enough energy into it," said Jon, "to be a real *atheist*. I never go denying anything. I just never give any of it a thought. Why isn't there a word for religious indifference?"

"So how do you resolve your moral dilemmas?" Peter asked. "What authority do you appeal to?"

"The light of pure reason," Jon said gravely.

Peter was amused but didn't smile.

"My word," said Mary.

Jon and Peter, however, knew they would be hitting this one back and forth for weeks. They always seemed to have some such little debate going.

Walter Bramford had stepped out of his office and was summoning Jon with a slight motion of his head.

"Oh, I'm supposed to see Mr. Bramford," said Jon, suddenly ill at ease.

Recently, Jon had been working for Walter almost exclusively when he was not working for Peter, and Walter was, as a boss, critical, driving, and something of a dictator—oddly authoritarian for someone whose private life was a little wild. Peter had noticed all this and had come to dislike seeing Jon with Walter. It offended his sensibilities. Two men, both about forty, comparably talented, and one ran the other ragged and insisted he behave submissively, smile politely, and do what he was told—or end up on the street. Peter could justify his own authority over Jon on the grounds that he was old enough to be his father. But aside from their positions in the firm, Walter and Jon were equals in every way. Not that you could accuse Walter of being mean to Jon; if anything, it was obvious that he liked him. Walter was just playing by the firm's rules, and he thought Peter should, too; he regarded Peter's ideas about work relations as mistaken and harmful. And Peter didn't hold that against Walter. But when he saw him ordering Jon around, it made him sick. He went into his office, closed the door, and sighed deeply.

When Peter left his office that evening, he visited Lesley again and spoke to Dr. Baird, who talked again of the possibility that Lesley would make a meaningful recovery. Walking slowly back to Riverside Drive with those words—*meaningful recovery*—in his ears, Peter again weighed his sins and his options. What would the Jews say about all this? And which Jews would be the most sensible? He had a feeling that Jews both made stable marriages and didn't judge divorcing husbands so harshly—an interesting combination that the nuns didn't really allow for. That system wouldn't work for the Catholic psychology, perhaps. Maybe he should strive for a more Jewish perspective on all this, as it seemed grossly unfair that he should be forced to bear Lesley *and* soul-consuming guilt: it should be one or the other, not both. That was as far as he got with this confusing moral question. He was distracted in the elevator by the presence of the woman he recognized as Edmond Lockhart's unexplained dinner guest weeks ago.

"You're Wanda," he said to her as they both stepped out on the twelfth floor.

"Yes," she said with a sidelong look at Peter, who was staring directly at her, making comparisons with Lesley. Wanda looked the way Peter imagined poetesses or off-Broadway actresses looked, wearing soft fabrics in those in-between colors that defied naming, skirt to midcalf, and undisciplined chin-length blond waves—dyed, of course, but attractively dyed. She had on snug-fitting, ankle-high laced boots. Lesley always wore heels, even with jeans, and her skirts were always short and slim to show off her legs.

"Edmond didn't see fit to introduce us. I'm Peter Frankl. I live here," he said, pointing to his door.

"Edmond's neighbor. And I'm Wanda Lockhart."

"Edmond's sister?"

"His wife." She smiled again, with a fitting awkwardness, given the unwieldy nature of the fact.

Peter had learned early in his legal career never to betray surprise. His shock was so great on this occasion, however, that he permitted himself to voice some part of it. "Impossible," he said, but his expression showed little change except a slight widening of the eyes.

"Edmond, actually, is just the sort of man who would invite his estranged wife to have dinner with his live-in partner and friends and relatives."

"That's not the most surprising part. I'm surprised that someone like you was ever married to him."

"I'm married to him now. We aren't divorced."

"I won't ask," said Peter.

"And you don't know what someone like me is like."

He conveyed skepticism with a tilt of his head.

"They're waiting for me," said Wanda. "Bye."

Peter found it all mystifying, but if they wanted to be mysterious, that was their business. He went into his own apartment and checked the messages, called his sister-in-law with the latest report on Lesley, tried and failed to reach Louis, who had finished his exams and would be home tonight or tomorrow. He felt, as he did most evenings, unsettled and something beyond lonely. The forsakenness of these evenings was eerie and portentous. To drive such feelings away, Peter usually read. Tonight he picked up a new history of the origins of the common law, but his mind wandered.

What would I be like, he wondered, if I had spent the last forty years talking to someone like Wanda rather than Lesley, who is so literal, so practical, so concrete about everything except, maybe, painting? But even her painting was coarsely naïve. Lesley read every novel on the best-seller list, but if you asked her about one, she'd either say "Good!" or "Boring!" She never had a comment. If you asked her why she liked a book, she was likely to say, without embarrassment, that it had a good plot or that she had cried or some dumb thing like that.

In fact, Lesley was really confusing to Peter. He still didn't understand how a woman as limited in so many ways as Lesley was—so dull and dull witted, inarticulate, so incapable of abstraction—could dress with such sophistication, decorate their apartment with such skill, produce paintings that made rich men open their wallets, figure out so accurately which schools the kids had to go to and how to keep business clients chatting comfortably, and, for that matter, add a column of figures in her head as fast as anyone he'd ever met.

Peter could blame his youthful weakness all he wanted, but the fact was that if he met Lesley today, he would probably still be misled. He would never have believed, if he hadn't lived with her, that human beings mentally constructed like Lesley existed. Now, at age sixty, he began to feel a sense of rage over the peculiarity, the unfairness, of the problems he faced with Lesley. As though being penniless and orphaned weren't enough, Peter had to have the additional bad luck to run into someone who fit into no discernible patterns of ordinary womanhood. Or was it possible that everyone's character would appear as unlikely as Lesley's if examined through the magnifying glass of marriage? Now Lesley, unlike him, had been very savvy when she was twenty, for Peter had turned into precisely the man whom the youthful Lesley wanted—whether she had brought this about or, perhaps, had simply always known him better than he knew himself.

Peter's thoughts having wandered far from the common law, he permitted them to turn again to the mysterious Wanda Lockhart, who was actually Edmond's wife! She was somewhat attractive to him, he recognized. Slender and altogether nice-looking, funny, maybe more the sort of woman he should have married, who would value his being something besides a good earner with a high standing in the hierarchy of the bar. But Wanda had married about as badly as he had—maybe worse. Edmond was intellectual, a writer, but a genuinely repugnant human being, small-minded and without self-respect.

Peter, tired and stymied, dozed off with his book on his chest and did not awaken until after 11:00, when the doorbell rang. Louis forgot his key, he thought irritably. But it was not Louis. It was Wanda Lockhart.

"May I come in for a minute?" she asked. She tried to look shy, but she wasn't really. Tired and gloomy as he was, Peter was glad to see her.

"I wanted to say that I'm sorry about your wife, and to apologize for all the misbehavior across the hall the last time I was there. You were so nice— when I thought about it afterwards I felt bad about your being treated to such an awful evening when you had so many troubles. Then I swore to myself I'd never go back to Edmond's, and I thought I'd probably never see you again." She stood in the foyer during this speech, her head ducked apologetically, clutching a handbag in front of her.

"But here you are back at Edmond's," said Peter.

"I won't deny it," she said with an elfin twitch of a smile.

"Come in?"

She insisted she had to be going but let Peter take her coat and show her into the living room. She even accepted a glass of wine. Within five minutes, she had stopped being apologetic and was mischievous again, and obscure, the way she had been that other night. She chattered away with gossip about Edmond. She giggled, telling how he had just now said, over dinner, that the experience of joy was a morally requisite immorality, to be sought and not found. Peter responded only with a lift of his eyebrows, which for some reason got her completely hysterical, making Peter laugh a little, too, and he wasn't a man who laughed much.

Edmond had undergone electroshock therapy a few years ago, Wanda told him, during a massive depression. He had a psychiatrist who didn't believe in talking about things—or in listening, either, for that matter. The psychiatrist told Edmond that his brain failed biochemically to process stressful experiences. He was still depressed, but he loved being depressed, Wanda insisted, and everybody should just let him enjoy himself. When he wasn't depressed, he tended to get mean. He was a cruel man.

"The real reason I left him," said Wanda, "was to keep him away from George."

"George?"

"Our son."

The remark produced a conversational syncope.

"My God. How . . . how old is George?" Peter asked to end the silence.

"George is nineteen. He's a mess. Edmond was horrible to him. But the first time Edmond really went to pieces, it was because he lost George."

"He loved him even though he was so cruel to him?"

"He probably did, but it wasn't so much the loss of a beloved son. He just needed someone weaker to be sadistic to or his internal balance got upset. But he soon found Ivy, and then he seemed okay again. He certainly doesn't love her, though, so it's been tricky."

"I'm not sure I believe what you're telling me. You can't really be so blasé about all this. But, assuming it's all true, why did you ever get mixed up with Edmond to begin with? Why did Ivy?"

"That's easy. I at least didn't know what he was like. I was young, and the bad stuff didn't start happening until we were married for a while. By that time I was in the habit of being married to him, and there was George to think about. I shouldn't have had George."

Wanda sounded so chipper that Peter dismissed everything she said. Even if it was true, it wouldn't explain why she continued to see Lockhart now, but he asked no more questions. Sitting on the sofa beside Peter, Wanda took off her shoes and tucked her feet under her with an agility that seemed young and appealing. And he, quite out of the blue, found himself yearning toward her despite his horror at the things she was saying. He wished he could help her or comfort her. The story she told, moreover, put his marriage with Lesley in a different light. At least he and Lesley had both been kind to the children and to each other, for that matter, even though they were so mismatched. Or maybe that meant they were not so mismatched. Maybe his marriage was as good as marriage usually got. Maybe only one couple in a hundred, or thousand, or million, had something more—just as there were people who could write doggerel, and then there were the Wallace Stevenses, and then there was Shakespeare.

Peter proposed this hypothesis to Wanda.

"I don't think worthwhile marriages are as rare as all that," she said. "You're making the classic error here. You're comparing marriages to one another, instead of to the alternatives of being single, or serial monogamy. When you start looking at what those lives are like, then you get a valid comparison. Samuel Johnson said that marriage has many pains, but celibacy has no joys. That's how you have to look at it."

"The alternative isn't celibacy anymore."

"It *is* celibacy for long stretches; the older people get, the longer the stretches—for both sexes. And being single wears you down. Single people suffer character deterioration."

"Nonsense," Peter said. Of course, Wanda was describing her own experience, and he felt sorry for her. He didn't really disagree, however, about the desirability of marriage. No, his longings were not for the single life, but for a different marriage, for some real company, some real understanding, and he had felt this way ever since he lost his parents. Tears stood in his eyes as he thought about all this, and when Wanda, who seemed touched by his sadness, put her hand on his shoulder, he had to tell himself to leave her alone. He so rarely felt the kind of feelings she was eliciting in him—never, he thought, alone late at night on the sofa with the object of them. And when she brought her knees up to her chin and tucked her skirt under her bare feet, he said, "Wanda?" and leaned over and kissed her. She was not surprised. She pulled his glasses off his face, the better to go on kissing, and curled up against him, fragrant and confiding. His heart beat too rapidly, and he thought about how Nelson Rockefeller had died in 1979.

He pulled gently away from Wanda and held her hands together between his. "Sorry," he said, and he put her hands down and put on his glasses. "I'm off balance these days because of Lesley, and maybe other things. I'm sorry." He could see in Wanda's face that she was a little disappointed, and he felt bad about that. He could also see that her mind was working hard.

"I'd talk you into it if I knew how," she said at last.

Was it that obvious that he was immovable? Peter wondered why she didn't at least try. But instead she put on her shoes, picked up her bag, and walked toward the door. He helped her with her coat and kissed her lightly on the cheek as they said good-night. When he opened the door for her, however, they were both startled to see Louis, bent, ready to insert a key in the lock. The three of them held their positions momentarily, and Peter's guilty conscience etched itself so clearly in his face that Wanda looked sheepish and Louis grave. Peter spoke first, sounding like a lawyer with a questionable client—confident but detached, unreadable.

"Louis, you remember Wanda—who we met next door?"

Louis nodded politely enough but did not smile, and when they all had gathered their wits, said new good-nights, and the door had closed after Wanda, he said to Peter, "There's lipstick on your mouth." He tried to sound noncommittal, but Peter could tell that he was angry and disapproving. What a switch—his son, Louis, morally disapproving of him!

"It's not what you think," Peter told him without great conviction, for actually it was fairly close to what Louis probably thought, depending on how Catholic you wanted to be about it.

CHAPTER 14

Lacking a steady boyfriend for the first time in her life, Mallory had begun to lean on Alexei. He pursued her, and she could not resist the pleasures of his company despite her awareness of being his elder and better. Their computer sessions ended, replaced at first by occasional, early-morning jogs together on the promenade. Twice, they went for breakfast afterward and ended up talking for hours. Then they had gone to a few movies. "It's like he's my best friend now," Mallory told her mother, "because Susan is always with Chris or with her mother in the hospital, and Sylvie is always with Alcott. For the first time, I'm the single one."

Mallory went home to her parents' cozy little fourth-floor apartment at 444 Riverside two or three times a week so as to immerse herself in the sanity, stability, love, and depth of thought and feeling that prevailed there, along with delightfully high culinary standards. Mallory recognized that much of her parents' culture had somehow failed to take root in her. Mallory could neither cook nor authoritatively dismiss Lacan. She knew very little of music and wasn't nearly the fanatic novel reader they both were; nor could she, offhand, recite a single line of poetry. But they adored her anyway, and this had the effect of making her suspect that she was actually quite wonderful despite these shortcomings, a continuing sense of which, nonetheless, tended to make her slightly irritable after an hour or two at home. Living there, although tempting, would have been impossible.

"That's good. It's about time," Ingrid said firmly. "Stay that way for a while."

"I suppose I will," said Mallory, "because I don't see anyone around to get interested in." The rest of Mallory's social existence had contracted, too; the crush of parties, lunches and dinners, and events that ordinarily filled her life had dwindled remarkably this spring. Everyone seemed to have less energy for it.

Ingrid was an affectionate mother who had been unwilling to look at her daughter with the dispassionate eyes of a psychotherapist until about a year ago. Then she had told her husband that she thought there were problems with Paul—with men in general.

"It's unlucky she was an only child," she had said. "It may be hard for us to let go of each other."

"Nonsense," Herb had said. "She's very separated, very independent. You wish it were somehow your fault so you could fix it. But this isn't psychological. This is reality, and I trust Mallory to cope."

"But is this poor Alexei having his heart broken?" Ingrid asked Mallory, recalling these words of Herb's with skepticism.

"I don't think so. He knows it's impossible. He's four years younger than I am, and he doesn't even have a BA. He has, basically, two years of classes at MSM—most of it was stuff like German vocal literature or phonetics and diction. He has absolutely no realism—to the point that there's something really nutty about it. I keep telling him to give it up and start doing something with his life. He's good with computers. There are still *some* dot-com jobs out there. I'm just starting to appreciate how intelligent he is. Did I tell you he's a grandmaster in chess? And he seems to be a sort of autodidact. A couple of times, he knew books I wouldn't have expected him to know."

"You know, Mallory, a lot of those chess people, and a lot of computer people, are almost idiots savants—ineducable people with inadequate personalities and a strange ability to play one game or think in terms of binary numbers. This man sounds like an eccentric of some sort—no one you should be mixed up with. What about his family? Who are his friends?"

"He doesn't say much. He says his mother is wonderful and his father is mean and crazy. He adores his grandfather, who lives with them, but he won't take me home with him. His grandfather was some kind of failed musician. I think Alexei works so much he doesn't have time for friends, but—"

"Be careful, Mallory. None of this sounds right to me. I don't understand what you're doing."

"The more I know him, the more I think he's . . . good. He's solid and good."

"Maybe. But then he's a good person with some bad problems in life. You don't need to take them on. Sweetheart, he's not someone who can do you any good."

"Maybe I can do him some."

"Beyond the pleasure of your friendship? Not possible."

"I'm not sure you're right. In any event, he's not going to do me any harm."

Mallory wanted to assume a higher moral position, but her mother made it hard for her by regarding any sacrifice on her part as at once dangerous and wrong, as though her highest duty, in deference to her parents' feelings, had to be to preserve her own interests. At the same time, Mallory felt, rather than knew, that Ingrid both thought her daughter's character a bit deficient morally and had no idea that she herself contributed to this deficiency. Mallory did not understand these things. She knew only that she felt increasingly irritable.

Mallory's conversation with her mother had ended there yesterday afternoon, and Alexei had spent last night with Mallory in her apartment.

He slept on this morning, in fact, while she awoke, made coffee, and reflected on yesterday's conversation with her mother. She began to grow uneasy about what she had done. She was no longer so sure that Alexei was not in love with her. And as she strove to decide what attitude to take toward him, it felt, in her imagination, hard and unkind to continue with the arm's-length gaiety and distanced goodwill she had adopted until now. She wasn't the sort to treat a lover that way. Attempting to explain her own conduct to herself, she decided that she had been overcome with desire. And wasn't that natural after months of unaccustomed deprivation? She had crossed a line last night, and she didn't know how to cross back. But she knew she had to, and she steeled herself to the necessity of feeling unkind.

She was drinking a second cup of coffee and reading the paper on the sofa, cross-legged in her pajamas, when Alexei finally awoke. She gave him a neutral look and in a nonchalant way offered him coffee and the front page, which she had finished. It did feel cruel, and especially so when she refused to respond to a kiss on her neck, right below her ear.

"What's this?" Alexei said eventually. "You're sorry?"

He looked severe, and Mallory, unexpectedly, felt a little intimidated. Before this, she had always felt that she had the moral high ground in matters of love. Nonetheless, she was relieved to have things out in the open and nodded to indicate that, in fact, she was sorry.

"But it's like a child, this sort of thing—not knowing your own mind and then acting strange this way instead of saying things. I should have known."

And Alexei hurriedly pulled on his shoes and left without a good-bye.

Mallory sobbed for a long time, until, intending to apologize, she tried to call him and was aghast to hear a recording say that his number had been disconnected. She couldn't find his name in the telephone book or online. It was horrible to think of having been intimate only hours ago with someone who might have just disappeared forever. Miserable with guilt and loneliness, she wanted someone to make her feel right again, but the thought of talking with friends, or even her parents, offered no comfort. The only comforting she craved was Alexei's.

Mallory spent the greater part of the next two days in tears. They fell onto her keyboard as she worked on a final draft of her latest assignment, now overdue, on how depression was being destigmatized. She e-mailed it to her editor, then gathered her courage and walked to the library on Broadway at 113th Street. She sat near the window on the second floor and waited for two hours, reading a copy of *Little Women* that someone had left on the table, but Alexei and the little boy never came, and she went home. Lying in bed, she wondered what Jo March would have done if Professor Bhaer had been not a learned, archresponsible, older man, but a boy younger than herself with no degree, no path-smoothing social status, and no plans that would allow him to occupy any place in life except at the margins or the lower levels. On the other hand, of course, Professor Bhaer would never have amounted to a damn if Jo hadn't bankrolled him in that school. Such silliness occupied her mind half the night.

On the fourth day after her night with Alexei, a Thursday, with an empty weekend looming before her, loneliness overrode shame, and Mallory had to tell someone—not her mother, who would both worry too much and indulge in some I-told-you-so's. She decided that Susan, good-naturedly melancholic and warmly supportive, was the person she wanted to hear her confession. Susan was free later that evening and asked her to come to dinner after she visited her mother. Lesley Frankl still lay in a coma at St. Luke's, but somehow everyone had been accustoming themselves to this terrible circumstance. Mallory knew that Susan now felt better when her friends confided their own problems in her. It made her feel more part of ordinary life. Susan would share Mallory's burden of her misconduct with Alex, lightening it enough for Mallory to function with something like her ordinary cheer until her bruised conscience stopped throbbing.

The two met at 9:00 at Susan's apartment. It was furnished far more luxuriously than the typical graduate student's. Susan had a good piano, a baby grand that stood in an alcove with a window seat off the dining room, and an antique mahogany table with four mismatched chairs, plus some Turkish rugs in warm colors, and a small sofa, all of which were things Lesley hadn't wanted after her redecorating a couple of years ago.

"I have a long story," warned Mallory after they had greeted each other affectionately.

"Love or work?" asked Susan.

"Not work, anyway," said Mallory. She told her tale frankly, omitting no conceivably relevant detail, while Susan, the only domestic member of their circle, with brisk competence did things with chicken, wine, flour, alarming-looking vegetables, and intimidating vials of spices.

Susan winced and clutched Mallory's hand when Mallory reported Alexei's accusations that last morning. Her obvious concern immediately relieved Mallory's sense of isolation, and her seriousness ratified Mallory's feeling that she was at a moral cusp. But when she had finished her recital, Mallory found Susan's first questions jarring.

"What kind of singer? Did he sing for you?"

Mallory was hurt that Susan was distracted by details that answered to Susan's musical obsessions rather than her own dilemma. She was usually more sensitive.

"I've never heard him. He takes lessons with some opera singer."

"Is he good?"

"Of course not—not that I've ever heard him. This teacher is some guy in the neighborhood who gives Alex lessons in exchange for chess lessons for his kids. It's not serious professional stuff."

"He lives in the barter economy. Oh, Mallory, you haven't done anything terrible. You've only been too nice."

"Nice!"

"You have a privileged life, and you tried to let him in on it," said Susan in a voice sweet with forgiving affection, "but he doesn't belong, and that's not your fault. You've been generous, but it only made him greedy. Doesn't it annoy you a little bit that he's so demanding and thinks someone like you should be with someone like him?"

Mallory felt relieved by what Susan said and was on the verge of regressing to a comfortable sense of self-love, when she imagined Alexei's take on their conversation. He would sneer at this quest for cheap self-approval and at the idea that Mallory was trying to be generous to someone with a blighted life. "That's twisted, Susan," she said.

"I'm only saying, you gave him something. You shouldn't feel bad because you can't give him more. It's sad but true that you don't owe him anything." Susan looked contemplatively at Mallory, however, for she half agreed that her explanation was morally twisted; but Mallory didn't usually demand to hear hard truths. She wanted to feel better, and Susan wanted only to help her feel better. Susan had a kind of genius, in fact, for disguising painful facts, seeing them as something other than what they were, and getting others to do likewise. Her friends thought it was one of the most lovable things about her.

"Look, it's obvious that you have no business with this guy. But I'm getting the feeling that you might be a little stuck on him. You are, aren't you. That's why he's giving you a hard time. He knows you like him."

"Anyone could be stuck on him. He's appealing."

"Come on. Good-looking, I suppose, and sweetly shallow?"

"You saw him—at my party."

Susan tried to recollect, then raised floury hands to her face in astonishment. "Him? Sylvie talked about him for a week. Sort of ridiculously good-looking? He got into a big argument with Chris about films and the arts. I didn't hear it, but Chris said he was really . . . ignorant and kind of crazy. Mallory, is that all it is? That he's so . . . ?"

"No! Absolutely not! You don't know him. You just don't understand. Susan, you know me better than that."

"Don't be mad," said Susan. She did know that Mallory wouldn't be tempted by looks alone, but it was a perfectly good out—both for saving face and for salving conscience. Susan was interested to see Mallory resist an offer of moral candy. It was as unprecedented as Mallory's getting involved in this sort of mischief in the first place—and *mischief* was the right word. This was a jam more appropriate to a girl going on twenty than a woman almost thirty.

"Mallory, I can't tell you how uplifting it is for me to see you take a misstep like this. I'm usually the one who does it. I'm always doing the wrong thing. Even with Chris, who is just about perfect for me, I'm always doing something wrong. I just don't seem to have the knack."

Mallory was, as Susan intended, distracted from her own guilt by Susan's confession that the affair with Chris was difficult. She wasn't surprised to hear it, however; Chris wasn't exactly the low-key, supportive type. But right now Susan was so upset about her mother that things might feel harder than they really were.

After dinner, the two of them sat cross-legged on the sofa, sipping wine until their talk grew soggy and grandiose.

"The thing is, Mallory," Susan said, "you believe in marriage but not love, and I believe in love but not marriage—at least for me."

"That could be," said Mallory. "But you're an anachronism. You believe in broken hearts and all that, which for anyone over thirteen is just sort of silly as far as I'm concerned. If people break up, they feel humiliated or betrayed or used or disappointed or lonely or whatever, but the only time their hearts break is when their parents divorce or die or something, and that's because feelings about parents always have this leftover primitive component."

"I've had a broken heart," Susan said, thinking of the college breakup that had left her in such deep mourning that she had refused to attend her graduation ceremony.

"You're abnormal."

"Mallory, don't get married unless you're in love. You can't really go back a few centuries to marriage as an economic alliance."

Susan's earnestness, Mallory thought, would have been embarrassing had anyone been present besides the two of them.

"I think good marriages are almost exactly that," she said, "with some friendship and goodwill and sexual compatibility added in. Your kind of love is just culturally defunct, like Freudian hysteria. You still see a case or two, but the social circumstances that made it common are gone."

"Nothing but that kind of love makes marriage worthwhile because it's a union of the flesh. That's what it's for."

"It used to be, maybe. Not now."

"Then do you plan on having extramarital affairs? I'm shocked," Susan said mildly.

"Of course not. Sexual variety isn't worth endangering a marriage for. You make some sacrifices to have a certain kind of life, and that's not really so hard for people who aren't going around falling in love. *That's* what makes marriages so unstable," Mallory said.

By this time, Mallory had put aside her guilty distress over Alexei, and even Susan was almost cheery for an hour or two, until the telephone rang, when Susan's face went pale. She let the answering machine click on, and they both listened to the voice. "It's Louis," Susan said with obvious relief. "I'll call him back later."

Mallory had recognized the voice, too. "Isn't he graduating around now?"

"I don't know how he did it, but he is. Commencement is next week."

"Will you go?"

"We don't know. No one feels like a graduation celebration. Poor Louis."

•   •   •

"I have to talk to you about something," said Louis's deadpan voice on Susan's answering machine. The words were unsettling; Louis had never before thought he had to talk with his sister about anything. Susan called him as soon as Mallory had gone and heard about his tense encounter with Wanda Lockhart and their father. She was sickened. It was incomprehensible that her father, of all men, would pursue another woman while his wife lay unconscious in a hospital bed.

"It can't be true," she cried, but there was no arguing with the report of the lipstick. She lay awake that night, struggling against a sense of malignancy that seemed to pervade the darkness of her room. She accused herself of being infantile and tried to be understanding—after all, her father was lonely and had legitimate complaints against her mother—but failed. By morning, Susan was in the grip of a new, sharp misery quite unlike her old sadness, which now seemed, in comparison, benign—almost contented.

Mallory felt better when she left Susan's apartment, but her mood steadily declined as she walked home, planning how she would explain herself to Alexei and, at the same time, fighting against a growing anxiety that she would never be able to find him again. She could try the library once more or go down to the fitness center on 106th Street. She resolved to try the fitness center first thing in the morning. And when she found him, he would have calmed down, and she would, above all, protect his feelings but at the same time make her intentions clear. This time he would not be able to accuse her of being false and childish.

At home, Mallory found messages on her answering machine from her father, from her editor, asking for some changes, and from Louis Frankl.

"I know I said April, but you know what's been going on. I just got back. So let's go out tomorrow, okay? I'll call again."

His voice was affectingly altered—slower, with a blue note in it now. You would have thought he'd been ill himself, instead of his mother. She dreaded the necessity of putting him off when he called tomorrow; he was already unhappy. How unfortunate that Louis was so different from Susan. She was subtle, fine, and good; he was a shallow, half-educated brat—slick and self-absorbed. On the answering machine, he hadn't even said who was calling, assuming she'd recognize his voice and remember every word they'd said months ago.

CHAPTER 15

The next evening, a Friday, Louis called Mallory, who had forgotten about him. She had gone to the fitness center that morning to inquire about Alexei and had learned that he came in on Fridays at 7:00 A.M. and Wednesdays at 4:30 P.M. She had just missed him. Later, after submitting one story and beginning research for another, she went to the movies with Sylvie Kimura, Alcott Adams, and some of Alcott's friends, one of whom showed an obvious interest in her. She intended to call Sylvie in the morning to ask about him; Sylvie would ask Alcott if she didn't know.

The telephone was ringing when Mallory opened her door. She kicked off her wet shoes at the doorway and ran to get it, leaving her dripping umbrella spread to dry in the hallway.

"I didn't wake you, did I?"

"I just got home," said Mallory. For Susan's sake, she tried to hide her chagrin at having picked up the phone. "How are you, Louis?"

"Bad. I'm just leaving the hospital. Want to go get dinner?"

"Sorry, I already had dinner."

"Then keep me company. It's pouring. Just someplace in the neighborhood. Let's go to the West End."

"I'm really sorry, but I'm awfully tired, and I have to get up early in the morning to write something."

Mallory made it clear that she was dismissing him with a lie, but he persisted. "Tomorrow night, then."

"I have plans. Sorry."

"C'mon, Mallory. When are you going to go out with me?"

"Louis, I told you months ago that I don't think it's a good idea."

"Do me a favor, okay? Let's go somewhere and talk, just once, and then decide. Just don't decide without talking to me one time. You don't know me. You think you do, but you don't."

During the silence that followed while Mallory thought this over, she heard Louis breathe a tense sigh into the phone, which caused her some anguish, but she knew better than to give in.

"It's not going to work, Louis. I'm very sorry, because I know how sad things are for you right now."

"All right," he said. "Maybe I'll call you in a couple of weeks."

"No, don't. It's a bad idea."

"All right." There was another exhalation and a click.

Mallory listened uneasily to the treble *plink* of rain on her windows and an accompanying bass of distant thunder. She had surely done the right thing, but again she felt unkind, just as she had with Alexei; and in her isolation it was hard to find her ordinary bearings. A series of further unwelcome thoughts came to mind, beginning with memories of Paul. After all these months, it was impossible for Mallory to conceal from herself that she hardly missed him, even though they had lived together for two years and for one of those had thought they would marry. She had suffered more over her awkward parting from Alexei, who wasn't even her boyfriend. She missed not so much Paul as being in a couple. He, finally, had protested one too many times that something was wrong. She had agreed, and he had moved out; since she had never really missed him, he had been right.

Now Mallory began to review breakups before Paul. She thought about her conversation with Susan and again doubted whether a healthy, normal psyche ever experienced either "falling in love" or "a broken heart," for she had not, and she was, in her own opinion, the sanest of her friends. The strength of love she knew only from her feelings for her parents; just thinking about those feelings made them surge. Mallory yearned to go home and see her mother and father. She vowed to call them first thing in the morning, and she would have dinner with them tomorrow night.

Checking her answering machine after talking to Louis, Mallory was dismayed to find a message from her editor demanding several substantial further changes in that afternoon's submission, which she had thought of as final. Mallory had put a bit of heart into the piece and thought the editor's comments wrongheaded. Drained and longing to rest, she wrenched her thoughts away from love and homesickness and, with loathing, retrained them on destigmatizing depression. She sat at the computer in pajamas rewriting until 2:00, then set her alarm for 6:00 and slept. When the alarm went off, the nausea of sleep deprivation overcame her, but she forced herself out of bed and went to work again. Frantic e-mails from the editor began appearing at 7:15, to which she responded at 8:00:

practically done—just give me a minute.

But it was almost 8:45 when she e-mailed the changes. In her fatigue and disquietude, she felt great relief at being free now to call her parents.

"I was thinking of coming home for dinner tonight," she said.

"Oh, sweetheart. We'd love to see you," said Ingrid on one phone, "but we're going out with the Sieverts." The Sieverts were dull friends of her parents who already had three grandchildren and liked to point out that Mallory was single and not getting any younger.

"Why don't you come along?" said Herb on the other phone. "They'd love to see you. We're having dinner, and then we're going to a concert at Alice Tully. I know I can get you a ticket."

Alice Tully Hall and dinner with the Sieverts, however, wasn't at all what Mallory had in mind. Nor was shopping for a graduation present for her cousin Elaine in the afternoon. Instead she said she would come to dinner on Sunday. Now a desolate, dull Saturday stretched before her. She didn't want to go back to bed. She was too tired to work on her pharmaceutical lobby piece. Nor could she think of anyone who would be available with whom she wanted to spend time.

I'll have a jog, she decided, and when I get back I'll call Sylvie.

The air was sweet smelling and pleasantly cool after the overnight storm, and the sky was still overcast. It was perfect jogging weather, and numbers of people were doing just that on the Riverside Promenade. Mallory felt clumsy from tiredness at first, but by the time she had gone south to 72nd Street and returned north, she felt better. At 112th Street, however, her equilibrium was disturbed when she saw Alexei playing chess on a bench with a small girl, while a tall teenage girl looked on and, judging from her expression, was teasing him while he ignored her. Mallory was so disturbed by the sight of him that she tripped and fell when she was fifteen paces beyond them, attracting unwanted offers of assistance from several bystanders. She laughingly refused help, insisting that she was not hurt. In fact, her hands and knees were bleeding and stung badly. Mallory was certain that Alexei had seen and understood what happened, which was humiliating. And he didn't come to ask if she was all right. That was peculiarly and unexpectedly wounding, although, after all, why should he—particularly when it was obvious that she was perfectly all right. Nonetheless, his indifference brought her near tears, and she limped home, where, after washing up and applying antiseptic, she fell into an exhausted sleep. When she awoke more than two hours later, she felt groggy and she ached. She tried to call Sylvie, but there was no answer. She could not remember another day as bleak and lonely as this one.

The doorbell rang. She knew that it was Alexei, and, yes, there he was when she opened the door.

"Hello," she said, resorting to the teenage convention in which one adopts a tone of sullen wistfulness in the first awkward conversation after a quarrel. She had no other resources at her disposal; her energies were absorbed in fighting off a debilitating longing that came over her the instant she saw him.

"You had quite a fall out there," he said, looking awkward.

"Come in? I've been looking for you."

"I know," he said. "They told me at the club, just now, that you were there." They sat beside each other on her sofa, looking ahead self-consciously instead of turning to face each other.

"Your phone was disconnected," she accused him.

"Yes. It's back on again. I was late on the bill."

"But you see, Alexei, things like that are the problem with you. Your phone gets disconnected, and no one can reach you. I have no idea where you live. You're not even in the phone book."

"I'm listed under my former roommate's name," Alexei said.

"But no one could possibly know that. How could anyone have a serious relationship with someone they have to leave messages for in tree stumps?"

"With a nobody. Why didn't you just e-mail me?"

"I didn't say that. I'm saying you're not responsible. You don't behave like an adult. You don't really understand how things work. I don't even know your e-mail address."

"Surely a reporter for the *Gazette* should be able to find that out easily enough."

Mallory turned to Alexei, but just then he got up and went to the stove, put on the teakettle, and began opening cabinet doors, looking for cups and tea. Unfortunately, this felt appealingly intimate and roiled her emotions. Her desolation vanished, supplanted by turbulence and longing.

"And what you said about being responsible—*that's* not true," he said, looking at her with a mixture of puzzlement, hurt, and severity. "I don't know anyone more responsible than I am."

"You have no plans for a real career. You probably don't live anywhere I'd feel safe walking to. Do you have an apartment or rent a room or what?"

"Surely your parents pay your rent here."

"They help a little."

Alexei snorted. "But I help my parents. I'm the responsible one, you see. And I *have* career plans. I'm going to be a singer in the opera."

"That's an illusion. It's absurd. There's absolutely no reason to think that will ever happen."

"I could fail, but maybe I won't. Is worth trying."

"You will certainly fail, so it's not worth trying."

"I have an audition tomorrow."

"For what? I'll bet it's one of those things where the performers chip in for costumes and scenery. What a waste of time."

"That's what my father said, too—a waste of time." Alexei chewed on his lower lip, holding back resentment. But even though Mallory saw this, she doggedly pursued her point, as though she would be justified in injuring him if she could make him admit that she was right.

"I knew it. You say your father is crazy, but the one objective fact you've ever told me about him makes him sound sensible. Milk or lemon?" he asked.

"Milk and sugar," she said.

They sat again on the sofa with cups of tea. She winced as she sat, because her knees hurt.

"Put antibacterial ointment on your knees," said Alexei. "Keep the skin soft with ointment, or you'll get scars." He took her hand for a moment and, looking at the raw skin on the palm, grimaced and laid it back on her lap.

"The problem is," he said longingly, "the real problem is . . ."

"I'd always be looking for someone else," she said.

"That would be a problem, yes," said Alexei wearily. "But why would you?"

"I want to get married and have kids and live the way I grew up."

"And you're so sure you can't do that with me?"

"Aren't you?"

"Not really. No. You only think so because you think you have to have everything easy. No risks, nothing hard—what is it, you have special trouble exemption?"

"Not at all. I expect hard things. But in my world the hard things aren't having no decent place to live and no degree and no chance for the career you want and no fallback or safety net. That's the whole point, Alexei. You don't have a clue about anything. The risks you're taking are so lunatic, no one can even respect them."

"What about your friend Alcott Adams? He's having hard time, trying to make films. Would you rule him out, too?"

"Him! He's got a little money, parents with lots of connections, two degrees from Yale. As soon as he decides he's not going to make it in films, he can move into a good job in public television or at some media corporation or any number of things. Most people would give anything to succeed as well as he's going to fail." Mallory was embarrassed to tell someone like Alexei, who faced such social and economic obstacles, that she and her friends sought successes of a kind that were reserved for class and privilege. But it was a fact, and it was precisely what Alexei didn't get.

"But he's not going to do that, you know—I mean public television or some corporation or whatever," Alexei said. "That's impossible for him."

"Believe me, he *is* going to do that. You can't tell about these things in one conversation at a party."

"You have hard ideas, Mallory. Why do you, when things have always been so easy for you?"

"This is futile, Alex. I wanted—"

"You wanted to convince me you're really, really nice person and I'm joke. But you're not very nice and I'm not very funny. I dislike these things you're saying, all about how contemptible people are superior. I don't respect it. And why do you think you can say such things to me—that my life and my hopes are absurd? Mallory, I don't think as well of you as you think of yourself."

He got up to go, and her eyes began to burn and then overflowed. Of course he was hurt; it was inevitable that he should retaliate. This time she had been frank, but he had still found plenty to disapprove of. Yet despite her wounded feelings and her own anger, she dreaded the moment when he would be gone. She remembered how she had felt, alone in her apartment, when he had walked out last week. Worst of all was her longing for him, which persisted through her anger and fed it, keeping her off balance. She followed Alexei to the door and grasped his arm, with a vague intention of trying to give this scene a different ending from the last time.

"Wait a minute, Alexei," she said. Unexpectedly, he turned and put his arms around her for a moment, which in her turmoil she found almost irresistible. She almost asked him to stay. The only safety here, she thought, wiping away tears when she was alone again, was in finding someone else.

As soon as she felt sure of her voice, she called Sylvie to ask about Alcott's friend. When it came to love and marriage, it was best to choose someone like oneself. Religion didn't matter—except that you should avoid really religious people. Race didn't matter. That's what her parents had always said. But Mallory belonged to a world with high educational, social, and cultural admission requirements. Mallory met them, and Alexei couldn't, and although that was unjust, it was not her fault and she was not obligated to take on his disabilities.

Alexei returned to his room on Tiemann Place, where he paced and muttered, then threw himself on his bed. He had to pull himself together for a chess lesson in half an hour and the audition in the morning, but the telephone rang shortly after he got home.

"It's me. It's Cora," said a shaky voice.

"Cora? You don't sound like yourself," said Alexei. He had to exert himself not to be rude out of disappointment that it wasn't Mallory.

"No, I've got a problem," she said in what would have been a reassuring singsong except that her voice shook.

"What's wrong?" said Alexei. He realized that she was trying not to alarm him. "Is this another computer emergency?"

"No, this is . . . Well, I fell off my loft ladder and I think something could be broken," she said in the same unsteady lilt, "and when I tried to get up I fainted, and I didn't show up at my job and I didn't even call." He heard her voice thicken with tears on the last words.

"Well, don't worry about that—you'll just explain later. You sound terrible. You need ambulance. Cora, you need someone there. . . . Can't you call someone . . . your parents, some girlfriend or—"

"My parents are in Idaho. You're the first one I could find, Alexei, but you sound like you're tied up. Don't worry, I'll—"

"Call ambulance. Wait—I'll call ambulance." Even this felt cruel, though. Alexei knew he should go over there, but he had to meet his chess student in fifteen minutes. And after that he had to prepare for the audition and then get plenty of rest. The audition, with a Brooklyn opera company, was the most serious he'd ever gotten, and even though Charles Braithwaite had said his chances weren't good and even though the opera company was small and obscure and tended to go in and out of existence, winning the part would give him significant onstage experience, which he badly needed. Besides, Cora was not even a close friend.

"No, no. Never mind, I'll—"

"I'll be there as fast as I can," he said. She was so appallingly forgiving, even in her terror, that Alexei was conscience-stricken.

He ran into the library on his way to Cora's and was relieved to find Vic sitting at his usual table. Vic promised to explain everything when Alexei's student arrived for the chess lesson, and he hurriedly pulled a twenty out of his wallet.

"If you have to, take a cab to the emergency room," Vic said.

Alexei took the money—he now recalled that he was broke and had even been counting on the chess lesson for money for dinner—and ran out again as fast as he could to Cora's place on 107th Street between Columbus and Manhattan avenues.

He waited with her in the emergency room half the night, held her hand until she went into surgery at dawn and again when she got out, and he stayed at her side until they finally found a bed for her. The doctors weren't too worried about the doubly fractured leg, but the concussion was serious; she'd have to be watched and have more tests. Of course, Alexei missed the audition. What would Charles Braithwaite say after he'd gone to so much trouble to set it up? Who would even believe that he'd been in the hospital with a friend? He should have left her and gone home. Once Cora was in the care of the doctors, what difference did it really make if she was scared or in pain or if she cried?

But Charles Braithwaite wasn't angry. He only said soberly, "Why didn't you call me? I would have had my doctor check in on her. You could have borrowed my car, Alexei."

The thought had never crossed Alexei's mind that anyone from Charles Braithwaite's world might be willing to help. People who were safe, who had resources—doctors to call, cars—generally resented doing favors for people who didn't. Although they could be generous to those as fortunate as they were, they thought that anyone who lived outside, on the edges, like Cora and Alexei, should learn to take care of themselves.

PART TWO

esley's eyelids twitched. Then they opened, and she spoke. "Henry? Judy?" she said.

"Judy's at home," said Susan, clutching her hand, but Lesley's eyes closed and again she was oblivious to words and caresses.

Susan sat alone in the hospital, glad not to face her father, but angry that he was not here. He had missed his visits several times in the past week. Susan watched tensely what seemed to be intelligent, expressive movement of muscles in her mother's face, so that she appeared almost to be frowning. The therapist said that such incidents would recur. She now expected Lesley to regain consciousness within weeks or even days. For Lesley had not only spoken, she had spoken sensibly, about the two people who had been with her at the time of the accident.

Peter was on his way to the office. He had walked a block in the direction of St. Luke's, then, instead of crossing the Columbia campus and going to Lesley, he abruptly turned south toward Samad's Deli. He disliked the campus at this time of year, a week after graduation, when everyone was gone. He missed the sense of high endeavors, the enlightened people walking in twos and threes, and the tidbits of overheard unworldly talk. He called Susan on her cell phone, knowing that she would be sitting at Lesley's bedside by now. Susan reassured him, but he heard the new coolness in her voice. Her unfriendliness was far more painful to bear than Louis's.

Louis was hardly speaking to him and had obviously told Susan the whole story about Wanda, because Susan was behaving strangely—quiet, brooding, accusing. Yet Peter couldn't protest his innocence, for he thought of Wanda constantly and fantasized committing with her all the crimes his children suspected him of. He wanted Wanda so much that there were times when he thought an affair might actually be worth estrangement from his children. Other times he had better sense. He wouldn't actually become an adulterer while his wife lay unconscious in St. Luke's.

"Look, Louis," Peter said to him one day, "what you saw was misleading. Nothing happened. Nothing is going to happen. You don't need to worry. Understand me?"

"Absolutely, Dad," said Louis, as inscrutable as ever, and nothing changed.

To celebrate Lesley's progress, Susan, Louis, and Peter gathered for dinner that evening at the Terrace, a Morningside Heights restaurant that Peter liked because, he said, it was like him, old-fashioned and stuffy.

"Well, kids," he said when the wine had come and he had poured a glass for each of them, "I think it's time to start being optimistic that your mother is going to be fine, or more fine than we ever let ourselves hope before." Peter spoke and thought his children's interests and wishes just as, when practicing law, he spoke and thought his clients'. Susan had often seen him do this without objecting, but now the doubleness of it outraged her. Louis's face was unreadable, but she suspected that his resentment exceeded her own. Susan knew that her father suffered under their angry mistrust, but there was nothing she could do. She looked down at her plate.

"So, Dad, what's this Susan was telling me about some program on terrorism at Columbia?" Louis asked, his face still expressionless.

"Well, yes," said Peter, smiling in spite of himself. "The Devereaux Foundation is funding a group of notables to study terrorism, and they've named me chair. I thought Columbia would never go along with it, but apparently Emma Devereaux knows someone there and convinced them I would act as a sort of liaison, administrative and nonacademic, and anyway, somehow she got them to agree. So, uh, it's going to be a lot of fun." He ended lamely as he perceived their ambivalence.

"Mother would hate the idea," said Susan. But she was distressed by this glimpse of her father's pleasure. It was obvious how much the seminar meant to him.

"She'd live," said Peter with an unconvincing chuckle. He was attempting to defuse things, but his remark produced a twitch at the corner of Louis's mouth, and Susan pursed her lips. In fact, the tension at the table increased to a point where it broke through Peter's satisfaction, and Susan, despite her anger, saw a kaleidoscope of hungers and despairs register on his face before he could banish them.

"I have such a headache," she said. "Does anyone have an aspirin?" The headache served as a useful distraction. After much sympathy, officious searching of pockets and bags, and pleas to the waiter, two aspirin were obtained and swallowed, and Peter regained self-possession enough to attempt a change of subject.

"By the way, Susie," he said, "one of the Devereaux Foundation ladies lives in your building."

"I'll bet I know who it is," Susan said. "She's thin, long hair pulled back, gray streaks . . ."

"That's her. That's Hilda Hughes. She runs away if you try to talk to her—a bit of a recluse, very shy and withdrawn. I tried to tell her about the construction plans for the building next door, in case she needs to pull out, but it got her so upset I was sorry I said anything. Do you know if she lives on the east or west side of the building?"

But Susan didn't. Louis sat silent, still wearing the empty expression he had developed in adolescence for family occasions, but his eyes darted from his father to his sister.

"Dad, this seminar sounds really good," he said at last. His voice was usually soft and sarcastic, but there was little sarcasm in it at this moment. Susan was surprised that he accepted the blow against their mother so easily. "And you know what you should do? You should get a story in the *Gazette* about it. Get some publicity so that people will pay attention to it."

"No, Louis, it's not that sort of thing," said Susan. "It's academic. Publicity would cheapen it."

"Well, sweetie," said Peter, "you may be right, but Miss Devereaux agrees with Louis. So we're going to invite press to the first meeting, at least."

"Make sure they're friendly," said Louis, averting his eyes slightly. "I know. Get Mallory Holmes to come for the *Gazette*. She's really smart, and she'd do a good job."

"But she just writes little health things usually," said Susan. "They wouldn't let her."

"It doesn't hurt to ask her to try, does it? Come on, Susan, she's your friend." Susan was suspicious of Louis's enthusiasm for this idea, and Louis knew it. The way to preserve his secret longer, he understood, was to make a show of openness. "I'll call her and ask her if she wants to do the story," he said, pulling a cell phone out of his pocket.

"Well . . . ," said Peter. He agreed with Louis that nothing could be lost by calling Mallory, and he had always liked Mallory. Louis understood that this was permission, slightly ambivalent permission.

"You know her number?" asked Susan.

"What is it?" asked Louis, who actually had the number on speed dial. Susan knew her brother well enough to guess that his calm was a ruse. He was interested in her friend, which surprised her and raised a little anxiety. She couldn't conceive of the two of them together. Mallory would have to turn Louis away, and Susan felt uncomfortable just imagining this. While her mind rapidly sized the dimensions of this unexpected situation, Louis left the table to make the call. He returned in what seemed hardly a minute.

"She'll do it," he said, pocketing the cell phone as he sat down. "I mean, she'll try."

"Reluctantly? Eagerly?" asked Susan.

"Are you kidding me? Your friend Mallory is very ambitious, and this is a nice chance for her. She said she has to go sell the higher-ups on the idea, but she thinks she might be able to pull it off," said Louis, and he smiled ingratiatingly, with just one side of his mouth. Susan recognized the lopsided, half-sincere smile as another of the expressions Louis reserved for family occasions. It was so innocent: tipping you off that he was conning you by using only half his mouth. Louis was always so transparently devious. Yet he had a different, whole, smile for their mother. Looking at her brother, Susan had the thought that he, too, was coming awake. But that raised the question whether he and his mother could both be awake at the same time.

CHAPTER 17

Their smiles invisible in the near darkness, Ivy Hurst and Edmond Lockhart descended the steps of Low Library amid a crush of people who called out flattering jokes and congratulations and, generally speaking, acted like iron filings in the presence of a magnet. As this year's Eisenhower Lecturer, Edmond had given a talk titled "The Eclipse of Joy." At the end, the audience had gotten to their feet and applauded with the self-congratulatory enthusiasm of people who have heard their own thoughts voiced. There had been an extraordinarily lively and good-humored question-and-answer period, then a champagne reception that was brilliant with scholarly stars. It might not be recorded in the *Times,* and then again it might, but it was nonetheless a historic moment. Edmond knew, as he walked down those steps, that now he was going to be remembered and he would be listened to in a new way. He had achieved a new status. He had observed others achieve it, coveted it, and now he had it himself.

"You've done it," Ivy said to him, glowing, when they were home again. "Now they all know what you are."

Edmond, for once, smiled and took her hand, delighting in new and profoundly gratifying emotions. A grating sense of inferiority had fled, and with it all his animosities and envies. He wished humanity well and forgave everyone their sins and flaws. In fact, he was struck at how he was surrounded by goodness. People were good and kind and did justice to one another. He savored the memory of how the audience had laughed at his wit, applauded his keen points, and stood clapping at the end; and how Arif Ahmed and Laura Bernhard had sidled up to him at the reception, trying to get near the bright center of things, where he was. He especially liked the ironic joshing at the end, when he was walking home and no longer expected to talk. At one point, still surrounded by his appreciative entourage, he had caught up with the great economist Joseph Madigan, now ancient and frail, who had sat right up front, where Edmond had been keenly aware of him. Madigan, hobbling along the sidewalk on Broadway, had turned to Edmond and, alluding to his own famous miscall on the direction of the economy back in the fifties, had said, "You'll find that it doesn't even matter if you're right or wrong." And everyone had chuckled, not because this was really so funny, but because that's how people reacted when a Big Man like Madigan deigned to poke fun at himself. Obviously, the laughter siphoned off some of the envy and hostility people feel for such a man; Edmond would have to remind himself to behave similarly. Clearly, however, Madigan was also making a comparison between his own status as a public figure and Edmond's.

Ivy was dreamy. "And all this on top of those reviews last week. Edmond, I can't tell you what it means to me to see you get the recognition you deserve, to see you completely happy, working so well, and everything just as it should be." Ivy knew that she lacked physical attractions and that, professionally, she would never be more than a minor figure in a minor field—no matter how many talks she gave at international conferences, or papers she published in learned journals. It was clear to Ivy that without Edmond she would fall to somewhere around the bottom quartile of the university's social/professional ladder. Therefore, she was never tempted to underestimate her good fortune in having a man like Edmond as her partner, and she was transported at times like this, when the world was at his feet and thus, in a way, at hers.

Edmond fell asleep a happy man, still turning over these jewels, one by one, in his mind. But at 2:00 A.M. he awoke, his breath catching with anxiety, his heart beating too fast. He could not stop thinking about Madigan's remark, which at the time he had taken as a welcome by one member of an exclusive club to a new member. But in fact hadn't it actually been somewhat hostile? Wasn't it just a sarcastic way of telling Edmond that his ideas were all wrong? With increasing discomfort, Edmond pondered this and then reconsidered some of his responses to last night's questions, which began to appear to contradict what he had said in his speech. He recalled a line in last week's *New Republic* review of his book: "Lockhart, however, never met a losing cause he didn't like. His praise goes to minor figures. He finds no merit in great ones." The reviewer had seen through him. Edmond broke out in a sweat of humiliation.

His mind sought out other humiliations. This business of Peter Frankl, a middlebrow nobody, using Edmond's own aunt and his own family's money to enter social and academic circles that Edmond himself was excluded from! Edmond had very much wanted to be asked to join the terrorism seminar; he'd once written a hard-hitting essay on the subject. Yes, maybe last night he'd given the Eisenhower Lecture, but that was nothing; it was already over. And Ivy thought that was good enough: $2,000 and a couple of bottles of champagne, no press. Ivy thought such inferior honors were good enough for him. Edmond, pursuing such wrongs and indignities, didn't fall asleep again until near 6:00.

Ivy slept contentedly the entire night and was still asleep beside Edmond at 7:00 A.M., when her clock radio went off to the sound of Bernstein conducting the overture to *Candide*. She awoke feeling happy before she recollected why. Then she remembered Edmond's successes last night and thought that the sassy, bracing music perfectly suited her triumphant mood. She sat up and reached for a robe on a chair near the bed. She had a tenure committee meeting first thing after breakfast.

"Get out," said Edmond. His voice came from deep in his chest, guttural and toneless.

"What?"

"I said get out. Turn off that noise and get out. You'll kill me. Someday you'll kill me."

She had not mistaken it; he sounded poisonous, and it frightened her.

"Edmond, what on earth—"

"For the last time, get out and shut up. I don't want to hear about your confusion and your surprise and all your petty feelings. I just want you to move your ever thickening self off my bed, turn off that noise, and let me get some rest."

Trembling, Ivy collected her clothes, showered, and dressed and was in her study stuffing a carryall with her notes, the files on the candidate, and the offprints of the candidate's articles when Lockhart appeared in the doorway, barefoot and wearing for the first time the plaid flannel bathrobe she had given him last Christmas.

"I'm sorry," he said in a hollow voice. "I had a very bad night, and I had just gotten to sleep. I'm sorry, Ivy. Don't go."

"I must be at a meeting in ten minutes. I must go," she said. Somewhat softened by his donning of the robe, she was nonetheless not ready to forgive and spoke in an excessively genteel voice, with a faintly anglicized accent, which she always did at such moments, feeling that it raised her above reproach.

"I'm not well. Can't you call and beg off?"

Ivy hesitated, then shook her head. "No, I can't. It's only an hour, Edmond, but I'll get out a bit early if I can."

"You'll try to get out a bit early. Oh, what generosity! What more could a man ask for? Tell me, how is it that a woman with absolutely no sense of proportion becomes a professor of the classical arts? Or is that why it attracted you? A sense of your deficiencies—physical and spiritual?"

"Edmond, what is this all about? You know that I'll have to leave if you continue. I can only conclude that that's what you want."

"So you always say, but here you still are. Why don't you get out, then? Just get out. Get out!" At the last words, he lost control and his voice rose from its smug baritone to a countertenor. Ivy gathered her things and trudged out, too overburdened, Edmond thought, with all those bags, and too pear-shaped to look as imposing as she obviously believed she did.

The truth was that she was more frightened than angry. He had sounded so crazy that she was scared, actually shaking, and did not know what she would do. Perhaps she should call his doctor. But she decided that before calling, she would wait to see whether Edmond would snap out of this, as he sometimes did. Yet because his disturbance seemed so much greater than usual this time, it was hard to imagine it would end quickly.

Seen through Ivy's fear, hurt, and agitation, the morning was oppressively brilliant. She crossed Broadway at 116th Street and passed between the great iron gates onto the campus, climbed the steps to Low Library, retracing most of the path of last night's triumphant procession, and went on to Schermerhorn Hall.

The candidate, Nancy Gettner, was a young woman—young and attractive—who had written a half-dozen scholarly articles and was well liked by her colleagues and students. The first two speakers at the meeting announced that they strongly favored promoting her to tenure and outlined the reasons that they had spelled out in their written report. It was apparent that most of the room were delighted with what they were hearing. Then it was Ivy's turn.

"All right, Ivy," said the chairman with a confident smile. He expected that Ivy, who was strongly feminist, would jump at the chance to tenure such a promising and delightful young woman. "Tell us why we're doing the right thing here."

Ivy looked grave. "In fact, I do not favor tenure."

The room grew quiet, and Ivy noticed Christie Blake and John

Cavendish catch each other's eyes. Then, obviously, they were scribbling to each other through the rest of Ivy's presentation, trying to make it look as though they were just taking notes on the discussion but gently sliding their notebooks to a position where the other could read it. This made Ivy's face burn. She had a right to be heard without winks or nods, and she really didn't want Nancy Gettner simpering around this department for the rest of her professional career. Ivy gave her comments in a state of irritation complicated by a lingering sense of eerie horror evoked by Edmond's behavior that morning. The case against Gettner was a very difficult one, too, but it was important to make a good presentation of her controversial position, and she was well prepared to do so.

Ivy first attacked Gettner's scholarly work. "She has no book," she pointed out. "Every other candidate for years has been required to have written at least one book."

"But this huge article in *Classical Arts Symposium* reflects more thought and work than most books," John protested. "It's already a classic. It's—"

"She wrote it ten years ago," said Ivy, "when she was in graduate school. She has produced nothing of that importance since. She shows no promise of being a productive scholar in years to come. She shows signs of being a devoted mother, which is lovely, but we are not permitted to tenure her for that. She will give birth in a few months to her second child. Since her first was born three years ago, she keeps the minimum in office hours, and she attends only required department functions. I am told that she is meeting with students in her home, with the child running around screaming."

"We can't base our judgments on anonymous hearsay."

"Then why not ask Nancy if it's true?"

"I used to meet students at home," put in Lou Staubach, "until I got scared by all the sexual harassment stuff, although in my experience it's hard to do a lot of sexual harassing with kids running around screaming." His belly rose and fell with a suppressed chuckle.

"It's not only unprofessional—it's foolhardy," Ivy went on, cool and firm, ignoring Lou, "and could involve this department in a legal nightmare. And I'll have more to say on a related issue in a moment. For the time being, my main point is that Nancy Gettner is going nowhere in her work."

"Ivy, I'll be honest. I can't believe what you're saying. What about this grant proposal? How can you argue with the quality of that?" asked John Cavendish.

"It's just a proposal. She'll write no book. She'll use the time to avoid teaching and to diaper babies. Essentially, she's arranged a two-year vacation. Or a paid two-year maternity leave."

Ivy's confident responses to Cavendish and Staubach emboldened other members of the committee, who felt about Nancy Gettner much as Ivy did but had feared the political costs of opposing a popular appointment. There were those who thought that several male members of the department wanted Gettner because she was so attractive and sweet and that the women were voting yes out of knee-jerk feminism. Tough-minded feminists like Ivy were so often useful in these situations. She could tear into Gettner without being suspected of sexism, and it would be easy to stand behind her; she would take the flak.

"I hadn't really focused on what Ivy is pointing out here," began Lester Kegan. "But, in fact, I've always thought of Nancy Gettner as . . . a lightweight—maybe just one of those people who do great work on a dissertation because the adviser is feeding them ideas, energy, helping solve the problems. Once they're on their own, they don't produce."

Clearly, several people in the room were thinking twice about their votes.

"I'm going to have to leave in a few minutes," Ivy continued. "I'm sorry, but I have illness to contend with at home."

There was a murmur of understanding and forgiveness, but Ivy noticed Christie scribble and John Cavendish's eyes slant to read what she wrote.

"I have just one more point, and it's one I'm sorry I have to make. But the fact is that, whatever we decide about her tenure, someone has to tell her to keep her hands off the students. She's always grabbing them or putting her arm around their shoulders. I saw her in the hall Friday, and she was actually hugging a young man."

"Danny Barth—because he got his fellowship," said Christie.

"That was two weeks ago."

"But she had just found out. Come on, Ivy. This is sleazy."

Unfortunately, Christie's last three words were too much. If she had just said "Come on, Ivy," and stopped, she might have drawn sentiment in favor of Nancy, but the last three words consolidated Ivy's support. Colleagues should not call one another sleazy in a public meeting. The majority condemned Christie Blake. A minority understood why Christie had made this mistake but had an ominous feeling that Nancy Gettner's appointment was seriously endangered by it. Christie felt what had happened and tried to fix it.

"I had no right to say that. I apologize. Look, Nancy is my friend, and my feelings got out of hand."

Worse and worse for Nancy, thought the minority. Now her support confesses its interestedness. Ivy tried to nod a cool acknowledgment of the apology, but somehow the insult, added to Edmond's cruel words of the morning, and the apology, undid her, and tears trickled down her cheeks. She whisked them away, but not before they had melted a great deal of negative feeling that had built up against her and her views on Nancy Gettner. Ivy made a dignified exit, muttering, "Excuse me," as she squeezed around chairs to get to the door.

The chairman said they'd have to have another meeting before they could vote, and all agreed.

"If she were my friend," Staubach said to Christie as they left, "I'd tell her to update her CV and get a ticket to the December meetings."

Ivy, having left early, could not yet bear to go home and face Edmond. It had all been so upsetting that she was still trembling. Yet she felt some satisfaction at the knowledge that she might still be able to derail Gettner's tenure. She bought a newspaper and went to the promenade on Riverside Drive, where she sat on a bench and read, worrying, however, that she would be seen after saying that she had to go home. At nearly 11:00, she called.

"There you are. Come home, dear. I've been missing you." He sounded normal again, calm and fatherly, and Ivy went home.

CHAPTER 18

Peter Frankl, all starch and creases, wearing a summer suit with a resplendent tie, left his apartment early one afternoon in June to attend the organizational meeting of the Seminar on International Terrorism. The participants were gathering for the first time to set up subcommittees and programs in preparation for the regular sessions, which were to begin the following January. There was no one at home to wish Peter luck as he set out, nervous but happily anticipating great things. He felt that his life would be fundamentally altered by this seminar—more so than by anything else since the birth of his children. He wished his father could have lived to see this.

The meeting was held in an elegant room in Low Library around a conference table large enough for all thirty participants and a crowd of onlookers. There were coffee and tea in silver urns on silver trays, and a gallery of distinguished visitors who sat in chairs behind the seminar members, away from the table, listening and occasionally tiptoeing in and out, clutching cell phones.

The atmosphere in the room was heavy with the importance of those assembled. There were reporters from the *Times,* the *Journal,* and two or three other papers. Mallory Holmes was one of two *Gazette* reporters. This is a big deal, she thought, looking around the room. She recognized the Nobel Prize—winning economist Joshua Newgate, New York ex-senator George Hume, a name-brand Columbia journalism professor, Avery Steinmetz, who for years had been a reporter for *The Washington Post.* There was the historian Lucius Polk; a civil rights activist who taught at the law school, Carlotta Salinas; and the Middle East expert Arif Ahmed. But most of the attendees had an anonymous sort of importance that was more intimidating. They knew things other people didn't. They pulled invisible strings. They wouldn't pander to reporters, and answered to no one. There was a thin, tiny, wrinkled woman in a peculiar dress, a plump elderly man who removed his coat, displaying red braces embroidered with gold stars. Mallory's eyes were drawn to one black woman in her fifties who projected great power and modesty simultaneously—like an ex-president or the queen of some tiny, armyless country.

Peter, having been introduced by Columbia's chancellor, made a short speech in fluent, succinct lawyerly style with a slight flavor of the Bronx. He thanked everyone, on behalf of the Devereaux Foundation, for undertaking to apply their wisdom and knowledge to the immense moral, social, and practical questions that terrorism posed. It was the foundation's hope that a group so talented, so diverse in its views and its fields of learning, would take the lead in developing creative solutions. Then he introduced the participants with brief biographies.

The stately woman in her fifties he identified only as Martha Lovett, a schoolteacher from Brooklyn who was here because no one who knew her would ever want to decide any important question without her advice. Another member, who was young and wore a wrinkled sports jacket and jeans, was introduced as Lester Maxwell, a philosopher and critic. But obviously there was more to his story than that. His name sounded vaguely familiar to Mallory. A talk show pundit, maybe? It would come to her, or maybe Howard Kappell, the senior reporter from the *Gazette*, would know.

"I'd be happy to take questions from participants first," said Peter. "Then perhaps they wouldn't mind a few questions from the members of the press whom we have invited to this preliminary meeting—before we settle down to getting ourselves organized."

Peter surveyed the room expectantly. At the opposite end of the table, two persons raised long, thin arms encased in black. Peter had already had a couple of encounters with this pair, named Smith-Smythe, who despite their physical resemblance were not brother and sister but husband and wife. They had twice demanded that he change the proposed date of the meeting and, although he had done his best to accommodate their wishes, had complained to the chancellor that he was disorganized and inconsiderate. They had also volunteered to serve as the group's "academic leaders," citing their superior qualifications and unparalleled devotion to the cause of ending terror. Although the Devereaux Foundation was grateful for their kind offer, Peter had replied, there was no need for academic leaders, as he himself, by arrangement with Columbia, would handle administrative matters, and each subcommittee would govern itself.

"Professors Smith-Smythe raise their hands. I'll let you two settle who goes first," Peter said. They had been invited to the seminar because, as Peter had just explained to the group, they had recently spent a year in Prague at the International Conference on Text and Terrorism, where their contributions had been highly prized.

"No offense, Frankl," said Chalmers Smythe, an unexpected testiness in his voice, "but perhaps you might just explain what right you have to admit or banish the press from our meetings."

Peter was taken aback by such an unfriendly question and the rude use of his last name with no honorific "Mr."

"I've been asked by the Devereaux Foundation and Columbia to set the ground rules for our meetings," Peter replied, managing to sound civil.

"We don't want press on a regular basis, Chalmers," put in George Hume, the ex-senator, "if that's what you're getting at. But I personally have no objection to their presence today. What could be the problem?"

"That's not the point," said Chalmers. "The point is, why should this man, or the Devereaux Foundation, for that matter, be making that decision? What other sorts of authority can they exercise without control? For that matter, does anyone here know the first thing about the Devereaux Foundation? How do we know they intend to allow this group to arrive at whatever conclusions it wants, freely, or whether they plan to control its deliberations and its output, along with how much publicity it's exposed to? I, for one, need a guarantee that—"

"They sent me a brochure about the foundation in the summer," said an expert in infectious diseases and biological warfare from the University of Texas, who was about thirty-five, plain, and guileless. She dug into a battered leather case propped indelicately between spread knees. "Didn't you get one? Here!" And she slid a brochure across the table to Chalmers Smythe.

"I should think that your letters of invitation made clear that it is precisely your untrammeled opinions that are desired here," Peter responded. His air of paternal patience, however, failed to disarm the Smith-Smythes.

"Forgive me, but some of us have spent years fighting unfreedom on campuses," said Teresa Smith, her voice wavering sarcastically. "We've seen all kinds of money come in and try to buy research, departments, expert opinion, chairs devoted to fascistic ideologies. What guarantee do we have that—"

"There are no strings attached to the money," Peter said patiently. "The money will not be withdrawn if the foundation should disagree with the conclusions of the seminar or any of its members. The financial arrangements that are already firmly in place would preclude its doing so, even if it wanted to, as the chancellor here will confirm. And, to my personal knowledge, the foundation doesn't want to. Its wish and intention is that the seminar bring together a variety of points of view in a situation of complete freedom. The basic format of the seminars was laid out in your letters of invitation. We naturally assumed that anyone who objected would have let us know earlier or would have declined the invitation."

"That sounds like a suggestion," said Teresa Smith. "Where does the Devereaux money come from, anyway?"

"Buttons," Peter replied. He was growing more and more irked, but a certain blandness in his voice was the only sign of this. "It's old button money—that's old money from buttons, not money from old buttons."

"Buttons?" she asked, frowning. "You mean . . ."

"Buttons—for clothes. Quite a progressive company, actually, union, good pension plan. They got out of ivory buttons on grounds of conscience long before the law was passed, but they still make leather ones, in case *that* bothers anyone," said Peter.

Some members of the seminar smiled, but the whole interchange had a bad effect on the tone of the proceedings. The Smith-Smythes were stone-faced, and several others looked nervous and uncomfortable. Peter knew that he had to get the Smith-Smythes to shut up or things would fall apart. "Further questions?" he said abruptly. "No? Then perhaps members of the pr—"

A young man from the *Times* was on his feet talking before Peter's last word was fully uttered. "Professors Smith-Smythe," he began in a manner poised coyly between aggression and ingratiation, which Mallory rather admired, "why are you getting involved here, anyway? What do you want this seminar to achieve?"

"Simply," Chalmers Smythe replied, "to help my fellow conferees achieve a more compassionate understanding of the despair that afflicts Palestinians and so many other Arabs and lies behind their resort to terror. I want to prevent this gathering from being used and manipulated by some of its organizers—who obviously have their own agenda here—"

Peter was outraged. But the poet Mark Bellini, something of a right-winger and given to social buffoonery and exhibitionism, cut Chalmers off before Peter could.

"That's very kind of you, Chalmers. And I hope to help you and our colleagues understand things, too. For example, I'm not sure *you* understand how helpful a few bombing missions against Mecca would be, especially if we could take out a historic mosque or two." Angry mutters, a few startled gasps, and a stifled titter or two greeted this. It was so offensive that Peter was too shocked to know how to respond. Lucius Polk, shaking his head in disgust, walked stiffly out of the room. His exit dismayed Peter even more than the juvenile left-right bickering. Polk was the ideal seminar member— tolerant and kindly, gentlemanly, rationalist, and independent minded.

"Keep in mind, Mark," Arif Ahmed replied coldly, "that the press may report your remarks, and the anniversary of September eleven is coming up."

"Wait a minute," Peter said with a hint of a snarl in his voice. "Threats of a terrorist attack are not a matter for joking. I'm offended, and so are a number of others present." Bellini was, of course, joking, and the joke was in very bad taste, but Peter thought that Ahmed's remark, delivered in an icy voice that conveyed a believable murderousness, was even worse than Bellini's.

"But jokes about murdering Arabs and Palestinians and bombing their houses of religion are, of course, quite acceptable," said Jack Dobbs, a left-wing scholar from the history department who was notoriously anti-Israel and had written that the United States was guilty of war crimes in Afghanistan. The Smith-Smythes' muttered echoes of this remark were audible around the table.

"What jokes?" said Bellini, munching a cookie. "I'm serious."

Peter, appalled and openly angry now, stood up at the head of the table. The chancellor, who had been sitting near Mallory, behind Peter, also stood and crossed his arms over his chest, looking stern—like a coach on the side-lines with a losing team that has just fumbled, Mallory thought. Sitting at Peter's back, Mallory and Howard Kappell exchanged startled looks. This thing was turning into a free-for-all, a joke.

"I'm going to cut this discussion off, ladies and gentlemen," Peter announced. "Let's move on."

Sarah Allen, the tiny, wrinkled woman in the odd dress, rose to her feet. "There's some tension here, some bad feelings," she said in an accent that sounded as though it belonged in a mountainside cabin in Kentucky. "I think maybe we should share a prayer to set things right." Looks of horror and disgust passed over the faces at the table. Peter, always ready with the right words in a courtroom, was at a loss here, and he saw he could not afford to be, for Sarah Allen was bowing her head, closing her eyes, and clasping her hands together.

"You know, I think we'll hold up on that one, Ms. Allen," he interjected at the last moment, as her mouth formed a pious O. "People just don't seem to be in the mood. All right! Let's set up subcommittee lists. Ms. Allen, what say I put you down for Islam and Modernity?"

Two hours later, at the end of the meeting, Peter had led the group through every task on the agenda, but the atmosphere remained tense and cold. He tried to right things in his final remarks, saying something good-natured about the dynamics of this very meeting illustrating how complicated their work was to be. But now he had qualms about the seminar. He was ashamed of having publicly shown temper—in thirty years of legal practice, he had never been that far out of control. And he began to wonder whether the whole thing wasn't just a bad idea—bringing together all these silly people who hated what the others stood for. What could they add to what think tanks and scholars and pundits were already saying? Why hadn't he told Emma Devereaux to can it? Why Columbia had nominated some of these people . . . That couple, the Smith-Smythes, and Dobbs were so abrasive. Bellini was a complete jackass, but inviting Bellini, along with two other archconservatives and a couple of rabid leftists, had been Hilda's doing. Wouldn't it be a good idea, she had argued timidly (after her first experience of jury duty), to force unreasonable people to deal, face-to-face, both with reasonable people and with their ideological opposites? Wouldn't it be useful to create a social environment where people's opinions have equal weight and their statuses are erased—kind of like jury duty?

The meeting was breaking up. People were shaking hands, chatting, milling around. Then Joshua Newgate came up to Peter, beaming, to congratulate him. He had expected something intolerably stuffy and boring, but everything was up for grabs with this group, he chortled. Peter felt better; after all, that had been the idea, sort of. His spirits rose further as he walked from Columbia back to Riverside Drive with Martha Lovett, who laughed uproariously about the events of the meeting as soon as they were alone.

"Maybe I should call the Smith-Smythes," Peter said, "and try to make peace."

"I'd just leave them alone," Lovett said as they turned south on Riverside. "Everything'll be fine."

"Thanks, Ms. Lovett," Peter replied earnestly. He guessed he must believe what she said because it made him feel so much better.

Peter headed north, walking briskly so as to avoid Edmond Lockhart, whom he had observed, when talking to Ms. Lovett, standing on the opposite corner across Riverside—almost as though he were lying in wait. They had not spoken since the night the Frankls walked out on his dinner party. In unavoidable encounters around the building, they had exchanged, at best, a cool nod or two. Now, however, it seemed that Lockhart wanted to make friends again.

"Peter!" he called, scuttling toward him without actually breaking into a jog. It was doubtful he could summon the energy for a full-out run. Peter pretended not to hear until Lockhart actually drew abreast. He looked worse than ever, absolutely ill.

"How is your wife?" Lockhart asked in a soft, mellifluous voice, and he put his hand on Peter's shoulder.

"Never mind my wife," Peter snapped. He disbelieved in Lockhart's concern for Lesley and found his touch distasteful.

"I understand, I understand," said Lockhart in the same soothing way. "Of course, it's painful to think of, but you must try not to worry, Peter. Worrying won't do any good." He looked at Peter sideways. "And how did your seminar meeting go this afternoon?"

"How did you know there was a meeting?" Peter responded belligerently.

"Oh, I try to keep up with my aunt's affairs. Who else does she have to protect her?"

"That's pretty good keeping up, Lockhart. You even knew the time of day."

"So how did it go?" Lockhart asked insistently.

Peter would not give him the satisfaction of an answer. "Look, excuse me, but I just remembered—I have to go to my daughter's place." This was not true, but he abruptly swung around and headed in the opposite direction. He could not endure Lockhart for another minute. Why was the man pursuing him?

Peter passed Susan's building without stopping. Lately he often walked the streets of the neighborhood, apparently aimlessly, but thinking of Wanda Lockhart and wondering just where she lived. He didn't admit to himself that this was why he wandered the streets, and certainly he never attempted to find Wanda's name in a directory, which would have made him confront his own purpose. Peter walked up and down blocks from 112th to 122nd and then walked east of Columbia and went a half-dozen blocks down Amsterdam, finally returning home feeling dejected and lonely. He had a moment's grateful, guilty relief, as he turned his key in the lock, that at least Lesley was not around to say that she'd told him so.

——————

CHAPTER 19

Not until Mallory and Howard Kappell had climbed into a cab together, after the seminar meeting, did Kappell let himself laugh.

"What a charade!" he cried. "Bellini playing Mussolini, and Arif Ahmed making threats and Hume sitting there with his eyes bulging out and Joshua Newgate giggling in a corner with some schoolteacher from Brooklyn. Who the hell put these people together in a room? Who is this character Frankl?" Kappell slapped his knee and then, as this did not adequately relieve his feelings, he slapped Mallory's knee, too.

"I've known Peter Frankl my whole life," said Mallory hesitantly, ignoring the clap on her knee. "He's my best friend's father—really a sweet guy."

"Sweet guy or not, we're gonna let him have it."

Mallory could not see why they had to let him have it, but assuming they did, she didn't want her name on the story. She couldn't criticize Susan's father in print. But she also didn't want to give up this, her first chance to do reporting with some political content.

"Howard," she said, stalling, "I want to be objective, but I can't really see why any of it was Peter Frankl's fault."

"Are you kidding? First of all, his prejudices were so obvious. Clearly, the group is overrun with right-wingers, and that's the way he wants it or someone at the Devereaux Foundation wants it. That's how these things work. And the idea that anybody ever made a huge fortune manufacturing buttons sounds crazy—that's a whitewash of some sort. Then here is a Jewish guy who is so obviously pro-Israel—"

"Wait . . . no, not really Jewish," said Mallory. She felt uncomfortable having this discussion with Howard Kappell, who was himself Jewish.

"What do you mean, not *really* Jewish? I'd stake my life on it that a New York lawyer named Frankl who looks and talks like that guy is—"

"His father was Jewish, an ex-rabbi, actually, but his mother wasn't, and he wasn't raised Jewish. They don't do bar mitzvahs or Rosh Hashanah, anything like that, and he doesn't think of himself—"

"Give me a break, Mallory. What point is there in pretending this rabbi's son is not Jewish?"

"I know the family well, and there's kind of an unusual history. . . ."

"All right, so they're secular. Mallory, where'd you grow up, anyway?"

"Here in Morningside Heights. I live in the Frankls' building. Of course, I understand about secular—"

"All right, all right. Look—you're off this assignment. You've got a conflict. I'm hereby taking over. Don't take it so hard. I understand how you feel, kiddo."

Mallory, however, was not sure that she understood how she felt. "But I'd still like to—"

"Here's an idea. You know the background on all this. You do some legwork for me. Your name won't go on the story, but I personally will make sure you get a decent break—soon—if you just help me out on this and do some fast work for me. I'd like this story to go in tomorrow, before it gets cold," he said, taking her hand and patting it in a fatherly way. "Here's what I need: the names of the responsible people at the Devereaux Foundation—the board, the executive director. I need to know who was in charge of this particular project, who's in charge of handling the foundation's money, who picked the members of the seminar, and anything you can find out about where the Devereauxes got their bread. I want names, addresses, histories, telephone numbers—right away."

Mallory had misgivings; indeed, she felt almost nauseated. But she undertook to gather this material for Kappell. There was no obvious way in which providing it would compromise her loyalty to Susan or Susan's father. Besides, if she didn't do it, he'd do it himself or find someone less sympathetic than she was to do it. If things went wrong, there would always be time to pull back later.

She went to work in the *Gazette* office and soon was speaking with Emma Devereaux on the telephone.

"Miss Devereaux, how was it decided to make Mr. Frankl chair of the seminar?"

"You say you know Mr. Frankl, my dear?" Miss Devereaux sounded ninety years old, at least.

"Very well," said Mallory. "I've known Mr. Frankl all my life. He's my best friend's father. I live in his building." She told these things to put Miss Devereaux off her guard but felt guilty enough about it to hope Miss Devereaux would not be fooled. However, she was.

"Well, then," Miss Devereaux said with affection, "isn't he a lovely man? And at first Columbia made such a fuss about Mr. Frankl being the chairman, although, as we repeatedly pointed out to them, he was not a stranger to the university."

"Why didn't they want him?"

"They had the greatest respect, but they wanted control in their own hands, as a matter of academic freedom. They said they couldn't sell their name and they couldn't let themselves be used for ideological purposes. Of course, we agreed with that. We wanted Mr. Frankl to be the leader because we know that he is so fair-minded and well-read and intelligent. We thought he'd help maintain balance in the seminar." Miss Devereaux promised that her secretary would fax to Mallory the names and numbers of all the board members and officers and referred her to someone named Hilda Hughes, who could tell her about how the participants were selected.

"Hilda made up a list of potential participants," said Miss Devereaux, "and then she took it to, to, uh . . . she gave it . . . at Columbia . . ."

"And then Columbia agreed to the names? Someone at Columbia . . ."

"Not all of them. I don't remember how many. Hilda and I sat down and talked it all over with them. My dear, you should talk to Hilda. I'm very bad with names. There were huge, long discussions about this name and that name."

"Miss Devereaux, can you tell me how your family made its fortune—how they acquired the money that they used to set up the foundation?"

"My great-great-grandfather made buttons, you know, very fine buttons and ordinary buttons, too, and various novelties. The family was always in buttons. They had several factories. And they had a few sidelines, related manufactures—those—oh, you know—those little—very popular, and—uh . . ."

"The money came entirely from manufactures?"

"Cuff links! Yes, originally. They were cautious, careful people, too, and they invested their profits, and they grew. And, of course, costume jewelry and . . . one of the most popular lines . . . You see, we've always lived fairly modestly, compared to some families."

Mallory sighed over the idea that the Devereaux fortune was the result of button sales, thrift, and wise investment. Next she called Wendell Ellery, who among his more sensible comments, in a conversation composed largely of overlong pauses and nervous exhalations, said that Frankl was a man of persuasion, the epitome. And then she called Hilda Hughes, who didn't answer; so she left a message on her answering machine.

"Wendell Ellery sounds rather crazy. I couldn't understand anything he was saying," Mallory told Howard. "I can't believe he's on the board of this rich foundation. Miss Devereaux is very elderly. She's open and honest, but it's possible she's a little confused. She told me that at first Columbia made a fuss about Frankl being chairman and had concerns about avoiding any appearance they were selling their name or letting themselves be used for political purposes. And she said the Devereaux people thought he'd help balance the group, but I don't think she meant—"

"See? Just as I said," said Howard Kappell with satisfaction. "They set up this academic seminar on terrorism, organized by a pro-Israel Jewish lawyer who thinks 'understanding' is figuring out how to slam Arabs and Palestinians. They let a lot of fools operate under their auspices, and the whole thing is a joke, but it's a respectable Columbia operation in the eyes of the world. I've been talking to a couple of the seminar members. They thought there was a lot of negative feeling about Frankl's appointment, and they were arguing that it is absolutely crucial to have a scholar with expertise on terrorism at the helm, some public intellectual. Otherwise, the whole thing lacks legitimacy and authority. The idea that some lawyer with simpleminded politics—"

"You know, Howard, I don't think Mr. Frankl is particularly conservative in his—"

"You let me worry about that," said Kappell.

"I feel uncomfortable with all this. Can you get someone else to take it from here?" Mallory asked.

"I can take it from here myself." Kappell sent Mallory home and called Orazio Cromwell, who summoned Wendell Ellery, and the three of them met at the bar in the Carlyle. Orazio chewed the stub of an unlit cigar and sipped brandy while his eyes shifted deviously back and forth. He had a bad cold, and his nose was red, but he had groaned and pulled himself out of bed when he learned that it was a matter of the Devereaux Foundation. Wendell looked directly at Kappell with narrowed eyes and a raised eyebrow, while Orazio avoided eye contact entirely.

"So what are you up to, Mr. Kappell? Who are you out to get, hm?" Orazio demanded hoarsely. He leaned backward on the bar, lit his cigar, and coughed a phlegmy, deep cough. Drunk, thought Kappell. A drunk, probably. Good God.

"Who are you out to get?" echoed Ellery with a sneer.

Kappell parted from them an hour later, rolling his eyes, and then tried to telephone Hilda Hughes. Hilda stood beside her answering machine and listened to Kappell's voice, as she had listened to Mallory's earlier, saying that he was from the *Gazette*. But she didn't pick up; she almost never did.

—————

CHAPTER 20

"When did you start that?" Mallory asked Sylvie Kimura, whose eyes were half-closed behind a spiral of cigarette smoke. An hour after Mallory had left Howard Kappell at the *Gazette*, she and Sylvie were in Morningside Heights, waiting to be served chicken burritos in the smoking section at Nacho Mama's. The place was a dim, noisy student hangout, grubby and cheerfully crowded. Sylvie, observed with pleasure by a young waiter who passed by, held her cigarette between her lips while she undid the thick black knot of her hair, retwisted it, and clipped it back in place, raising and showing off a full bosom and exposing two inches of slender midriff.

"When I was fifteen. We used to go around the block and smoke after school. One drag, I loved it. My mother begged me to stop. She still begs me to stop. But, really, I'd rather die young." Sylvie smiled at the expression on Mallory's face when she said this.

"You're a *nice* girl, Mallory," said Sylvie with affection, thinking how rare it was to meet with anyone who was just the nice girl she appeared to be. Mallory wanted no truck with death, and Sylvie knew that attitude was often at the core of niceness. Sylvie was almost as interested in niceness as in death and respected both—though she knew she was too fond of the latter to have much of the former.

But Mallory, whose still raw feelings from Alexei's accusations had been freshly salted with guilt about the aid she had been giving Kappell, winced at Sylvie's words. "Do I deserve that?" she asked. She looked drained and weary.

"I wasn't being sarcastic," protested Sylvie. "It's just that I know that I myself am not very nice. What's wrong, Mallory?" Sylvie meant it. She knew plenty of people like herself, who were drawn to death and things near it, but unlike Sylvie, they usually assumed that all apparently nice people were hypocrites. Sylvie would not be tempted into such a self-congratulatory stereotype, and Alcott, too, never made that mistake. He did not underestimate Mallory.

"Just some annoyances at work. So Alcott got a backer for the new film?" asked Mallory.

"Somehow, yes, he's come up with money. There's a real script—he's working it over. He's got a payroll. He's hiring extra crew, and he was auditioning last week, this week. It's going to be a real film. It's a big deal."

Mallory smiled congratulations at Sylvie, and Sylvie responded with only a brief, polite nod—betraying in this way just how big and important it all was.

"Oh!" said Sylvie, remembering. "I saw your friend, that impossibly attractive one from your party. He was down there last week with the core crew, acting like he belonged there. I forgot to ask, but it looks like Alcott maybe gave him a job. I'll remember to ask him tomorrow." A waiter slammed plates of fat burritos, beans, and rice in front of them, and Sylvie stubbed out her cigarette. Mallory had been ravenous, having had no chance to eat since morning, but this news subdued her appetite.

"How strange! But maybe not so strange. Alexei always needs work, and he's so energetic and organized, and he likes being helpful. I can see him running around a movie set, pushing things and keeping everyone on schedule. Maybe he'll actually develop a trade and support himself. He just did a couple of years at the Manhattan School of Music, you know, and he's sort of floundering through life." Mallory found it jarring that Alexei had turned up that way among her friends, but she tried to sound as though this were merely interesting.

"What does he do?" Sylvie asked.

"Odd jobs. He wants to be an opera singer. He's sweet but clueless." Mallory let nothing enter her voice that might betray the nature of her connections with Alexei.

"Can he sing?"

This was the very question Susan had asked, and Mallory gave the same answer. "Of course not. I've never heard him, but I'm sure it would be embarrassing."

"I like opera," said Sylvie. "It's not cool. I like it very much."

"What's the story with Alcott's friend Sean?" asked Mallory.

Sylvie noticed Mallory's quick shift of subjects but chose to ignore it. "He's a scriptwriter," she replied. "He looks cool, but he's not, and he's a few years younger than you. Also, I don't think he has any intention at all of being a couple with anyone for a long time. But you never know. And it certainly doesn't mean you shouldn't. . . ."

Mallory sighed. She thought it did mean she shouldn't. Why was it that she found herself without a single decent romantic possibility now, when for the first time in her life she wanted to find someone to marry? Sylvie was so lucky. It was interesting to watch a skeptical, touchy person like her cope with so much contentment. But the future of this union between Alcott and Sylvie was hard to predict, seeing that neither of them was dreaming of a nice co-op somewhere and a baby or two. On the other hand, now that they had found each other, it was equally difficult to imagine them parting. Certainly neither of these hard-to-please people was likely to become interested in anyone else.

"You know, Mallory, I'm not the sort of person who was likely ever to find anyone," said Sylvie, who, it seemed, was having her own reverie about couples. "If I weren't with Alcott, I'd be alone. You're different. There are lots of possibilities for you."

"But, unlike you, I want to get married, and that's a different proposition."

"Then why didn't you marry Paul?"

"I could have, easily enough. I insisted on breaking up, but only because he was so dissatisfied. If he could have been contented, I think I would have been, too. But I didn't cry when we broke up. He knew I wouldn't, and that's just what bothered him."

Sylvie nodded thoughtfully and said nothing. Paul had been much more unhappy than Mallory, no doubt about that. Mallory was frank about things like this. Sylvie herself would have found it hard to admit that her capacity, or perhaps her need, to love was as attenuated as Mallory had just implied hers was. Mallory was nice, but a little hard, perhaps. She never needed anyone, which was odd, such hardness in someone so nice and pretty and normal. Sylvie took in a breath as it hit her: that was the big attraction! That was what so many guys liked about Mallory—and also why it never worked out. She really didn't need anyone.

"Is Paul in the film?" asked Mallory.

"I don't know," said Sylvie, tucking her insight away for discussing later with Alcott. "They're just casting now. I think he wants a part—I know he does, but there might be some hurt feelings this time. Alcott has more friends than parts, and he doesn't think some of the friends act so well—even if they'll work without any pay."

Mallory knew that this was one great reason why Alcott had hired Paul in the past and grew sad thinking about how hurt Paul would be, to be left out now because Alcott could afford to pay for someone better.

She and Sylvie said affectionate good-byes over the din of the restaurant, and Mallory went home, where, despite her unsettled feelings about Sean, Paul, Alexei, and Howard Kappell, she fell immediately into a blank sleep. She did not wake until the telephone rang at 9:30 in the morning.

"Hi," said Louis.

"Who is this?" asked Mallory.

"You know it's me. Come on," said Louis.

"Louis," said Mallory, "it's not polite to force me to guess, is it?"

"I'm not that big on etiquette," Louis said. "No, wait—I know one favor deserves another. That's etiquette. So you owe me one, because I heard you're doing the story on the Devereaux seminar."

"No," said Mallory. "I was there, but a senior reporter is going to do it, because so many name-brand people are involved." Her usual frankness failed her; she felt too much discomfort about her involvement with Kappell's story to tell Louis the truth.

"That's too bad. Anyway, I tried, so you still owe me one. Come on—have dinner with me tonight."

"I'm busy tonight. You didn't really think you could bribe me into having dinner with you, did you?" But Mallory's voice was not as convincingly firm as she knew would be necessary to dissuade Louis.

"Not really, but what's the big deal, Mallory? I'm an old friend. You like me."

"I don't know about that."

"Look, I want to get married."

"You've changed, huh? Good luck."

"To you. I want to marry you, and you won't even let us get the ball rolling here."

"Thanks, but no." She made this feint at taking his declaration as a joke, though he seemed to mean it, because she owed it to Susan not to humiliate him. But she began to fear that things with Louis might escalate in unpleasant ways. Obviously, he got more and more interested in her just because she kept turning him away. Of course, he would respond only to a hard-to-get woman.

"Come on. I'll be a big success—I'll be just like my dad. We'll have kids, a big co-op. You have to use your imagination, look ahead a little bit."

"Louis—"

"I love you. I *know* you, and I love you. Those other guys only think they do. You know, you're trickier than they realize. You're a nice tricky girl, a tricky nice girl." But there were no daggers in his voice as he said this. On the contrary, he sounded admiring and amused. Mallory considered hanging up, but, she reminded herself once more, he was Susan's brother. Besides, after having possibly contributed to injuring his father, perhaps she owed him something. She was stymied by the guilt-provoking subtexts of the conversation.

"I'm having dinner with my parents tonight," said Mallory. "Look, Louis, I'm being straight. I just don't want to go out with you."

"I have an idea. I'll come to your parents', too."

Mallory thought this over. Her parents were not exactly short on penetration and social skill. Their presence might help deflate things. She could enlist their help in discouraging him. It would be the easiest way, and she would alert them to the situation in advance.

"Hold on," she said to Louis, and she called her parents on her cell phone.

"Mom, would you mind if I brought Louis Frankl to dinner tonight? I'll call in a minute and explain everything."

"Of course not, sweetheart. Fine. But, Mallory, did you see that your CDC vaccinations piece is on the front page of the Sci-Tech section this morning, with photographs and a chart? It's beautifully laid out, and you did a superb job with it."

Mallory was, at first, elated to hear this and impatient to retrieve her *Gazette* from the foyer. Then she recalled Kappell's promise to make sure she got a break and again felt queasy.

"Louis," Mallory said into the other receiver, "they said all right. So I'll meet you there at about seven."

"Right." And he clicked off. He had tried to sound casual, but Mallory heard the tension in the word.

"Dad, I'll visit Mom early tonight, and I might be gone before you get there," said Louis a few minutes later at the breakfast table, where his father sat sipping coffee and reading the morning *Gazette.* His anger against Peter had slowly waned as he convinced himself that there had been no more visits with Wanda Lockhart. Although under the circumstances he could forgive his father's having been tempted, he thought he couldn't overlook actual adultery. "Hey, is that something by Mallory? Is it any good?"

"It's amazingly . . . layered, subtle, or something. She's awfully young to be so . . ."

"Tricky?"

"That's too negative. She's not deceitful. She's just cagey, very cagey, in the way she's written this—with the politics of the debate and her opinion so evident, and still it's objective. You know the CDC guy was a good guy and the other guy was an ass, but it's all respectful. Very well done."

Louis listened so intently to his father's words that an unaccustomed frown line appeared between his eyes, and then he nodded brusquely. Peter laid down the Sci-Tech section and picked up the City section, where on the front page was an "Uptown, Downtown" column by Howard Kappell. It was devoted to yesterday's seminar meeting. Peter's heart began beating faster. "The real-world stakes may seem small," Kappell began, "but the principles involved are large." After describing how the Devereaux seminar came into existence, Kappell claimed that it was being derailed by a group of right-wing nuts who wanted to bomb Mecca; that it was a fraud, being in reality nothing more than an underhanded attempt by a few wealthy right-wing people to use the prestige of Columbia University to support and spread their pro-Israel, anti-Islam pro-war politics; that Columbia had violated academic principles by letting an outsider control one of its academic functions; that Frankl, who was the foundation's lawyer, was outrageously unqualified to serve as chair of such a group and obviously had used his position at the foundation to promote himself and his political views. Without saying it in so many words, the article implied that Frankl supported extreme right-wingers like Mark Bellini and had probably had an undue influence on the selection process for the seminar.

If this seminar was to continue, at a minimum Frankl should resign as chair and Columbia should insist on more control and should replace Frankl by someone with scholarly expertise on the subject of terrorism, preferably someone well-known and generally respected by the public. And Kappell thought that the responsible parties owed it to the public to explain just how many buttons had been manufactured and sold to create the Devereaux Foundation's half-billion-dollar endowment. Columbia University, surely, had an obligation to learn the real source of every penny used to fund this endeavor. But perhaps even more important, someone should make sure that the Devereaux Foundation officers were competent and not subject to corrupt pressures of any kind. It would be a betrayal of the public interest if a great fortune, ostensibly dedicated to the promotion of art, scholarship, and religion, were to be squandered and misused.

Peter fell back in his chair, with such pain in his face that Louis half stood, afraid his father was having some sort of attack. Louis reached for the paper and began reading. Prejudice, stereotype, innuendo, and half-truth, Peter thought, and I have no chance of setting any of it straight. Accused of being extreme right-wing after voting Democratic for nearly forty years! Why did Kappell think he knew Peter's views on Israel? Because he had a Jewish name? Was it really true that if he objected to one view, he could be assumed to favor any others he hadn't mentioned? Certainly that's how Kappell's mind seemed to work. And how on earth would he ever explain all this to his law partners! For it would have to be explained.

Peter's thoughts turned from his own interests to those of the Devereaux Foundation and the prospect of an investigation into its affairs. Kappell's hints of mismanagement might mean that he had gotten to poor Orazio Cromwell. Peter groaned aloud at this realization and the grim probability that the oddities of the Devereaux board members would be publicly exposed. In the worst case, Miss Devereaux could lose control of the whole thing. How sad if Hilda's eccentric approach to project funding were to be replaced by mainstream, bureaucratic thinking and the Devereaux money allotted to the reasonable, unobjectionable projects that cautious people without imagination favored, or to the finger-in-your-eye kind of art that those same people, for some reason, had for a century regarded as "innovative."

Had Mallory gone along with this stuff? He didn't want to believe it. He thought of calling Mallory, then decided that he could not scold Susan's friend. The telephone's ringing interrupted these thoughts.

"Daddy, have you seen the paper?" Susan asked, her voice tense.

"I've seen it, sweetheart," said Peter calmly, so that she would not know how wounded and worried he was.

"I called Mallory. She's so upset," Susan said. "What a schmuck."

"Please, sweetie, there's no need for language like that," said Peter.

"What language?" Susan asked. "Did Kappell call you?" Her anger against her father was, apparently, forgotten in outrage over this public attack against him.

"No."

"He wrote that stuff without even speaking to you? You have to do something, Daddy—make some calls and see what's going on here."

"Sweetie, it would be a waste of time." He described the events of the seminar meeting.

"You should throw them out," said Susan.

"That wouldn't be wise or right," said Peter, to whom it was self-evident that it would be a mistake to take Kappell's bait and show any perturbation about this.

Louis, staring at his father across the table while Peter spoke to Susan, had still said nothing at all, but Peter wouldn't have expected him to.

Morris Malcolm, looking over the Sci-Tech section of the morning newspaper, remarked to his wife, Merrit Roth, that her former student Mallory Holmes had written an excellent article about the CDC and vaccinations, and he handed it over to her while he took a look at the City section. Merrit and Morris were at their own breakfast table, just a few blocks away from the Frankls' apartment. As Morris read the newspaper, he peeled and sliced bits of apple for a child in a high chair, and Merrit nursed a plump baby of about three months and nibbled on toast.

"And here's Howard Kappell," said Morris, "fussing about some grant or something that the college accepted to run a faculty seminar about terrorism. All these famous names—Teresa and Chalmers, of course! Oh, my God. Listen to this." And Morris read the "Uptown, Downtown" column to Merrit.

"He makes it sound like someone at Columbia got snookered by the Devereaux group, doesn't he? What's he up to?" said Merrit. "It seems as though he thinks Teresa and Chalmers should chair this thing, but I'm surprised he'd get that close to coming out for them in print. That's almost a breach of journalistic ethics, because they go way back with him. Besides, they could be a real liability. Did you see that strange thing they wrote in *The London Review of Books*?"

"I'm not surprised. I never believe a word Kappell writes. He doesn't care about truth. He doesn't know the meaning of the word," said Morris, a molecular biologist who thought that, in the new millennium, only a few scientists like himself clung to that archaic idea, "and he's pretty fuzzy on right and wrong, too. They're schmucks, all three of them."

"Could you please refrain from using that word in the presence of the archangel? Do you want him saying that at school someday or in front of your mother?"

"What? Schmuck? I don't care. And my mother wouldn't even know what it means."

"Please, Morris."

"'Muck?" said Gabriel, who was nearly two, looking tentatively at his father.

"All right, all right," said Morris, a suppressed snicker in his voice. "No I-told-you-so's." He kissed his son, whom he thought a very clever little fellow. "I've got to get to the lab. What've you got planned for today?" He was frequently worried that his wife, who had been something of a public intellectual herself until Gabriel was born, would become unhappy staying at home with two babies. She used to turn out award-winning books. Now she was a contributing editor for an online journal called *Tablet* and was lucky to produce three or four short articles a year. They were always begging her for something that was two weeks late.

"I'll try to get in some writing, assuming Clem sleeps. Then, this afternoon, Anne is going to bring Stuey and Gilbert, and we'll take all of them to the park for a couple of hours."

"That sounds nice. I mean, does that sound nice? Is it—"

"Stop," said Merrit. But, still sitting at the table nursing Clement, she turned up her face for a kiss. Later that morning, when both babies were sleeping, Merrit began sorting papers in her office and found a fall issue of *The London Review of Books*, which she opened to the peculiarly unpleasant essay by Teresa and Chalmers. Then, reminded of Mallory Holmes's article in the Sci-Tech section, she went back to the newspaper and found Mallory's e-mail address at the end of the article. Mallory was delighted to hear from her. They agreed to meet for coffee at the end of the summer, as Merrit and Morris planned to spend the next few months in Oxford and were about to leave town.

Even before he left home for the office, Peter began trying to contact the Devereaux Foundation board, beginning with Hilda. He sent her three e-mails describing the Kappell article and demanding that she call him immediately. Hilda, who was sitting at her desk, fortified by a mug of strong tea and a plate of buttered toast with cherry jam, was not alarmed by the unnecessarily . . . *muscular* message of the third.

Hilda—call me NOW or else.

She had not yet seen the paper, and felt sorry for Peter, but she wasn't worried. Who cared what newspapers said or what people who read them thought? Having to greet one's neighbors in the hallway, or ask after their relatives, or make dinner conversation—*those* were real trials, which others apparently endured with superhuman courage.

"Oh . . . dear," she said to Peter, mustering, unconvincingly, the strongest tones of outrage and dismay that her mild voice could convey. "My goodness. But . . . well . . . isn't it good that the seminar isn't too . . . conventional and hidebound? We'll get real dialogue if we can deflate some egos and get people out of their socially predetermined ruts. Don't you agree? I think we should be pleased."

"Look, Hilda," Peter said, "that's just childish. You don't seem to understand that this is a big problem. I have to resign as chair. I should never have let you talk me into that. You and Emma have to think of someone who inspires complete trust to replace me—someone who can keep the whole thing sane, maybe one of the seminar members. This is more than bad publicity. There's a threat here. If someone decides to start looking into the Devereaux Foundation affairs, it's possible Emma could lose control— temporarily or permanently. You could lose your job."

"I'm surprised that you, of all people, are that cynical," said Hilda. "Anyway, Peter, I'm sure that Emma will want you to continue. I'll tell her what you said. But she'll never accept your resignation when you've been unjustly accused and suspected." She had never before called him Peter. She was coherent and articulate, even a little assertive. As distracted and annoyed as Peter was, he noticed this and told himself that he should have known that a sensible mind was concealing itself behind all Hilda's silliness.

"She's going to have to," Peter replied. "I'll talk to her myself later on, but you tell her first. Tell her I resign the chairmanship and that's it."

Hilda promised again, and although she still doubted things were quite as serious as Peter claimed, she also agreed to have Miss Devereaux call a meeting of the board later that very day.

Perversely, Peter felt calmer after the absurd conversation with Hilda, but he barely had time to knot his tie and pack his briefcase, ready to set out, when his firm's senior managing partner, Mort Whitehall, called—obviously from a cell phone, as he was being driven to work. The connection was poor.

"Wha . . . hell is . . . ," Mort said. Going through the Eighty-fifth Street underpass in Central Park, Peter thought.

"Your guess is as good as mine," said Peter, making an effort to sound composed. Of course his partners would be upset, because something like this hurt the firm's reputation, and that dipped into their pockets.

"Why would you gas in public about your politics, for chrissake?" asked Mort, his voice fully audible now through the static. "You of all people should know better than—"

"I did no such thing. It never happened, Mort. The whole column is a lie."

"Get real, Peter. This was a public event. There were fifty or so people there. It can't be an outright fabrication."

"It might seem unlikely," said Peter, "but Mort, how likely is it that *I'm* misleading you? You've been working with me for thirty years or so. Don't I have more credibility with you than some idiot at the *Gazette*?"

"Peter, if you could hear what other people are saying, you'd think I'm your best friend. Of course, everybody knows you've been under a lot of stress.... My advice to you is to go in to this meeting—"

"What meeting?"

"—of the senior partners at lunch—and tell them the article is exaggerated, but you're going to stop working for the Devereaux Foundation board just for the sake of appearances. Then maybe we could get someone to write something for *The American Lawyer* saying—"

"I'm resigning from that seminar, but I'll continue to represent the foundation. They need me, and anyway, if I don't, it'll look like confirmation of what the piece said."

"You're giving up the client and getting off their board. Call me when you get in. We'll talk," Mort said, and there was static-free silence.

Mort was ticked, but Peter was, too. Indeed, he felt a whole new order of anger. His body felt like molten metal. He could have said just about anything in that state, so it was probably a good thing that Mort had hung up.

When Peter left the firm that afternoon, his partners were dissatisfied with his account of the foundation, his role there, and the events of the seminar meeting. Most of them thought that, finding a few hundred million floating around in a power vacuum, Peter had done what came naturally—more or less manipulated the old lady, put his political buddies into the seminar, and all that—which would not have bothered anyone except that he let it get into the papers and make the firm look bad. A few of his partners thought that it was kind of a shame, but he had no right to take risks with their wallets. His absurd insistence that he hadn't done this was rather despicable, and his obstinacy surprised them. Obviously, the guy was succumbing to the stress of his wife's medical problems. In the end, the partnership were persuaded to do nothing, at least for the time being, by the combined efforts of an unlikely team: Harry Rothenberg, a respected partner senior even to Peter, and Walter Bramford, who despite his relative youth was as powerful in the firm as Harry.

Harry knew that Peter was telling the truth.

"We've worked with Peter for thirty years," he pleaded. "There isn't a man of higher integrity in the city. There is no rational choice here except to believe him and defend him."

Walter, on the other hand, knew that Peter was telling the truth, but he implied the opposite. He spoke up as soon as Harry sat down and argued forcefully that whether or not Kappell's article was true, the firm's interests lay in backing Peter 100 percent. Privately, Harry doubted that this really was in the firm's interests, but the right thing to do, he told himself, was to support Peter, and he didn't give a damn why anyone else wanted to as long as they did. He doubted that Walter believed in his own argument. Walter was doing what he could to help a friend, just as he would never pass up an opportunity to hurt an enemy. Morally simple-minded, to be sure, but straightforward.

Walter walked out of the meeting at Peter's side, obviously in a state of high self-approval, and looked sideways at him with something like tenderness.

"But you're going to have to be careful from here on out," he said almost kindly, as though Peter were a youngster and he an old man who had just given him an unearned second chance. This was exasperating, and it was humiliating to be under Walter's protection.

"Thanks for the advice, Walter," Peter said, "but you just publicly implied that I'm a liar, and I kind of resent it. I'd rather be believed than helped."

"I know that, Peter," said Walter. "But no one really cares whether or not you're telling the truth. That's irrelevant." He gave Peter a friendly little smile, quite unoffended, and walked off briskly, hands in pockets, eyes on the ground.

"Do these people know me at all?" Peter asked Harry, who had come up behind them and overheard their exchange.

"This way of thinking, this moralism of yours, is just foreign to them," snarled Harry Rothenberg, who had majored in philosophy at Harvard in the fifties. "Why don't you understand that? You've worked here for thirty years. Do you not know these people at all?"

There was an envelope on Peter's desk when he returned to his office, addressed in block print to "Peter Frankl—personal." He tore it up and threw it in the trash without reading it, but it made him nervous. There hadn't been physical threats yet, but what if this nut worked himself up enough to take a shot at Peter?

"Did you see anyone in my office?" he asked Mary. "There's another one of those notes."

"Good heavens. No. No one. Just Jon—he left a file. What did it say?"

"I didn't read it. Threw it out," he said. "Whoever it is just wants to upset me. Why should I let him? Mary, cancel my appointments from three-thirty on. There's a special meeting at the Devereaux Foundation this afternoon."

"Oh dear, Mr. Frankl, do you think you should—" Mary stopped herself. Who was she to tell Mr. Frankl what he should do?

When Peter arrived at the meeting room of the Devereaux Foundation, there was a haphazard, lackadaisical mood among the board members, a being-held-after-school mood. Hilda, Emma Devereaux, Wendell Ellery, and Orazio Cromwell, who had a red nose and a large box of tissues, were there, and haste was evidenced by the absence of pastries, coffee, and the usual stacks of handouts. The room was stuffy, the air conditioner having been switched on only moments before, the lights were off, and stacks of untidy files sat on the floor at the other end of the room. Peter looked around and thought that at all costs—indeed, at whatever cost to himself—this board, with its eccentrics and dimwits, must not be exposed and endangered. *He* could stand being falsely accused, but his heart would break if he was responsible for *their* being publicly shamed or for Miss Devereaux's losing control of the foundation.

Peter by now had learned of Kappell's interviews with Cromwell and Ellery and was pained to hear that Mallory herself had called Emma Devereaux and Ellery and that Hilda, who could have straightened the whole thing out, of course had failed to answer the telephone. Obviously, Mallory had some significant involvement with the story after all. Had she been truthful with Susan? Peter explained what had transpired at yesterday's seminar meeting and passed a copy of the newspaper column to Orazio, who was the only one present who had not yet read it. Hilda stealthily bit her fingernails and tried to look concerned. Ellery looked shrewder than ever and drew doodles of dragons, and Orazio blew his nose constantly, creating a repellent heap of wet tissues on the tabletop.

"Orazio, do try—oh, what is it, Bon . . . Bone . . . what is the name of that . . . ," said Miss Devereaux, "try taking . . . mm . . ."

"I don't believe in cold remedies," said Orazio in a hollow, nasal voice, holding up his hand to forestall suggestions. "They prevent your body from doing its natural thing. A little brandy, that's all."

"It's just a silly article," said Hilda. "It's insulting and aggravating, but no one will remember it next week."

"It undermines my credibility, the foundation's credibility, and the seminar's credibility," Peter insisted. "We can't afford to ignore that. Emma, you have to call the Columbia people and talk about my replacement."

". . . Bonafed," said Miss Devereaux. "It dries you right up."

"No, certainly not. I never touch any of those things," Orazio repeated defiantly.

"Certainly not!" echoed Ellery, vigorously cross-hatching his drawings.

"You are entirely right, Ellery. We can't replace him," said Miss Devereaux. "No, no, no!"

"I told you so," said Hilda in an undertone. Lately, she really did talk more, Peter noticed.

They argued until long past sundown before Miss Devereaux would agree to accept Peter's resignation as chair of the seminar. "I'll speak with . . . with Mr. . . . with . . . Hilda and I will speak with the Columbia people, and then we'll meet again. But right now I must go. They're waiting for me at home. I vote against anything else," Miss Devereaux said, and toddled out. The others soon adjourned. They could never seem to accomplish anything once Miss Devereaux left.

Peter walked up Riverside Drive in a trance of concentration, his eyes on the ground. Those people were children. He had to act like a responsible adult and protect them, their respectability, their money, and their work. It went against the grain to give in to Kappell's sleazy pressure and resign from the seminar, but it was necessary to maintain the seminar's effectiveness and respond to the charge of having used his position for self-serving purposes—for wasn't there some truth to that? But as for stepping down from the board altogether, that he couldn't do until he found some way or someone to protect these innocents.

CHAPTER 21

Ivy looked at Edmond and saw that he was worse. His face was so doughy and bloodless that she struggled against revulsion. He was spiraling downward as madly as he had the other time, years back, when they had given him electroshock, which had also revolted her. The idea of burning out parts of one's brain was something she could hardly think about, and when you were talking about the brain of one of the most subtle minds of a generation . . . It was simply unfathomable that Edmond had done it, but he had, and entirely voluntarily.

Edmond had been all for it. He had been downright chipper when he came home after the treatments. But he didn't remember that he'd been writing a book. He never did remember anything about that book and eventually threw all his notes and drafts in the trash. He still couldn't remember things—their trip to Spain, his son's operation—but he hadn't minded the memory problems. Ivy thought that a brilliant man's agreeing to such treatment, in preference to therapy or drugs, was a kind of self-mutilation, and she blamed the doctors who did not realize it. These are scientists of the mind? she had asked herself, watching Edmond's skillful manipulation of the psychiatrists, who loved this highly cultivated patient, his affectionate dependency, his fatherly advice as to the necessity of pulling out all the stops in his treatment. He had presented himself as what they believed in and wanted to see: a high-functioning, decent man who was essentially normal except for a couple of tragic kinks in the brainworks that acted up every now and then. But they had been, psychologically speaking, babes in the wood. Edmond had been in control of it all, feeding them the justifications they believed in and getting exactly what he wanted.

That was almost eight years ago, and to this day none of their friends knew that things had ever reached such an extreme. Now, however, they were reaching that point again. This time, Ivy thought that she might have to run away. Wouldn't it be better to live alone in some kind of peace than observe and share, through Edmond, in such monstrous things? And there was this: he was not her husband and refused to be. She didn't have the authority to approve or block treatment. She wasn't obligated to see this through. But when Ivy calculated the costs of losing Edmond, the loneliness, insignificance, and relative poverty that she would return to, she couldn't give him up. She'd tried to leave him before; both times she'd come back, chastened by her solitary unimportance and need, which outweighed the humiliations of life with him.

"Edmond, you must try to find a doctor, someone you can talk to. There's something bothering you, I can tell," Ivy said at breakfast one morning.

"You have the causal relation reversed," Edmond said contemptuously. "Something—everything—is bothering me because I am depressed. I am not depressed because of the things bothering me. I will not go through the rigmarole of consulting a psychoanalyst or a therapist or any other shaman that you might want to sic on me."

"Edmond, it seems obvious to me that all this began the morning after you gave the Eisenhower Lecture. It was clear as day. And there's a little pattern like this. You—"

"Shut up, Ivy."

Ivy froze. She reasoned, however, that it was his depression talking and restrained her feelings.

"I've probably been in ten therapists' offices," Edmond continued. "No two of them say the same thing. None of them has ever helped in the slightest."

Ivy summoned her courage. "Please try to restrain your rudeness. I understand that you're not well this morning, but it's still hard to take. Edmond, my honest opinion is that most of those people you went to veered towards quackishness. Why not try to—"

"Of course they were quacks! All of them are, which is why I long ago vowed not to subject myself to the indignity of psychotherapeutic prying again. At least electroshock is a real medical treatment offered by real doctors who don't try to invade my privacy or pretend they know my thoughts and feelings. Of course, emotionally it's painful to go through it—you can't begin to understand just how painful, how it fills me with horror to be forced to subject myself to such . . . degradation." Edmond's brows drew together, and there was a small, wry smile on his colorless lips.

"I don't know, Edmond," Ivy said, mumbling, out of fear of his temper. "You say it's all so awful, but you don't act as though you really mind."

"You *choose* to see indifference," said Edmond, "instead of courage, just as you're totally unsympathetic to what I go through on account of burdensome and anguishing family responsibilities."

"Oh, Edmond, why can't you just leave your aunt Emma alone? She has plenty of people to look after her." Again, she spoke in something of a whine, fearing an outburst, but Edmond did not explode this time. He left the room. Soon Ivy heard his footsteps and Burke yelping joyfully in the hallway and knew that he was going out for his paper. In a few minutes, looking out the window, she saw Edmond, with Burke tugging on the leash, emerge from under the awning of the building beside Peter Frankl, who was dressed in a suit and carrying a briefcase.

"Looks like rain. Are you sick?" Peter asked Edmond, who was standing on the sidewalk at the corner, waiting for the light to change. Edmond's face was as gray as the sky. Peter was rather pale himself this morning, and there was no spring in his step, but he felt a paragon of health and energy next to Edmond.

"Yes," Edmond said noncommittally.

"You should see a doctor," said Peter with an assumed heartiness. He half hoped to increase Edmond's sense of debility. Something about him made Peter want to squash him.

"I have."

Maybe the man really had some chronic disease, but to Peter, his colorless, sagging flesh and sunken eyes suggested mental, not physical, misery.

"I see the *Gazette* is objecting to your running the seminar," Edmond said. He avoided Peter's eyes, but this thought, apparently, roused him to the extent of a momentary smirk, quickly suppressed. "You'll have to resign, you know," he added gravely.

Peter, who felt oppressed by these lugubrious morning encounters with Edmond Lockhart, which had resumed after a pleasant hiatus, strode off without responding, but he didn't go to the subway. Instead he walked past the subway station at 116th, crossed Broadway, and walked up to the Jewish Theological Seminary at 122nd Street, where he had an appointment with the elderly rabbi, scholar, and theologian Eli Friedman, who used to play cello in his father's Wednesday night string quartet.

Friedman was the last living friend of Peter's father. He had been considerably younger than Leonard Frankl and was probably in his eighties now. Peter called him every other year or so or dropped by to see him at JTS, where he had taught Jewish philosophy when he was younger and now held some emeritus post. Peter felt the need to talk to someone older and wiser, even though he was at an age when he himself was supposed to be old and wise, and Friedman was a man his father had thought highly of.

Friedman was ruddy and jowly, with wispy white hair through which the dome of his head shone a wholesome pink, wire-rimmed glasses, and large, protruding eyes. He smiled genially to see Peter, reminisced about his father, and led him to a coffee machine.

"Now let's sit somewhere and talk," said Friedman. "This is a nice room here, and no one will be using it this morning. Don't you like it?"

Peter did like the room, which was lined with books and had a small conference table at one end and upholstered chairs and a sofa at the other. Rabbi Friedman stood unconventionally close, so close that Peter could smell aftershave or cologne—some century-old smell of European gentle-manliness—and he could read the letters on the monogrammed linen hand-kerchief tucked into Friedman's suit jacket pocket in the old-fashioned style. But, though Peter was initially surprised by finding his face so near to Fried-man's—to the top of his head, actually, as Friedman was considerably shorter than Peter—it took only moments for it to seem natural. They sat down, Peter in one of the chairs and Rabbi Friedman on the sofa, grasping Peter's arm to lower himself. He responded affably to Peter's polite inquiry about his plans for the summer.

"We're always in town until August. This year the doctors are telling me I shouldn't travel, but we'll see about that. They don't have good doctors in Europe? What could be healthier than the mountains in . . . You look so much like your father now! So what is it? Someone getting married? Some-thing like that?"

"No, Rabbi, I wish it were something as happy as that. I'm here because I have trouble, and I want your advice. I was going to say I have three big problems, but sometimes I think it may be all one big problem."

The rabbi's white brows rose into a shaggy tepee shape, and he nodded and folded his arms to listen. Peter began with the story of Lesley's acci-dent. "Now," he concluded, "in the past week or so, the doctors are starting to say they think it's possible that she'll wake up."

"Thank God!" exclaimed Rabbi Friedman.

"Wait. I expect you'll despise me, but the truth is I don't want to be married to her anymore. With her gone, I feel free to think my own thoughts for the first time in nearly forty years. I feel as though I've been in a coma myself and just woke up. But I hate myself for this so much sometimes, I wish I were dead."

"Nonsense. I don't understand anything. Why don't you want your wife anymore? Ah! This could be some paradoxical reaction to her illness, you know. I've seen such things."

Peter shook his head no. He told Friedman that Lesley was a good person, a bit spoiled, but a loving mother and a supportive wife. He tried to explain her character in neutral terms, but Rabbi Friedman stared at him skeptically and rubbed his enormous forehead and wagged his head. "I just don't get it," he said. "How can this be? This sounds like something made up—like a story."

"I know," said Peter, "but it's all true."

"Of course you're sincere in everything you're telling me. That's not what I mean," said the rabbi. "What about the newspaper article I saw? Maybe that business is upsetting you and getting you mixed up?"

Peter dismissed this idea with a wave of his hand. "It's upsetting me, but it's not mixing me up. On account of that article, my law partners are furious and insist I get rid of the client. They could force me out if I refuse. Actually, I might not mind that so much, but Lesley would be furious. She'd turn the kids against me, and I couldn't stand that." Peter explained everything: his dislike of his firm, the strange anonymous notes that sounded as though he wrote them himself, the Devereaux Foundation and what it meant to him, how Lesley hated his going there.

When Peter had talked himself out again, Rabbi Friedman voiced some incomprehensible syllable—"umf," Peter heard—followed by a faint, whistling sigh.

"That Kappell," Friedman said after thinking, "why does he hate you?"

Peter thought this was beside the point and was disappointed in the rabbi, but he answered respectfully. "I can't figure it. Apparently he decided—I don't know why, because it's not true—that I was favoring the right-wingers in there and that I was too pro-Israel. Of course, you know I don't like the settlements, and I—"

"Don't start on that. It doesn't matter, anyway. The man doesn't care who you are or what you think." They had argued about Israel in the past, and the rabbi was a less skilled political debater.

"Of course not," said Peter. "He thinks he's the only individual in the world. The rest of us are generics—we're types. There are Jewish opinions, and I have a Jewish name. That's enough for him, even though I'm told he was informed of the family situation. You're right—he wasn't interested. You know, it's very annoying being saddled with all these assumptions. On the one hand, according to the tenets of Orthodox and Conservative Judaism, I'm not even Jewish. On the other hand, if Hitler ever came back, he'd send me and my wife and my kids straight to the camps."

"Kappell thinks like the terrorists, like Nazis—Goering, you know—*he* gets to decide who's a Jew and who's not. I told you when the kids were babies that you should convert."

"Convert to what? I'm an atheist."

"Reform Judaism?"

"That would be pointless, Rabbi."

"Fair enough," said Friedman with an air of surrender. He was a Conservative Jew who thought that Judaism without God was a contradiction in terms.

"Let me ask you, Peter. With your wife unconscious in the hospital for so long, it wouldn't be surprising if you . . . if you . . ."

Peter now explained, with a blush, about Wanda. How terrible it sounded spoken aloud. "So in fact I haven't ever been unfaithful to my wife, but my kids think I'm a skunk. I can't blame them. I'm unfaithful in my mind all day, all night."

Rabbi Friedman relaxed when he heard the Wanda story. "Now it all makes sense. The main thing is, you didn't actually destroy your family or hers. So why all this guilt? This is way too much. A little guilt—yes, fine. Just don't overdo it."

"You don't get it yet, Rabbi Friedman. The problem is that I *did* destroy my family—but long ago. Until just a few months ago I had no idea. The main thing I worried about was why my kids weren't getting married and never had anyone serious in their lives. Now everything is going wrong—my marriage, my job, my kids. But it's turning out that it's all the same big problem—me. I'm the problem."

"Wait, wait, wait. It can't be true. Listen, Peter, I'm glad you came to see me, but it's all too much. I need to think, and I have an appointment soon. Give me a couple of days. Can you come back on Thursday morning?"

Peter promised, although it troubled him that the old man, for some reason, appeared to take his dilemma personally. Maybe Friedman was beginning to understand that there was no way out. Lesley, like other married women her age, depended on Peter not just materially and socially. Her persona fed on him, and because he knew how hard it was to sate her hungry little soul, how much it took out of him, he also knew that he would destroy her if he left her. Peter was condemned to continuing in an unhappy marriage, while being deprived of consolation in his children or his work, and to being completely despicable at the same time.

And, in fact, when Peter had gone, Friedman thought to himself that there was little to be done about all this. He blamed himself harshly for not keeping better tabs on Peter when Leonard Frankl died. Obviously it had all been up to him; he had been criminally irresponsible. Would he have behaved differently if the boy had been Jewish? But he blamed Leonard Frankl, too, for having a child when he was so old, and then dying and leaving him alone, with nothing, and for mixing the boy up about who he was, where he belonged, and what he was supposed to do with his life. Friedman felt a little bitter against his old friend Leonard.

CHAPTER 22

For more than ten years, Hilda had been in psychoanalysis with an elderly woman who she believed to be the last of the émigré psychoanalysts of the 1930s and 1940s. Dr. Margarethe Stoller had been a protégée of Anna Freud, both in England and later in the States, even though she remained independent when the British Psychoanalytical Society split into two factions, Miss Freud's and Melanie Klein's. Hilda had chosen to be psychoanalyzed with Dr. Stoller because she wanted a rigid, classical Freudian of the clichéd type that still inspired *New Yorker* cartoons. They were hardly to be found anymore, but Hilda wanted none of this flexible, humanistic stuff.

Dr. Stoller's appearance certainly suggested that she was just what Hilda was looking for. She clumped around her office in heavy brown leather shoes with thick leather soles and buckles (Hilda often wondered, admiringly, where she found them), wore her white hair in a long braid coiled at the nape of her neck, and still spoke with a strong German accent. Her office, however, was small, dark, and surprisingly messy, with newspapers, journals, and cups of stagnant dark liquids standing here and there instead of curios and mementos of world travels. In technique, she was old school in some respects, but not all, which Hilda found annoying. However, having long ago given up any hope of being "cured," whatever that might mean, she enjoyed her daily conversations with Dr. Stoller and lived cheaply to support this expensive habit, and when Dr. Stoller's improper techniques ruined the theater of the whole thing, she exhorted her to strive for better.

Dr. Stoller had tried to analyze Hilda's wishes for an old-fashioned, silent, perhaps even harsh and uncomprehending analysis, as well as her decision to continue analysis indefinitely, or at least until such time as Dr. Stoller retired, but without good result.

"You like things the way they are," she had said to Hilda last week. "You don't wish to be different. You intentionally went seeking the silliest form of treatment you could find that would be intelligent enough for you to make a pretense of being serious." Her voice was raspy and shaky now, but it hadn't been ten years ago.

"Why would I like things the way they are?" Hilda had said, luxuriating on Dr. Stoller's couch, crossing her ankles on the little cloth provided at the foot. "My life is a succession of pains, privations, and humiliations. I don't enjoy them at all."

" 'Enjoyment' is not the right word for a masochist's satisfaction in her sufferings. But, joking aside, Miss Hughes, *masochism will get you just so far.*"

Hilda had heard something urgent in this speech, which had replayed in her mind a hundred times over the weekend, with appropriate diacritical markings, as usual: "Chōkĭnk assīt, *măssōkĭsm vĭll kĕt yù chüst ssō fä.*" After all these years of timeless discussion, why had Dr. Stoller begun to seem rushed, unwilling to wait for the psyche to move at its own pace—not that *Hilda* believed in that, but Dr. Stoller was supposed to. Was she responding to something Hilda had said or what?

On Tuesday, Hilda showed up early for her session. "What did you mean," she began, " 'just so far'? Where does it get you to, and why isn't that far enough?"

"I didn't say it wasn't far enough," said Dr. Stoller. "That's for you to judge, isn't it? But let me try to answer your question . . ."

Hilda was shaken by Dr. Stoller's willingness to answer. She should ask, instead, why Hilda wanted to know or . . . or . . . whatever clever counterquestions psychoanalysts asked to frustrate you in the way they were supposed to. Offering gratification, in the form of answers to questions, was a terrible thing to do—downright dangerous to the patient. Dr. Stoller had done such things often in the last few sessions. Was she giving up on Hilda? It was a little provoking.

". . . about masochism. It is a solution to a conflict, but a costly one. It deprives you of what you really want and bribes you with a sense of triumph in your own defeat. This, of course, inspires impatience in others, who naturally find the masochist's sense of victory repugnant, especially when coupled, as it so often is, with a call for help and sympathy."

Hilda flinched at the word *repugnant* and thought that now Dr. Stoller had forsaken neutrality and come close to offering a negative moral assessment of a neurotic position. "Even masochists deserve sympathy, I think," she protested.

"The question is, sympathy for what?"

"If you're going to give lectures, Dr. Stoller, you have to be more down-to-earth. This is too abstract for me."

"This man Frankl you've been mentioning. When he told you all those interesting stories, you were tongue-tied. He sensed in you an intelligent listener, so you immediately behaved in such a way as to induce him to think you silly and unintelligent."

"Yes, but I couldn't help it."

"You could, though. And now you have to decide whether you will continue to settle for so little, when you might have so much more."

"Well, Dr. Stoller, after all these years, we're exactly at the same point we started at. You're still talking about choice, and I still think I behave the way I do because I was born with a lot of weird wiring. I have a dozen personality tics, and despite the fact that my crushes never go anywhere, I'm gay—although I give you credit for not pushing for nurture over nature on that one."

"Crushes? I know of only one crush."

"The number is irrelevant. My point is that we should both be worried about helping me live within my limits, which no doubt reflect a combination of screwed-up nature and unnatural nurture. I came to treatment because I hoped to get over enough of my inhibitions to have a relationship. I don't say it's your fault that it failed. But lately you're pretending things are better when they're not. You've never talked as though treatment were about to end before. What is this all about?"

"Your analysis *is* almost over, Miss Hughes. You have choices, you understand a great deal about yourself, although you pretend not to. You no longer need the sort of help I can offer. And, by the way, whatever biological endowments may dictate in the lives of others, I feel quite confident that in your case they are irrelevant."

"I can't believe it! All you have to do is look at me to know that's not so." Hilda laughed.

"You often derive pleasure from my holding what you regard as incorrect views. But that surprises neither of us anymore. Really, the only thing left to talk about is the choices you are going to make. I will accept them and do my best to analyze them with you until the very last minute of our time together."

"*I don't get this, Dr. Stoller!* Nothing's changed. Why are you pretending there's this big development when everything today is the same as it was last week and last year and the year before that?"

"Not at all! Obviously, something has changed. Just look at the invitation to lunch from the young woman last week."

"Peter Frankl's daughter?"

"Who else? And this second encounter with Peter Frankl. You said he backed off with his hands in the air and said—"

"What are you talking about? When he told me to sell my co-op? He regarded me as some sort of lunatic."

"Not at all. That's not at all what he did, as you well know. And what about this seminar you set up, with him as chair?"

Hilda grew calm. "Are the Frankls what's got you all fired up? No, Dr. Stoller, you're grasping at straws. Oh, I see. I'm terribly sorry, but there's nothing in it. Oh, my goodness." And Hilda laughed, quietly this time.

"What effect did the Frankls have on me?"

"You're completely misinterpreting everything. Peter Frankl just wanted to talk to someone who didn't matter at all."

"A few days ago," said Dr. Stoller with an odd air, "I saw a newspaper article that attacked Mr. Frankl. I'm surprised you haven't mentioned that."

"Oh, Dr. Stoller, what is happening? You're not supposed to introduce the subject. That article was all lies. It got the poor man so upset, he resigned as chair of the seminar. He keeps saying that Miss Devereaux could lose control of the foundation and then I might be fired."

"None of that worried you enough to mention it here?"

"Of course not. We've done nothing wrong. Mr. Frankl is a worrier."

"Wasn't it odd to put Mr. Frankl in charge of the seminar?"

"Yes. We do many odd things. That's our modus operandi. You see, Dr. Stoller, he is really a remarkable man, even if he hasn't the background some people think they want. We didn't want background. We wanted a good, clever man, and he was the best and the cleverest we could find."

"Such odd policies can be risky—throwing small fish in the tank with big ones."

"Mr. Frankl a small fish? He is so strong-minded, so protective of others, and smart that we think of him as very big. But, of course, he has no name or public reputation, has he. He wouldn't have been so vulnerable to newspaper lies if he had. I see what you mean—oh, dear. Well, he's such a worrier that Miss Devereaux hasn't told him that her nephew Edmond has been hounding her again, especially since that article came out. He's positively demanding that she retire before something terrible happens, but it's so obvious to me that Edmond just wants to take over himself and that he's delighted with the whole mess that I don't let what he says worry me a bit."

Dr. Stoller was silent after this speech until it was time to announce that the session had ended. Hilda felt melancholy when she left, which was unusual. She returned to Morningside Heights and put in four hours with Miss Devereaux at the foundation office, during which she was uncharacteristically absentminded. She was going to lose Dr. Stoller, the stable center of her life, the only human being with whom she felt entirely comfortable and could speak openly. Dr. Stoller was going to pretend that Hilda was cured.

When Hilda returned home that evening, feeling weepy, she stopped for an ice-cream cone and was still licking it, swallowing tears with the cream, when she reached her stoop. Finding it hard to manage her briefcase and cone and fumble for keys at the same time, she sat on the stoop to finish the ice cream before going in. She licked her fingertips delicately, felt the evening breeze on her face, and watched the sun set beyond the treetops of Riverside Park, beyond the Hudson. The sky at the horizon showed golden through the leafage, blood red over the treetops, then higher up turned purple and shaded into a deep indigo. Hilda's tears flowed. The sky blurred, and the pleasures of the ravishing sunset, the crying, and the ice cream merged poignantly in her consciousness.

No sooner had she made herself comfortable there, however, than she saw two figures turn the corner onto 114th Street from Riverside and knew, before she could see their faces, that they were Peter Frankl and his daughter, Susan. Hilda began to tremble and felt the blood roaring in her head. All right—this was just too peculiar, that there were now Frankls wherever she looked, whereas she had lived near them for decades and never seen them at all. Yet study the thing as she might, from all directions, her encounters with Peter and Susan Frankl appeared random, meaningless. Dr. Stoller shouldn't put ideas in her head. She used to discourage Hilda from seeing significances that weren't really there; now she was actually suggesting them herself. Hilda didn't know what to do. Perhaps Dr. Stoller was, at last, growing . . . too old for this business.

While her thoughts ran this course, Hilda quickly arose, snuffling and hurriedly crunching the last bit of cone, and dug frantically for her keys in her large, crowded handbag. The tears overflowed and began to trickle down her cheek just as she opened the door, before the Frankls were close enough to see her face or speak. She trudged up the stairs to her fourth-floor studio, not trusting the elevator to come quickly enough. Two minutes later, someone rang her doorbell, and she heard voices, male and female, out in the hallway. Hilda stood inside her room, arms folded across her chest, staring at the door. A second later, a loud knocking followed, and then she heard Peter Frankl's extraordinarily loud voice.

"This is pretty damned silly, Hilda. We saw you go in, you know, and there's a lot to talk about. We're going to 107 West. Meet us for dinner—at *nine!*" The last words were called out with impressive volume, very slowly, so that she had to understand them. She heard muttering and shuffling, and then a note slid under her door and there were fading sounds of steps and voices. Hilda strove to find the note terrifying, horrifying, but could dredge up no such interesting feelings about it. After standing there indecisively for several minutes, she picked it up and read:

107 West—Nine PM
Peter and Susan

After thirty years of marriage, Herbert and Ingrid Holmes were still sweet on each other and held hands when they went on their daily walk down the promenade all the way to 79th street and back to 116th, near 444 Riverside Drive, where they lived in the small apartment where Herb had grown up with his parents. Ingrid and Herb did everything together. They saw their psychotherapy clients in next-door offices and attended chamber music concerts and members' special previews at the museums. For over thirty years, they had laughed at the same stories and found them more and more funny as years passed, so that now, a mere allusion to an amusing event or jest of a quarter century ago could convulse either of them.

"Herb, remember," Ingrid would begin, and one corner of Herb's mouth would begin to turn up, "remember when your new client came to my office by mistake? And I was expecting the bathroom renovations person? And I said, 'Oh, I'm *so* glad to see you. You're the only one who—' "

Here they were already both suppressing snorts, and Ingrid's voice sounded choked.

" 'You're the only one who would actually . . . actually come . . . to my office.' " By this time, they would both be holding their sides and wiping tears from their eyes. "And then I said . . . 'I cut out some pictures of . . . of toilets I'd like . . . to show you.' " The last words would be shrieked, and the two of them would be overcome with such violent paroxysms of laughter that speech was impossible.

By the time she reached her teens, Mallory had begun to find the whole routine revolting, especially at night when that hilarity issued from behind closed bedroom doors. Now, however, she was beginning to think it unbearably, sweetly sad, for lately she had often had the thought that her parents were no longer young and one day would leave her alone. She had noticed their gently swelling midriffs and how the color was gradually fading from their skin and hair, leaving them anonymously gray, less like her particular parents and more like generic old people. If this was how their own daughter could perceive them, she realized, horrified, how hard it would be for the rest of the world to understand that they were real persons, lovable and good. She could just imagine what they would say about such fears.

"Of course!" her mother would say, turning up her palms to indicate stoic acceptance. "But the real problem is when older people see themselves that way."

"Which your parents are in no danger of doing, ever," her father would add. What did people do who did not have her parents? she would think, feeling so much affection for them that the rest of her life seemed, for the moment, insignificant. What else could be as real or strong as her passionate love for these good people?

In her parents' kitchen that evening, Mallory told her mother, Ingrid, all about the situation with Louis while Ingrid was preparing to pound a piece of raw meat with a wooden mallet. Mallory said nothing about the Kappell fiasco; she felt too ashamed of her own role in it, and there were more immediate problems to deal with. A mix of spicy and sweet cooking odors complicated the atmosphere, which was slightly hazy with steam and smoke.

"My goodness, sweetheart. If you're not interested in him, you shouldn't have invited him over here. He'll get the wrong message." Ingrid pounded the red slab furiously.

"No, he won't. Mom, I just did it so you and Dad could help. You're both fairly skilled at getting people to see and accept unpleasant realities. Why not? And I don't want to offend him. He's Susan's brother. But he can't be all that offended if I ask him to dinner with my family. I can show some respect, and he can't come on to me."

"Hogwash, Mallory. I would never have agreed to this if I'd known what was going on. As soon as your father gets home, send him in here." Flipping over the pulpy mass, Ingrid resumed her attack.

"Don't leave me alone with Louis!"

"You'll have to be alone with him for two minutes. There's the buzzer. That's him."

"How I dread this!"

"Mallory, what I don't like is that this is underhanded and sneaky. Why can't you be straightforward with him?"

"I *was* completely, brutally, straightforward, and it didn't work. The next step will be, he starts getting mad." Mallory scowled. She was almost as annoyed with her mother as her mother was with her.

"Unless he is really demented, he will accept a straightforward, unequivocal no on your part, and I remember Louis. I don't think he's demented."

"You're not allowing for his being so upset and so determined."

"Yes, I am."

Mallory went to the door and admitted Louis. A slight movement at the corners of her mouth was all she allowed herself by way of a smile in greeting. She was surprised at how tall he was. She had been thinking of him as not much above her own height. He was carrying flowers wrapped in paper, and he was dressed in the handsome suit and tie he had worn to work. He surprised her by a quick kiss on one cheek and, simultaneously, with his free hand, a brief caress on the other.

"Fast work, getting those flowers," she said, refusing to thank him.

"They're for your mother, not you," he said.

Mallory led him into the kitchen to Ingrid.

"Louis, how nice to see you, dear. How lovely these are! Any news about your mother?"

Mallory now regretted not having asked him this. She never had in any of their conversations, although she always asked Susan. She avoided being friendly to Louis in any way so as not to encourage him, but this now struck her as appalling, ruthless. As soon as her mother asked the question, sadness and anxiety appeared on his face, replacing the vaguely wise-guy, louche expression he had worn as long as Mallory had known him. Magic! Both her parents were like that with people. Louis now exhibited a perfectly unhappy boy's face. Even Mallory felt for him, and her tenderhearted mother went over and gave him a quick embrace, holding her sticky hands away from his crisp shirt.

"She comes nearly conscious now, for a couple of minutes at a time. The doctors say the movement is in the right direction," Louis replied. It was a relief to hear him speak straightforwardly for a change. Altogether, at this moment he appeared a more reasonable and sympathetic human being than Mallory was accustomed to think him. What a mistake it was to bring him here, she thought, realizing that her mother would of course bring out the best in him.

"Oh, that's encouraging. I'm so glad. Sweetie, get Louis something to drink. Are you starving? Try one of these," and she pointed to a plate of puffy-looking things that, he and Mallory discovered, contained some creamy crab concoction. They simultaneously nodded their appreciation to Mrs. Holmes with full mouths, and feeling trapped by their absurd synchrony, Mallory knew that it was hopeless. She would get along swimmingly with Louis all evening. Her parents would think he was a sweet boy and feel sorry for him, suffering with his desperately sick mother and Mallory's rejection. They wouldn't blame her, but she would nonetheless feel like something slimy with too many legs.

Mallory's father burst in. "I forgot it, Ingrid. Completely forgot it. Now don't fuss. Come on, Louis," he shouted, shaking Louis's hand vigorously, "we'll run down to the market. Be back in two minutes." Louis strode off with a quick grin at Mallory. "She needs cardamom seeds," they heard Herb say as the two went down the hallway.

"Well, I didn't expect him to be this nice," said Ingrid.

Mallory shook her head dismally. "He's not," she said.

"I think he probably gives you a very hard time."

"No, he's just completely obnoxious."

"That's what I mean. That's his version of giving you a hard time," said Ingrid.

"It's not endearing."

"He's doing the fairy-tale bit—he's seeing if you'll love the prince, or perceive the prince, when he's disguised as a—"

"I can't believe you're going to say that."

"What?"

"Frog."

"I was going to say," said Ingrid, "a poor woodcutter or tailor or whatever the poor young men always are in those stories. You're going to have to prove yourself to him."

"You really have it backwards."

"Mallory, I'll make a prediction."

Mallory shrieked childishly. "How can you do that? It'll be a fate hanging over me if you make any prediction about me that has Louis's name in it."

"What are you talking about? I was only going to predict that Louis will be a more heavyweight character someday than you'd expect. Also, although I know much of what you told me about him is perfectly right—he's not the world's deepest person—he's also not quite as lightweight as you said. You have to allow for how much he's going to change when his career advances and he gets married and has children."

"He's thirty-two, mother, not a kid."

"But he's still going to change, and he won't be punished for being so slow to grow up. I wish more girls understood how these young men transform. They usually develop their paternal qualities in the marriage, whereas the girls already have maternal qualities in courtship. Do you know what your father was like when he was young and single? *I* do, and it wasn't so impressive."

"I refuse to believe that life is so unfair. Besides, you're mixing up paternal and maternal qualities with husbandly and wifely ones."

"They go together, and that's good because it means there's a coincidence between the capacity for marriage and the capacity for child rearing. And"—here Ingrid, hearing Louis and Herb return, signaled Mallory with a nod and altered the flow of her thoughts—"we'd all be happier if we understand our locations on this complicated map and navigated accordingly."

Mallory was less annoyed at being lectured than saddened by realizing how little her mother understood the new generation, who were never going to assume parental and marital roles of the sort she had in mind. "Your map doesn't show a few new turns in the road, Mom."

"Take these nibblies out—no, ask your father to come in and help me, and then we'll all talk for a while. You can't invite Louis over and hide out in the kitchen."

"So you tell me, then," Herb was saying in the living room, when they were all reassembled there with a plate of the little crab confections and glasses of wine, "*why* would an Eagle Scout engage in such destructive business frauds? Why did any of them do those rotten things? What do they say about it in B-School?"

"It's no big mystery." Louis spoke languidly, leaning back, while Herb spoke energetically, leaning forward, his eyes fixed brightly on Louis's face. Louis, Mallory thought, was trying hard to convey a lack of interest in the subject so as to get off the spot. But that wouldn't work with her father.

"So what's the explanation, then?" Herb said, genially expectant, as though he really thought that Louis were going to enlighten him.

"Yes, what's the explanation?" Mallory echoed somewhat aggressively, glad to have her father witness Louis's incapacity for adult analysis and conversation, even though it made her a little uneasy to watch Louis squirm.

"Well . . ." Louis sighed. Mallory caught the tension in his sigh and tried to feel no mercy. Louis could say nothing worth hearing, and his listeners were sharp and sensible. So let him feel inadequate and learn to think of Mallory as over his head. "I knew guys like that at work before I went to B-School."

"Yeah?" Herb said with encouraging, genuine curiosity.

"Yeah. And, uh . . ." Louis stretched and yawned just slightly. Mallory observed that he was attempting to disguise his long pauses as profound ease. Mallory stole a glance at her parents' faces and saw that they realized as well as she that Louis was stumped. She began to feel uncomfortable and was on the verge of speaking herself, to end Louis's misery, when he finally continued.

"I mean, there's just not much to say about them. I mean, they were always like that—you know, they would buy a term paper off the Internet or copy on a test. That's just how they grew up. When I was a kid I used to wonder about it, and I remember I thought that kids probably just stopped doing that when they grew up. But they don't. You know what I mean?"

"I do," said Ingrid earnestly.

"Ah," said Herb, nodding his interest. "And why are they like that? Why do so many kids turn out like that?"

"That's your department," said Louis, obviously feeling pleased relief at the apparent success of his remarks.

"But I just don't know any of these guys."

"Well, I'm not much of a psychologist," said Louis, again causing Mallory, who was excruciatingly aware of how gratuitous this disclaimer was, to cringe for him, "but, uh, I think—maybe this sounds sort of silly—but their fathers never told them not to. Maybe their fathers even . . . you know what I mean?" And he indicated paternal sins with his hands.

Mallory, who had no idea what he meant, stared at him.

"I know exactly what you mean," said Ingrid. She did, too, Mallory thought with a sigh. She always knew what everybody meant.

For Mallory, the dinner was punctuated with a series of such moments of discomfort, followed by rescues of varying degrees of success, with the result that she was feeling drained when, soon after they left the table, Louis said, "I have to run. I want to drop in at St. Luke's for just a minute. The night nurse will let me in to see Mom. C'mon, Mallory, I'll walk you home."

Mallory shook her head. "No thanks," she said politely, "I'm going to help with the dishes." For a moment, she feared that her parents would insist that they needed no help, then realized that, of course, whatever they thought of Louis, they would never do anything that would look as if they were encouraging him.

Louis looked at her and tilted his head a fraction of an inch, and she plainly heard his voice in her mind: *Come on, Mallory.* She experienced the strangling sensation that a woman feels when she is pursued by a man she looks down on. Mallory felt bitter against her parents for failing to understand her position. Then an odd thought passed through her mind: She had never had that unpleasant, suffocating feeling about Alexei. She did not think she would, even if he had continued to pursue her. Why was that?

"Thanks," Louis said to Herb and Ingrid as he left, in a tone of voice that curiously combined cool and sheepishness, making Ingrid wonder whether those qualities were not, psychologically, quite close to each other. Of course they are! she decided, thinking it through, and made a mental note to bring this up at a clinical seminar she was attending at Columbia Presbyterian that term.

The three Holmeses at first went silently about clearing and washing up. Then Herb said, "That kid has been messed up somehow, and it's a shame."

Mallory shook her head at the excess of sympathy in this. "Dad, you know *he's* one of those regular guys who buy term papers on the Internet."

"No way," said Herb, and Ingrid, too, shook her head, no way. Their naïveté was aggravating. Mallory had often noticed that they failed to detect flaws in people of her generation, as though their blind parental partiality extended to anyone who might be remotely like Mallory in relation to them. Or was it simply that they were being venal, approving of a rather inferior man just because he was a rich investment banker? After all, her mother had actively objected to Alexei, but not to Louis, essentially on class grounds.

CHAPTER 24

"Here's a moral question for you," said Rabbi Friedman to a group of men assembled around a table. "Say a man is married to a shrew— a terrible wife." Not that Lesley Frankl was a shrew, but just for the sake of argument, he thought to himself. "He manages to stick with her until the children are raised. Then he wants out, but by that time he's old, she's old— too late for her to start over, presumably, but maybe not for him. What should he do? Can he get divorced? Is adultery such a big deal after the child-rearing years? Let's have a comparative discussion."

This was Rabbi Friedman's regular Thursday morning ecumenical discussion group, composed of clergy from the neighborhood, including two wishy-washy Protestants from Union Theological Seminary, one devout colleague of the rabbi's from Jewish Theological Seminary, an earnest young Episcopalian priest from St. Ursula's on Broadway down at 113th, and two Catholic priests who were becoming increasingly shifty-eyed in the wake of ever more frequent newspaper reports of scandals in their church. The group had been meeting for years, with little change in membership. Everyone was an atheist except for the Episcopalian and the two rabbis.

Last time, they had argued fiercely about the attack on the World Trade Center. Four against three, with the Catholics and the Protestants tending to collapse any moral distinctions that justified counterattack. Greg Merriweather, the young Episcopalian, allied himself with the rabbis, read aloud from Niebuhr, and grew teary arguing for the importance of slivers of moral difference. Rabbi Friedman didn't really understand taking it that hard, for this was nothing compared with some of the things he could remember. His own wife had fled Austria as a young woman, and all of her family that were left behind were killed.

After today's meeting, his old friend's son, Peter Frankl, had to be dealt with. Although Eli had always liked the young man, not so young now, he dreaded this conversation. A man who decides at sixty that he's stifled and unfulfilled—at sixty, when his prime working years are ending and the main business of love—sex and babies and all that—has already happened! Going back on all that at sixty was a cruel thing to everyone, especially the woman, who would probably find no new mate. Even if she did, he wouldn't be the father of her children; the one who remembered her young womanhood, her motherhood, her friends, her parents, the past, and all who had died. Peter held the threads of his wife's life in his hands and was threatening to cut them. A strong, healthy woman usually bled to death, in spirit, under such a misfortune, and this woman was almost dead already anyway. Rabbi Friedman had discussed the whole thing with his own wife in the interim, and his attitude toward Peter was more complicated today. All the relevant facts were not known.

The Protestants from UTS had a ready answer to the rabbi's moral question. They were certain that the man should divorce his wife. He had already gone beyond the call of duty. Why should an error of youth force gratuitous suffering in age? Let the woman bear the consequences of her own sins now that the children were adults.

The Catholics thought he could not. Marriage was a sacrament, not a civil contract that could be broken because someone decided he didn't like the deal. One of them read from a Bible he had brought along. "It's in Matthew, of course. Everyone knows this passage." And he read:

> The Pharisees also came unto him, tempting him, and saying unto him, Is it lawful for a man to put away his wife for every cause? And he answered and said unto them, Have ye not read, that he which made them at the beginning made them male and female, And said, For this cause shall a man leave father and mother, and shall cleave to his wife: and they twain shall be one flesh? Wherefore they are no more twain, but one flesh. What therefore God hath joined together, let not man put asunder.

> They say unto him, Why did Moses then command to give a writing of divorcement, and to put her away? He saith to them, Moses

because of the hardness of your hearts suffered you to put away your wives: but from the beginning it was not so. And I say unto you, Whosoever shall put away his wife, except it be for fornication, and shall marry another, committeth adultery: and whoso marrieth her which is put away doth commit adultery.

"That could not be clearer," said the Catholic priest when he was finished, "aside from that bit about the hardness of heart, which never makes much sense to me."

"That's too Jewish, is why," said Rabbi Friedman. "What that means is, that what Moses did, letting men divorce their wives, was sort of like ... legalizing marijuana. Moses says you really shouldn't smoke this marijuana at all, but I know your weakness of will. You're going to do it anyway, so I'm going to regulate it. I'm going to tell you how, where, and when. So, out of realism, pragmatism, Moses gives them a regulation rather than make a futile prohibition. The same with divorce: you shouldn't put your wife away, but I know your hardness of heart, your meanness, so here's a regulation. That's what it means. Very Jewish, that remark is. We accept human nature."

Rabbi Friedman picked up another Bible to read the interesting passage over for himself. He felt annoyed that the Catholic priests were, in general, forgiving of the shepherds' sins and not so forgiving of the sheep—and in the part of life of which they had least experience, too, where humility would be appropriate.

"Ah-hah! Wait!" said Rabbi Friedman, reading. "There's more to this. Of course. Listen:

His disciples said to him, "If such is the case of a man with his wife, it is better not to marry." But he said to them, "Not everyone can accept this teaching, but only those to whom it is given. . . . Let anyone accept this who can."

"Very, very Jewish all this is. See, he has it all ways. He says flatly: Except where someone commits adultery, divorce is wrong, and that's all there is to it. *But* this is a very, very hard teaching to follow, so it's just for those who can do it. Heh, heh. I feel sorry for you gentiles trying to figure this out."

This last comment, and the chuckle, annoyed Greg Merriweather, the Episcopalian, who remarked that many of them *had* managed to figure it out and promised to bring in a learned commentary on that passage at the next meeting.

"I would be delighted to read that," said Rabbi Friedman with indefea-
sible goodwill. He had hoped to hear ideas that would help him deal with
his friend Peter, and he certainly had. Obviously, poor Peter was a man to
whom the hard teaching was given. He had to stay married because he could.

"Peter," he called out warmly when he saw him exit the elevator as he
was returning to his office.

"So what's new? How is Lesley?" he asked genially when they were settled on the sofa in the same pleasant room, drinking coffee, and he listened
attentively to Peter's report.

"I want to talk about your wife," Friedman continued, unexpectedly
turning sober. "Last time you talked about too many different things and
you confused me, saying they're all the same. Now tell me. Is there anyone
you might be interested in besides this Wanda person? You know, I'm wondering if you don't need just a friend—a woman, not an old man like me,
and not this obsessing all day, all night nonsense."

Peter refrained from smiling but thought that Rabbi Friedman really
was very old. "If I stay married to Lesley, I can't be friends with women—
not *really* friends. It would be infidelity."

"You have to get divorced to have a friend? I don't mean have an affair—just someone to talk to. What's so terrible about talking?"

"Ordinarily nothing. But in my case it would immediately lead to more
intimacy with another woman than with Lesley, which would be abandoning Lesley. I know this from experience."

"Having a friend is abandoning your wife? You're exaggerating terribly.
Married or not, everyone is entitled to a friend. Why not? Some nice, bright,
middle-aged lady, who would go to a concert or lunch or talk with you
about books, or someone in the neighborhood who would take a walk with
you. It could be doing her a favor, too. I'll bet you already know someone."
Rabbi Friedman smiled encouragingly, and Peter was touched at his well-
meaning naïveté.

"I used to try to have friends, but I always found myself turning into
someone Lesley didn't know and couldn't live with. That's just as bad as divorce—becoming a stranger to your wife."

"Peter, you can't believe that you're obligated to live a charade because it
makes Lesley feel more comfortable," Rabbi Friedman said. "Lesley doesn't
sound weak or brittle, but you wouldn't be obligated to erase yourself even
if she were. Marriage is not a suicide pact. I'll tell you something else: What
you're telling me is the strangest, most strained stuff I have ever heard out of
the mouth of a disgruntled husband."

"Lesley would probably like it if I were more like . . . like Henry. That's the husband of her best friend, the one who was driving the night of the crash and died. He was her idea of a good, fun husband. The three of them, they were very simpatico."

"Absurd," said Rabbi Friedman.

He sounded disdainful, even a little irritable, and he sighed wearily. Again Peter regretted having burdened him with problems that he seemed to take personally for some reason.

"You're mad at me?" said Peter.

"Yes, I suppose so—for reasoning like a fifteen-year-old. And all this business about wishing you hadn't been a big lawyer and hating your firm— it's the same thing. You think you have to work for truth and goodness and all that, but you have a childish idea of what decent work is. You should see through your father's foolish ideas by this age."

"My partners probably see it your way, but I don't hate my job because I think I *should* do something else, Rabbi. It's because it really is a dreadful place, but even if it weren't, I'm unable to care about it, which—sorry to whine—for a man like me is pretty painful. And of course people have a right to be themselves in marriage. It's the bad-faith way *I* got married that's the problem. I misled Lesley and her father and took their money, so I owe her the man they bargained for. That was the deal."

"No, no, no. They were just smart investors. You gave them back with interest. You have a right—an obligation, really—not to play this game anymore in your marriage. And if you stop this childish attack on your firm and your work, you'll get along better with Lesley."

Peter thought this over. "The minute I imagine her back in our apartment, I feel a big door in my mind slam shut. It opens only when she's gone."

"Maybe you should see a psychotherapist."

"A psychotherapist? I'm here seeing you."

"All right, all right. But mental doors slamming shut and such things— please, Peter. Think of your father. Imagine him acting with your mother the way you do with your wife. Impossible!"

Peter took a few seconds to reply. "Sometimes I wonder about his first wife, though." His father's first marriage still felt like a forbidden subject after all these years.

Friedman now recalled that the older Frankl *had* suppressed himself in his first marriage. In fact, Friedman used to wonder why he had not asserted himself and forced his first family to accommodate him. Why couldn't he even have chosen a less restrictive type of Judaism, so that everyone could have lived more comfortably—rather than break so violently with his family and faith? But Leonard had insisted on strict Orthodoxy, even though, Friedman had reason to believe, he regarded it as hogwash. These Frankls couldn't seem to manage in-betweens, give-and-take, comfortable, human-scale compromises, and Peter had taken this family trait into his marriage with painful consequences. Friedman said as much.

"That sounds reasonable, Rabbi," said Peter, "but my father's dissatisfactions had nothing to do with what kind of Judaism he practiced. It was just being a Jew. That was the thing he had trouble with. He thought the rules of decency didn't belong to any religion in particular. He would have understood that it would be faithless, and cruel, to remodel my marriage the way you want me to. It would make Lesley's deficiencies clear to her. She'd see how I've always looked down on her and her father, her whole family."

"Maybe it wouldn't make her deficiencies clear to her. Maybe it would only make it clear to her that you think she has a lot of them," said Friedman. "The problem here is that you were just too young. If you had waited, you would never have made these mistakes. And where were the old people who should have been helping you—like me? Well, it's a mess."

"So there's no way out. You agree now, right?"

"The way out—if 'out' is the right word here—since you've already decided to stay married, is to figure out how to have less deprivation in your marriage and then see where you are. Don't be false with Lesley if she wakes, and find a nice, middle-aged woman to be friends with. This will help you more than you think, although not as much as you'd like. And you have to get rid of this lunatic idea that you owe Lesley the man she thought she was getting"—Friedman was trying to sound encouraging again, but then he seemed to lose steam—"maybe."

"Maybe!"

"That's my answer. Because I still smell something wrong in your story. There's some twisting here, but I don't see what. If I have any further thoughts, I'll call you."

"Don't look so worried, Rabbi," Peter said, supporting him by the elbow as he struggled to rise from his low seat on the sofa. "I didn't think you were going to be able to fix things for me. You know, all this stuff that we've been saying today and the other day—I didn't know it. It helps me just to understand a little."

"I know. You would have gone to your grave unconscious. You're acting just like your father, who would have said, I have to do this because God wants it—and you don't even believe in God."

"Of course I don't, any more than he did—or you do."

Rabbi Friedman shook his head slightly and sighed.

They agreed to meet again in a few weeks.

"Then," said Friedman, "we'll discuss your children. We'll take this one subject at a time, and we'll see if, as you say, you're the only problem."

CHAPTER 25

One Saturday evening, Susan Frankl and Sylvie Kimura sat cross-legged in Susan's window seat, holding playing cards; on a cushion between them that served as a table sat a cribbage scoring board with pegs and a saucer full of ashes and butts. The window was open, and Sylvie was lighting a cigarette.

"You're going to burn up your cards, Sylvie," Susan warned her. "Twenty-five."

"Go," said Sylvie.

Despite the summer heat, Susan had cooked dinner for Alcott and Sylvie, relying on the weatherman's promise of a cold front by afternoon. Now, at 8:00, a clap of thunder tardily announced the change of weather, and chill, unruly bursts of wind filled the room. Alcott, too, was late. The financial arrangements for the new film had begun to unravel, and he could not afford to ignore a summons from his backer that had come just as he and Sylvie were preparing to go uptown from the Village.

Susan assured Sylvie that the dinner would hold until Alcott arrived, and the two of them had been sipping wine and playing cribbage for nearly an hour. Susan wouldn't hear of Sylvie going down to the stoop to smoke in the rain. Her apartment, snug and filled with cooking odors, felt doubly welcoming now that it was so wild out-of-doors. Rain, confidences, and wine all poured freely.

"I haven't played a card game, any game, really, since high school," Sylvie said. "No one plays games anymore, Susan. Just video games."

"I like games," Susan said, dealing deftly.

And Sylvie remarked to herself how Susan's phoniness, her repugnant pseudoaplomb, fell away in the game. Susan-the-gamester had an authentic, barbed way of talking and sharp-edged competence.

"When I was growing up," Susan was saying, "my mother—cut, Sylvie—was dissatisfied with everything about me. I wanted to play the piano and she wanted me to dance. She was always trying to cut my hair off. She gave up and left me on my own when I was about six. She just kind of canceled my childhood. My father was the opposite. He thought everything about me was perfect. He was—he is to this day—so miserable if he thought anything was going wrong for me, especially my love life, that I couldn't let him know. So growing up, I never had anyone to lean on. I was always on my own—like you, but for different reasons."

Sylvie nodded, thumped a card down on the pillow, and blew smoke into the rainy night. "Um, this is a run, right?"

"Yes, you learn fast. When I met Chris, I thought—I'm not alone. I can talk to him. But after just a few weeks, he began to find me frustrating. I'm too moody, and he doesn't like my taste in anything—music, fiction, movies. Last week, he said I should think about going to medical school. He said I was getting this musicology degree only because my father wanted me to. He didn't think I had a scholarly bent or a lot of musical insight." Susan sounded as though she expected Sylvie to be amused at this.

"Chris is a suburban aesthete with arrested development," Sylvie said blandly. "He wants to be more cool than anyone else, and he thinks that means liking the latest thing before anyone else and getting bored with it sooner than anyone else. He doesn't really have tastes. My deal, Susan."

"That's rather harsh, isn't it?" she said. She thought she should be offended out of loyalty to Chris, but, disconcertingly, she wasn't. "Besides, he's probably at least partly right. My father always regretted that he didn't become some kind of scholar or teacher, and I think it might well be true that I'm just trying to give him a vicarious experience of something I have no real vocation for—not to say that I don't love what I do, but love and talent are two different things."

"No, they're not. People can't really love work they can't do. They can only love the idea of doing it. Look, I get the idea, Susan," Sylvie said, stubbing out her cigarette, "and I don't like it. You can't listen to Chris when he says that stuff, or things could turn out wrong. I know what I'm talking about."

"Sylvie, I'm perfectly capable of— That's Alcott," said Susan, interrupted by the buzzer. She pressed the button to admit the caller, but when she opened the door, Chris, not Alcott, stood there dripping.

"Were you here last night?" he said without preamble, and he walked in without invitation.

"I thought you were in Cambridge," she said. Timidly, she made as though to embrace Chris, but he moved past her. Susan's card-player edge was already gone, Sylvie noticed, replaced by a nonchalance so false that a less loyal friend than Sylvie might have found it a bit disgusting.

"I ran all the way from a Hundred and Tenth in this deluge and all you can say is—" Chris broke off when he saw Sylvie standing at the window, looking at him with an expression so blank and cool that Susan thought he would certainly infer they had been telling stories about him. This was hard to watch, Chris's sweet boyishness, his civilized ease, subjected to such an openly hostile suspicion—and all on the basis of Susan's stories, which were probably prejudiced and inaccurate.

"Hi, Sylvie," he said, and walked around the room. He looked appealing, with the refined near homeliness of his face, wet hair slicked back, and a wet shirt that clung to his slender form. He observed the table set for three and, behind Sylvie, cards scattered on the window seat.

"I really am glad to see you. I'm just surprised that you didn't go to Cambridge," Susan said. "I'm having company—Alcott will be here in a minute."

"Changed my mind," he said matter-of-factly, and wiped rain off his face with a tissue he took from her desk drawer. "You're playing cards? Susan, you are really—" The buzzer rang again.

"Alcott," said Sylvie, in such a pregnant voice that Chris turned and looked at her.

"I'll come back later tonight," said Chris.

"No, stay!" Susan replied, her voice tight with anxiety. "We're just having dinner. I'll set another place."

Once more, when she opened the door, she was surprised not to see Alcott. Instead, Alexei Mikhailov was getting off the elevator; he gave an awkward smile as he walked to the door. He was hardly wet at all. "Alcott dropped me off," he said, his handsome features twisting into some sort of unpleasant grimace, which Susan diagnosed as a product of shyness. He had met Susan only once before, at Mallory's party. "He asked me to just tell you he's trying to park. He'll be here in a minute."

"Alexei," said Sylvie, "it's bad news, isn't it."

He nodded and avoided looking her in the eye. "Let him tell you."

"Please, come in," Susan said, but the invitation sounded forced and saccharine. Alexei looked from Susan to Sylvie to Chris and flushed a little at Susan's obvious reluctance.

"I have to go. I'm really late," he said stiffly, with a hint of an accent. His eyes swept Susan's rooms involuntarily, as this might look as if he would like to come in, but he couldn't help staring at the cards scattered in the window seat, the piano, and the place settings on the table. Again he made the indescribable grimace, of mixed scowling, perfunctory smile, and something vulnerable, and turned to go. Susan saw that this was because he felt unwelcome, and she was ashamed. But it would be so hard for them to talk with him there. His manners, moreover, verged on the uncouth.

"Alexei!" said Chris genially from the other side of the room, where he was sitting on the piano bench. "What's up?"

The trace of excess ease in Chris's voice grated on Alexei. "Good-bye," he said to no one in particular, neither ignoring Chris nor responding to him. He fumbled with the locks on Susan's door until she opened it for him, then left with a final nod to Susan.

Susan, Chris, Sylvie, and Alcott had a great deal to discuss when Alcott finally arrived, as rain soaked as Chris had been.

"My backer is pulling out," Alcott said, pacing up and down Susan's living room. "He says he has no faith in the script and everything is being mishandled." Alcott was restless and agitated, though, not depressed, and wouldn't accept sympathy, not even from Sylvie; he pulled away when she tried to put her hand on his arm.

"There's still a chance he'll change his mind," he insisted, as if Sylvie were arguing with him, although she had said nothing. "When he thinks about it, he's going to see that legally he can't do this no matter what his lawyer's telling him."

"If you lose him," Susan asked, "can't you find enough money to finish somewhere else?"

"I'd have to can the whole thing. I'd never pull together that much money for a project that already has one serious vote of no confidence."

Susan didn't ask what the film was. You never asked Alcott, and he rarely told. Only a few of the people working on the film, in fact, would understand more than a couple of scenes and fragments. The money problems and the backer's threats, however, could be, and were, openly discussed and occupied them all through dinner.

"What happened to Alexei?" Alcott asked abruptly when the subject had been exhausted and the meal nearly consumed. "Didn't he come up?"

"He said he couldn't stay," said Susan, once more ashamed that she hadn't made the invitation with more enthusiasm.

"Is he still seeing Mallory?" asked Chris. "She really had no business getting mixed up with him that way." Susan looked at him despairingly across the table. She could never make Chris understand that couples had private communications. Mallory wouldn't want her little affair getting around, and here it was being broadcast from Susan's table by her own boyfriend.

"Mallory and Alexei?" asked Sylvie, frowning. "What is this?"

"But it's an interesting mistake for Mallory—very interesting," Chris continued, ignoring Susan's signals. "Here's our reliable, good, nice Mallory, who always knows where people went to college and whether their parents are rich and would rather write dreck for the *Gazette* than political analysis for an e-zine. She doesn't often go wrong, but when she does it's for sex with almost an embarrassingly good-looking and sweet, uneducated, broke guy who is, shall we say, no 'challenge' for someone like her—she's totally in control. What an eye-opener."

"Unfair! Unfair to Mallory," said Susan, shaking her head, despite the fact that she herself had had similar thoughts that she had more or less expressed to Mallory herself.

"Unfair to Alexei, too," said Alcott, staring belligerently at Chris.

"Totally off," protested Sylvie, "on both counts."

"But, Susan, you yourself told me that she didn't take him seriously," said Chris.

"Oh, I just meant that it's not a big deal for her," said Susan, trying to soften this, which had been another comment meant only for Chris's ears. "She likes him, and she thinks he has a lot of natural ability. She says he's definitely smart."

"But in fact she can't really take him seriously," Chris added. "He's just not from her world."

"You may think that way," said Alcott with a hint of contempt in his voice, "but don't slander Mallory." Neither Alcott nor Chris, Susan realized, really knew Mallory, but Chris understood her better through what he'd heard from Susan. She wished he would keep quiet about Mallory and Alexei. Still, Chris didn't mean to be unkind, and Sylvie and Alcott themselves were condescending when they insisted on judging Alexei by different criteria from those they used to judge their real friends and themselves. In the long run, Mallory's attitude might be kinder; Alcott and Sylvie would draw Alexei in and increase his ultimate sense of exclusion and disappointment. Obviously, Alexei suffered from his awareness of his handicaps, and no amount of tolerant, condescending affection could change that.

"Susan, did you know," Sylvie asked, "that Alcott has hired Alexei?"

"I heard something about it," said Susan, not wanting to divulge another word of what Mallory had told her. She wanted them to talk about something else.

"I need a cigarette," said Sylvie. She lit one and went again to the window seat, followed by Alcott, who also took a cigarette from her pack and sat beside her to smoke it.

"What are you doing?" Sylvie protested, aghast. "Put it out. Don't be ridiculous. Is it because you're tense about the money?"

"I'm doing it because you are. I can't let you die alone, can I? If you smoke, I'll smoke, too. I used to smoke, actually."

"This is coercion," she said, looking fierce, "and I don't like it."

"I didn't think you would."

"Come on, put it out."

"We both smoke, or neither smokes. I've thought about it, and that's the only way."

Sylvie snatched Alcott's cigarette from his hand and angrily stubbed it out in the saucer.

"I knew I could count on you," he said, smiling, and he tore away her own cigarette, leaving the filter between her fingers, and crushed it, too, into the saucer.

"Let's discuss it later," she said. She flushed angrily, and Alcott made a show of being unconcerned.

Late that night, Susan played solitaire at the table and felt low, ruminating on how quarrelsome the evening had been and feeling guilty for Chris's gossip about Alexei and Mallory. I suppose I have to let Mallory know, she thought. Chris, however, was in a good mood. He sat at Susan's desk and tinkered with a printout of the last scene of his newest play, a sort of counter–love story that he thought had a good chance of being produced.

"I don't need to ask how it went today," Susan said, seeing that he was closing up his laptop. "You're so up, you couldn't go to Cambridge."

"No, I had to see you," he said. "I can't tell you how annoyed I was when I got here and you had all these people over—and I was ready to jump into bed." He put his arms around her and pressed his face against her neck.

"You were so annoyed, you told everyone about Mallory and Alexei? How I wish you hadn't done that."

"You don't need to make such a deep, dark secret out of something like that. It's not a big deal. You know, it's also very annoying the way you sit here for an hour playing this idiotic game."

"But you should let me make that decision," Susan said as she gathered the cards from the table and put them in her desk drawer. "Mallory is my oldest friend, and she told me this in confidence. She'll be upset when she finds out."

"So don't tell her."

"I don't want her to find out from someone else, which she definitely will sooner or later. I want her to know that I wasn't just ignoring her wishes."

"So you're going to tell her I'm the bad guy? That's nice." But, seeing Susan's expression darken, Chris retreated. "Look, I'm sorry. That wasn't fair. I'm really, really so sorry, but I had no idea you regarded it as a sacred trust or something. Look, I feel terrible. Don't be mad, Susan."

Susan forgave him, but not herself. From now on, she would be more reserved with such confidences. And she would arrange no foursome dinners with Sylvie and Alcott.

CHAPTER 26

P eter Frankl tried to explain it to Lesley again, but she stared and frowned at him irritably.

"You're talking nonsense," she said. "I want Louis. He'll do it." She was sitting upright in her hospital bed, which had been raised to its highest position. Her scrubbed face, without makeup, looked particularly ravaged when it expressed, as now, suspicious annoyance, and her hair, unprecedentedly long, stood upright in dark clumps that showed starkly white roots.

Peter tried again to make her understand, with shorter sentences. "Susan can't come yet. She's in a meeting until noon. Her meeting is uptown. She can pick up the things because she's uptown. Louis is at work downtown. He'll be there all day. He—"

"What work? Louis at work?"

"Louis works at Hartley Stanton Thornwick."

"No one told me about that."

"I think we did, but you've had a lot on your mind."

The therapist, a thin young woman with two tiny silver rings in her left eyebrow, intervened. "Mrs. Frankl, you need to be quiet and rest. You've been talking all morning, and you're wearing yourself out. I'm going to ask your husband to leave so you can eat lunch and have a nap."

"No, he's going to stay, because it's not lunchtime and I'm bored silly. I just want a few things from the drugstore and from home, and I don't see why that's such a big problem or why someone can't—"

"Susan has your list, and she'll be here in an hour or so. Lesley, I have to go to the office now."

When Lesley regained consciousness, Peter had taken almost two weeks off work and spent every day with her in the hospital. Now he had urgent business to tend to. His partners were pushing him harder on resigning from the Devereaux Foundation. He had just learned that for weeks Edmond Lockhart had been pressuring his aunt Emma, too, to resign from the foundation's board. Columbia had received three letters of complaint from seminar members about the preliminary meeting in June. Tending to Lesley all day long, while coping with these anxieties, had exhausted him. Even Peter's ample store of patience was almost depleted.

"But when will you be back? Not until seven? What am I supposed to do until then? Peter, bring me my flowered robe when you come, and call Becky. I need my cell phone so I can keep it in my lap. I can't *reach* that one. Why don't you *think* of things like this? I can't believe you really have to work. Wait . . . oh . . . Oh, I have it, never mind the cell phone. It was under the sheet. What's Susan's number—wait, it's on here. I don't remember how to—"

Peter kissed Lesley on the cheek and walked out while her words still flowed. He had to, because they would not stop. As he walked to the subway, Peter thought longingly and guiltily of the peace that had prevailed in their lives during the time Lesley was unconscious. He had come to experience it as normal. Lesley had begun talking in a rambling way when her eyes were still closed. For several days, she lay there half-conscious, talking away, half-responsive to things that people in the room said, weaving phrases overheard into her stream of garbled words. Even now, she went into and out of sleep without seeming to be aware of it. She was half drowsing and muttering when Susan arrived and came alert when she kissed her cheek.

"You were supposed to bring me things: deodorant, lipstick, my purse. I need some magazines and some videos. I'm all alone in here, completely bored, completely—"

"I brought you all that," said Susan, fishing in a large bag, "but I wasn't sure which lipsticks you'd want. You're pale, so lighter ones, right?"

"Oh, now she's the cosmetics expert, too, besides the musicologist, whatever that is. My daughter is so much smarter than I am. I like bright lipsticks, of course. Anyway, why shouldn't I be pale since I never get out of here? You can't imagine how frustrating it is having to rely on someone for every little thing—give me . . ." And Lesley reached for the mirror and a lipstick. She was shocked when she saw the frame of pure white around her face. "What happened? How—"

"We'll have someone in to color your hair, as soon as you're strong enough," Susan said. "If you want, I mean." At first they had tried to keep Lesley away from mirrors. Fortunately, she forgot a great deal at the beginning. This was the third time she had discovered her undyed roots.

"Have I lost my memory? How long have I been here?"

"Mommy, they said it's natural to forget for a while. You were in a coma since March and you woke up the second week in August. Today is August twenty-sixth."

"Henry and Judy?"

Susan hesitated. "Judy's at home. She's fine. She'll be in to see you any day now. She's just waiting for permission from your doctor. Everyone's been asking about you, all the neighbors." Lesley looked frustrated and confused, but Susan, by chattering, succeeded in making her forget that she wanted to know about Henry. "Aunt Rita came for a while, and she's been calling every day, and . . . You know, it's a funny thing, Mom, but when you were unconscious, you know what you said? You must have said it a dozen times: Top drawer. Isn't that funny?"

Lesley frowned. "I never said that."

"You did—really. Ask Daddy. We'd come in and kiss you, and you'd say, 'Top drawer.' "

"I didn't say any such thing. Why would I say that?" Lesley grew irate. "Your father doesn't know about it."

"Well, maybe not." I shouldn't have said it was funny, thought Susan. That probably hurt her feelings, and I certainly didn't think it was funny at the time. Nonetheless, Susan was surprised at how vehemently her mother denied what was obviously true. She supposed that Lesley disliked hearing how helpless and out of control she had been. Such trying interchanges with her mother had been occurring several times each day, and Susan was growing accustomed to placating her when she was irrationally obstinate. Lesley had been captious and demanding almost from the moment of awakening. After only two weeks, both Susan and Peter dreaded her ceaseless talking and her demands. The therapists, too, who had tended her so faithfully during her long unconscious period, now seemed to find the sessions with Mrs. Frankl difficult, and the neurologist who headed the medical team asked Peter, gingerly, after a long—unnecessarily long—examination of her, whether he had noticed any . . . personality changes.

Peter answered without embarrassment. She had always talked a lot, but he thought she talked even more now; she had never been quite so demanding, although she had leaned that way; she had always been sharp and impatient, but she had never been as angry and irritable as this.

"This could all reflect a high level of frustration," said the doctor, "as well as unresolved anger about the accident or envy of people who don't have her troubles—any number of things. Or it could be physiological. But whatever it is, in my opinion it's likely to go away. What we have to do now is try to increase her strength and reduce her frustration. There's no reason why she couldn't be walking around in a relatively short time, using a walker, and that should help a lot. I can't make any promises, but I wouldn't be surprised if you have her home in a few weeks. I don't know whether she'll ever be one hundred percent. Only when we can do finer testing will we see if there are any worrisome deficits. But for now, confusion and forgetting are to be expected, and you shouldn't worry unduly."

Peter wondered privately whether Lesley's volatility was in part a response to her family's having fallen out of the habit of accommodating her. But he thought it wise to encourage the medical staff in its impression that the difficulties were the result of her injuries.

He did not know how he would bear to have Lesley at home, unable to go anywhere or entertain herself, demanding constant attention. He had contacted a home nursing agency but worried that Lesley would be so difficult that no nurse would stay with her. What would he do then? He might have to take a leave of absence until she got better. And what if she never did? What if he was forced to retire and devote himself full-time to nursing Lesley—and she continued her nonstop talking? In comparison with that, even his work at the firm seemed a life of ease and satisfaction.

"If there is a God," he said to Rabbi Friedman a few days later, "He is unforgiving." On this visit, he and Rabbi Friedman were strolling round the conference table in their usual pleasant room, arm in arm. They had decided that the conversation flowed better when they moved.

"Wait," said Friedman. "She's probably going to improve and get back to normal. Besides, you've got money. You'll pay whatever it takes to have someone look after her—possibly a great deal if she continues to be so impossible. Be sensible, Peter. It's you who are piling on the punishments for your sins. Quitting your job and nursing your wife full-time—completely out of the question. Now, what have you done about getting involved with a new friend, someone you enjoy talking to and like to spend time with? If you're really interested in being good to Lesley, you'll do this because, unless you do, you're not going to be able to stand it. You'll end up leaving her. Could it be that this is what you want? You'll make it all as horrible as possible, so that it will feel as though you were forced to leave her?"

"I've actually imagined having an affair just so Lesley would find out and leave me."

"Don't be so sure she wouldn't choose to overlook it. Many would overlook a great deal to keep their homes and the status of a married woman. Maybe she'd even want this for the children's and grandchildren's sake. Let's turn and go the other direction."

"Women like that don't have such a keen sense of their rights as Lesley. Besides, having deceived her and deprived her of any chance of real love and real respect, it would be too much if I killed the marriage because the whole thing didn't work out for me."

They paused and looked out the window at a group of musicians walking past, carrying instrument cases. "Where is your father's viola?" Friedman asked. "It was a good instrument. Why didn't you ever learn?"

"It needs some work, but I have it. They couldn't afford to give me lessons. He tried to teach me, but he was impatient, and I couldn't get it."

"Too bad. Well, now the topic is your children. That's enough walking, don't you think? It makes me dizzy after a while, going in all those circles. Let's sit for a minute."

The two took their regular places on the chair and the sofa, and Peter laid out the children's history as uncompromisingly, when it came to his own defaults, as a tough-minded prosecutor.

"Rabbi Friedman, I wrecked my children because of my problems with Lesley. It was a bad thing to bring children into such a dishonest marriage. Susan is a good girl, but so unhappy. Louis has some devious quality to him. That was no way to bring up a boy, estranged from his father."

"Well, I have to agree with you that there you're to blame. You had no right to sacrifice your son to your sense of sin—even assuming that self-sacrifice made sense. And why are you so critical of him? There's nothing wrong with working for Hartley Stanton Thornwick."

"Of course, I never talk to him this way. For that matter, until all this happened with Lesley, I never thought things were so bad."

"I don't know if I think so now," said Rabbi Friedman, looking at Peter with rueful skepticism. "I don't know if I believe anything you say."

"You have to believe that things are really as bad as I'm telling you," said Peter. He was teary now about both his children, but mostly about Louis.

CHAPTER 27

ALEXEI MIKHAILOV, TENOR
STUDENT OF CHARLES BRAITHWAITE
VOICE RECITAL
BACH
HANDEL
SCHUMANN
PROKOFIEV

ANNE BRAITHWAITE, PIANO
SUNDAY, SEPTEMBER 15, 2002
4:00 P.M.
ST. URSULA'S EPISCOPAL CHURCH
BROADWAY AND 113TH STREET

Mallory did not want to attend Alexei's recital, but perhaps she had to. Ordinarily, she would have called Susan to talk over such a question, but she and Susan, for the first time in their lives, had not been on comfortable terms for several weeks. First, the Kappell story in the *Gazette* had given her a bad conscience toward Susan, and later, she was offended by Susan's confession that she and Chris had told everyone about Mallory's encounter with Alexei. Not until the day before the recital did she put aside these feelings and call Susan.

"It's going to be an embarrassment," Mallory told her. "Susan, in all likelihood, he can't sing, and I have a strong premonition that he'll have a lot of soulful, sentimental Russian ideas about what music should be. It might be kinder if I didn't go."

"Well, I'm going," said Susan, taking Mallory by surprise. "Sylvie and Alcott asked me to come along with them."

Mallory's embarrassment only increased on hearing that so many of her friends planned to attend. She knew that Alexei had been hired on Alcott's set, but it was nonetheless startling to learn that Sylvie and Alcott would actually show up at his recital, and they must surely understand his recital would be something strange. But that, Mallory realized, was probably the explanation. They loved strange things, those two, and Alcott was probably interested in Alexei just because he was such a peculiar person caught in such a painful and, alas, absurd bind. They were being nice, but Mallory, who could not help liking Alexei and retaining a kind of respect for him, found their willingness to treat him as a curiosity, on display in this ill-judged way, morally suspect. But I, she thought, have no room to look down on anyone else for behaving badly to Alexei.

"I'm curious to hear him," Susan said. "You never told me he was Charles Braithwaite's student."

"He didn't tell me. Anyway, I wouldn't have recognized the name if he had. Who's Charles Braithwaite?"

"Ask your mother, you vulgarian. He's a Met singer, a baritone. He's the kind of singer musicians love, cerebral, romantic at the same time, and really good-looking—irresistible. People come from all over to study with him. I have friends who have friends who know him quite well."

"You're kidding me."

"I'm not kidding you."

"But, you know, none of this changes what I said. I told you, Alexei coaches this guy's kids in chess. It's not as though they have a professional relationship."

"I have a feeling you're right, but we're all going, and it might be a nice gesture on your part, especially since Alexei invited you. Maybe you could make friends again. Actually, looking at it from another angle, your absence might be conspicuous, since we'll all be there."

"I was just having the same thought. I might come. If I do, I'll look for you."

And Susan knew from this that Mallory would be there. Of their circle, in fact, only Chris, who would be in Connecticut with his parents, would be absent. Susan missed Chris on Saturday night but was just as happy to attend the recital without him on Sunday. She hadn't liked Chris's superior air with Alexei that night when Alexei had dropped by, and Chris was no opera fan.

Now that her mother was back at home, even though she was not yet entirely herself, Susan, for her own part, did feel more like herself, less strained than in the long months of Lesley's hospitalization. Things were more relaxed with Chris; Susan thought it a good sign that the two of them felt easy enough to spend a lot of time apart. She still hadn't tried to arrange a meeting between her parents and Chris, which, she knew, was beginning to be a little peculiar. Well, she would get to work on thinking of the right occasion for something like that. Her mother was in no shape to meet anyone just yet, and for the time being that served as a perfectly respectable excuse. She dreaded her father's looking at her and Chris, however, in light of the question of marrying or not marrying. That wasn't how things worked anymore. The decision to marry or not would be the last one they made, following, not preceding, decisions about sharing an apartment, reconciling career plans, and having children. Chris and Susan were so far from having mastered even the first item on this list that her father's way of looking at things would seem absurd. Chris's parents had quite different expectations and perfectly understood the correct sequence of decisions. They didn't expect Chris to marry anytime soon. They wouldn't object but might be a little surprised if he ever wanted to marry Susan. Susan was the academic type, and the Frankls' ample income was just modest comfort compared with the Wylies'. The Wylies were big money, old family.

All the Braithwaites, except for the baby, Gilbert, went early to St. Ursula's on the day of the recital so that Charles and Anne could help Alexei warm up. The little hall, in which small recitals and concerts were often given, had a good warm sound, not too liquid, Alexei thought. He was in voice and unexpectedly excited by the prospect of singing here. He'd given recitals when he was at the Manhattan School of Music that were attended by a dozen or two voice students, and he'd performed minor roles in a couple of amateur productions around the city. But there was nonetheless a thrill in seeing the room fill with people, most of whom he didn't know. Who would come to hear him sing?

From the cramped backstage area, Alexei could look at the audience unobserved. Cora Bledsoe was sitting near the front in an aisle seat, a crutch on the floor beside her, next to Victor Marx. She was apparently telling him something about the program as she tapped it with her forefinger. Alexei had written his own program notes, with Cora's editorial help, and he watched Vic's face hopefully for signs of interest or approval, but he was distracted by seeing Sylvie and Alcott come in with Susan, followed by a group of Charles's other students. There was Mallory, with an older man and woman—her parents, obviously. That was surprising and discomfiting. A priest came backstage and was hailed warmly as "Greg!" by Charles and Anne. Greg the priest then went back to the audience, apparently intending to stay and listen. The Braithwaites seemed to recognize other faces in the audience as well. Had they shanghaied everyone they knew? Then there were all those perfect strangers, people who seemed to have come because they saw one of the home-printed flyers with which Alexei, Stuart, and Ellen had papered the neighborhood. Alexei wondered if he had been right to keep the whole thing secret from his own family and was glad that he had, right or wrong. He grew more and more excited, until he began to tremble a little. Then, suddenly, his limbs went rubbery, and things seemed dreamlike and outsized. He wasn't sure he would be able to sing in this hyperexcited condition. He was still able to observe, however, that his reaction was odd. It was such an informal, really trivial occasion—a neighborhood recital before sixty or seventy people.

Charles and Anne both seemed to know how he felt. Charles came over and said things with an unprecedentedly encouraging smile and then went to sit in the audience, the children on his left, Vic on his right. Alexei had no idea what Charles had said, but he felt the friendly intentions. Anne stood backstage with him, listening to the audience gradually hush. She tucked her music under one arm and held Alexei's hand tightly, smiling—no, she was actually almost laughing for some reason. "Alexei, it's going to be fun," she said, and that got into his brain. Fun? Maybe they were having fun. But if Anne hadn't been there, he would not have known when to walk out. She looked at her watch, then at him, and nodded, and, Alexei leading, they strode onto the stage.

Mallory, Ingrid, and Herb watched him expressionlessly. Ingrid and Herb, unlike their daughter, were serious lovers of bel canto, which gave an interesting edge to their curiosity about this young singer. Ingrid knew the whole of her daughter's history with him, and what Herb didn't know, he suspected.

The stage was small and low and held nothing but a small black Steinway grand, which looked rather scuffed but, Anne had determined, was in good tune. Alexei, by Anne's orders, was dressed in a casual black shirt and jeans, and she had unbuttoned his cuffs and rolled them up a turn or two— a maternal intimacy that she took without asking permission. In the audience, Charles was beginning to feel helpless, more nervous about this recital than about his own performances. He had somehow fallen into an almost desperate yearning for this difficult student to succeed; he was overfond of him. Charles was so tense, in fact, that he was slower than the rest of the audience to realize that Alexei was, as his daughter Jane said later, making magic. His stage demeanor was an unlikely but charming combination of matter-of-factness and excitement, and his wish to be liked came through in an appealing little grin at the sound of the welcoming applause. When his pure opening tones, young and strong, broke on the audience, they were already half willing to be pleased. The hall was so small that every vocal nuance was audible—the shape and texture of every tone, every stirring resonance, all those intimate sensations of the live voice not captured on recordings. And Alexei was near enough to absorb the listeners' reactions and sing in a dialogue with them, adjusting volumes, tone colors, and tempi responsively.

To this sophisticated crowd, it was soon obvious that Alexei's musical grasp and passion were something unusual. People found themselves thinking, before half the program was finished, that this was one of those unpredictable small, memorable occasions that sometimes happen in music, and they began to congratulate themselves on being there. At the close, having believed in what Alexei was singing and fallen a little in love with the young singer, the audience responded with a rush of applause and appreciative murmurs, and people called out casually to him, as though he were an admired and familiar friend.

"I just had a little informal recital in mind," Charles said afterward to Anne, "because I had to see what he'd do in front of an audience. But he turned it into a debut." It was the most charming New York debut either of them could remember, despite the fact that there would be no review in the *Times* or the *Gazette* and no invitations to repeat the performance.

Mallory had been dragged to enough concerts by her parents to realize that, after all, Alexei could sing very well and he was something of a natural on a stage—at least on the rickety little stage at St. Ursula's. Just how well he sang, she estimated by observing her smitten parents' reactions.

Sylvie and Alcott were the first to rush up to grip Alexei's hand and hug him after three encores—when Charles signaled him to stop, fearing vocal strain. They left him to receive more good words from appreciative fellow musicians, strangers, and other happy friends. Susan stood by shyly, waiting her chance, and in a pause darted forward and said, "Alexei, that was an hour I'm going to remember all my life." She was overwhelmed by Alexei, by his musical mind. He was so beyond anything she might have expected. She felt, now, small in comparison with him. She wanted to say more but couldn't find words and stood there looking at him almost tearfully. He shrugged and smiled and glanced around, hoping to find Mallory with Susan, but Mallory had left with her parents. This was disappointing, and he realized that he had had some stupid idea that she would be impressed and change her mind about him.

Cora and Vic were last to come up to congratulate Alexei, having been so affected by the performance that they sat for a while to recover themselves. Cora, for once without a smile, had a faraway look and wet tracks on both cheeks.

"Well," Vic said to her when at last their concert mood began to break.

He liked to listen to music but never knew how to talk about it. "Now what made that so . . . I guess it was all about things I could never put into words."

"Redemption? Love?" asked Cora, a fresh overflow of tears threatening as she spoke.

"Well, yes, maybe," Vic said matter-of-factly, rising at last, holding out a hand to Cora, and nimbly retrieving her crutch despite his eighty years. Cora tended to gush, but, he thought, it came from the heart. "Sometimes we historians make things harder than they have to be, don't we."

"I am *so proud* of you," Cora told Alexei. He was embarrassed by this, as it suggested she had rights in him. Besides, only people in Disney movies talked like that.

Vic was amused at how the sophisticated young Russian recoiled from this socially naïve sentimentality, but of course, Alexei was wrong if he thought her musical judgment was naïve. He put his arm around Alexei's shoulder and said, "You know what she said? She said your singing is about redemption and love."

"Yes?" said Alexei noncommittally, but he smiled at Vic and embraced Cora. He was surprised at how happy he was that the two of them were there.

"Now what happens to that kid?" asked Herb as he, Ingrid, and Mallory strolled down Riverside Drive in the autumn dusk, looking at the remains of a wan sunset across the river. "Just what happens to all that talent? In Morningside Heights—at least in central Morningside Heights, I can't speak for the north or south—he's a star, but there are probably only a half-dozen places in the whole country that can come up with a hundred people who would take the time to go hear an unknown boy—young man—sing that kind of stuff on Sunday afternoon."

Mallory kicked at dry leaves on the sidewalk and agreed somewhat bitterly. Privately, she was acknowledging that all the unpretentious, more or less plebeian sweetness and charm in Alexei that she had held cheap—of course she had—were precisely what had made a room full of people fall in love with his singing. Listening to him and watching him, she had found it hard not to feel all her own longings for him reawaken. After all, she was still lonely; many months later, she had found no one else. Only poor Louis continued to pursue her: he called and they had ridiculous conversations for which she had less and less patience.

Now *there* was an unfortunate comparison. Louis's narrow soul, his pitiful attempt to appeal to the part of her that had responded to Alexei, and only to Alexei—with the size of his bonus, no less. This last thought took Mallory by surprise. Even though she had never really allowed herself to have a love affair with Alexei, it was quite possible that he was the only man

she had ever been in love with. And this thought led her to the equally disquieting one that she had never wanted love before and therefore had never
demanded it. For a moment, she wondered whether it might not be worthwhile to go with Alexei and have those well-known struggles together—of
the young artist and the young journalist, with babies stacked on cots in the
living room—but her father brought her back to reality.

"It's not like it used to be," he was continuing, "before rents got so high,
competition so stiff, and opportunities so rare."

"He's knocking on the door of a mausoleum," Mallory said. " 'Oh,
please, admit me to this tomb so I can be part of this dead enterprise.' And
he can't even get in."

"Not a dead enterprise, Mallory," said Ingrid. "Contracted, maybe, but
such good things don't die."

"Mother, of course they die. There is one classical music radio station
left in all of New York City. All the arts, your kinds of arts, are dying. They
lasted just long enough to sing their death throes in modernism, and now
they're about gone. Your whole life is about ghosts—even your profession.
Psychotherapy is done, because everyone knows physical therapies and drugs
are more successful."

"Sweetie, that's not only a very pessimistic kind of thinking, it's an ill-
informed one, and I don't buy one word of it," said Herb. "These things are
indispensable to a kind of human character that is still around. They'll survive because those people are strong and find what they need eventually, even
if the world doesn't always make it easy for them."

"Daddy, I hate to tell you this, but character types die off, too. Your
kind, the kind that need these things, are a dying breed. My generation has
had to be practical and nose-to-the-grindstone. Rents are too high for us to
indulge ourselves the way all of you did."

"I don't like hearing that I'm a dying breed," said Herb mildly, "and
from my own daughter. It's bad enough knowing that I'm dying, let alone
my breed, too. And I thought you were my breed, to tell the truth."

"I don't know," said Mallory, who in her misery was inclined to strike
out at the pair whom she had always expected to protect her from sorrows.
"Actually, I doubt I'm any more like you than . . . than Louis is like Peter
Frankl, whom I . . . Oh, never mind." She had still not told her parents the
ins and outs of the Kappell fiasco.

"Have you heard from Louis?" asked Ingrid, adding, to sound more
nonchalant, "Look how dark it's getting, and it's only six." She, too, was
pained at the things Mallory was saying but had more of a grasp on what
was behind it than her husband.

"Louis thinks I should marry him," Mallory said. "He told me he makes lots of money. He told me the size of his bonus. He actually thought that might persuade me."

"Well, I thought you just said, more or less, that it would," said Herb. "Isn't that what you meant when you—"

"No, it isn't," Mallory snapped.

"In any event, I still think you underestimate Louis," said Ingrid. "When he tells you about his earnings, he's not trying to impress you with what a wonderful guy he is—I don't think so, anyway. I think he's trying to tell you that he can offer you the setup that you need. He's saying, I can pay for you to have this low-paying, high-status, meaningful career. He thinks it's so obvious how much you need help that he doesn't even need to explain it. He's telling you he'll let you live in some kind of luxury while you do this. You'll have a nanny and a housekeeper."

Mallory petulantly denied this, then said impulsively, "That's what Alexei needs, though, isn't it—some rich woman who'll give him a setup, as you call it."

"Mallory, you're determined to be dense and unpleasant," said Ingrid. "There is nothing wrong with exchanges of assets—emotional, physical, material, intellectual—in marriage, if and when the marriage is built on a moral foundation of love, mutual respect, equality, and all those other things that I hope we taught you to demand. There is everything wrong with mutual exploitation. It offends me to hear you pretending that you don't know the difference."

Mallory was shamed by her mother's rebuke, but the truth was that she really had taken her mother, in speaking of Louis, to be suggesting that it wasn't so awful to offer, and thus by implication to accept, a financial bribe as an inducement to marry, that this was realistic and down-to-earth. Despite her mother's chiding, Mallory was not at all sure that there really was much difference between mutual exploitation and a complementary exchange built on a "moral foundation." People convinced themselves that they loved what they needed or wanted, that was all. They never said "Oh, but our moral foundation is lacking—let's forget it." Mallory herself had always been like that, at least until Alexei came along. The temptation to succumb to her desire for him, contrary to all her interests, was eye-opening. Until that happened, she had thought of love and passion as naturally puny phenomena that had been culturally, conventionally, inflated—or as outmoded emotional by-products of psychological underpinnings that had long since disappeared. These things didn't happen to the post-Freudian, post–sexual revolution generations, who saw through it all and were not about to risk jobs, status, or advantageous liaisons for the sake of venerable myths. As far as Mallory was concerned, the absurd obsessions of stalkers and preteens were all that was left of the driving power of love.

"Understand me," said Ingrid. "I would be upset if you told me you were going to choose someone like Alexei because it would mean you'd have more difficulties in life. Besides, you've told me things about his history and family that make me wonder how easy it would be to be married to him. There has to be a volcano there, with all that trouble behind him and such unusual charm before an audience at his age."

"Believe it or not, he's easy to get along with. Why should charm mean a volcano brewing?"

"It often means an excessive desire to please, or excessive narcissism."

"Not Alexei."

"Or a great deal to sublimate," said Herb.

"That might be true," said Mallory. "Tell me, Mom. Would you be equally upset if I were to fling myself at a limited person like Louis Frankl?"

Ingrid had to give this some thought. "To be frank, probably not—if you mean someone with stable, reliable career plans, even if he wasn't the most poetic and sensitive soul on the block. You know I don't think Louis is as limited as you do. No, I would not be *equally* upset. But I doubt that I'd be happy, either. Surely life will offer you more comfortable choices, maybe someone who has some poetry and a little money or some earning potential both."

"I doubt it. The reason is, I can't compete for the man who has some of both. That man is not going to choose me."

Her parents rushed to assure her that he would, but she persisted. "No, you just described Chris Wylie and Alcott Adams. Chris preferred Susan, because he thought she was deeper than me, and Alcott wanted Sylvie Kimura, who really is braver than I am and smarter than almost everybody and devoted to her writing. He wasn't interested in me."

Ingrid and Herb exchanged glances, horrified at this reasoning, but it was pointless to argue with her when she was in this mood.

"Sylvie and Susan are the luckiest women I know," said Mallory.

CHAPTER 28

"Mother, the hot water is off in my building this morning," said Susan into her cell phone as she turned the corner onto Riverside Drive. "I'm on my way over to take a shower, all right? Don't be scared when you hear me come in."

"I don't know why you think you have to have that apartment anyway, since you can't pay for it and you spend half your time—"

Susan clicked off in the middle of Lesley's reply and pocketed the phone. When she walked into her parents' living room, she was surprised to find Edmond Lockhart with her mother, sipping coffee. Susan hoped her mother would not begin to impose on all their neighbors, but if she had to inflict her personality problems on someone, she could not have made a better choice than Edmond Lockhart. Oddly enough, he looked cadaverous, while Lesley, who was still quite weak and had so recently been near death, appeared glowing and energetic, at least compared with her visitor. She had colored her hair, put on makeup, and regained some muscular strength. Lesley could walk short distances now using only a cane—a walking stick, she insisted everyone call it. The personality problems, however, as the doctors called them, were not improving in tandem with the physical ones. They recommended psychotherapy, but even a hint to Lesley along these lines elicited explosions of wordy rage. Lockhart stood when Susan walked in, although it appeared to take all his strength.

"Hello, darling," said Lesley, who remained seated and held up one arm to invite her daughter's kiss. "I ran into Edmond on my walk with the nurse."

Susan nodded noncommittally to Lockhart, whom she had not seen since the night of his wretched dinner party. She dreaded being trapped into sitting and talking with the two of them and excused herself, sidling out of the room. "I won't interrupt. I'm just here for a shower because the hot water's off in my building, and I have to run."

"How's the dissertation?" Lockhart said with languid politeness as she left.

"Fine, thank you," she said half over her shoulder, mimicking his manner so as to show as little interest as he had.

In the hallway outside Susan's old room, she noticed that the door to her mother's studio was open and peeked in. Perhaps if Lesley began doing some painting, that would siphon off some of her raging verbal torrent. In fact, there was a new painting on the easel, obviously unfinished, in a fairly violent palette unlike Lesley's usual colors. Susan studied it doubtfully, but she was glad that her mother had resumed this outlet. She headed back toward the living room, intending to praise the new work, but paused just around the corner, for she heard them talking about Peter and Aunt Emma, who, Susan knew, was Emma Devereaux. She was also aware that her mother angrily resented her father's escalating involvement with the Devereaux Foundation.

"He's always there," Lesley was complaining. "His secretary told me he was there three hours Tuesday morning and all Thursday afternoon, and half his firm isn't speaking to him, but he's very arrogant and picking fights with everyone. I tell you, I'm worried sick about him." Susan thought, however, judging from the way her mother's voice rose at the end of this speech that she was less worried than wrathful.

"Well," Lockhart began, clearing his throat importantly, "the foundation is a big operation, and Aunt Emma has been running it like a kaffeeklatsch. I'm sorry to keep coming back to this, but I do blame Peter for this and for the damage to the foundation's image. I put him in over there so he'd help me control things . . . get the place under control, and look what he's done instead! They eat cookies and hand out tens of thousands of dollars to crackpots. And to think of his actually taking charge of that seminar and forcing prominent people to associate with quacks and charlatans."

"What? Quacks and charlatans?" asked Lesley, who was still easily confused and got lost when she tried to switch trains of thought.

"One of them is a schoolteacher named Martha Lovett who used to be my aunt's housekeeper, and there's some blogger named Lester Maxwell who considers himself a philosopher and publishes his thoughts on the Internet, where he's developed a little cult following. They're both full-fledged members of the seminar. Maxwell sat right next to Senator Hume. Even the security implications of that . . ."

Lesley was genuinely shocked.

"My dear, I'm truly sorry," Lockhart continued, "to speak this way about Peter, but it's all so frustrating. And it looks as though he'll get away with everything."

"But you shouldn't give up," Lesley said. "You have your aunt to protect. If there's trouble, she'll be blamed."

"Yes, and things are completely out of hand. If he'd just help me convince her to retire! She's far, far too old, and Peter just doesn't control her. He lets her have her way and keeps around all those strange people she put on the board."

"Well, Edmond," Lesley said, pouring coffee into his cup, "you're very nice to put it that way. Some people might think Peter likes having an incompetent at the head of things because then he can run things. He has his own little foundation to play with, doesn't he? He can be a big shot, a do-gooder, and pretend he's some fancy patron of the arts and hang around with famous people."

Lockhart mumbled something here, and Lesley's voice dropped, too. Then Susan heard: "That's a . . . a disturbing idea, Lesley. Perhaps you're right, although I shudder at being forced to be so harsh with her. Maybe there's no other way. On the other hand, quite frankly, I think Peter will be better off if we manage to rein him in a bit as well—despite some collateral damage at his firm. I do so hate to be the cause of the smallest harm to Peter."

"Whose fault is it all? Whose fault?" Lesley cried. "You have your aunt to take care of."

Susan tiptoed back to the shower, so angry and disoriented by what she had heard that she feared she might actually faint. There was a roaring in her ears that wouldn't subside. She soaked a towel in cold water and buried her face in it. In half an hour, she left through the service entrance, calling a listless good-bye to her mother from the hallway.

When Chris came by that evening, Susan was quiet and melancholy, but she told him nothing about the morning's eavesdropping. Nor had she called Mallory or Sylvie to try to talk about it. Except at Alexei's recital, she had seen neither of them for weeks, although she thought that she, and not they, was the one holding back. She spent many solitary hours, therefore, attempting to digest and master what she had overheard, but the more she tried, the more she felt the world ominously off-kilter. Her sense of down and up, right and wrong—everything was skewed.

Even her immediate impulse to tell her father began to seem questionable after four or five hours of brooding on the subject. Susan could not bring herself to expose her mother, especially given her father's apparent temptation to infidelity. He might leave her mother, divorce her. Over and over, this idea registered as by far the most distressing in all her miserable day-long ruminations. At the age of twenty-nine, Susan could not bear the thought of precipitating a breach between her parents, especially of turning her father against her mother.

"You look terrible. What's wrong?" Chris said with a hostile undertone, throwing his coat on Susan's bed, where she lay, trying to read. He was tired of Susan's off moods. As far as he could judge, there was never sufficient reason for them. Or even if there was, there came a point when someone could be more trouble than she was worth.

"Things at home," she said. "I'd rather not go into it." Seeing his impatience, she roused herself to attend to him and the present, which satisfied him, and soon he was reporting on his latest efforts to interest producers in the new play. It was often easier to listen than to ask for Chris's understanding, and in the past, Susan had done so without resentment. Tonight, though, she grew sullen as Chris talked, and her mind wandered.

Then Susan suddenly saw why it all went wrong, why she and Chris weren't interested in listening to each other. It came to her like a revelation. They lived too separately, and that created an atmosphere of stasis, emptiness. When you lived apart, you couldn't develop the kind of domestic intimacy that feeds limitless interest in another person. You needed all those petty interchanges that people always complain about—over meals and toothpaste and wet towels.

"Chris," Susan said, "do you want to move in together?"

Chris took several moments to reply, during which Susan studied his face anxiously. "I've thought about that now and then," he said, "but I've always decided against it."

"Why?"

"Because I'm not sure where we're going."

"Me neither. But that's why I thought maybe we should move in together. I think that's how people used to settle things like that. They just thought: We'll team up. They didn't wait for a train of events to come by and carry them along. They went and bought a ticket."

"Very cute, but it doesn't make sense. You should have a reason to move in together—like you're going to get married and raise kids."

"I don't want to marry you, either. But something's wrong with the way things are."

"What are you saying?"

"Maybe we should break it off."

"You're really crazy, Susan. Are you threatening? Move in or you'll break if off? Why?"

"You're right. That's too extreme. But let's change things."

"Why? Look, you have to say what's on your mind. This is just a guessing game for me—and a pretty upsetting one."

"I have a feeling that we're just hanging out together until you meet someone you really want to marry and settle with, and I don't like it."

"I should've known. Oh, man."

"I know you don't really love me."

"Let me ask you—do you love me, really—whatever way that is? Maybe you don't."

"Maybe you're right."

"That's nice. Do you mean that?"

"I'm sorry. Really I am. But, Chris, don't you have that feeling? That it's either up or out with us?"

"No, I don't. We've only been going together for six months. Where's the fire?"

His eyes, she was startled to see, were filling, and guilt swept over her. She had actually thought that he might be relieved that she offered him an out. She, too, grew teary and in a moment was in his arms. When he left in the morning, she felt closer to him than she ever had but no less convinced that their feelings for each other were not what they should be—what they should be, at any rate, if they ever were going to marry. But why, Susan thought, should marriage be the touchstone for someone like me? How unlikely, when you thought rationally about it, that someone like me should marry.

CHAPTER 29

At 7:00 A.M., Peter left Lesley asleep in their king-size four-poster bed and tiptoed out of the room. Since her return from the hospital, he had a hard time falling asleep with Lesley because he didn't trust her body. He doubted that it could get itself asleep and awake in the ordinary way without going wrong. All the pills she took, all the doctors' sober cautions, reinforced such doubts. The result was that he, and not Lesley, had developed insomnia. He took hours to fall asleep; he awoke at any noise and at the earliest light, alert to danger. Today, as always, he retrieved the paper from the hallway and joined Louis in the kitchen. Louis, who had still not found himself an apartment and did not seem to be looking for one terribly hard, made coffee, and they each poured bowls of cereal. This private, shared breakfast had become a routine, and as a result, Peter thought, he had had more conversations with Louis in the past month or two than in the preceding decade. He had gone out of his way to show a respectful interest in Louis's work during these breakfasts, and their talk had progressed from a few hesitant remarks about headlines to what were for Peter eye-opening political and social debates that sometimes lasted as long as ten minutes. Louis had quirky opinions, from Peter's point of view: he disliked prisons, the death penalty, the income tax, and gun control.

This morning, Louis took the Business and Sports sections while Peter looked at the front page, the Arts section, and then the City section, where, on the front page, there was another of Kappell's "Uptown, Downtown" columns. Peter was always tense when these appeared, but none of them had reverted to the subject of the seminar—until this one, in an "Afternote" that appeared at its foot.

> To revisit a subject that was discussed here some time ago, here is an update on the Devereaux Foundation, which has funded a seminar at Columbia University of academic and political superstars, charged it with studying international terrorism, and made sure it has a questionable political tilt. The good news is that Peter Frankl, whose chairmanship of the seminar was unwise and improper, has resigned. The bad news is that he's still overseeing matters at the Devereaux Foundation, where, according to informed sources, senility, venality, stupidity, dishonesty, and plain childishness and foolishness allow him a clear playing field. Also, Columbia needs to review the membership rostrum of that seminar carefully. Enough said.

"My God," said Peter.

"What?" asked Louis.

Peter shoved the paper across the table, and Louis read.

"Huh," said Louis with the vacant, hostile look Peter had first seen on his face in adolescence. For once, Peter was sure that he was not its object.

"It's my fault," said Louis. "It was my idea to call Mallory and put them on to the story."

"It's not your fault. Possibly it's Mallory's fault."

"She can't stop him."

"At any rate, she *didn't* stop him. Just after the first seminar meeting, she called people at the Devereaux Foundation, and obviously she fed Kappell information. I don't know exactly what she told him, but she was at least working with him then."

"I don't believe it," Louis said, turning pale.

"Emma Devereaux and a couple of others told me she called them."

"I knew she was tricky, but I can't believe she'd mess *you* up."

"That's probably going too far. I don't think she meant to hurt me."

"I'm gonna call her."

"I wouldn't. Leave it alone, Louis. What's she going to tell you?"

But Louis had made up his mind. He went to his room and called Mallory, even though it was not yet 8:00. She was sleeping.

"Did you know about this Kappell column?" he asked.

Mallory recognized Louis's voice. "What Kappell column?" she asked. She sounded hoarse and groggy.

"He's got another attack on my father and the Devereaux Foundation people." Louis read Kappell's "Afternote" to her.

"Oh God. Look, I can't go along with his attacking your father, but he may really be on to something with the people at that foundation."

"No, he's not. You don't know anything about it."

"I know a little. He probably knows more."

"He's going after them because someone wants him to. This doesn't make sense otherwise. You know that. Don't get tricky with me, Mallory. I know you too well, and I'm better at it than you."

"*You* don't know anything about the Devereaux Foundation."

"As a matter of fact, I do. I've known about it for years, from my dad. You've made a big mistake with this. These people don't deserve what you're doing to them. Stop it, Mallory, because it's not nice."

"Louis, it's not me. I didn't even know he was going to—"

But Louis had hung up. Mallory had never known Louis to be angry before. He sounded almost contemptuous—and she had always taken him to be amoral. Now even Louis was her moral superior. This reversal of their previous roles humiliated Mallory. At the same time, she thought it unfair that for such a small crime she should appear so hugely guilty and feel so immensely unworthy. And why wasn't time curing the whole problem, as it cured other problems in Mallory's life? What was *she* supposed to have done about the whole thing, anyway?

A few days later, on her way to meet Merrit Roth for coffee, Mallory resolved to tell her the entire story, hoping Merrit might find a way to absolve her former student. Perhaps she would tell Mallory that such was real life, filled with moral ambiguity, that there was no way to keep your hands clean, that Mallory should not worry so much. Mallory had always greatly liked and admired Merrit Roth, so brilliant and sparkling, so pretty, and had written one of her best undergraduate papers for her.

Mallory was waiting in the café and greeted Merrit warmly when she arrived, looking harried, with a stain of curdled milk on her shoulder. No, Merrit said, she wasn't teaching at Columbia, hadn't taught anywhere for more than three years, during which she had gotten married and had two children, but she was an editor for a well-known online magazine, *Tablet*. Mallory thought that Merrit looked tired and thin but happy; and somehow their roles were reversed. Mallory, with her serious *Gazette* job and careful grooming, felt older and more respectable, even though Merrit was a dozen years her senior and had a couple of famous books to her credit and a big name. Writing for a scrappy online journal like *Tablet* hardly fit Mallory's image of her former professor. It was frightening to think that marriage and the family could do this even to someone like Merrit Roth. Merrit made it easy for Mallory to approach the delicate subject of Howard Kappell and the *Gazette* by mentioning at the outset that she had seen all Mallory's articles. She listened sympathetically and encouraged Mallory in her hopes of moving into more significant subject areas, and she looked serious when Mallory began telling the Devereaux Foundation story.

"A while back a friend called me and told me his father was going to organize an important faculty seminar at Columbia, and he suggested I come and write a story about it. When I asked the *Gazette* for permission, they said a senior reporter was already in charge but I could go and work with him."

"Howard Kappell?" said Merrit. "I've seen a couple of articles he wrote about it."

"What a memory you have."

"He did something on it just a few days ago, and I happen to know Howard, and . . . But go on."

Mallory described the inaccuracies in Howard Kappell's original story, the prejudice Kappell had displayed talking about Frankl after the seminar, her own relations with Peter Frankl, and her respect for him. She related her conversations with the Devereaux people and how she had finally begged off any further involvement. And she told what Louis Frankl had said to her after the second Kappell piece on the subject had appeared a few days ago. She wanted Merrit to know everything so that she could size up the situation correctly and give her absolution.

"He's sort of a slimy guy, Howard," said Merrit.

"How well do you know him?"

"I used to know him pretty well, but we're out of touch now. In fact, I always used to run into him at the Smith-Smythes', who, I see, are part of the seminar. I don't see them anymore, either."

"He never mentioned knowing them. How strange."

"He knows everyone. He wouldn't publish this stuff if he hadn't convinced himself there's something to it, but that doesn't mean there *is* something to it. He's a crooked guy, in my opinion. He twists things."

"I'm beginning to appreciate just how true that is. He should have told me he knew them."

"They're big on the terrorism circuit. They're always involved. Last fall they came out with a strange essay in the *LRB* that comes awfully close to justifying the Palestinian suicide bombers and al-Qaeda, too. It's all odd," said Merrit. "So what do you propose to do about all this?"

"Me? What *should* I do? I don't know of anything I can do."

"Don't you want to try to set the record straight?" asked Merrit.

"You don't understand, Professor Roth. This is the real world. Kappell is not going to sit back and let me call him a sleaze. Nobody at the *Gazette* pays any attention to what I think. I could damage my whole career over something like this. I have to ask whether this is a cause that's really worth it. I don't know any reason to get behind the Devereaux Foundation people."

"But you have reason to question Kappell's motives for maligning them. And what about your best friend's father, whom you so admire? Look, Mallory, I'll confess *I* have something of a personal interest in this situation. My second book, the one that got the Bridgehaven Prize, was written on a Devereaux Foundation grant. I know those people—at least I knew the ones who were running things then. They're a little bit crazy, and sometimes they fund garbage, but as far as I'm concerned, overall they succeed better than anyone. I'm appalled at what Howard is doing to them. Someone should write something on the other side of this."

"Professor Roth, the other problem with this is that there's no percentage in arguing with spin," Mallory said. "All you can do is counterspin. It's degrading and futile."

"How can a professional journalist function with so little faith in the printed word—and the truth? I'm not sure that at your age you've earned the right to be as cynical as that, Mallory." Merrit was smiling, but Mallory sensed a judgment behind the friendly words. She was dejected not only at having failed to get absolution from Merrit Roth, but in learning that even she was too interested in this situation to be genuinely objective.

"I have to try to think this through," Mallory said. "Is it okay if I call you again?"

Merrit shook Mallory's hand warmly. "Of course! I hope you do because I'll be curious to know what you decide to do. Feel free to disregard anything I say, too, Mallory. You're the one on the line."

CHAPTER 30

Hilda arrived late at Dr. Stoller's office. This had happened only twice before: the first time when she got stuck underground in the subway fire of 1991 and the second in 1996 when she was in a meeting at the mayor's office that went on for an extra hour. On those two occasions, Hilda had finally arrived at Dr. Stoller's office panicked and crying, and there was much analysis of how needlessly strong, how incapacitating, her emotions had been.

Today, Hilda expected to feel the same way and geared herself for frantic emotions, but she could come up with nothing more than a little tame regret about keeping the doctor waiting. She had simply gotten interested in a story on the Arts page at breakfast and, feeling relaxed, had lost track of the time.

"I know what you're going to say," Hilda began affably. "You're going to say that it's possible to be self-defeating by being overrelaxed as well as by overreacting."

"Self-defeating? What was self-defeating?" (Vät väss sĕlff-dĕffĕtĭnk?)

"Missing part of my session, of course, the most important thing in my day, the thing that gives my life shape and meaning."

"Hmm. Not really."

"Oh, so we're back on that kick."

"It is not a kick, but a fact. There was nothing self-defeating in this. It just didn't mean very much to you to get here on time this morning, which is fine, quite as it should be. I don't know why you insist on continuing to come at all, especially when you're going to need the money to pay for a new apartment."

"I'm probably going to be homeless. I can't find anything affordable in Morningside Heights."

"Fortunately, once you stop analysis, you'll be able to afford much more, won't you? My goodness, let's calculate—you pay me how many thousands every month?"

"I thought we agreed that I'm probably going to lose my job. Anyway, I'm not stopping."

"Very soon now, you are. Let's set a date, in fact."

"Oh, I suppose we should," Hilda said, suddenly straightforward. Both of them found it refreshing to hear her speak unaffectedly. "If I don't get fired, maybe I really could have a nice place," she continued after a silence, "which is at least some compensation for the fact that I'd be alone there— not that there's anyone I would have the remotest interest in living with. Today's lesbian women are so conformist and conventional. They were cheerleaders in high school, and now they want to have two kids and go to religious services. None of them want to get mixed up with someone weird like me. They say lesbianism is normal—which, to me, is like a kleptomaniac insisting that he's just a regular guy with an unusual hobby."

"Lesbianism is innocent—not like stealing."

"But that doesn't mean it's normal, for heaven's sake—except in the minds of people who think that everything abnormal is bad. To me it's abnormal *and* innocent. I don't want to be normal. Not me—no way."

"This is the new line of defense? Before, you were alone because your choices were socially unacceptable. But now you're alone because they are so acceptable. The result is the same, though—the world imposes loneliness on you. But despite your excuses, you're changing recently. Your life is different."

Dr. Stoller was exaggerating, inflating two or three unsatisfactory encounters into something significant—and casting her out at forty-eight, an age when even social butterflies and mothers of six and ex-cheerleaders found it hard not to be lonely. Like many other psychoanalysts, she was so satisfied with her narrow little insights that she preferred not to perceive that Hilda had shed her fear but remained in isolation. Indeed, maybe all that had happened was that Hilda had learned not to be afraid of what was, unavoidably, her permanent condition. Hilda couldn't convince Dr. Stoller of this, however, so she changed the subject.

"I've had a dream so crass and obvious, I'm ashamed to tell it."

"Yes?"

"I buy a hot dog at the corner stand down by the Devereaux Foundation, and it is indescribably delicious."

"Hm."

"I'm walking along the street eating this, when Julia, the one I had such a crush on in college, Julia walks up to me and looks at me very oddly, very ambiguously, intensely. I can't figure out what she's thinking. I wonder if maybe she disapproves of my eating on the street."

"Then?"

"That's all I remember."

"So what comes to mind?"

"Oh, come on, Dr. Stoller! When something is this obvious, we don't need to beat around the bush."

"You mean hot dog as phallus?" asked Dr. Stoller.

"Yes. In the dream I'm acquiring one by primitive means. What else?"

"What else? Precisely! What else comes to mind?"

"The Devereaux Foundation meeting."

"There would, perhaps, be quite a delicious treat there?"

Hilda was mentally writing diacritical markings for "Děr vút bē kvīt" when she thought, with a start, Frank-I—frank. Good Lord!

Dr. Stoller said nothing, but, Hilda thought, her silence was insufferably smug.

"So aren't you going to bring up this new newspaper article?" Hilda went on, so as to cut off any aggravating discussion. "Now I really am worried about us all, but not as worried as you would think I should be—at least not for my own sake. I do worry somewhat—actually a great deal—about Peter and Emma. Let's talk about that, Dr. Stoller. Why is it that I'm not scared for myself when this disaster is looming over me? Joblessness, homelessness—it doesn't scare me a bit."

"Because you would like to have all your troubles moved from inside to outside? Because the trouble satisfies your masochism? Maybe was even caused by it, at least partly?"

"Ah!" Hilda cried, clapping her hands on her cheeks. "Oh, it's so true. I'm going to go right home and become terribly upset."

"That would be wise," said Dr. Stoller gravely. She knew that Hilda's pretended shock was intended to conceal the real thing.

Hilda rode home impatiently on the M4, although usually she savored the trip, delighting in the freedom to let her mind wander without feeling that she should be doing something else. She got out at 113th Street and went home to begin reading fifteen or twenty proposals that Miss Devereaux had handed to her at their last meeting. But when she sat at her desk, she felt so melancholy that she could not work. This was unprecedented.

Usually, Hilda was happiest cozying at home with a box of chocolate truffles, reading proposals, feeling both useful and safe from calls, visitors, or other intrusions. But now, she thought, calls or visitors wouldn't be so unwelcome. She was restless and lonely and, as she had predicted, frightened of the threats looming over her. Only the urgency of a deadline kept her reading until almost 5:00 P.M., when she decided to get some air. She pulled on her coat, put $20 and her keys in her pocket, and went outside, where it had grown cloudy. A strong, chill wind blew off the river and pushed at Hilda's back, as though urging her toward Broadway to buy chocolates at Mondel's. At the door of the shop, though, she changed her mind. She trudged back down 114th Street to Riverside Drive, head lowered against the wind. Her eyes teared, her nose dripped, and she dabbed at them now and then with a small linen handkerchief edged with lace. The resemblance in this to weeping began to make her feel like weeping.

This latest batch of proposals was discouraging, she thought, striding along the promenade, graying locks rising high around her ears with every gust of wind; many were offbeat and quirky, and the rest were trite. She didn't feel like recommending any of them to Miss Devereaux, especially after that second article in the *Gazette* and especially while Edmond Lockhart continued to perch himself at his aunt Emma's elbow, like some overgrown vulture.

One of the proposals was about mice—painting mice. A lady wanted a travel grant to go to South America to paint the mice there. Then there was a composer who needed funds to work on a suite for whistle, sticks, and tin cans—completely tonal, though. Hilda wondered if the foundation wasn't acquiring a reputation for giving only rare, eccentric grants, and whether that wasn't her fault. She was the one who had insisted they offer two years' support to the man writing a book on haunted houses of Marin County. Although she had never funded anything sillier than that, it seemed all too possible that a few odd whims of hers were going to cost everybody their positions and reputations. She should have talked to the *Gazette* reporters when they called and straightened them out. She had trapped the Devereaux people, like dolphins with tuna fish, in the net of her own madness.

Hilda felt all but desperate to find some valuable new work, something to prove that the foundation was worthwhile and save her friends. Wasn't there anyone who needed money to make something true or good or beautiful? Perhaps she and Miss Devereaux no longer knew how to find or attract the people—for there must be such people—who were doing things they wanted to help, people who would not otherwise get help. Perhaps Hilda should have focused on this growing difficulty earlier. She had not noticed, until just this moment, that their proposals had declined so seriously in quality. Hilda clumped briskly south on the promenade, and then north again, puzzling over these matters. When she got home, an hour later, it was nearly dark and she had an idea—quite an interesting, hopeful little idea.

At her stoop, she rang Susan Frankl's bell and was pleased to find her at home. Susan was equally pleased to see Hilda and made a nice cup of hot tea, and they had a long, confidential talk.

hris was bringing Susan home to meet his parents in Connecticut. On a clear Saturday morning in early October, they drove for two hours, at midday arriving at a large house set in the midst of rolling green acres. His parents were often in Manhattan during the week now, but as a boy, all through his boarding school years, Chris had thought of this house as his real home. It was located outside an old Connecticut town in a neighborhood filled with similar houses, each surrounded by acres of green, tree-shaded lawn from which the dead leaves had been scrupulously raked, it seemed, within the last half hour. The quiet was such that one could not imagine the leaves had been blown away by any of those loud machines.

Susan looked especially pretty, but she felt more calm than she thought she should. On the other hand, Chris did not seem to think that this meeting meant much, and perhaps that was what made her calm. As far as he was concerned, the purpose of the trip was only to satisfy Susan's curiosity about how he had grown up, among what sort of people. If they decided to move in together in a year or so, at least his parents would know who she was, and it would all be easier. It was just an afternoon in the country, that's all, which he took as lightly as he took most things.

Chris's father was older than Susan's—late sixties, perhaps, slightly sunburned, with receding white hair; and his mother, who had that perfectly natural-looking streaked blond hair that so many rich suburban ladies resort to in middle age, was at least ten years younger. She was thin, wore a silk-tweed sweater over capri pants, and on her fingers had sparkling rings that Susan knew were "good," as her own mother would have put it. Mrs. Wylie's eyes were sharp, her smile of greeting ever so faintly sarcastic, and she looked at Susan without speaking. Mr. Wylie, on the other hand, grinned and spoke heartily.

"Chris," he said loudly and with a rising inflection: Chris?

Chris kissed his mother, who then spoke to him. "Do you think Susan is hungry?"

"Are you hungry?" Chris asked Susan, although she stood between him and his mother.

"A little."

"Mariposa is making lunch for us," Mrs. Wylie told Chris, "and it'll be ready soon. Why don't you show your friend around?" Her walk, as she left, was graceful in a slightly mannered way.

"Well, Susan," said Mr. Wylie, "you and Chris met . . ."

"At Yale," she said with a friendly smile, and noticed that Mr. Wylie was obviously reassured by the Yale connection and indifferent to the friendliness.

"In my day, you couldn't meet girls at Yale," he said. He laughed a CEO laugh, Susan thought, to show that the king was relaxed and everyone could stop worrying, and then he disappeared into a room off the high-ceilinged hallway in which they were standing. Susan took it that conversation was not intended to begin until lunch.

Chris's room was large and opulent and had the same pored-over look as her own parents' apartment, with a painting and curios that were carefully uncoordinated with the wallpaper, draperies, and carpet. There was a four-poster bed and a breakfast table, with overstuffed chairs at either side, before a window that overlooked the lawn behind the house. It was all pretty in its way but held little trace of the boy Chris might have been—except for a single photo, which Susan studied with great interest, that showed him at about four on a bicycle with training wheels—or of the man he had become, for that matter. Curiously, aside from this absence of the artifacts of childhood in Chris's room, Mrs. Wylie's style and taste were not fundamentally different from Susan's mother's. Could it be that Chris saw something of his mother in Susan? The thought was not pleasing.

"Where are all your trophies and pennants and stuffed animals and kid books?" Susan asked affectionately. "I get to see all that, don't I?"

"Packed away somewhere, I guess," he said. "Mother no doubt thought she'd get me to come home more often if I had a grown-up room to stay in."

"That's unusual," said Susan, betraying her discomfort with the coolness of this house and its inhabitants in spite of herself. She hoped that she would find a way to like his parents before she was forced to give him her opinion.

"Not really," said Chris.

Maybe he already knows, thought Susan, that I don't much care for them. "Show me the library and the garden," she said.

They were standing in the garden, breathing in the scents of earth and vegetation, when a maid called them in, and they found lunch served in the dining room, although, as Mrs. Wylie said, they often had lunch in the breakfast nook because it was cozier. The dining room was, in fact, rather grand for the occasion, but the table was pretty, set with brightly colored Japanese porcelain. Mariposa served.

Over lunch, the Wylies asked what Susan's father did and showed, with slight nods, that they knew his eminent firm. Susan withheld the further information that would cue them to his importance there and in the city bar, too, put off by what seemed to her condescension and arrogance. Chris, however, added these tidbits to her pleasant but brief responses to their inquiries. They relaxed further, and Mrs. Wylie, finally, spoke to Susan.

"And what do you do? Are you in theater, like Chris?" she asked, holding her sarcasm in abeyance out of respect for Peter Frankl's prestigious partnership.

"No, I'm in graduate school in musicology, writing my thesis now."

"I've never heard of anyone studying musicology," said Mrs. Wylie, slipping back into a slightly mocking tone.

"Maybe that's good. Maybe it means there's a shortage of musicologists," Susan said, despite feeling instinctively that jokes would be disruptive of the Wylie household's domestic culture. If Mrs. Wylie heard Susan, however, she showed no sign, just smiled the same faintly snide smile before, during, and after Susan's words; Mr. Wylie gave a brief, deflating, executive chuckle. Chris gave Susan a sarcastic, questioning look. He didn't recognize the rebellion in her joke, she realized; he thought it was just a social mistake—a piece of nerdiness. She felt both foolish and frustrated. The rest of the meal was spent balancing on the brink of dangerous, truth-screaming silences. Chris and his father traded enough small talk about the Yankees to prevent the pauses growing dangerously long. At one point, there was a temporary release of tension when Mrs. Wylie thought to ask Chris if he'd picked up a painting she was having framed in the city. He hadn't, and this permitted an almost normal interchange of mild accusation and apology.

"They're not just ordinarily boring, you know," Susan told Chris later, when the two of them were alone in the library, and she asked him right out how those two people had ever produced him. She was surprisingly aggressive in her dislike.

"You don't need to tell me that they're limited," he said. "Do you think I'm blind? They're a pair of blank checks."

"And why doesn't your father write one to produce your play?"

"No way. He hates what I do."

"I've always wondered about that. You never tell me anything at all about them."

"Look, Susan," he said, all at once becoming cheerful, "the easiest answer to your question is that they *didn't* produce me. I was a mess growing up, and they just paid the bills for people who would straighten me out. I had nannies and shrinks and teachers and lessons, and my parents just kind of managed the staff. They're good at delegating. If it wasn't for all the shrinks and hired help, I would have ended up as nutty as my sister."

"You never even told me before that you had a nutty sister."

"Why should I?"

"Because I have no way of understanding you if you don't tell me the basic facts of your life. Chris, a lot of the time, I get the idea that you wish I'd stop trying to make a love affair out of our relationship, but I don't know what you'd prefer." Susan knew that these words might force a breach, but she felt reckless. Chris grew either thoughtful or angry, she could not tell which.

"What a bad idea it was to bring you out here," he said at last.

"Because you don't want me to know your family?"

"You're going to run out on me. Just don't spout psychobabble at me about it."

"I'm not—unless you want me to. Not at all."

"I think you are. Look, this is not the time and place to try to have a serious talk. Wait'll we're out of here."

Susan accepted a moratorium, knowing they would have a long drive back to the city.

The additional hour that they spent in the Wylies' home seemed like many times that to Susan, and as the time to leave grew near, she felt like a drooping plant that someone had watered. When they actually stood at the door, she watched herself, helplessly, grow lively and overtalkative, in something like an ecstasy of hope and warmth at the prospect of escape. She so sparkled in her good-byes that she actually elicited an answering glimmer in Mr. Wylie's eye. Mrs. Wylie, once more, did not speak and smiled an almost imperceptibly sarcastic good-bye. When they were in the car, driving off,

Chris admitted that it was deadly in his parents' home, deadly, dull, and empty.

He drove fast through the countryside, and they both enjoyed the sensation of flying away. But Susan again broached the subject of his having never told her anything about his family or his past, and of their never discussing what they could or should mean to each other. Although they talked about these things, with long pauses, for most of the drive home, Chris's contributions were languid and forced, and they reached no conclusions or insights. He kept reverting to good cheer, which Susan now recognized as a dodge. Without it, he got slow and dull in speech but drove faster than ever.

Traffic was heavy on the Cross Bronx Expressway, and it was dusk when they exited onto the Henry Hudson. As they joined the four-lane phalanx of traffic surging south along the western edge of Manhattan, the cars, close and fast moving, made Susan think of stampeding bison and movies in which Indians ran herds over cliffs to kill them.

"We're coming up on the place where your mother was in the accident, aren't we," said Chris.

His tone of voice, full of good-natured interest, was jarring to Susan and somehow made her fearful. She gripped the seat belt with one hand and the edge of her seat with the other.

"Chris, you're doing eighty. Slow down. Can't we get off this? Let's take Broadway down."

"Are you out of your mind? That would take hours. We're going to exit in a couple of minutes. Relax. You're just getting upset remembering your mother's accident. You're absolutely safe. I'm a really good driver."

"I wish you'd go slower."

"It's safer to keep up with the flow of traffic."

"You're going faster than the traffic."

Chris glanced at Susan. Her cheeks were wet and her face distorted with suppressed sobs.

"Susan, calm down! Look there's the Riverside exit. We're almost—"

"Take it! Take Riverside, Chris!" Susan cried.

"Don't be ridiculous, Susan. Jesus. Just a couple of minutes and we're off this thing. Everything is perfectly all right."

Chris kept looking over at Susan, almost curiously. Later, neither of them could say how it happened, but they knew that Chris's front bumper tapped the rear bumper of the car in front of him, and both cars swerved. It was frightening, especially at such high speed, but no harm apparently was done yet. Then the other driver motioned at Chris, but Chris ignored him and half smiled at Susan, who wept silently and gripped the armrest. Still gesturing and looking furious now, the other driver maneuvered his way behind Chris's car and accelerated enough to hit its rear bumper with considerable force. Chris's car struck the car ahead of him, and there was an instant pileup. Air bags exploded open, and in what seemed only seconds police and ambulance workers were swarming over the scene. Susan and Chris were rushed to St. Luke's. Chris refused to see a doctor and seemed both unharmed and unfazed by the collision. The police concluded that he was a victim of road rage and were not inclined to be hard on him. Susan was being examined when Peter arrived, white-faced even though he had been told that she seemed to be only shaken up and bruised.

"This is a bad way to meet, Mr. Frankl," Chris began in the waiting room. Peter, who was at least four inches shorter than Chris, looked up at him with a not very friendly expression. Chris had a cell phone in one hand and a diet soda in the other. "I don't want to make excuses," said Chris, "but I think it happened because Susan got so hysterical."

Peter listened coldly to Chris's account of Susan's growing terror and then grew serious at the story of the assault by the other vehicle. "You told all that to the police?"

"Yes, but obviously I didn't get the license plate number, so I doubt there's anything anyone can do."

Peter thought that Chris wasn't necessarily at fault, but he still felt unfriendly.

"Where had the two of you been, anyway?"

"We went to visit my parents in Connecticut. Just a little drive to the country. Anyway, I have to take off now. I was just waiting for you to get here."

Peter was taken aback. He was leaving? While the doctors were still examining Susan after an accident in his car?

"Daddy, let's don't tell Mother," Susan said when she came out, a bandage across one cheekbone. The doctors had said she should see her own doctor immediately if she experienced any dizziness or headaches, but they thought she was all right. "She doesn't need to know. I'm fine. I'll say I got the bruise in a cab or something."

Peter, who had already made up a story to tell Lesley about the telephone call and why he had to go out, agreed readily. Lesley had recuperated well, but so much of her continuing disability was emotional that a shock might set her back.

"Where's Chris?" Susan asked, looking around the waiting area at the emergency room.

"He said he had to go. You didn't even know he was leaving?" Peter's evident dislike and disapproval of Chris anguished Susan.

"He was upset, Daddy. Don't get the wrong idea. He behaved completely responsibly."

"Maybe I'm just a nervous father, Susan," he said, "but I'd bet a lot that guy is missing a screw somewhere. And if you were so scared on the Henry Hudson, why the hell didn't he get off when you asked him to?"

"You're judging him under the worst possible circumstances. For my sake, please try to be a little more understanding."

There was a little fire in Susan's voice that Peter had never heard before, and he decided he'd better back off. He frowned at her, then said, "C'mon, honey, I'll take you home."

Peter tried to believe that Susan had been so afraid of an accident that she had caused one, but he couldn't fully credit this theory. Chris's calm indifference—about Susan, about the shocking vehicular assault on the Henry Hudson—told him that there was something more to this. On the other hand, there really were people out there committing murderous acts with their cars, and maybe that explained the whole incident.

Such things happened in part because the Henry Hudson was just a bad stretch of highway. Why, back in the thirties, when it was built, the speed limit was probably only forty miles an hour, and there were probably a tenth as many cars then, maybe even fewer. Driving now was an endless series of negotiations over road rights, in which the borderline insane struggled to enforce their need for superiority. No wonder so many of them lost control in their cars. They were just like the World Trade Center murderers. They all killed people they thought had put them down. They had no more reason than that. Osama bin Laden was not so hard to understand. It had nothing to do with religion. He had a few loose screws, and it was perfectly obvious why. The guy was one of fifty-four kids, for heaven's sake, of a man who kept a stable of wives. Even dogs don't have fifty-four puppies. He must have felt like dust under his father's feet or more likely, fatherless. There certainly wasn't any dad taking little Osama out to play catch in an oasis or something. How was a boy supposed to grow up normal when his father was a father like a stud horse is a father?

Peter might not have the greatest relation with Louis, but at least he had played catch with him. Every Sunday Peter had taken him to Little League, and every summer they went to Yankees games—because the boy was crazy about that stuff. Unfortunately, Peter himself not only had no interest in sports, but looked down on them, an attitude that Louis had surely detected. And he had always been a little down on Louis, too. Yes, granted,

Louis was no Susan, but a lot of people would be very happy to have Louis for a son. Good athlete, MBA from Harvard. From this thought, however, Peter all too easily recalled things about Louis that he disliked—and they added up to his being his mother's son. Perhaps some of his resentment against Louis was really resentment of the mother who wanted him for herself. But at least, Peter thought, I took him down to the park. I did do that. And I was faithful to his mother.

Edmond Lockhart, with Burke on his leash, fell in step with Peter as he turned the corner on Riverside Drive. Lockhart's expressionless face shaped itself into a sardonic smile at the sight of Peter, and a manic glint shone from his eye.

"So the *Gazette* isn't going to let you off easy, I see. I told you, Peter. I don't like to say so, but you've brought all this on yourself. You're very Jewish, you know. You don't think so, but you are."

"What are you talking about?"

"I think you know what I'm talking about. You were in a situation where you had to rise above your ethnicity, and you failed."

"You're an embarrassment, Lockhart," Peter replied. He waved Lockhart into the elevator and, to avoid a tête-à-tête, let the door shut and waited for the next car. Herb Holmes appeared at his side just as it arrived.

"So what do you know, Peter?" Herb asked with neighborly indifference.

"Oh, a few lines of poetry," Peter replied, and he recited as they rode up:

> *For shameless Insecurity*
> *Prays for a boot to lick,*
> *And many a sore bottom finds*
> *A sorer one to kick.*

"No doubt about that," said Herb.

CHAPTER 32

When her father had gone, Susan called Chris and said that the accident was her fault.

"Remember what you said before about my acting things out in little dramas?" Chris replied.

"What are you saying?"

"Nothing. I was just thinking about how wild it was that I actually drove you to Connecticut to meet my parents."

"I don't see any minidrama in that," Susan said. "Are you coming over later?" She had told her father that he would, but she knew that he might not. She asked timidly so that he wouldn't think she was demanding that he attend her—the way her own mother demanded her father's attentions. She and Chris had a loose connection that did not easily accommodate the idea of obligation, even under the present circumstances. Therefore, she now made a point of showing that she made no claim to his company, and he made one of refusing to visit her at a time when ordinary consideration made it obligatory.

"I don't know. I might stop by."

"Fine," she said. "Whatever." Of course, he was not coming. She was now careful to speak in the casual, self-possessed tones that she knew put him at ease.

Peter called his daughter several times that evening, stopping only when Susan told him that she wanted to go to sleep. He dropped by early the following morning, Sunday, to check on her, carrying the Sunday paper and a satchel of magazines and books to entertain her that he had selected from his own shelves. He had in his pocket a pair of eyeglasses that he had had made up for her that week, and he showed her that he was putting them in the drawer of her nightstand. Louis came, too, about an hour after Peter. Both Peter and Susan were surprised at how shaken Louis was by the news of Susan's accident. He's better than that Chris fellow, anyway, thought Peter. He's here, after all, and he cares enough about his sister to be a little upset. Nothing wrong with that.

Peter called home from Susan's to check on Lesley, and the housekeeper told him that the gentleman next door had taken Mrs. Frankl out for a walk.

"Edmond Lockhart?"

"Yes, I believe that's his name. The man across the hall."

"Lockhart, right. He's pushing her in her chair?"

"Yes. I see them out the window right now, going down the promenade. Don't worry. It's not so chilly, and she's all wrapped up. She needs to get out sometimes," said Yolanda, who was feeling slightly defensive.

"Of course. I'm just surprised that he'd do it, Yolanda. That's absolutely fine. Will you tell her I called and hope she had a good walk? I'll just stay here at Susan's, since Lesley is out, and visit for a while. Tell her she can call me at Susan's if she needs me, all right?" Peter was pleased at how this had worked out, but Susan seemed less than well pleased when he told her.

"There's nothing to worry about," Peter told her. "She doesn't even need anyone with her. She's fine, sweetie, your mother's just fine." Susan responded, however, with only a tight little pull of the lips.

"Now I'm going to ask . . . ," Peter began when the two of them had settled comfortably at Susan's table while Louis turned on the television to watch a game. Peter felt more at home in Susan's apartment than he did in his own, and that freed his tongue. "What's up with this Chris guy? Are you serious about him or what?"

"You're being unfair to dislike him without really knowing anything about him," Susan said. Despite her own misgivings, she was irked that Peter had any. He probably blamed Chris for the accident.

"Why?" asked Peter. "He doesn't seem to care about you the way he should, for you to be as serious about him as you look like you are. Are you really?"

"I don't know. Probably. Daddy, I think you could be wrong about this."

"He doesn't even pretend to have the right feelings. Where is he now? Why isn't he calling you? Use your head, kiddo. This is not how a guy treats the girl he loves. Frankly, it would be bad behavior even if you were just casual acquaintances."

Louis, his arms spread out across the back of Susan's sofa, had turned his head to listen to this. He had not often been party to intimate conversations with either Peter or Susan, let alone both at once. He got up and sat at the table with them.

"I think he doesn't know how people behave when they love each other. He's just learning that."

"So much the worse. I don't like to interfere, but my advice to you is— it's good advice and you should listen to me—find someone else. Louis, what do you think?"

"The guy is definitely a jerk."

Peter's heart warmed at these words from Louis, and he gave him an almost imperceptible nod of his head in approval. Both Louis and Peter felt that for once they were together in something. Susan, on the other hand, for the first time felt somewhat estranged from her father.

"You don't know him at all, Louis," she cried in dismay.

"I know he's not here right now," said Louis. "And I thought he seemed like a jerk at Mallory's party last spring. Sorry, Susan. What were his parents like?"

Susan gave a vivid description, thinking to create sympathy for Chris.

"That might explain why he is the way he is," said Peter. "And it makes me feel a little sorry for him, but it doesn't explain why you would get mixed up with him. What does the guy do, anyway? He's a playwright? What kinds of plays can he write with blind spots like his?"

"Experimental theater is what he does."

"That confirms a prejudice of mine."

"But you're getting this all wrong, Daddy. Chris actually agrees with what you're saying. He doesn't want to be like his parents. He's doing everything he can to be different. He's superior to them in a thousand ways. Chris isn't about money and status. He really cares about theater and the arts. He has profoundly good values."

"Isn't the word for someone like that an aesthete?" Peter asked. "I wonder if all aesthetes are the children of amoral businessmen—that or divorced parents who drink, which is what I used to think. But maybe it would be better if we dropped the subject for a while."

"I thought you always wanted your children to be involved in art and scholarship and all that."

"I did, but not that kind. What Chris does, as far as I'm concerned, is not as good as what his father does, which at least could possibly contribute to someone's well-being, somewhere. Maybe he helps people get fuel oil for their furnaces or something."

"Do you think *I'm* an aesthete? I don't believe I ever heard you use that word before. You should have warned me against it when I was little."

"Sweetheart, you are everything that guy Chris is not, and it hurts me that you don't see it."

Susan sat in offended silence. He was changing the ground rules of their relation somehow. She felt betrayed and exposed and grew even angrier. Peter cast about for some way to make peace. He looked at Louis, who met his glance with a slight lift of the eyebrows, which almost made Peter smile. He felt grateful affection toward his son.

"Susan, I have an idea," said Peter. "Let's go on a trip—you, me, Louis, and your mother. Someplace wonderful. Paris or Rome or . . . wherever you like. Stay in some terrific resort, or some great hotel, get away from our worries."

"I'm a teaching assistant this term. I can't go anywhere. And is Mother really well enough?"

"Don't say no so fast. When's your last class before the holidays? Your mother would be absolutely delighted."

How Victorian, Susan thought: whisk his daughter away from the temptations of an unacceptable suitor and cure his invalid wife at European spas. But what would make *him* happy? she asked herself, beginning to feel remorseful about her surge of anger toward him. He was my father and mother both, she thought.

"I think Mother would like Chris," Susan said. The words came out more aggressively than she had intended.

"I'm sorry to say there's a good chance she'd be impressed with his money and his career," Peter said after a stunned pause. "She might overlook the rest. You know your mother, Susan. She has blind spots. That doesn't mean you should. That shouldn't tempt you to stick with a guy who's not right for you."

"But he's more right for me than anyone I've ever met. I'm a little odd. Most people can't get past that, but Chris likes it. Besides, it might be the first thing I've ever done that Mom would really approve of—if I married Chris."

"Married! Susan, don't lose your common sense. This is twisted thinking." Louis gave a little sigh here, and Peter chose not to meet his eyes this time.

The telephone rang, and Lesley demanded that Peter return home. He left reluctantly. "Are you having any company for the rest of the day?"

"I'll stay for a while," said Louis.

"And Chris will be by later tonight, so I'll be fine," said Susan.

Peter approved of Louis staying and would even rather have Chris come than allow Susan to be alone. He had thought of calling Mallory and asking her if she could sleep over at Susan's, but he felt awkward suggesting that now.

When the elevator opened on Susan's floor, Peter found himself face-to-face with Hilda. She did not startle and shriek at the sight of him, but her face tightened in some unreadable fashion.

"We meet again," Peter said lamely, for it seemed clear, at least, that Hilda was not pleased to see him.

"We meet over and over," she replied. Her tone of voice was as inscrutable as her expression.

"Returning your videos?" he asked, pointing to the red bag she carried that was marked with the video rental's familiar logo. "I'll walk you." Lesley could wait half an hour.

And all the way to 105th Street and back, he regaled Hilda with the news of Susan's accident, Chris's behavior at the hospital, and Susan's defense of it afterward. Hilda was less than delighted to have his company but nonetheless absorbed every detail.

When Peter had gone and Louis had returned to watching his game, Susan sat at her table, shuffling a deck of cards and pondering. Her just-discovered wish for her mother to approve of Chris warred with anger about her mother's betrayal of her father, and she weighed, as she had a hundred times before, telling him that he overestimated the loyalty he owed his wife. If he left her, she thought, I could devote myself to making him happy. That would probably be better than devoting myself to Chris, but it would be another Victorian scenario, she realized: a daughter refuses marriage so that she can take care of her aging, loving, kind, generous father. He wouldn't let me, though, she thought. And besides, maybe he wasn't paragon enough to justify sacrificing her life for him.

Chris showed up at around 10:30 P.M., when Susan, having decided he was not coming, was already reading in bed. He hadn't said, for sure, that he would. He sat on her bed, drank a beer, and made jokes.

"You look like someone beat you," he said, his finger tracing the arc of the bruise across her cheek.

"I'm telling everyone you did it."

He laughed, and Susan saw that he particularly liked her having said that.

"I spent all day with the new readers," he said.

"And the reading for the producer is when?"

"Probably Thursday. Then he'll take a couple of days to think about it. So I might know by early the week after next whether this is going to happen."

Susan read pessimism in his face behind an expression that was supposed to be impassive. Recalling her recent conversation with Hilda Hughes, she considered suggesting that he call Hilda, who was looking for valuable new work; then, as she imagined Hilda meeting Chris, she thought better of this. Hilda would never fund something Chris wrote; she wouldn't care for his plays any more than her father would. Hilda had told her they never supported anything that was, or called itself, experimental. Well, sooner or later the older generation had to loosen the purse strings, recognize that times and tastes had changed, and give the kids a chance to do it their way. Why not try to persuade Hilda? When she asked herself this question, Susan discovered what she had never before admitted to herself, that she did not believe in, did not really like, Chris's plays, either. She could never argue persuasively that anyone should sink cash into one of them. Chris, of course, would say that he didn't ask anyone to *like* his work, that *liking* was not the point at all. But that was getting sort of metaphysical. Susan tried to assuage her guilt toward Chris with the thought that in the end he might well find support for the new play, and it would be better to have real commercial backing. If and when that was ruled out, she could reconsider talking to Hilda.

CHAPTER 33

The entire Frankl family sat in silence at the dining room table while Yolanda served. Lesley glared at her plate. Peter and Susan stared out across the river at the lights in New Jersey, and Louis looked at each of their faces in turn. The three of them awaited Lesley's next volley.

"Whose fault is any of this but yours, Peter?" she asked when Yolanda left the dining room. "You insisted on butting in where you had no business and getting in over your head, and it did nobody any good. You never do anybody any good."

"Never?" said Peter, poking listlessly at his salad. That morning he had received a letter from Irving Frankl, a half-sibling he had not seen or spoken to since their father's death. Irving excoriated him for his shenanigans at Columbia and the Devereaux Foundation. "When I saw the article in the *Gazette* yesterday, I decided that I had to write and urge you to stop this nonsense. You have no idea," Irving wrote, "what damage you are doing to the image of Jews in the mind of the public. I hope you don't deceive yourself that my father would have approved of what you're doing. You are a disgrace to his memory."

Peter had learned yesterday that after Kappell's second article appeared, Edmond Lockhart had told his aunt that if she did not resign from the Devereaux Foundation, he would initiate proceedings to have a court declare her incapacitated and call on the attorney general's office to seek her removal as chairman of the board. Of course, Edmond had assured her that she need not worry about abandoning her ship: he himself would put aside his own work and devote himself to administering the foundation. It was time for others to continue her work.

Peter thought that Edmond would never succeed in these legal threats, mainly because his aunt was not incapacitated and the attorney general would have better things to do with his time; but that didn't matter. She would have to resign. The very threat of such an ordeal would probably frighten her into compliance, and if it didn't, the strain of it might well kill such a frail old woman. Hilda was surely going to lose her job. Peter had seen real fear in her eyes for the first time, which simultaneously assured him of her sanity and unnerved him. Who else but Emma Devereaux would ever hire her? Would she become homeless and brush her teeth in the fountain at 120th Street? No, Peter himself would not let that happen, and neither would Emma. Poor Emma. She was rich and would suffer no financial harm, but she thought everything was her fault. In fact, none of the Devereaux people blamed Peter. They all kept apologizing for causing him so much grief. They said that they should have followed his advice. How often he had warned them! This was touching, but Peter was well aware that it had been his job to prevent just these things from happening and that he had failed.

"Lay off, Mom," said Louis. He rarely had dinner with his parents, but Susan had begged him to come and help stave off his mother's assault, which had already lasted an entire day. Lesley looked at Louis, startled into silence by his siding openly with his father. Peter, too, looked at his son curiously.

"Who do you think you . . . ," Lesley began, her volume amplifying as her sense of betrayal grew, but Louis was determined to end the harangue.

"So how bad are the books over there, Dad?" he asked, drowning out Lesley's voice.

Peter realized that Louis had a good businessman's sense of how things worked. Not that he had underestimated Louis's ability that way; he had merely taken it for granted. He didn't particularly admire business talent.

Lesley, too, always easily distracted, apparently wanted to know how bad the books were, for she went silent and listened, frowning suspiciously. Susan sat, morose and silent, and stared at her mother.

"Oh, the books are in fine shape," said Peter. "They're not going to find anything wrong there. I'm a good lawyer, Louis. My client's affairs are in order."

"Then I don't get it."

"Edmond and his lawyer just want to get Emma and Hilda out of there—all of them, but especially those two—because although the books are perfectly in order, they clearly record, for example, that the foundation disbursed twenty thousand dollars to someone writing a book on haunted houses in Marin County. There're a few other things like that."

Louis laughed. "But who cares?" he asked.

"Edmond cares. I think Edmond has hired a real lowlife as a lawyer—which is surprising because the whole case here is bona fides. Without knowing what's going on, I smell a rat."

"Me too," Louis said.

"What are you talking about?" Lesley demanded, her face reddening. "Why don't you just leave the Devereaux Foundation alone, Peter—for your own sake? Whatever happens, you just keep sticking to them, when it makes no sense. You're going to destroy your whole career for a room full of crazy people." She was incensed that Peter refused to honor a formal request by his partners to end his representation of the Devereaux Foundation. Even Harry Rothenberg had voted for this. Walter Bramford had been the sole holdout—why, Peter didn't know; maybe he just liked being contrary.

"Mother, please," Susan said, "let it drop. Let's change the subject." Both Peter and Louis noticed a new sharpness in her tone.

"You never want to discuss anything honestly. You never want anything out in the open, Susan," said her mother, glowering at her. "Hide and pretend—that's what you've been like since you were—"

"Mom, shouldn't you stand behind Dad on this? He's really doing what he has to do," said Louis.

"I will go down with the ship," said Peter, looking at Louis appraisingly. No one—let alone his son, Louis—had ever fought his fights before, and here he was, going against his mother in defense of both Peter and Susan. Lesley would take it as a betrayal.

In fact, Lesley was so furious that for once she said nothing, but, leaning on her walking stick, left the table without excusing herself. Susan sat looking anxious for a moment, then got up and followed her out, leaving Peter and Louis in silence. They still had not spoken when Susan returned in a few minutes to get a tray of food for her mother, which she carried out, saying as she left, "She shouldn't skip her dinner."

"How's your love life?" Peter asked Louis when Susan had gone. He put the question innocently, as though it were not a remarkable departure both from their usual style of conversation and from the subject at hand.

Louis looked off to the side, ate a bite, and considered. "Not great," he said with a shrug, and there was such stoic misery in his eyes and the set of his mouth that Peter sorrowed. Louis was lonely. He couldn't win love.

"Look, Dad, I'm meeting some people," Louis said, laying his napkin on the table and rising.

"Sure, Louis," said Peter. "I'm really glad you stayed for dinner."

"Yeah," said Louis with a sideways nod and another shrug that acknowledged his father's appreciation but refused any credit.

He doesn't exactly have a way with words, Peter thought, but could there have been a more becomingly modest response to a father's gratitude? It was downright delicate. All in all, the kid did have some good points.

Peter walked to his bedroom. The door was shut, a light showed through the crack, and TV voices were audible. The thought of lying in hostile silence side by side with Lesley, watching Fred Astaire and Ginger Rogers, was intolerable. He felt restless. I'll go out for a little walk, he thought.

Lately, he regularly went out for an evening walk, during which he thought incessantly about Wanda Lockhart, even though he had never once seen her since her visit months ago. Tonight, just before going out, he looked up "Lockhart" in the telephone directory. He was equally disappointed and relieved that there was no W or Wanda—not that he would have called, anyway.

The air was cold, and it was windy as Peter, hands in pockets, trench coat collar turned up, went down Riverside and then up 107th, past the Devereaux Foundation, and then to 114th, past the building where Susan and Hilda lived their lonely lives, and then past the West End, where Louis was trying not to be lonely. There was no comfort to be found anywhere, not in thoughts of his wife, his work, or his children. I've failed, Peter thought, in just about every important way there is to fail. He walked back to Riverside and to his own building, hoping that Lesley would be asleep. There in the lobby, reading in a visitor's chair, was Wanda Lockhart. She looked up at him and smiled.

"I've been waiting for you," she said. "I was at Edmond's. The doorman thought you'd be right back. Walk me home?" She reached for a bulging book bag that sat at her side.

"Let me carry that for you," said Peter, and she readily handed over the bag, which was unexpectedly heavy. "What are you doing with all these books?" he asked. "What do you do for a living, anyway?"

"They're just novels I'm borrowing to take with me on a little vacation," she said. "The two good things about Edmond are his library and his trust fund, which keeps me off the job market. Sometimes he cuts me off, but I always manage to get him to turn the tap back on."

"Is that what you were doing that night? When you came visiting?"

"Why, yes, that's right. He was so mad at me after you walked out on him." Wanda laughed mischievously.

"And where are you going on vacation?" he asked, determined to take advantage of this chance encounter to satisfy as much of his curiosity about her as he could.

"To Edmond's place on the Cape."

"With George."

"Not if I can help it." She laughed again. "I've got George in a program upstate for a couple of months . . ."

Peter shook his head. She was leading him down 115th Street. There was that peculiar sense of humor again and an almost brazen display of low-mindedness.

". . . which is really lucky, because Edmond often likes to stay at his Cape place at this time of year, when it's cold and lonely and gloomy, you know, but this year he's got too much business in town." Wanda went poker-faced and looked sideways at Peter. "Now how did a smart lawyer like you let Edmond get the better of you?"

"Are you sure he's got the better of me?" Peter asked.

"Quite sure," said Wanda with an air of knowing secrets. "There's my place," she said, pointing to the other side of the street.

Peter's heart vaulted and skipped, then settled into a nervous but steady allegro beat. He set down her book bag while she pulled keys out of a shoulder bag. He didn't know whether he would go up or not, or what he might do if he did go up. Unexpectedly, Wanda stepped close and leaned against him for a moment, so that he could smell her hair and skin again, the same smell as before. Peter's desire for her made him breathe hard, and involuntarily a little noise, a needy little rattle, escaped from deep in his throat. Yes, he decided, horrified at himself; he *would* go up.

"I'd ask you up," said Wanda, "but I'm expecting a date."

Peter was mortified but relieved. "Well," he said lamely. This was what happened when you let your fantasies get out of control.

"Don't take it so hard," said Wanda with a slightly superior but kindly air. "I was waiting for you because I have to tell you something. Look, Peter, you've got to give in to Edmond. Make Emma resign. She's old. This is the only thing that makes sense. Promise me you'll do that."

"No, Wanda, I won't promise you that. It would be unethical," Peter explained respectfully, as though Wanda, understandably, had overlooked this. Why should Wanda take such an interest in Edmond's troubles with his aunt Emma? Or was it that she thought she was being helpful to Peter?

"You've really got to, Peter," Wanda said. "He's got you over a barrel.

Look, you have to or I'm going to tell everyone we had an affair. Now how about that?"

"What?"

"You heard."

"You mean blackmail?" Peter was more disbelieving, even curious, than angry.

"I guess. I don't know the technical term for it." Wanda had a vaguely awkward air, as though she were not certain what demeanor best suited making blackmail threats.

"Whom are you going to tell?"

"Miss Devereaux, your wife, your kids, your law partners."

"But I'll deny it. It's a lie."

"Mostly, but not a hundred percent a lie, not a bald-faced lie. Anyway, no one will believe the truth because your story is inherently just not very believable—that someone goes to the very edge of temptation and doesn't fall off. What's believable is that people fall. My story is much more plausible. You're really cornered, Peter. You have to give in." Wanda spoke rather impatiently, as though Peter were contemptibly naïve.

"He threatened to cut you off, didn't he."

But Wanda only laughed, waved good-bye, and was gone.

Peter's obsession with Wanda disappeared as quickly as she did, and as soon as she was out of sight, he began to wonder about it. Just what had been the attraction? He had known all along, on some level, that Wanda was peculiar, cold, and not exactly big on principle. No, Wanda's behaving as she just had and her marriage to Edmond were not hard to understand. Peter's yen for her, though, that was a mystery.

Earlier that evening, while Peter, Lesley, and Louis had been dining, so had Edmond, Wanda, Ivy, and Edmond's lawyer, William Reed—Reed, they all called him. Reed had a struggling solo practice in which he had been forced to accept several dubious clients. He represented, chiefly, the owner of a dozen soft-porn magazines and several "financiers" for whom he set up limited partnerships as tax shelters of questionable legality. "No guarantees!" he told these flinty-faced men who made millions through dubious investment vehicles. "I can't guarantee they'll withstand a challenge. But I *can* guarantee that if they don't, the downside is you just pay up." This, of course, was not true, but Reed could not yet afford the truth. Edmond Lockhart had been referred to him by Edmond's accountant, who owed Reed a few favors.

Reed readily accepted this work, and for a fairly low fee, as he recognized Edmond's naïveté instantly. Just as quickly, he decided he must make the Devereaux Foundation his client as well. With its huge endowment, he could practically live off its fees alone. He could say good-bye to the sleazy investors and the rickety tax shelters and the soft-porn moguls and hang out with respectable people. He knew right away that the old lady was not incapacitated, but she was too old, for chrissake. He didn't blame Edmond at all. They'd scare her out, and everyone would thank them. At least, they would if they could get rid of this guy Frankl—a very stubborn guy. Reed heard the fascinating story of the two newspaper articles.

"Well, it's a lotta bread for him," said Reed.

"No," said Edmond. "He donates his services—pro bono."

"He's extremely upright. In fact, I kissed him," said Wanda, "but I couldn't get him to go any further. Incorruptible. Or very repressed."

Edmond was angered by this story and demanded details, but it made Reed thoughtful; he had a private, intense conversation with Edmond, followed by a tête-à-tête with Wanda. Ivy observed his maneuverings suspiciously. She had long ago accepted Wanda's occasional presence as the price she paid to live with Edmond, but Reed and all this Devereaux business was a painful new tax on that luxury.

PART THREE

CHAPTER 34

Sundays in Morningside Heights, people with real jobs slept late. But on the fringes of the neighborhood lived those with day jobs and odd jobs who got no weekend rest—dancers who processed words and proofread documents for IPOs, poets who walked dogs, and painters who swabbed floors and waited tables. Alexei's weekends were full of sessions on the promenade or at the health club with fitness clients and trips to apartments all over the city, where he set up computers, fixed crashes, and retrieved files for panicked writers and professors, and instructed lawyers on how to project their voices.

Chess brought him to the Braithwaites' door early one unseasonably chill Sunday in October. He found the household in a chaos of preparations, and soon he was walking to the subway station at 116th Street, holding hands with Stuart on his left and Ellen on his right. Both children were bundled into coats that concealed all natural signs of sex, size, and shape and loudly insisted on artificial ones. Ellen's was a satiny pink, with big-eyed floral-patterned animals appliquéd on the pockets, while Stuart's was navy and gray with multiple zippers and flaps and so many pockets that any object thoughtlessly deposited in one was in danger of being lost forever. Alexei was less well dressed, in a thin, short jacket, and he hunched his shoulders against the unusual cold. The train was long in coming and crowded; Ellen sat beside Alexei, who put his arm around her protectively, and Stuart, who was small for his five years, sat on his knee. The children chattered excitedly over the noise of the train. Alexei was taking them down-town to the Marshall Chess Club on Tenth Street to play in their first tour-nament.

He had explained the procedures to them over and again, and he re-peated them now, winding up with admonitions to stoicism. "If you lose, do you cry?" he asked. "Even if it's because you made a silly mistake?" They shook their heads, grim-faced at the thought of making a silly mistake. "If you cry, though, that's okay," he added inconsistently, but the children loudly denied the possibility of this happening.

It seemed colder and lonely in the Village. The people, the restaurants, and the businesses were stylish, and all projected an air of disillusionment. Tenth Street, which was deserted, was lined with brick and brownstone row houses and trees that had begun to drop their leaves. The wind whipped up and down, and the visitors from Morningside Heights felt the local melan-choly take hold of them.

None of them were smiling when they reached the Marshall Club's town house, and Stuart and Ellen drew closer to Alexei when they entered. Inside, despite high ceilings, carved woodwork, and other signs of a gentle-manly past, the place was noisy, dim, and dingy. Notices and clippings about chess were everywhere—score sheets, contests, anecdotes, cartoons, announcements of events all over the world. Game tables were set before benches that ran the perimeter of its walls.

The noise emanated from two or three dozen scrappy-looking children, most of them behaving with an intimidating knowingness. A boy about Stu-art's age immediately approached him. "Play me!" he demanded, and Stuart, happy to comply, was instantly at home, but Ellen stood by shyly and watched the two small boys, unwilling to leave Alexei's side to find a game of her own.

Alexei, scanning the room, observed several adults he knew, including at least two who were, by American standards anyway, famously eccentric. Al-though well worth playing, they made him uncomfortable and, seeing them, he grimaced. When he was younger, Alexei had been troubled by what peo-ple so often said of chess players, that the most brilliant were simply autis-tic, or nearly so. Perhaps he, too, with his exceptional skill in chess at such a young age, was diseased, not talented. At least, Alexei thought, I'm not with-drawn or weird like Sergei Ivanovich Petrov, whom he had observed playing at the other side of the room, or the famous Boris Tarlov, whom he had once almost played. Alexei was the opposite, hungry for company and affection, although not so good at finding it lately. But maybe they were, too, and per-haps, after all, he *was* like them. Or it might be that he had some other brain dysfunction, not autism. He certainly had a number of capacities in chess and in music that were suspiciously suggestive of atypical brainworks—freakish memory feats, multitrack concentration, and absolute pitch. Someday, Alexei imagined, this overlapping constellation of abilities, found occasionally among the upper echelons of chess players and musicians, might be traced to a specific genetic endowment—a dysfunction, perhaps, that eventually produced fatal illness or even madness, and pregnant women would take pills to suppress it. Alexei's habit of doubting whether he was brilliant or simply mismade, exacerbated by a series of misfortunes and disappointments, had to some extent curbed an early tendency to egoism, but in the chess world he was remembered as the conceited child star he used to be.

"Look who's here!"

"I don't believe it."

Alexei didn't look toward the first voice, but he recognized the second one.

"It's No-Show! Where you been?"

A tall, gangly man with bent shoulders and a crooked, angular face quietly announced, "Mate!" at a table near the door, then looked at Alexei and the Braithwaite children.

"Alexei Nikolaevich, those aren't yours?"

"Of course not. They're my students."

"Ah! Come play."

"In a minute. I have to help them first."

The children's noise subsided abruptly when the first game assignments were posted a few minutes later. Alexei showed Ellen and Stuart the list of pairings, with their names, their opponents, assigned tables and colors—black or white—and pointed out where they were to record the results of the game. He led them to the tables and made sure they were supplied with chess clocks, pencils, and forms for recording moves. Then he smiled and whispered, "Good luck."

Back at the tall man's table, Alexei sat down to play, and a group gathered to watch that included three or four taciturn, grave men and one perfectly round, fat woman who was so short that she stood almost eye to eye with the seated Alexei. The faces of the onlookers were composed and neutral, those of the players concentrated, but nonetheless it was evident that the game stirred excitement.

"It has to be short, Sergei Ivanovich," Alexei said to the man, "because soon I'll have to work with my students."

"Blitz game, then?"

"Well, five minutes each," said Alexei.

"You're white," said the other, pressing buttons on a chess clock.

Alexei's hand hovered for a second over a pawn and then shoved it forward with the peculiar deftness of serious players.

When Stuart reappeared ten minutes later, Alexei held out his arm to the boy. "Well?" he asked in a low voice, while his opponent, his face rumpled and grooved by the intensity of his thought, considered his next move.

"I won," Stuart said in a loud whisper, trying to suppress his triumphant smile on the theory that Alexei would think this highly mannerly. But Alexei reacted with a delighted grin.

"Congratulations. I want to hear all about the game. But first watch while I finish playing—no talking." Stuart leaned against Alexei's arm to watch. Ellen returned some minutes later, looking sober, and Alexei, seeing her face, made a move—at which two or three onlookers inhaled and exhaled and rubbed their chins—and then turned to talk with her.

"Just absurd," the round lady whispered. "That's Alexei Mikhailov, you know. He's good but he's wild, and he has big ego problems. He won't play if he thinks he'll lose."

"So?" Alexei said to Ellen. She shook her head, eyeing the portrait over the fireplace indifferently.

"It doesn't matter if you lost, Ellen. That boy had a high rating, but you . . ." Alexei looked over the page of recorded moves that Ellen clutched. "You made him work for that win, didn't you? This looks very good."

"That's right, honey," said the little round lady, who had turned to listen. "You're lucky you got to play that boy, because you want to play the best players you can. That's how you learn. People fight for the privilege of playing great players—at least, usually they do," she said pointedly, with a side glance at Alexei, "even though they'll probably lose." Alexei ignored the indirect communications in this speech and nodded at Ellen. What the lady said was true.

Despite the spectators' predictions, in another few minutes Alexei announced, "Checkmate. It was a pleasure, Sergei Ivanovich, but you'll have to get even some other day. Excuse me, please." And the onlookers leaned closer around the table to analyze the game, while Alexei led Ellen and Stuart to another table.

In the end, Ellen and Stuart each won two games and lost two, placing in the respectable middle of the tournament's final rankings. "Very good," Alexei said, "especially when you've never played in a tournament before." While the children chattered excitedly and Alexei packed up, preparing to leave for home, Sergei Ivanovich Petrov was limping his way toward them, and now stood slouching beside their table.

"Alexei Nikolaevich," he said in a gentle voice, "will you play in Berlin in December? You could get an appearance fee, I'm sure, and Marfa would—"

"It's very annoying you don't stop this. I'm done with that. Leave me alone." The children, who had never heard Alexei snarl as he did now at Petrov, were startled and fell silent and stared.

"*He'll* be there."

Alexei didn't respond to this information.

"You should come. Think it over," Petrov said.

"Why should I?"

"You're playing better than him."

Alexei shook his head and grimaced. "How would you know, anyway?" he responded.

"I do. I also know why you didn't come the other time."

"No, you don't."

"I do."

"I don't believe you know, but if you do, keep it to yourself."

"I always have. But I could help you put a stop to it if you want me to." And the man limped off.

"Who is that man? What did he mean?" asked Stuart.

"He's someone I used to see at tournaments. It was just some grown-up stuff he was talking about," said Alexei, shouldering the backpack and leading the children downstairs to the door.

"Are you a grown-up?" Stuart asked hesitantly when they were outside walking, three abreast, down the block, past all the stoops and patches of garden in the front of the row houses. The day's light was almost gone, and the half-bare black branches of the trees, under the streetlamps, made an eerie latticework over their heads. Although the children were still too excited to be affected, Alexei found himself growing despondent again. He had to conceal it, for the children's sakes, but Stuart's question hatched a little worm of anxiety in his brain.

"What kind of question is that?" he said testily. "What do I look like?"

"You're big enough, but your clothes are like a kid's and you don't have a home or a wife or kids or a job."

"Oh. So, well. I have lots of jobs, and as for the other stuff—nevertheless, I'm grown up. Lots of grown-ups don't have all that." Alexei felt humiliated at failing Stuart's test of adulthood. "If that's what grown-up is, Stuart, then being poor is the same as being a kid." Stuart did not understand this, but the precocious Ellen got the gist. She thought about it, holding Alexei's hand.

"So are you going to get married, Alexei?" she asked as they headed down the steps to the subway.

"Yes," he said firmly, although he had just been thinking that Stuart's analysis of his social position was all too similar to Mallory Holmes's. His melancholy turned into fear, and he was not accustomed to feeling fearful. Alexei did not want the false youth that, among the educated poor, lasts into deep middle age. He had never set out to live on the edges of society, the way some did, making virtues of insecurity, powerlessness, and poverty. On the contrary, he had intended to grow up fast, accomplish great things, rise high, and do good—all that.

"Who are you going to marry?" Ellen asked with a silly smile.

"Don't get personal," he said. He had thought a great deal, since that unhappy talk with Mallory, about how young women did not find him an attractive prospect. Perhaps this was how compromises in life got forced. He could struggle on with poverty and uncertainty, at least for a while yet, but the loneliness was going to defeat him. He couldn't manage alone.

Alexei stood in the Braithwaites' apartment just long enough to explain to Anne that the children had performed commendably in their first tournament.

"Do you think you'd like to do it again someday?" he asked Ellen and Stuart.

"I want to do it *every day*," said Stuart. "It was the best thing in my whole life."

"I want to play in lots of tournaments," said Ellen, twirling with excitement. "Mommy, you have to come see."

"I *will* come see," said Anne, and she followed Alexei to the door, having detected his gloom. "What's wrong?" she asked.

"Nothing," he said. "I'm going to be late if I don't run." He couldn't talk to Anne about all that right now. He might whine; he would certainly sound childish.

"Alexei, I almost forgot in all the chess excitement. We're having a Thanksgiving dinner, and we want you to come—about seven-thirty. I know it's a long way off, but I wanted to ask you before you made other plans." Actually, this was a thought of the moment, inspired by a wish to cheer up the forlorn young man, but Anne quickly concluded that it was a good idea from all angles. "And bring someone if you want. Bring a friend, you know. Just tell me if you decide to." She had long been wondering about the state of his love life. If there was any little nudge she could give things . . .

"Well, I guess," Alexei said, "I could come, yes. Thank you very much."
He was most curious to attend a Thanksgiving dinner at the Braithwaites'.
He had been at several Braithwaite family dinners, but this would be different, and he was relieved to have an excuse to avoid his own family. Anne was
gratified to see Alexei brighten appreciably.

Although Alexei had said he was late, in fact he had nothing to do but
go home to his room on Tiemann Place and make something to eat on his
half-size stove. He resolved, as he walked, to arrange a rematch with player
#17 in his Internet chess club, to whom he had lost last week. The game
with Petrov had gotten him in the mood for more. By now, Alexei had become an avid participant in this online group. He had played often enough
to know that there could be hardly more than fifty or sixty members, and a
number of them, at least in Alexei's estimation, were among the world's best
chess players. This he knew because by now he had played so many of them
and also because it was possible to observe club games in progress and to get
records of other players' games. He even thought he recognized a player or
two, on the basis of their preferences for unusual nineteenth-century openings. The club had become important to Alexei. It provided the pure joys of
playing without any nonsense. Of course, it was not nearly as good as playing face-to-face, but it was still very good.

Why should he bother with the tournament in Berlin, in fact, when he
could play such good players whenever he wanted? There were times when
he almost decided to go—particularly when he learned the amount of the
money prizes. With that much cash, he could give a lot to his mother, silence
his father's reproaches, and still have a great deal left over—perhaps enough
to get a better apartment and pay Charles Braithwaite for a while without
having to untangle so many people's computer wires. He could certainly
take a girl to dinner and buy a few tickets for concerts and operas. He knew,
however, even while tempting himself with such thoughts, that he would not
play in Berlin.

He could hear his telephone ringing as he stood in the hallway unlock-
ing his door.

"I've been calling you all day," said Alcott Adams irritably. "When are
you going to get a cell phone or an answering machine? I've been going crazy
trying to find you. Can you come down here tomorrow?"

"Impossible. Tuesday I could come. What's up?"

"I may have new money for the film."

"You're unbelievable! You already found new money? How is that possible so soon!"

"I'll tell you when I see you, but we're organizing and we've revised the script. I think you should be there."

"Me? If you think so. But you can always fill me in on anything later. When will you start filming again?"

"I'm not sure. Very soon. But you should be there. Look, I really want you to be there. Can you make it Tuesday, then? Around eleven? Actually, now that I'm thinking, Tuesday is better than tomorrow."

"All right, if you think it would be useful. I'll see you then." Alexei couldn't bring himself to say that he'd rather not come until the new money was a sure thing and Alcott really had some work for him to do. He didn't have nearly as much time to hang out in parking lots and lounge on stoops and park benches or sit around drinking too much coffee, scheming and pipe dreaming, as Alcott seemed to think, and for that matter, he had never been sure what it was he was supposed to be doing for Alcott. Most of the time he dragged cables and lights around without any idea why they were to go one place rather than another. Yet Alcott had several times insisted he attend smoky talk sessions at various sidewalk café tables, just as he was doing Tuesday. Alexei liked Alcott but did not understand why, when it came to filming, he always had to be surrounded by an entourage or why he felt entitled to so much shoring up. And Alexei most certainly did not know why *he* had to be part of the entourage. According to Sylvie, when Mallory found out that Alexei was helping out on the set, she had decided that he should make a career of it. Hearing this, Alexei had seethed. Working on Alcott's sets for low and erratic pay had felt like doing an onerous favor. He knew, though, that everyone else thought he was the one receiving the favor. It all grated. Still, he would go down there and give Alcott a hand once more. What else could a friend do?

CHAPTER 35

"What's a six-letter word for an Arab despot?" asked Lesley at the breakfast table on Saturday morning. She had taken up crossword puzzles after having read that Alzheimer's disease was less common among habitual crossword puzzle solvers; perhaps it was also good therapy for the postcomatose. Peter encouraged this new hobby, for it kept Lesley silent for minutes at a stretch. On this occasion, she had been working the puzzle for more than half an hour and had interrupted Peter with questions some forty times. With heroic patience, he gave her answers or sometimes, as on this occasion, grunted in an excellent imitation of fascinated ignorance, without actually thinking or interrupting his reading.

"Oh, I see—wait. Is there some despot named Hassan? You're wrong, Peter. It isn't 'venal' in four across. Why did you say that? It isn't even close. Next I need eight down: 'a man after his own heart.' What on earth is that supposed to mean! You know, these puzzles are really . . . I mean, it's no fun if you have to be a mind reader. A good puzzle should just challenge your vocabulary, your basic—"

"Would you look at this?" said Peter abruptly. Unshaven, he was reading the *Gazette Book Review* over his third cup of coffee. NPR's *Weekend Edition* was on the radio at a subdued volume, and a man's somber voice could be heard reading tonelessly, although only occasional phrases could be distinguished. Lesley, who sat opposite Peter in a flowered silk robe and slippers, looked up expectantly.

"I don't believe it!" Peter said. "Edmond Lockhart has written a memoir about his depressions called *Confession*. A depression confession, for God's sake. You'd think there were enough of those out there already." Peter had woken that morning undecided whether or not to confront Edmond. Of course, Edmond would deny that he had put Wanda up to anything; and if Peter again refused to help him remove Emma from the board, Edmond might simply make Wanda do her worst. No, the best thing would be to stall for time and avoid confrontations. In the meantime, however, Peter's outrage was mounting, and his loathing for Edmond was limitless.

". . . legacy of pain and loneliness . . . ," said the NPR voice.

"Why are you always so nasty?" said Lesley. "Depression is so misunderstood and stigmatized. I mean, these people are miserable. They can't help it, and people *blame* them for it. Ivy really blames Edmond."

"Don't believe everything Edmond tells you, Lesley. I doubt Ivy has enough sense to blame him. And frankly I wouldn't be surprised if depressives' books and memoirs weren't actually the *source* of stigma about depression. People read a few pages and then think how terrible it would be to have to listen to him all through dinner. This reviewer says, 'Despite the author's medications, the book reeks of depression and has the same appeal, or lack of it, according to one's taste.' "

". . . diminishing hopes in the face of lost . . . ," mourned the NPR baritone.

Lesley looked her blank look at Peter, which meant that he had transgressed and she was politely restraining her disapproval. For once, however, Peter was not silenced by it. Lately, he was more and more unwilling to grant Lesley an excess share of the familial airtime.

"She says it's a genre. She's right!"

". . . the positive and active anguish that William James . . . ," put in the radio voice.

"She says people who write this stuff try to disarm your skepticism by confessing things that no one in their right mind, no one with half-decent manners, would confess in public. This is supposed to make you think there's nothing they're not telling, but in fact they're often not telling lots of important things, maybe none of the really important things. Beautiful, Stoller, whoever you are, exactly right. . . . It's like copping a plea. I bet she's a lawyer—no, a psychoanalyst. . . ."

"Peter, what do you know about it? You're no doctor. You just hate Edmond because of the Devereaux Foundation trouble."

". . . lethargy of misery . . . ," the voice droned.

"What are you talking about, Lesley? I've disliked the man for years.

Look, I'm sure depression is terrible and shouldn't be stigmatized, but that doesn't alter the fact that depressed people write whiny, self-serving books. I mean, if being depressed made them appealing and insightful, they wouldn't be taking little yellow pills, would they? Now my opinion is, the pills reduce the pain but don't change the underlying—"

"Do you realize, Peter," Lesley said, "that you talk a lot more now than you ever used to? You talk a lot, you know."

Peter stared at her. "*I* talk a lot?"

"... long-standing obstacles to ... ," intoned NPR.

"I don't really care to hear any more of this."

"Yeah, let's turn it off," said Peter, frowning, and hit the radio's off button. "Why do all those NPR essay voices sound so dreary and refined? They all sound alike—sort of like Edmond, actually."

"I meant *you.* Turn the radio on, Peter. I was listening to that." But Peter ignored this.

"Look, Lesley, I think you just don't like to hear anything bad about your new buddy. But you know what? Now that he's on soma, I think he's crazier than ever. That grin he has lately gives me the willies. He doesn't seem to realize that I'd be a bit ticked off with him for trying to destroy me and my client. He's started making strange remarks and doing strange things."

Louis, who had walked in on this debate, bare-chested and wearing pajama bottoms, laughed at this speech of Peter's and leaned over his shoulder to read the review. It was gratifying to Peter, having Louis laugh like that, but Lesley was angry.

"Louis, you just show how shallow you are when you laugh at someone like Edmond Lockhart, who has more brains and education than anyone in this family no matter how great they think they are. You don't really understand the discussion."

"Oh, I don't know ... ," Peter began.

"I understand it, Mom," said Louis mildly, sitting at the table and pouring a glass of orange juice. "I've just always thought Lockhart was an ass."

"Get out of here—or get dressed," said Lesley. "What a nerve to come in here half-dressed. You get on my nerves, Louis. I don't know what went on while I was in the hospital, but you act like some kind of Neanderthal and like you think you're some big intellectual with all your intelligent opinions."

"That will be enough, Lesley," said Peter, half rising. But Louis seemed to ignore her. He drained his glass and left, with a glance back at Peter. Peter himself was shocked at Lesley's venom against Louis, and it occurred to him, for the first time, that he had never in all Louis's life had reason to think that Lesley was genuinely nice to the boy. Lesley wasn't the softhearted type. What kind of life had his son lived? Peter felt a chill thinking about that and vowed privately to talk to Louis about it as soon as he could.

"Who do you think you are, Peter? I'm tired of the disrespect I get around here. I'm ill, and everyone is giving me a very hard time. He shouldn't come to the table half-dressed. What were you saying before? What things was Edmond saying?"

Peter judged the depth of Lesley's interest in Edmond from the fact that she had remembered the thread of the conversation before Louis's interruption.

"First, yesterday he comes up to me at the corner while I'm waiting for the light to change, and he says, 'Peter, Peter, pumpkin eater,' and laughs like he's a real wit. Then he tells me how he thinks the doorman is very sexually active."

"I think you're distorting everything. You know," said Lesley, growing more and more angry, "I don't like what you're saying at all. He doesn't take Soma, by the way. It's Zoloft. He started out on Prozac, but he had to switch because . . . well, I don't really know why, but Zoloft is just as effective."

"Lesley, soma isn't real. It's the drug they take in *Brave New World* to . . . Wait, you don't mean some drug company actually named something . . . ?"

"I never read that book. Anyway, Peter, it's mean to make fun of people for being sick."

"Look, my opinion is that whatever Lockhart is on is loosening his lips and deadening his mind. When I talk to him, he doesn't seem like himself anymore—he doesn't seem like the guy I know."

"He says *he* feels like he's really himself for the first time in his life. But you just want to think bad things about him, Peter, just like you always used to put down Henry Rostov."

"Henry! I never put down Henry. Why would I? Maybe I said he bored me. That's not really a put-down."

"You know it is!" Lesley's face reddened, and she slapped her hand on the breakfast table.

Her fury reached such a peak, in fact, that Peter was alarmed.

"All right, honey, don't get upset. Look, I'm sorry—you're right. I shouldn't talk that way about your friend, should I? I apologize, from the heart," Peter said.

Lesley was slightly mollified, but she still glared at him, flushed and fierce.

"Look, Lockhart's a brilliant, prominent man, isn't he? Maybe I'm envious. You've got an envious husband."

This approach was more successful. Lesley grimaced and nodded, although not graciously, switched the radio back on, and returned to the crossword puzzle.

"... reading from his memoir, *Legacy of an Unfinished Childhood* ...," said an affectless female voice.

The incident was over, but it left Peter unsettled. Lesley never used to shout, but maybe he never used to provoke her so much. Lately, he had a ready truculence, a kind of pleasure in striking out. Just now, he had purposely been needling Lesley—until her rage frightened him for her sake.

It was uncomfortable that his wife was so thick with a man he was quarreling with and had despised for years—a man who, moreover, had always despised her, as far as Peter could tell. What on earth could have produced this friendship between two human beings who were so ill suited and opposed, in every way, as Edmond Lockhart and Lesley?

While Peter pondered this conundrum, across the hall Edmond Lockhart and Ivy Hurst, who had returned late the night before from a trip to Edinburgh, were also reading the review of *Confession* in the *Gazette Book Review*. Ivy had seen it first.

"Edmond! You're in this one. Here it is!" she had cried.

But why hadn't his publisher sent it to him in Edinburgh or let him know when it was appearing? He should have checked his e-mail while he was away. He snatched the *Book Review* out of her hands and began reading avidly. She could tell by his face that it was bad, but not how bad. Timidly, she leaned in close to read over his shoulder, but he twisted away irritably.

"Who is this woman, this Stoller?" he asked, his voice tremulous, after he had scanned the review. "A practicing psychoanalyst? Why on earth would they have someone like that review this book? That's like asking Hitler to evaluate the Nuremberg court."

"It's only one review, dear. I hope you don't let it upset you. The book will be well received generally. I feel confident that it will. No one is going to second this."

"It's the *Gazette* review. It will be influential."

"Maybe there'll be a better *Times* review."

She reached for the paper, which was lying on the table in front of Edmond, but he clutched it and would not let her pick it up. She looked at him with a mild, questioning expression. "Can't I read it?"

"Shut up, Ivy. I can't cope with your stupidity and insensitivity just now."

Ivy's face went gray, and its flesh seemed to slacken. She walked clumsily out of the room, almost stumbling, and went into the bedroom, where she sat on the bed. She picked up the telephone but let it lie in her lap while she stared at the wall. These scenes, the distressing visits from Wanda and that horrible lawyer of Edmond's—it was all too much for her.

Edmond, in the meantime, had also picked up the telephone; he punched in a number from memory.

"My dear," Ivy heard Edmond saying when she put the receiver to her ear. She was about to reply, when someone else did.

"Hurry up," said Lesley's voice.

"I need you. Can you meet me?" he asked in a whisper that made his voice crack.

"I think so. But not until later—one o'clock?"

"Yes." The word was faint but rich with emotion.

Across the hallway in the Frankls' apartment, Peter called to Lesley, "Who was it?"

"Carla," said Lesley languidly. "About a print."

That afternoon, when Edmond went out, Ivy began making her own phone calls. She was on the telephone for more than an hour, at times in tears. When she hung up, she pulled several suitcases out of a closet and packed them with clothes. She went out and returned with boxes, which she filled with books, folders, and papers; last of all, she removed a computer backup tape from her desk drawer and tucked it into her purse. All this she did at such a brisk pace that sweat formed on her upper lip, and finally she was physically drained. Despite her great efficiency, when Edmond returned at twilight, the van that was to carry off her belongings had not yet arrived. At the sound of his key in the lock, Ivy, who had hoped to avoid a scene, despaired.

She ignored Edmond, continuing her final errands. She retrieved some medicines and toiletries from a cabinet in a bathroom, then wrote a check for her share of that month's expenses and left it on Edmond's desk. He, though, lost in satisfied thoughts about his afternoon's activities, did not grasp the meaning of her bustling activity until he walked into the bedroom and saw the four bulging suitcases, plus a number of large bags stuffed with clothing and other belongings. Even then, it took him several moments to register what was happening.

"I'll send someone for the computer and desk, and those shelves, and the other furniture that's mine, and these paintings," she said in her slightly Oxonian accent, pointing to the bedroom wall.

"Send someone?" asked Edmond, confused. "What's this?"

"Someone will come Monday for the rest of my things."

"You're leaving?"

"Obviously."

"But this is monstrous. Out of the blue, you're walking out—after ten years?"

"Not exactly out of the blue, but, yes, I'm walking out."

"Oh, my God. Oh God, help me!" Edmond staggered to the bed, where he collapsed and began to sob loudly. "Ivy! Oh, Ivy!"

Ivy looked troubled and hesitated for a moment, but the buzzer rang at that very moment, and she instructed the doorman to send up the porter and the man who had brought the van. There was no going back. Even without this latest atrocity, she had been telling herself that it was time to go. Soon Ivy, the van man, and the porter were busily loading up the service elevator. Each time they returned to the apartment, Edmond's sobs, from the bedroom, were clearly audible. The porter and the van man, however, after exchanging looks, chose not to hear; and Ivy, although she could not help shuddering as Edmond's noisy grief actually increased in volume, did not go in to comfort him. Nor did she leave a telephone number or address where she could be reached, as she had done on the other two occasions when she had left Edmond.

Edmond, believing that he had successfully concealed from Ivy his affair with Lesley, reacted to Ivy's departure as though he really were as innocent as he thought she believed he was. Pacing in his partially emptied apartment that evening and observing the many signs of her absence, he looked in vain for a note that would say what set her off or where she had gone. Briefly, he wondered whether she was angry about their spat over the review, but, finding no way to capitalize on that theory, psychologically speaking, he quickly dismissed it in favor of a more gratifyingly sinister one. No, he thought, she simply never loved me. It was my success she loved, my worldly stature. When I was beaten, scorned, no matter how unjustly, she left without a word of explanation or warning. I was living with a monster of narcissism. I never understood my own rages, my interminable melancholy, but it all makes sense now. Oh, yes! How else can a man feel when he is living with a woman who intends to suck him dry and then cast him aside, a woman as coldhearted, as manipulative, as false, as any he ever read about in a novel? But I love her! I love her so totally. She must come back.

Edmond went to the telephone and called Lesley.

"My dear," he said.

"You can't do this," muttered Lesley's voice. "Even *he* will catch on if you keep calling me."

"Something has happened. Ivy's gone. Come over, can you?"

"Oh, that sounds like fun, but I'm still not going out much," said Lesley's voice, loudly. "Let me take a rain check, and I'll call you back."

"All right. As soon as you can." But now that Ivy was gone, Edmond found he had no reason not to be aware that Lesley was a very inferior woman to Ivy. Lesley was even older than Ivy, although with a rather nice figure—quite honestly with a figure much nicer than Ivy's. But Lesley was coarse, uneducated, not very bright, whereas Ivy was a refined woman, a scholar, a woman who could understand and help him—personally, editorially, in every way. And Lesley was sick, which was most inconvenient and dismal. It didn't fit with Edmond's self-image that he should have to render physical aid to someone, particularly to a woman with whom he was having an affair. It was inappropriate somehow. He doubted very much that Ted Hughes, for example, ever had to push Assia Wevill in a wheelchair to sneak out on Sylvia Plath. Or what about Bertrand Russell? You couldn't imagine him having to spend ten minutes helping Lady Ottoline Morrell or Vivienne Eliot get out of a cab, or holding them upright on an elevator ride. It made his current affair seem ridiculous, not impressive and intimidating like other well-known men's affairs. Why couldn't he have had an affair with a healthy young beauty? Of course, there were other ways to look at this. There was the "man of hearty appetites" point of view, which was how he usually chose to look at it: like Don Juan, he loved them all—big, little, old, young. Edmond was crushed, however, to realize that he could no longer find comfort in considering himself a man of such hearty appetites that he even had a taste for old, sick women. And Ivy suddenly seemed, in her absence, haloed, golden, valuable, everything that was good and comforting and desirable. Oddly, his depression, which he thought had maintained an uneasy backroom coexistence with his Zoloft-driven mood, lifted—and in the middle of a catastrophe like this one! Whatever biological or chemical snafu produced it, his melancholia, without warning, inexplicably, ceased, and, miserable and lonely but not at all depressed, Edmond sat looking out his window at the lights across the river.

CHAPTER 36

L ouis called Susan and made a squash date. It was not their first. Louis, who in his own way had always been fond of his odd little sister, thought she would gain social ease and become more outgoing if she played more sports. Susan had progressed very little despite his squash instruction. Her feet were curiously immobile, her reactions so bizarrely slow that the ball hit her more often than she hit the ball. "Stop thinking so much!" Louis would say. "Don't analyze. Just hit it!" Every twentieth opportunity or so, Susan's physical instincts would come alive, and she would make a quick, hard hit that brought a smile to his face. "Okay!" he would shout, his voice reverberating in the court. "Now you got it!" Although one or two such strokes were usually the limit of her success, Louis never lost patience or hope. Today, they spent half an hour on a Columbia squash court; then, red-faced and sweating, they went for showers and afterward walked together down Broadway to Taci, a small, dark neighborhood restaurant with indecisive décor, where in the evening you could listen to opera singers, live, while dining.

They ate salads and pasta and toiled unsuccessfully to make small talk, while Louis kept one eye on a television screen over the bar.

"Susan, is Mallory seeing someone?" he asked abruptly. "Or was she? I think so, but who is it?"

"You mean Alexei?" Susan was not as surprised by his question as he thought she would be.

"Who's that?"

"She wasn't really seeing him," Susan said, feeling her way carefully. "I think he wanted to, but she wouldn't."

"I think she likes him. Who is he? What's he like?"

Susan had long suspected that Louis himself was interested in Mallory. He had to know how things were, so she explained the whole thing: Mallory's brief involvement with Alexei, Susan's own deep admiration for Alexei's talent, how attractive he was and likable, too, although odd and foreign. But he had problems and Mallory was not interested in him and didn't consider him her equal. "So he's no competition, really, but I don't think she'll ever accept you, either." Although this was the first time that Susan had ever acknowledged knowing about Louis's interest in Mallory, they both acted as if it was not.

"She should, though. She's making a mistake."

"I think she wants someone who's more . . ."

"Somebody with a name—some artsy type or some writer or whatever. See, you say this guy, Alexei, is the real thing, but *that* doesn't really interest her. She wants money and status. She doesn't give a damn about art."

"You're being a little rough on her, Louis. You know, she was interested in Chris before I got together with him."

"She would be. He's rich. He does lousy plays, but idiot critics like them, and that's all she cares about. She doesn't really like what he does. It doesn't matter to her."

"Chris's plays are hard to like, but they're brilliant. She admires him. So do I."

"You're nuts, Susan. But not the same way Mallory is. You think you owe him something, I'll bet. You think he needs you."

"Chris would never get over it if I left him. Besides, I'm not going to be like Daddy and marry someone who's from a different planet, who I can't talk to." This subject felt dangerous to both of them. They never discussed their parents' marriage, or the suffering that its divisions had caused them, or even their respective loyalties to one parent.

"Neither am I," Louis said after a tense pause. "And that's why I want to marry Mallory. She's a lot like me, you know." He again pretended to be distracted by the hockey game on the television.

Marry Mallory! Mallory a lot like Louis! As far as Susan knew, they had never had so much as a date. What was he thinking of! Yet another miserable situation in the Frankl family. But she could not hurt her brother's feelings and said nothing.

"How's your paper? Your dissertation?" Louis asked after another tense silence, pretending that they hadn't just stopped short at the edge of a conversation precipice. Impetuously, she decided to tell. It was time everything was out in the open, at least between her and Louis.

"Louis, I've got trouble," Susan said. "Ivy Hurst, you know . . . Edmond Lockhart's beloved . . ."

Louis liked Susan's sarcasm. Susan was so much fun and so sweet; if only she'd let guys get to know her, she'd be really popular.

"She's on my committee, and she's demanding that I change the whole thing. She thinks I'm wrong about a big chapter that's the basis for more than half of the thesis, and it's the only really original and interesting part. It has a comparison between the development of singing techniques and the playing techniques and sound and structure of stringed instruments in Renaissance Italy. It's kind of a weird point—you know me—and it's hard because I have to get people to imagine how things probably sounded . . . to prove this point, that point. Ivy says unless I change it all she'll fail me. I'm almost positive *she's* wrong. I'd lose two years of work if I tried to change it, and I still believe in it. My main adviser says he agrees with me, but he can't get her to back off. It's almost like she's out to get me."

"What are you saying?" he said. "Why would she be out to get you? Not because we all walked out that night at dinner?"

"I think that's probably a lot of it—along with this business with Daddy and Edmond Lockhart at the Devereaux Foundation. I'd guess she's just completely prejudiced against me. But don't tell Dad. He'd be so upset, and there's nothing he could do."

"That really stinks," said Louis.

Susan, unexpectedly, was comforted by Louis's sympathy. It had the effect of encouraging openness. "And there's something else," she said. To Louis's surprise, tears filled her eyes and her lips pressed together in an upside-down bow. She looked the way she did when she was five years old and got her oversensitive feelings hurt.

"Come on, Susan."

Susan told him about the conversation she had overheard between their mother and Edmond Lockhart. "She talked terribly about Dad. She put Edmond Lockhart up to something. She treats Dad so badly, but he just accepts anything she does, as though he thinks he's always in the wrong, like he owes her for something. Sometimes I've been tempted to tell him, but then I just can't bring myself to do it."

Louis looked wounded.

"Oh, Louis, I'm sorry I told you," she said. "I never should have told you."

"No, no," he said. "It's just that it makes me feel sorry for her."

"You mean because it's like we're all ganging up on her and don't love her?"

Louis nodded and grew pale at these words, which were so accurate that they undermined his attempt to suppress his emotions.

"That's why I didn't tell Dad," Susan said. "But why would she do something like that? Why does she resent him?"

"It's some ego thing," he replied. "She hates the fact that he's better than she is. She smells that that's a good thing there, over at the Devereaux Foundation, good people doing good stuff. I realized this when I was a kid—she hates people who are too nice and good, like Dad. She feels inferior. She didn't really want me to be like Dad."

"She thinks, 'He hath a daily beauty in his life / That makes me ugly,' " said Susan. "I didn't think you understood that."

Louis thought, as he often had before, that Susan's social life would improve if she wouldn't go around saying nerdy things like that. He didn't like her condescension very much, either. "You thought I was just naturally shallow, right? You probably also think I don't know that's from *Othello*."

She protested, but actually it had seemed that way. Louis was just made more like their mother. That was what she and her father had thought. And she was amazed that he recognized the line.

"One time," said Louis, "she told me to say I had to go to the doctor so I could skip a test at school because I didn't study. And I said I didn't like telling lies like that, and she smacked me—really—here," he said, pointing to his cheek, "and she said not to pull any more garbage like that and all the smart kids did things like that. But secretly I never did cheat—like that was my private little rebellion. With girls, though, I used to act the way Mom liked. I guess I thought they'd like it—*she* did. Actually, some girls really do."

"How could this go on right under Dad's nose?"

"She was sneaky, and he didn't really want to know. See, Susan, he feels bad always being so superior to her."

"Edmond Lockhart doesn't want him at the Devereaux Foundation because *he* thinks he's superior to Daddy," Susan said bitterly.

"That's how it works," Louis said. "If you want to go for something good and get somewhere, you get everyone mad. Everybody wants you to stay put."

"Not everyone," said Susan tearily. She loved her brother.

Louis left the table and walked toward the men's room. He did not return for ten minutes, until Susan was so worried that she almost went to check on him. But he finally reappeared at the table, holding their check, his face still bloodless.

"You know, people shouldn't just let other people get screwed over and not try to help them out. That's the worst—when everyone just looks the other way and pretends it's not their business."

"But what should we do? Tell Dad?"

"He might leave her," Louis responded in a flat voice.

"She treats him so horribly."

"I don't know," Louis said. "Never mind. Let me handle it." This was an unprecedented thing for Louis to say, but then the whole conversation was unprecedented.

"Also, I have another idea," he said, looking at her obliquely. "This guy Alexei. Why don't you ask him to help you with your paper?"

"With my dissertation? Help me with what?"

"With the singing stuff. He's a singer, isn't he? And smart? Maybe he'll do a little recording for you. Just get a tape recorder and—"

"Louis, he'd think I was crazy," said Susan, horrified at the thought. But she felt another burst of love for her brother, with his naïve ideas about how things worked. "See, it's not like that. . . ."

"You said you really liked him, and he's talented and nice, so what does it hurt? I'm going to be talking to him anyway. I'll let him know you're going to call."

"Why are you going to talk to him?" Susan asked. "You're not going to talk to him about Mallory? . . ."

"Don't worry about it," said Louis.

When they stood up she hugged him, even though she knew that would embarrass him.

That night, Louis called Mallory and asked for Alexei's phone number, letting her infer that he needed help with his computer without actually saying so.

When Alexei's telephone rang, he was just about to begin an Internet chess game with player #17, but he answered anyway. He was too lonely to let a call go by.

"Who?" he asked. He had no recollection of seeing Susan's brother at Mallory's party.

"Mallory says you know a lot about computers," Louis said in his dead-pan voice.

"More than Mallory, anyway," said Alexei.

"Well, I'd like to talk to you," said Louis.

"Sure. When, where?" said Alexei, picking up a pencil and, for the first time, taking his eyes off the screen, where #17 had still not registered a move. They quickly agreed that Alexei would come to the Frankls' apartment the following evening.

CHAPTER 37

Susan felt foolish when she rang Alexei's buzzer. They had met on two or three occasions, but never alone and never for a reason of their own.

Louis had made this improbable meeting unavoidable by handing Alexei a copy of the chapter of her dissertation that Ivy had attacked. "Susan wants to talk to you about it. She'll call you," Louis told him, and Alexei thought this strange. He recalled Susan's inhospitable behavior when he had gone to her apartment on the evening when Alcott and Sylvie were visiting her. By late that afternoon, however, Alexei had read the fifty pages of typescript and, to his surprise, found it intriguing, even enlightening. He would never have guessed that Mallory's closest friend could be as musically knowledge-able and sensitive as Susan showed herself to be in this essay. He was am-bivalent about the discovery, however, for he assumed, based on her behavior that night at her apartment, that her attitude toward him would be the same as Mallory's. Yet he could not comfort himself, as he had with her friend, by dismissing her as shallow and ignorant, with a sense of entitlement out of proportion to her merits. Unprotected by a sense of superiority, Alexei ex-perienced an uncomfortable combination of envy and admiration.

But he also understood now that she really did need help, although he had consented to read the chapter only because it would have been rude to refuse. No one but a singer, he thought, could explain certain aspects of this topic. Susan was making a point about the connection between the development of certain techniques of bel canto, of string instrument construction and playing techniques, and of composition during a period of great musical change in the Renaissance. Her idea was beautiful—which for Alexei was the next thing to true. He had a few things to tell her that might help: a reference to a book that Charles Braithwaite had made him read, one specific thing about singing techniques, and one general thing about her argument.

When, with a restrained, hesitant smile, Alexei opened his door to her, he was struck by how attractive Susan was, which further undid him. Mallory had so outsparkled her friend that he had not noticed that Susan was sort of pretty. Imagine a woman as good-looking as that, with the intellect that was evident in the pages he had read. He had drawn up a mental comparison of Susan with her friend, relying on information fed to him by Susan's brother during an unusual and long conversation a couple of days ago, while poring over a computer that didn't seem to have much wrong with it. He decided that Mallory and Susan were friends because of their differences, not their similarities. Compared with Susan, Mallory was clever, fun, and attractive—attractive in the literal sense. She drew people to her and stood out and got noticed, whereas Susan, at least in Alexei's limited experience of her, drew back and watched. Mallory did not have Susan's depth, not because she was less bright, but because she was not capable of such sustained interest in distant subject matter. Susan was an intellectual, and this quite dazzled Alexei, who could and did read things as weighty as Susan's chapter with pleasure, and comprehendingly, too, but could not conceive of writing such a thing, could not even fathom how a person began. He was all but overwhelmed by his despairing admiration. He had to strangle a silly sense that something unfair was going on.

Alexei, reflecting on all this as Susan stood uncertainly at the open door, made an awkward beginning by failing to say anything for a long time after his initial "Hello." Seeing him so ill at ease, however, Susan felt less embarrassed at having come and walked in, uninvited, and looked around Alexei's room. The floors and walls were rough and bare. There was a battered upright piano against one wall, a music stand, and music in stacks and rows on the floor beside the piano. Next to the sink, dishes had been washed and set to drain on a small rack. There was an old oak dresser on which a chess game was laid out and a daybed that doubled as a sofa, with a low table in front of it. One wall, lined entirely with boards set on cinder blocks to form a desktop and shelves, was devoted to an elaborate computer setup and books—chess books, music books, novels, and a great deal of poetry. The place was ticky-tacky, but he had obviously tried to make the most of it.

"How do your neighbors stand your singing?" she asked.

"Fortunately, most of them are gone to work all day, but there are a couple who sometimes are a bad problem. I'm always trying to do them favors so they won't complain to the landlord."

Now, still without an invitation, Susan had made it all the way to his sofa. On a little table before it, he had gathered his copy of the chapter, pencils and paper, a plate of sweet cheese tarts, and tea things. He was orderly and hospitable. She admired and took pleasure in these preparations and happily accepted a cup of tea. "Who made these?" she asked, sampling a tart. "You? Really?" The cookery was particularly impressive to Susan, who was usually the only person who could cook in any gathering of people her own age. She wandered to the piano, where a book of Schubert sat open, and played the opening bars of *Winterreise.*

"Nice," he said. Even in those simple notes, he recognized polished, conservatory playing. It set up a strenuous discord in his mind: someone from that other world where Mallory, Louis, and all those people lived surely belonged to him—more to him than to them, in fact.

"Not really. Someday I'd love to hear you sing that," she said.

"Would you play for me?" he asked, and then blushed and hunched his shoulders self-consciously because this was more than a polite request. He was always desperate for an accompanist.

Alexei did not know how to open the subject of Susan's dissertation. He was not used to receiving guests, and Susan's presence in his shabby room made him acutely aware of being at a social disadvantage. When he had stood for a moment in her apartment, it had seemed marvelously luxurious and tasteful. That such plenty, such security, beauty, and sophistication, belonged to someone hardly older than him, and not to the parent generation, had made him feel hurt and shy. Mallory's place, which was smaller and less richly furnished, and Mallory herself, had not had quite that effect. Yet at her party back in March, he was aware that he had been invited in defiance of class distinctions whose subtleties he did not entirely grasp. His first two years in the States had been spent at the Manhattan School of Music, an institution that recognized and elevated talent and talent alone and was full of immigrants like himself. It was only through Mallory that he had had any contact with privileged castes in this country. Until then, he had hardly known they existed. Their attitudes seemed to him similar to those that Party members used to have in the Soviet Union, except that their sense of having all things due them appeared even more profound, for here it was mitigated and restrained by no proletarian sympathies, such as those that were so widespread in Soviet Russia, despite the system's blatant hypocrisies.

Like all young Russians, Alexei had learned the flavor of the old Soviet society even though he had been so young when it all collapsed. Society hadn't collapsed, at least not wholly, when the government did.

Susan's manners, however, were different from the others'. She by now had wandered from the piano to the chess board on the dresser, which she studied curiously.

"Game in progress?" she asked.

"I have a chess correspondent," Alexei said, "in Russia. He's old and doesn't have Internet."

"Whose move is it?"

"Mine. I'm white."

"So," said Susan, frowning in concentration, "will you do bishop to G5?"

"No, you don't play chess, too?"

"Very badly."

"Just like the piano, I'm sure," he said with a wounded half-smile. "Yes, bishop to G5, I think." He felt it unjust that she also played chess at least well enough to recognize the Queen's Gambit. It wasn't fair that privilege should also be virtuous, pretty, and multitalented. But such thoughts made Alexei feel small and left him tongue-tied; he welcomed the distraction of the doorbell ringing.

"I'm not expecting anyone," he said, frowning, as he went to answer it.

The visitor was Cora Bledsoe, who was on her way to MSM and had stopped by to drop off cookies she had baked for him. In Alexei's small room, she seemed particularly radiant and plump; and her manner and appearance—her very frankness and lack of a social façade—so obviously placed her beneath Susan's social set that Alexei was damp with sweaty embarrassment. Cora was blind to this level of social reality, of course, and that was one of the very things that diminished her status, but it also freed her to feel an instant liking for Susan. And although Susan was shy at first, she soon warmed to Cora.

Before leaving, she favored Susan with a nutshell history of her life, a thorough review of a concert she'd attended last weekend, and the entire story of her night at the emergency room with Alexei, including a recital of his speeches and actions—despite his efforts to cut her off. She mourned his missed audition, which she had learned about from Vic. She had even called the little Brooklyn opera company to explain Alexei's absence, but they said the part was gone—they were sorry.

"Isn't that terrible?" she said, leaning toward Susan with a stricken expression.

Susan had to admit that it was, and she was pained to hear that Alexei had lost such an opportunity, although a candid woman-to-woman disclosure of this sort required her to respond with absolution. "It wasn't your fault, though," she said feelingly.

"It didn't matter. I didn't really have a chance," Alexei muttered.

Cora's stories let Susan know not only Cora herself, but also Alexei, both through what she learned of his behavior and through Cora's perceptions of him, which she integrated with her own. By the time Cora left, Susan knew Alexei better than she had any right to: kind, boorish, grumpy, affectionate, egoistic, loyal, and trustworthy—she put the puzzle pieces together according to a pattern disclosed in Cora's affection.

Alexei was restless and flustered when Cora was gone. He wondered if Susan would think Cora was his girlfriend. Susan, to whom it was evident that she wasn't, wondered if Cora thought—or even hoped—that Susan was. They tried to resume talking but managed only a frail, disjointed conversation until Susan, picking up the copy of her chapter from the table, plunged into the story of her troubles with Ivy Hurst, going all the way back to the dinner that the Frankls had walked out of months ago.

Alexei listened with a puzzled frown; now it was his turn to take in Susan. He was still oppressed by the fact that Mallory's friend, and Louis's sister, was this pretty, unassuming girl who played chess and chatted easily with Cora and had so much musical sense that it gave him the false feeling that he knew her well. She wasn't proud and superior at all, any more than her brother, Louis, who was so obviously fond of her. When he and Louis had spoken together, Louis had praised her talents and merits and several times had disparaged that fellow Chris she was going with. Alexei himself didn't care much for Chris.

Susan was saying that she had a meeting with Professor Hurst the following Monday and intended to try to persuade her to change her mind. Soon the two of them were deep into the material. Alexei observed curiously how Susan was transformed when she began to talk about the music. She spoke with warmth and energy; she was open and looked appealingly into his eyes for signs that he understood. And he did. Having heard Ivy Hurst's challenges, Alexei urged Susan to stick to her guns. He was outraged. Hurst's objections were, musically speaking, entirely ignorant. He couldn't believe it! Couldn't Susan get a new outside reader? He had some very definite ideas about responses to Hurst's criticisms, and Susan listened carefully to his explanations of vocal technique and his thoughts about her account of the musical ideals that had guided development of the violin. She smiled when he sang some of his explanation and was pleased at his general point, which was that even if her thesis could not be absolutely proved by the historical evidence currently available, it was valid by aesthetic standards. The facts Susan had focused on cried out for historical explanation, too, because this dovetailing of ideas in separate musical realms was too significant to be dismissed as mere coincidence, and she was the first even to notice it. This was by far the best talk about her work that Susan had ever had, and it left her exhilarated.

"I once told a friend of mine," she said, "that I had never been able to talk to anyone the way I could talk to her, and she said, 'Oh, everyone tells me that.' But I do feel that way about you."

"No one tells *me* that," he said, half smiling. Her openness was seductive, yet he was suspicious of it—even a little angry. In Mallory's case, it had turned out to indicate a kind of disregard, a sense that he was beneath her and that therefore her normal patterns of distance and standards of restraint did not apply. With Alexei, Mallory had permitted herself the kind of intimacy a superior has with social inferiors—something Alexei had read about in novels—except that she had thought she was being democratic. Neither of them had understood what they were doing. At this moment, Alexei felt very much like kissing Susan, who was sitting here on his sofa looking at him with big, dark eyes, smiling; but, remembering Mallory, he did nothing of the kind.

Susan, for her part, aware of a special warmth for Alexei, thought to herself, I must have been desperate for someone to talk to about this. I never realized how much it would mean to me. She was not really surprised that Alexei was so bright, not after hearing him sing in that cerebrally passionate style. But it was surprising that they were so completely on the same wavelength, that she felt so comfortable with him. She would have said "like a brother" except that she had always felt that she and her brother had little in common.

"How much music does Chris know?" asked Alexei.

Susan responded by making a circle with her thumb and forefinger.

"So he tries, but he just doesn't have the background to go into it with you?"

"He doesn't try. He finds my interest in it incomprehensible. He thinks I should go to medical school and not waste time quarreling with Ivy Hurst." She laughed at Alexei's expression. She had never expected Chris, or anyone else, for that matter, to be interested in her obscure ideas about Renaissance music.

"Why medical school? Are you also scientific?"

"No, no. He thinks I have a caretaker bent. Don't worry. I'm not going to medical school. But, you know, I never expected anyone to pay any attention to this stuff I'm writing about. I went into it with the idea that it was my solitary passion. But, of course, on another level, I don't understand why the whole world isn't just dying to know the answers to these questions."

Alexei nodded at that, a downturn at the corner of his mouth conveying, miraculously, both that the whole world *should* wish to know this and that she was kidding herself if she thought she didn't mind pursuing her work as a solitary passion. She had noticed at the recital that Alexei had a great ability to convey complicated ideas and emotions efficiently, understatedly, with his face as well as his voice, and it struck her that he could never be very effective as a recorded singer. Or, at least, he would never be as effective on a recording as in person.

"To me," she said, "all these little moves forward are miracles, and particularly now, when . . ." Susan's voice petered out in the middle of this speech, and she felt foolish. He probably had his own sophisticated views of the contemporary music world, and who was she to sound off in front of him?

"This is all true. Don't stop," Alexei said. "And I'm glad you try to figure it all out and write it down—and that there's a place in the world for you to do this."

He seemed wistful saying this, and Susan felt another wave of warmth for him. She had admired and liked him before, but now she felt an affection. He was good. Such a sudden, strong liking was a rare and happy experience for her; and she thought immediately that Chris had to get to know Alexei. She expected Chris to come pick her up and hoped he would come soon so that they could visit for a while before they left.

In fact, Chris buzzed up just as Susan was trying to reach him on her cell phone.

"Alexei!" he said, walking in, his hands in his pockets and head tilted to the side appraisingly. "I hear you were a big smash at that recital."

Alexei did not smile. He heard an undertone of condescension in Chris's voice and saw it in his posture. So did Susan, and she tried to stop it.

"Chris, Alexei has just done more to help my thesis in two hours than my adviser did in two years. Really! I'm not kidding. He may have saved the whole thing." Her voice pitched too high, and she heard herself pleading for Alexei and knew this was false, all wrong. She couldn't think of anything she could say that would fix things.

"Great," said Chris, too kindly, so that this word, too, implied a multitude of things that made Susan to fight for Alexei and made Alexei become even more cool and unsmiling. As they were saying good-bye, however, Alexei had a thought.

"Susan, I'm invited to Thanksgiving dinner at the Braithwaites'. Do you want to come with me? I would like you to talk to Charles about all this. He'd be very interested, and he's really scholarly, you know."

Susan was bewildered. She looked at Chris. "Charles Braithwaite? But I'm not invited."

"They told me I should bring a friend. They'll be happy to see you. I know them very well, and they'll be really glad if you come. I teach chess to their kids, and I take lessons with him, you know. It's in the evening—seven-thirty."

"Well," said Susan, stymied as to how to interpret the invitation. She had a moment's social anxiety as well, wondering if appearing anywhere as Alexei's guest would be consistent with her own sense of social dignity. Maybe *she*, too, would get treated like a personal trainer or a computer repair person by the Braithwaites, which would be quite humiliating. But she was disgusted with herself for such doubts and, moreover, realized, as Alexei had, that if she said yes, it would set things right between them and salvage the groundwork of friendship that had been laid before Chris's presence raised questions as to their equality. Besides, she wanted to avoid going to Chris's parents', and she could easily see her own family in the afternoon, before the Braithwaites' dinner. Therefore she announced, decidedly and with sincere pleasure, "Yes, of course, I'd love to meet them. She played at your recital, didn't she?"

"Good. Then I'll call you," Alexei said, and smiled slightly and nodded to the two of them as they left. Alone again, however, within five minutes he wished he hadn't invited Susan, who might turn out to be just like Mallory—nice in manner, but ruthlessly self-interested in reality.

Chris, with Susan on the street, was puzzled and irritated. "*That* was strange—asking you to a dinner without me when I'm standing there in front of him—at someone else's house, yet. What's this all about?"

"Just what it looks like. I was telling him how I didn't have anyone to talk to about my work. And they're musicians, and he thinks I'd like them and could talk to them about it."

"He's a good guy," Chris said after they had walked in silence for more than two blocks.

"An astonishingly good guy."

"He still works for Alcott on the set sometimes, doesn't he?"

"So I've heard."

"Would you like it if I gave him work, if this play of mine gets off the ground? I could find something for him to do. I know you'd like to help him out if you could."

"I somehow doubt he'd take the job." Susan knew she should thank Chris for this; he was attempting to be generous to please her. But she couldn't bring herself to say the words.

"I somehow think he'd go down on his knees for a real job in a real production at union wages," said Chris.

"You don't know him."

"Neither do you. But I've known a million guys like him."

"No, you haven't."

"My argumentative one, that's not what I want to talk to you about." Susan smiled, which inspired him to put his arm around her waist as they walked.

"Susan, I've thought a lot about all the things you've been saying, and you're very smart at figuring out this stuff that goes on between us. But sometimes I see you giving up on me. I've seen you put things aside, when you know they're not right, and just act the way you think will make me comfortable. But in the long run it doesn't really make me comfortable because it means you're giving up and you might leave me, and I couldn't bear it if you did. I just couldn't bear it, Susan."

Susan saw that his eyes were swimming. She had never realized that he had any idea that she was humoring him or that she actually often did give up on him. She had never been sure that he understood how hard she was fighting for him. But he did. She threw her arms around him.

"So I want you to move in with me, because I'd feel more sure of you. Don't you think it's time?"

Susan did indeed. This speech of Chris's upset all the pessimistic ideas she had had about him lately. Her thoughts, however, jumped immediately to her father. She had to try to make him understand. He wanted Chris to treat her more the way *he* did, which was sweet but not a realistic expectation for relationships in the new millennium.

"So when?" Chris asked, frowning and smiling slightly at the same time, his eyes still overbright. They both took it for granted that Susan would move down to the Village, where Chris lived, because his loft there was five times the size of her apartment. She would subway up to Columbia. Susan had never been in love with the Village, but she'd get used to it.

"Let me think. It's hard to say. I have to decide what to do with my place first."

"Hang on to it. It's a nice place. It could be our uptown pied-à-terre."

She agreed that she should keep it, assuming that her father consented, which he probably would. He would want to ensure that Susan had a place to go back to if she needed it.

That night, she called her friends to tell the news. Mallory, whom she hadn't spoken to for weeks, had seen this coming for a long time. In her opinion, Susan and Chris were a natural couple; it had been obvious the minute she saw them together. But she was sorry that Susan would be so far away. It was pleasant living as they did, as neighbors, here in Morningside Heights. She knew she would miss being able to run over to Susan's, and have her drop by. Susan would not necessarily be at home in the Village, with its bohemian, beat, and hip antecedents. It might not be a good match, Mallory thought, geographically speaking. Why couldn't they move up-town? However, Mallory talked only about how glad she was that Susan and Chris were going to make a couple and how right that seemed to her; and because she loved her friend, she knew what things she should say to make her happy. Susan, of course, heard much of what Mallory did not say in her pauses and overtones and ellipses.

After this conversation, Susan remembered with some embarrassment a discussion with Mallory about Alexei months ago in which she had ac-cused Mallory of having let herself be seduced by his good looks. Mallory had told her that she didn't understand, which she certainly hadn't. Susan wondered if it would be out of place to raise all that with Mallory now. Perhaps she could do Alexei a favor with Mallory. But, recalling the things she and Louis had said about Mallory at that strange lunch at Taci, she decided that was not possible. Mallory was never going to be seriously in-terested in someone with no degree and no prospects, whatever his talents and good qualities. Besides, trying to sell Mallory on Alexei would be dis-loyal to her brother, even though there was no chance for that to work out, either.

Sylvie was less enthusiastic about Susan's moving in with Chris than Mallory had been. But she was touchingly happy that Susan was moving to the Village, where she would be near her and Alcott, and therefore spoke only about this welcome aspect of the news.

"The sadness down here is reassuring," Sylvie said, "because, you know, as long as the world is chaotic and cruel, and love is rare, everyone might as well act like it."

"But every now and then," said Susan, imitating Sylvie's cool drawl, "someone gets lucky."

Sylvie knew that Susan was talking about her, Sylvie, not about herself. "Every now and then," she agreed with an unusual bashfulness. "We got re-ally lucky, Alcott and me, by the way. He went and talked to your eccentric friend, you know, from the foundation."

"Hilda Hughes!" Susan said. "Why didn't you tell me?"

"Hilda Hughes, yes. She practically threw the money at us. We've just been frantic, getting things going again."

Susan realized with a pang that Hilda wanted to be sure they got the money before she was fired.

"She liked the proposal," said Sylvie.

"Which you wrote?" asked Susan.

"Which I wrote. I wrote it faster than I wrote my senior paper. Do you remember that?"

"I hope it was better than your senior paper." Susan heard a ripple of giggles from Sylvie, who hardly ever smiled.

"It must have been."

"This is such good news, Sylvie, I don't know what to say. Let's celebrate when I'm in the neighborhood this week."

After Susan had talked to Mallory and Sylvie, she thought about calling her father and telling him of her plans to move but decided to put it off. She had to consider more carefully just how to break this to him. Instead, thinking of a sudden possibility, she called her brother.

"You don't seem terribly surprised," she said to Louis.

"Mallory told me," he said. "I called her just now."

Susan knew better than to ask any questions. "Can't you be glad for me?"

"Sure, yeah. If you like him, that's the main thing, and he likes you. Sure." Louis was determined to be neutral.

"Louis, I'm not ready to tell Daddy yet."

"I won't mention it."

"I need a day or two to figure out what to say to him."

"In your shoes, I'd need a month or two. This is going to hit him hard, Susan. If it were me, he'd say I never had any sense anyway. But with you, it's gonna hit him right in the stomach."

Susan thought about this as she lay awake beside Chris that night, restless and undecided how to talk to her father. Sometimes she thought that she might be taking it all a little too seriously. After all, she wasn't going to marry Chris. She was just going to move in with him. How serious was that? She didn't really know.

CHAPTER 38

The following Monday morning, Susan arrived at her parents' apartment just in time to kiss Lesley good-bye as she left with her nurse for physical therapy. A moment later, she stood at the door of the library and watched her father at his computer, a tie hanging over his shoulders ready for knotting. Peter was often gloomy these days, but he beamed when he saw his daughter, and she dreaded her task.

"One second," he said. He guessed that she had timed her arrival to find him alone. Susan gathered herself while he finished his message, then without preamble told him her plans to move in with Chris.

"It's a bad decision, sweetheart," Peter said. "It's the wrong thing." Susan obviously expected him to be unreasonable and uncomprehending and was doing her best to handle him. He found it maddening, being treated like a retarded police sergeant—and by Susan, the one he loved most, the understanding one.

"How can you be so sure? Why is it you think I have such poor judgment? After all, I know him very well, and you're going on the basis of a thirty-second encounter under extremely stressful circumstances."

"And a few poorly timed absences, plus some unencouraging things about his background you yourself have told me, along with my instinctive reaction to him. In my business, you get good at that. Susan, this guy will make you unhappy. I'm sure. I think you know it, and for reasons I don't get you're ignoring what you know."

Susan deliberated with her head bent, and Peter knew that she was hurt and soon would be angry.

"I have a better chance of being happy with Chris than you had with Mother," Susan said, taking Peter by surprise, "and you made it work. You raised a family and stayed together."

"Susie, you're way off," Peter said. It stung him to hear her justify herself with an appeal to the model of his own marriage. This was where he had gotten by putting a good face on things for the sake of the kids. Although it was probably too late to try to put her straight, he decided to try, circumspectly. "Actually, things may have been a lot worse for us than you ever realized—not that I want to whine. I just want you to be aware that maybe there was more trouble than you understood."

"Daddy, I was, and am, quite aware of what went on, maybe more aware than you were. You did far more damage by enduring it all in silence than you ever would have by . . ." Susan paced nervously, unwilling to say more.

"See, that's the thing, isn't it? I'm not sure, either. I've asked myself over and over. Should I tell my daughter that her mother is an unusually limited human being not capable of offering her much in the way of love?"

"You know and I know that that's not the half of it. Maybe the rest is for another conversation, but it's a long overdue one as far as I'm concerned. For now, here's the thing: I care far more for Chris and share far more with him than you ever did with Mom. Our compatibility is infinitely greater—socially, aesthetically, every other way. He's my kind. But you marrying Mom was like . . ."

While Susan searched for an adequate comparison, Peter waited expectantly. He had had no idea that this was how she saw things.

"Like Captain Picard marrying a Klingon woman or something," Susan said finally.

"I can't believe that with an education from two great universities you can't come up with a more literate analogy than that," said Peter. He wanted to lighten the tone of their interchange but couldn't resist adding, his bantering tone dying away, "And it's not so kind to your mother. There isn't really any need to be so harsh, is there?"

"Whatever you say," said Susan. His stubborn blindness, passivity, and manipulability enraged her, and for a moment she was tempted to tell him what she had overheard between Edmond and Lesley. She would have liked to make him look and feel as injured as he really was, expose him to his own suffering. But as long as his ignorance brought him any comfort, she would not take it away from him. Nor would she risk being the cause of his abandoning her mother. Susan gave Peter an ambivalent kiss on the cheek and left.

She walked to the Columbia campus, where unfortunately she had an appointment with Professor Hurst. It would be hard to talk about Renaissance music with her mind revolving on the things her father had just said to her so unequivocally: "bad decision" and "wrong thing." He shouldn't have opposed her so openly and unqualifiedly when he knew that she was not going to change her mind. Susan mourned the Victorian necessity of throwing off her father to keep her lover. Her whole life was an anachronism.

When Peter finally set out for his office that morning, an hour later than usual, he spied the nurse already wheeling Lesley down the block toward home, and he barely escaped around the corner before they could see him. Peter was so disgruntled by Susan's news and their near quarrel that he knew he would have no peace of mind for days to come. Susan was already unhappy with Chris, and with his flat-out warnings he had succeeded only in helping her avoid facing that; now she could fight her father instead of Chris. Chris had more than ordinary human deficits. With him, Susan might live precisely the stunted life that Peter himself had, without companionship or affection . . . without—why should he be so loath to say this even to himself at this point—without even ordinary decency and kindness in her partner. Still, she hadn't said she would marry the guy, which would have been worst of all; and maybe the fact that she didn't seem anxious to marry him showed that on some level she knew it was all wrong. Peter had a book in his briefcase that he had checked out of the library—Marcus Aurelius. Why not give stoicism a chance? he had said to himself, and made a mental note to ask Rabbi Friedman what he thought of it.

Susan arrived at Ivy Hurst's office and knocked tentatively on the thick oak door. When an authoritative voice commanded her to enter, she opened it with respectful caution and peered in.

Ivy sat before her in profile, at a broad desk in a wide chair, which she filled entirely. Generally speaking, it was impossible not to notice that Ivy was oddly shaped, narrow-shouldered and flat-chested yet so broad in the hips that to Susan it always seemed as though her upper and lower halves belonged to two different women. Susan had noticed this against her will, as it was a crude and ungenerous observation. Yet on the present occasion she was helpless to avoid forming the opinion, as she stood beside the desk, waiting for an invitation to be seated, that the divergence between Ivy's upper and lower halves had increased, the one having grown lesser and the other greater. Susan fastened her eyes on Ivy's face in an attempt to censor this unpleasant perception, but Ivy's face inspired her with further unworthy reflections.

Ivy looked haggard. Her newly trimmed boy-cut was particularly short, upright, and bristly and made an unpleasantly vivid contrast with the sagging flesh of her face. Her eyes were red-rimmed, their sockets dark and hollow. The fiercely unfriendly expression on her face alarmed Susan. She must be unwell, Susan thought. "Is this a bad time?" she asked respectfully.

"It's nine-thirty," said Ivy with an air of sardonic contempt, "which is the time we agreed on."

"Yes, I only meant . . . ," Susan began, and then stopped. The truth could not be uttered, and no plausible falsehood occurred to her. "I wanted to speak with you about the questions you raised about chapter three, and several related issues as well."

"I think my remarks were very clear. What didn't you understand?" Ivy's voice, a contralto that was somewhat hoarse and harsh on this occasion, contrasted most unpleasantly with Susan's silken, good-natured soprano. Ivy was sensitive to such things. She noticed the contrast, and it increased the unfriendliness in her face.

"Oh, I understood them. They were very clear, yes. But I have a few reactions that I want to talk over with you." Susan tried hard not to appear hostile or confrontational. She smiled hopefully, but Ivy glared back.

Susan realized, with a shock, that Ivy disliked her and meant her harm. This wasn't someone being misled by emotion into making a shallow misjudgment. This was a woman who knew just what she was doing and was going about it in a calculated way. It was a ghastly realization. This is an enemy, she thought, my first real enemy, and she trembled. Without waiting any longer for an invitation, she sat on a narrow chair beside Ivy's desk. Of course, nothing she could say would change Ivy's mind. Ivy was going to try to stop her from getting her degree no matter what Susan did or said. How could she feel so much hatred for the mere daughter of the man who had offended her? It was downright Homeric.

Susan thought all this while digging in a carryall for papers, but she did not know how to have a polite discussion with someone who wanted to destroy her. She began, lamely, to explain why she thought the fundamental ideas of her third chapter were sound. While Susan spoke, Ivy began rummaging through a desk drawer. Susan cut off her sentence to wait for Ivy to finish.

"Go ahead, go ahead," Ivy said, pulling out folders.

"I was just saying," said Susan, "that the real purpose of the thesis is to explore the separate roots of these common developments, so that they can be seen to—"

"What common developments?" asked Ivy offhandedly, going through the contents of several folders. Susan could see that they contained photocopies of journal articles. The folder on top was labeled *Ousia*. Obviously, it had nothing to do with Susan's thesis. Susan had until this moment given Ivy the benefit of the doubt: perhaps she was searching for some document that would be relevant to her objections to Susan's work or to Susan's responses to her objections. But no, she was simply doing little chores while Susan struggled to offer fine-honed explanations of the reasoning at the core of her thesis. She was paying no attention at all. Susan stopped speaking again, waiting for Ivy to cease examining the folders.

Ivy looked up archly. "Well? I'm all ears, Ms. Frankl."

"Actually, you seem too busy with something else to be all ears, Professor Hurst. I'll come back another time when you aren't so tied up." Susan rose, gathering the notes and text she had laid on the desk beside her and haphazardly crushing them back into her bag.

"I'm a busy woman, and I agreed to meet you, here and now, to listen to all your complaints," Ivy said. Something satisfied could be heard in her voice, behind its unconcealed threat. "If you aren't interested in following through, you can't expect me to waste my time scheduling another meeting. I am dismayed, though, that you would show up in my office so completely unprepared as you obviously are to deal with the serious objections I've raised to your thesis."

Susan looked down at Ivy, who remained seated and smiled slightly at the humiliation and rage apparent on Susan's face. Susan managed to make it into the hallway before her fury turned to tears.

She could not avoid a bitter, daunting struggle, and she might lose! Susan yearned for help, for comfort. She couldn't call Chris, who forbade calls when he was working and wouldn't see something like this as an emergency. She couldn't call her father, either, not after this morning's disagreement. She was tempted to call Alexei, who had seemed to be so interested and so angry about Ivy, but feared that would annoy Chris. Sylvie, she decided, who had some firsthand experience of injustice and petty cruelties, was the one she wanted to talk to. She would have to learn a little of Sylvie's toughness.

Sylvie, however, didn't answer, and neither did Mallory. That night, when Chris came, at about 10:30, Susan was still on the telephone, calling around trying to learn whether it was possible to remove a member of one's dissertation committee. The consensus was that it was not, although every-one knew of instances where members had resigned. "She will definitely not resign," Susan was saying into the telephone as Chris sat on the bed beside her.

"Have you had dinner?" Chris asked when she hung up.

"I'm not hungry," Susan said.

"I've been trying to call you since about nine. Do you realize you've been on the phone for an hour and a half? And you didn't answer the cell."

"I left it in my coat pocket. I didn't hear it. I'm sorry, Chris, but some-thing very bad has happened. I've got serious trouble."

"What is it this time?" he asked wearily.

"This time? I thought this was the first time I'd ever said that."

"Susan, when do you not have serious trouble? Your mother spends months at death's door. Your father is publicly denounced. You get hysteri-cal and cause car accidents. Ever since I've known you, it's just one damn thing after another."

Susan looked at the floor, an icy tightness constricting her chest. She wanted to reply, but all the responses she could think of seemed futile. If she got mad, he would back off. If she threatened to leave, he would admit that he was wrong. If she tried to make him understand how distorting, un-friendly, even cruel, those words were, he would laugh and shrug.

"Look, sweetheart," said Chris, coaxingly now, and he squeezed her arm. "I've had a rotten day myself. I don't want to bore you with the details. Frankly, I just don't have it in me to listen to yours right now. Why don't we both just put it behind us? I'll go grab something to eat. We'll go to bed."

"The deal fell through?"

Chris didn't answer.

"I'm sorry, Chris." Susan knew not to press him to explain what hap-pened. Chris put on his coat and ignored her.

"Be back," he said. While he was gone, she debated whether to forgive him for his insensitivity. She had wanted something out of him at a time when, understandably, he had very little to give. In good relationships, surely such lapses should be overlooked. By the time Chris came back, smelling of beer and onions, Susan had forgiven him.

CHAPTER 39

Peter saw Hilda in a café on Broadway as he passed on his way to the subway. She took a cup from the counter clerk and went to sit in an armchair, her back to the window. He stood a moment and considered before going in. By the time he had bought a cup of coffee and approached Hilda, she was engaged in lively small talk with a well-dressed woman in her forties who was nibbling on a bagel. Peter was surprised to see Hilda being so sociable. He stood a few feet off and debated whether he should walk out or speak to her about Emma. After all, at this moment she seemed to be so entirely relaxed. Why remind her of problems and spoil her morning?

Her voice carried to him clearly, and he heard her say, "Really? I got back from Capri last week—I always come back early in November. I spent only two days in Rome," which astonished him, as he knew that she had been in Manhattan last week. Her tone of voice, self-possessed and worldly, was quite as astonishing as what she was saying.

The other woman spoke then, something about that time of year in Italy, and Hilda, leafing through a newspaper with what Peter perceived was a pretense of casual distraction, responded in the dogmatic yet ladylike manner of society women he had known, "I always spend Christmas in London with my sisters, and I love the way it closes down so completely. It ensures that everyone remembers the feeling of precommercial life." Then for some reason Hilda turned around and saw him. She blushed and said dejectedly, in a voice more familiar to him, "Hello, Peter."

"May I join you?" he asked, looking for a chair and letting her know with a scathing look that he had overheard something.

"Please, take my chair," said the woman with the bagel as she stood to go.

"What the hell was that all about?" he asked Hilda, staring at her and frowning.

"What do you mean?" asked Hilda, not meeting his eyes.

"Let me ask you, have you ever been to Capri?"

"No."

"London?"

"No."

"You really ought to go sometime. But I wouldn't recommend Christmas, unless you've got relatives or close friends there. By the way, do you have any brothers or sisters?"

"No."

"Hilda, playing around at being crazy like that, when you're not, is just juvenile. All it does is destroy your self-respect. Cut it out. Are you going downtown, maybe? Taking the subway?"

"Yes."

"Come on. Oh, Christ!" Peter was watching a woman entering the café.

"What?"

"There's Wanda."

"Who's Wanda?" Hilda asked in a depressed voice, stuffing her newspaper into a carryall.

"Someone whom I barely know in a very complicated way."

Hilda's expression changed from melancholic to penetrating. Damn her, thought Peter, watching Hilda figure out half of the whole complicated mess just by watching him and Wanda react to each other, for now Wanda had seen him and flashed her mischievous smile. She looked fresh and pretty—blond, cheeks pinked by the cold.

"Peter," said Wanda.

"Wanda, how are you? My old friend Hilda Hughes."

"Hilda," said Wanda, acknowledging the introduction with a polite nod and a civil inflection in her pronunciation of the name. Wanda's lively eyes darted from Hilda's face to Peter's and back, trying to interpret the mystifying, fading clues there of something in the way of a recent emotional encounter.

"Can you stay for another cup of coffee?" she asked Peter.

"No," he said. "How's George?"

Wanda laughed. "Despite everything, I'll bet you're some lawyer, Peter." With what elegant economy Peter had signaled that his feelings were in all respects unchanged! "And if the world operated on schoolboy rules, what a winner you'd be! Listen, you'd better call Edmond this week. He's not going to wait much longer."

Hilda, walking beside Peter down the subway steps at 110th Street, was experiencing an unprecedented envy. If only she could talk to people the way Wanda had—but when she tried, one of those silly charades started up. How very grown-up Peter and Wanda had been together! How Katharine Hepburn and Spencer Tracy! Why was she, Hilda, condemned to lonely, endless childhood while everyone else had grown up decades ago and had long been enjoying the privileges of adulthood? How she yearned to share them! Peter was right, absolutely right. Her neurotic games were the behavior of a woman who wouldn't grow up. But never before had she experienced this as something painful. It had always been the other way around. Hilda told herself that she was entitled to refuse to grow up because her childhood had been so deprived, but she had by now caused far more harm than she had suffered. If soon she were to be unemployed and homeless, it would serve her right but wouldn't much help the people she had injured. Never once in her life had she even dreamed that she could hurt someone with her silly games, especially Emma Devereaux and Peter and the others at the foundation.

Peter saw the tears standing in Hilda's eyes, and over the roar of the subway train, each of them gripping an overhead bar, she heard, out of a long string of words he uttered: "Hilda . . . a long time . . . you." She felt indescribably comforted, and his face, watching hers, showed relief.

CHAPTER 40

Funding had flowed almost immediately from the Devereaux Foundation into Alcott Adams's new film production. Emma Devereaux was enthusiastic about this latest project, especially as everyone kept telling her that it might be their last one. Mr. Frankl had been right—he always was—when he said they shouldn't have him chair the seminar meeting. Now Edmond was threatening to have her declared incapacitated and the newspapers were calling for the government to come in and look at their books! As though every penny's fate were not recorded there, duly and properly! As though their programs were not published in press releases just as soon as they were funded, and in all their annual reports as well! But Mr. Frankl, although he was always looking so tired lately, promised to stand by her, so come what may, she would not resign. Indeed, if she hadn't learned never to disagree with Mr. Frankl, Miss Devereaux might not be *quite* as worried about all this as he was. He was such a worrier. But as none of them had done anything even remotely wrong, what could be the problem? And since she was not at all incapacitated, why should she fear Edmond?

Now, feeling anxiously ambitious for the new film, Miss Devereaux did allow herself to hope that it wouldn't be cold or dark or cruel or incomprehensible, as were the works of other young filmmakers who used to apply for their grants. Miss Devereaux wished that movies could become more the way they used to be—say, like *Brief Encounter* or *His Girl Friday*. Hilda had said that the one Alcott Adams wished to make was worth a chance, but she hadn't looked Miss Devereaux in the eye when she said it. Miss Devereaux knew very well that this meant that Hilda liked it but thought Miss Devereaux would not. Still, Miss Devereaux was sanguine, for Hilda had found the young man through Peter Frankl's lovely daughter, a remarkable young woman who was devoted to the study of Renaissance music and, according to Hilda, played Bach on the piano like an angel. What better recommendation could there be? Mr. Frankl's brilliant daughter thought the film quite worthwhile, and that should be good enough for any of them.

Early one cold, bright morning in November, Miss Devereaux had the idea that Hilda should visit the set and see how things were coming. They had been filming for several weeks, according to Hilda's reports, often in Morningside Heights where Hilda lived. Miss Devereaux called Hilda and said that, if it was not inconvenient, Hilda should spend some time observing the production and let her know if it was going all right. If things looked bad, perhaps Hilda could guide them a bit. Or perhaps Hilda could bring Mr. Frankl's daughter along, and *she* could influence them. Yes, decided Miss Devereaux as she spoke with Hilda on the telephone. Could Hilda please arrange to bring Susan Frankl with her? If so, she would send a car to pick up Susan in the Village.

Hilda felt no alarm about the necessity of observing a filming and having to speak to the people involved. In fact, surprisingly, she felt a great wish to do just that. It would be a happy change of pace from sending job résumés out into the abyss of the job market, in anticipation of her firing by Edmond Lockhart. She got Susan's new number from Peter, whose voice became strained when giving it. He certainly disliked Susan's having moved in with this fellow.

Susan and Chris, at 10:30 A.M., were both still fast asleep when Hilda called, and Chris answered groggily. He managed to convey contempt for the caller, Hilda thought, in very few words. Susan, however, sounded glad to hear from her.

"Go to the site? But are you sure they're filming today?"

It had never occurred to Hilda that they might not be. She readily agreed when Susan, who had all the cell phone numbers, volunteered to call Alcott and find out if they were filming, where, and whether a visit would be agreeable. Wouldn't this be better than showing up unannounced?

"Much better. Yes, Susan. Find all that out, and call me back."

Susan called back within the half hour. They were indeed filming—and in Morningside Heights, near the corner of Riverside and 115th, and it was lucky they had called, because there would probably be almost no filming left to be done after today. They had been able to salvage a great deal from their earlier efforts. Perhaps they could all go for dinner later, someplace in the neighborhood, and have a good talk then? Susan would try to set it up with Alcott and Sylvie and some of the other people. Hilda, far from feeling panic at this suggestion, was instead inclined to feel delighted with it. Susan herself was all too happy to abandon her struggles with her thesis and join this expedition. The only thing that kept her spirits from soaring at the chance to get away from her desk and be amused, in fact, was the feeling that she was responsible, at least indirectly, for the Devereaux Foundation's handing a few hundred thousand dollars to Alcott. What if the film was a dud?

Susan had hardly spoken to her father since she had moved into Chris's loft three weeks ago. Several times, she had gone so far as to pick up the telephone, but she didn't know how to talk to him now that, for the first time, they had less than perfect amity. Instead, she chose to wait and to communicate through her calls to her mother, unpleasant as these were. Susan had to admit that while she was enraged with her father's slightest error, she easily tolerated her mother's sins. Because her father was good, she demanded a great deal of him, but she made no demands on her amoral, indifferent mother. Her mother did not disapprove in the slightest of her moving in with Chris. She had even come to visit and had praised the apartment, which was thoroughly, cleverly, downtown. In fact, Lesley had been so pleasant that Chris had said afterward he couldn't believe she was the woman Susan was always complaining about.

Susan arranged a dinner meeting with Hilda and Sylvie, who said that Alcott and several others might or might not join them, depending on how things went. It occurred to her then that she might invite her father, too. With Hilda and the others there, the tensions would be diluted and perhaps she and Peter could ease their way back into friendly relations. She called her father at his office.

"Daddy, it's Susan."

"Why are you speaking to me?" he said, and she laughed.

"I'm not," she replied. "This is purely a business call."

Peter agreed to meet them for dinner that evening, not mentioning that this would mean canceling dinner with a client. He wouldn't tell Lesley either, because he wanted to see his daughter without her. He used not to be underhanded like this, but now it seemed the lesser evil.

Chris was at Susan's side as she hung up.

"What're all these phone calls about?" he asked. He was annoyed at having been woken.

"Sorry, sweetheart, but I'm arranging to spend the day out. I'm going to visit Alcott's set with someone from the Devereaux Foundation. They asked me to, for some reason. And then I'm going to meet my father and Sylvie and maybe some other people at dinner."

"And you don't want me to come, obviously."

"Let me make friends with him again. Then we'll arrange something a little less haphazard, with Mom, too. Don't you think that would be better?"

"What makes you think I care if I ever see either of your parents again?" Chris said, and Susan realized that of course Chris was bothered by her seeing their mutual friends, not her father, without him. She had been aware for some time, as well, that he was deeply envious of Alcott having found money, while his own chances of getting something produced any time soon seemed to grow more remote every day. Of course, this whole expedition, which promised to bring her so much pleasure, was galling to him. She had been insensitive.

"How come you know these people at the Devereaux Foundation?" Chris demanded. "What on earth do you have to do with Alcott's film?"

"I told you. My father is—maybe was—on their board, and the woman who really has the say over who gets money lives in my building. I met her through Daddy, and we got to be friends. She's eccentric, but I like her."

Susan's heart was sinking as she spoke, for all at once the fact that Alcott, and not Chris, had gotten Devereaux money began to seem an enormous betrayal on her part. Why had she never mentioned to Chris her role in putting them in touch with each other? Why hadn't she simply begged Hilda to look at Chris's script or just sent it to her? She was so sure that Hilda would dislike it. Now it would look as though Susan had schemed behind his back and shut him out purposely, when in fact she had been astonished to learn that Hilda had actually called Alcott Adams after hearing Susan mention his name. Then Susan remembered that she had done more than mention his name. She had said he was a major talent, with a kind of genius. At the time, she had not thought of this as disloyalty to Chris. She had had no idea when she said it that Hilda was fishing for names of people to contact. Did she owe it to Chris to think, or to tell Hilda, that *he* was a kind of genius? Perhaps she did owe him a chance to capitalize on her connection with Hilda.

"So she found Alcott through you, didn't she." Chris had followed her thoughts through the emotions he had watched cross her face.

"So it seems. I just mentioned him to her once, and then one day she told me that she'd called him. I didn't tell her to. The thought never crossed my mind. I mentioned you, too." But this sounded defensive and shouted of things unsaid. She had, in fact, told Hilda that her boyfriend was a playwright, but she had voiced no enthusiasm for his work. "Chris, my father told me that this foundation is really, really old-fashioned, conventional, and hidebound. They usually fund things like classical ballet and early music festivals and rhyming poetry in sonnet form about love and nature. They would never have been interested in stuff like yours."

"But they're interested in Alcott's, which isn't any of those things."

"It has occurred to me that they just don't really understand that." Susan saw, however, that this simply raised the question whether they might not have had a similarly happy misunderstanding of Chris's work—if she had praised his play instead of Alcott's film.

"Why didn't you ever tell me about this?"

"I had other things on my mind. It wasn't any big deal," Susan said, hearing her own voice involuntarily confessing that she had wronged him, although, she protested to herself, she hadn't really. She hadn't!

"Well, the little good girl isn't necessarily always so nice, is she," said Chris. He sounded gloomy and sarcastic, but not enraged. Surely, though, if he thought her guilty of this, wasn't his reaction inappropriate? Why wasn't he angry?

"You don't believe that," she said firmly.

"What don't I believe? That you helped Alcott get a grant instead of me? Of course that's what you did. Otherwise you would have told me all about it."

"But if you believe that, you should hate me. You should throw me out. We can't live with something horrible like that between us."

"What are you talking about? And you're the one who's always insisting on learning how to forgive and forget, and sticking things through."

Chris dressed quickly and pulled on a coat. "I'll see you later, I guess," he said, and he was gone—unshaved, unfriendly. He sounded just as he had when he left yesterday, with almost the same words. Although he believed she had betrayed him, he felt nothing more than annoyance. Susan's moral sense was offended. He *should* believe in her innocence. But, granted that he didn't, then he should demand, or at least want, remorse and repentance from her. Chris didn't care whether she was good or not. That didn't mean anything to him. Susan found this incomprehensible.

It was already past 2:00 when Miss Devereaux's car delivered Susan to Hilda's. The two of them grasped hands affectionately and agreed that they had best proceed immediately to the corner of Riverside and 115th, for it was likely that the filming would stop once it grew dark, in a couple of hours. Hilda put on a stylish coat—very long, of fine black wool—a slouchy hat and tight leather gloves and wound a velvety black scarf around her neck. Susan was curious why, at last, the old pilled seventies' houndstooth had been retired. How different Hilda looked wearing such good-looking things. Hilda saw Susan's appreciation. "My new clothes for job hunting," she explained, pretending to be unembarrassed.

"Do you think he'll have those enormous white trucks," Hilda asked Susan as they walked to Riverside Drive, "and tables of food, and all that stuff you see when they're making movies?"

"I doubt it will be anywhere near so elaborate. My guess is one white truck, or maybe a van with some coffee thermoses."

"I wonder if Alcott Adams will have a moral to his story."

"Well, the film won't be amoral. But I don't expect a story with a clear moral point. I hope that's okay."

"I don't really have any expectations one way or the other. Just curious."

Hilda's question unnerved Susan slightly, so recently had she found herself disturbed by what seemed amorality in Chris. Here again, a comparison between Chris and Alcott was called for, and as before, Alcott came off better. Susan knew that Alcott was intensely moral, even moralistic. She recalled hearing an outraged tirade against his former girlfriend, whom he had called a Salome.

They found the production crew just where it was supposed to be. There were no white trucks—just three vans, one of which was Alcott's own. Cords snaked along sidewalks and gutters. Lights were rigged at the stoop of a brownstone. Several people were eating sandwiches, standing at the open door of one of the vans, and Susan detected Alcott's voice, rising out of a jumble of voices, "How can his nose still be red, for God's sake?"

Alexei, wrapped in a blanket, appeared at the door of another van.

"Why are you blaming me," he said, "when you ask me to stand there thirty minutes for no reason, before there's even a camera?" How odd, Susan thought, that Alexei of all people would insist that he's too cold to come out and work—and when everyone else is bearing it.

"He's not blaming you," said Sylvie, who was standing behind Alexei. "Don't be irritable, Alexei. He's just impatient to get rolling. You know what? If we don't finish, tomorrow I'll bring you one of those ski mask–type hats that go over the nose. Okay?"

"I'm not half as irritable as he is," said Alexei.

"Sorry," said Alcott, trotting up to the van. "Very sorry. Look, I'm tense. Come on—we're ready."

This was a great deal of bending on the part of Alcott. Susan wouldn't have known he had it in him. She was struck by this catering to Alexei.

Just then Alexei saw Susan and gave her a quick, curious smile. He wasn't angry at all, Susan realized. He was just making sure Alcott didn't start throwing his weight around. But she was still confused about what was going on. It sounded as though Alcott were intending to film Alexei, which would be very odd.

Alexei threw the blanket into the van and walked into the frigid air wearing only a thin jacket. He took the steps two at a time and waited on the stoop while Alcott shouted directions preparatory to shooting: Alexei was certainly acting in the scene. The cameras were pointing at him. A woman, between forty and fifty, opened the door of the brownstone. Alexei was speaking; the crew was keyed up. Then the tension let down, and everyone slouched and lounged and moved around again. Another break, Susan and Hilda guessed. They had no idea what the action was.

"They've cast Alexei in a part," said Susan, in her excitement squeezing Hilda's hand. "I'm so pleased. I'm so happy."

Hilda stood on her toes, trying to get a good look at the man Susan was speaking of. "That handsome one on the steps is Alexei? Is he good?"

"He's actually a singer," said Susan, "an extraordinary singer in my opinion, but it doesn't surprise me that they gave him a part because he probably can act, too. Opera singers can often act, can't they? Not that he's actually ever sung in an opera—it's a long story. I'll tell you all about him when this is over. I know him a little."

"It doesn't surprise me, either," said Hilda, "because he's so good-looking."

Hearing the note of appreciation in these words, Susan was touched; how sweet of this middle-aged gay woman to take what she imagined was Susan's view of an attractive young man. Alexei was standing at the head of the stairs, shoulders hunched against the cold, hands in his pockets, concentrating very intensely and staring at the ground, occasionally muttering a word to himself, suddenly looking odd and foreign, the way he had struck her before she knew him.

Susan remembered the surge of affection she had felt for Alexei the last time they were together—the night she had decided to move in with Chris. Since then she had spoken to him just a few times, briefly, on the telephone, when she had called with questions her adviser had asked about some part of what Alexei had told her. Seeing him here, in these apparently happy circumstances, made her feel that same warmth toward him. She recalled with satisfaction their date next week to attend the Braithwaites' Thanksgiving dinner and resolved to find an opportunity to talk with him before the day was over. It was just as well that Chris had not come.

Sylvie appeared beside them, the curves of her figure obscured by a thick down coat and her face covered by a scarf wrapped up to her eyes, which, however, showed a smile quite as clearly as the concealed features could have done. Susan introduced her to Hilda, who shook hands cordially.

"This is the script," said Sylvie through the scarf. She stood next to Hilda so that Hilda could read the tattered typescript, on which various lines were struck and rewritten in ink.

"Did you write the script, Ms. Kimura?" asked Hilda.

"Rewrote it with Alcott," said Sylvie.

"What's Alexei's part, Sylvie?" asked Susan.

But at that moment filming resumed, and Sylvie trotted to Alcott's side beside the stoop. "You can look at this if you'd like," she said as she ran off, handing the script to Hilda, who read:

GAYLIN: It's me.
CHRISTA: I see it's you.
GAYLIN: Aren't you going to ask me to come in?
CHRISTA: Go away, Gaylin. I don't want you here.
GAYLIN: I'm having a hard time. I'm sick. . . .
CHRISTA: Get out.
GAYLIN: Mother, please. . . .

"Oh my," said Hilda, distressed for Gaylin's sake and reading with difficulty in the cold wind. Sylvie reappeared in a moment and, after apologizing politely, asked if Hilda would mind letting her take back the script after all. She had to change something. Handing it to her, Hilda said, "It seems rather a sad story."

"Parts are," said Sylvie. "Overall, no."

"Gaylin's not at the center of things?"

"That bit is nothing you can judge by. Would you like to meet Alexei and Naomi?"

Susan and Hilda met a half-dozen actors and actresses. Alexei broke into a broad smile at Susan's approach and gave her a quick hug. *He likes me,* she thought with a melting feeling. *I should get out and see people more often.* Later, she and Hilda read a few more snippets of the script, heard about various scenes finished and one yet to be done, and when it was dark left the crew at work, with plans to meet several of them for dinner on Broadway at 8:30. In the meantime, Hilda would return home and Susan would go to her old apartment to warm up. The two of them agreed as they walked home that despite elements of disorganization and little quarrels that seemed continually to erupt, the group as a whole inspired confidence and hope. Susan, feeling vindicated, confessed to Hilda how she had worried that the whole thing would not meet her expectations.

"Oh, you shouldn't have worried about that," said Hilda. "It wasn't your idea to give them the grant. You have no responsibility at all. We didn't give the money expecting that the film would be a success, although we hope it will. We just wanted him to have a chance to try."

Back in her old apartment, Susan took a hot bath and fell asleep on the sofa for over an hour, with the feeling of collapse that comes on returning home after long traveling. When she awoke, she couldn't face going back downtown later that night. She called Chris and left the message that she would see him tomorrow.

CHAPTER 41

———————

They gathered that evening at the Heights, on the second floor overlooking Broadway, around tables pushed together in front of the windows.

"Where's Chris?" Peter asked Susan. He was trying to be more accepting.

"Not coming," said Susan, as though this were nothing.

"Louis is going to meet us here," said Peter. "He had no plans, so I told him to come." Susan was glad to hear it. Now that she and Louis had become better friends, she liked having him around, even if some of her friends didn't.

In the end, they were eight: Susan, Hilda, Peter, Alexei, Sylvie, an actress introduced only as Naomi, and, half an hour later, Alcott, and much later, when the others were nearly finished with their meal, Louis, who knew everyone at the table except Naomi and Hilda. Hilda observed that Peter had succeeded in pushing his troubles aside for the moment. He was more cheerful and lighthearted than she'd ever seen him, but maybe this was normal for him when he was socializing. Hilda herself felt inexplicably at ease, considering that she hadn't had dinner with friends since graduate school over twenty years ago.

The film people, natural exhibitionists, were not displeased to have been observed that afternoon or, now, to have a sympathetic and amused audience for their tales of frustration, with which they entertained the company throughout the evening: the elderly lady who, annoyed at their half blocking the sidewalk, encouraged her dog to pee on the equipment; the homeless couple who kept stealing food and anything else not nailed down; the compulsively talking madman who had to be shushed and shooed away once an hour.

"Finally, I had to hire him," said Alcott. "Just a small part."

"You're not kidding, are you?" asked Naomi, the woman in her late forties who played Gaylin's mother.

"Of course I'm kidding," said Alcott, peeved. "What's wrong with you, Naomi?"

Naomi looked exasperated. Sylvie, though, Peter noticed, snickered at the interchange between Alcott and Naomi.

Hilda and Peter listened and laughed and asked questions, the last of which, of course, was when they would finish.

"Very soon," said Alcott, "so Alexei can go to Berlin."

"Berlin?" Peter asked Alexei, who had been deep in talk with Susan from the time they all arrived. "Seeing friends?" Peter had met and liked Alexei when he visited Louis, and his first impression was confirmed on observing him this evening. He had a pleasant, unassuming air for such a good-looking, obviously bright kid. And then there was something faintly outlandish about him that attracted Peter. He was struck by Susan's demeanor in talking with him—bright-faced, animated, and unself-conscious.

"Oh, no. I'm not really going to Berlin," said Alexei.

"See, Mr. Frankl," said Alcott, "he doesn't look the part, but he's a chess master—a grandmaster—and he should go play in this big international tournament and beat this certain guy he has a long history with."

"I'm really not going," said Alexei. He strove to sound unruffled, but his irritation was obvious. "I don't play tournaments anymore—not for years. I used to."

Louis, who had come in a short while ago and sat on Alexei's other side, listened closely to this interchange, his eyes darting from face to face at the table.

"If you beat that person," said Hilda with avid interest, "would you get a chance to play the world champion?"

"Oh, no, no," Alexei said with a polite smile. "Just a . . . a fairly big champion—maybe someone who would play the world champion, and I would get beaten, of course."

"That would be good publicity for the film, if you won that Berlin tournament," said Louis in his first remark of the evening.

"Yeah," said Alcott. "It would be good in the write-ups: 'Chess Champ Stars in Indie Film.' "

" 'Stars'?" asked Susan. "Is he the lead, Sylvie?"

Louis waited until the center of the conversation passed down the table, then asked Alexei privately, "Why not play?"

"It's a long story," he replied.

Louis, who was seated to Hilda's left, turned his attention to his father, who was on her right. It was so noisy that he could just make out the gist of their conversation: something about the Devereaux Foundation problems. But he could see that his father was talking animatedly with Hilda, and after a while Peter shook his head and shrugged, as though to say he gave up. An idea dawned on Louis. He likes her, he thought. He likes that she's quirky. He's having a good time. Here was what his father was like without his usual ironic, cheerful tolerance and mournful stoicism, when he wasn't twisting himself into a shape that suited his wife.

Then Louis looked across the table at his sister, whom he had observed earlier in intense conversation with Alexei. She had just learned that Alexei was playing the male lead in Alcott's film and was looking incredulously from Sylvie to Alexei. Alexei, however, was staring into a glass that he was rolling between his hands, obviously uncomfortable. He still hadn't recovered from having the conversation focus on him a minute ago. That was odd, for someone who wanted to make a living on a stage.

"This is my son," Peter said belatedly to Hilda, reaching so confidently for the check, past Alcott, that there was no arguing with him. "My son, Louis. Louis, this is Hilda Hughes, who for the time being is still with the Devereaux Foundation. She lives in Susan's building. And you're too late for dinner."

Louis grinned at Hilda, and she thought he was very handsome and charming. He said nothing to her, however, until they all stood to go, when he asked hopefully, "Uh, read any good books lately?" She looked up at him, puzzled, with her head tilted to one side, slightly thrown by both his awkward timing and his tone of voice.

"Yes!" she said after considering for a moment. "Oh, yes. The most amazing book!"

Louis, eyes wide, nodded expectantly and took out a pen, ready to write on a napkin.

"It's called *The Betrothed* by Alessandro Manzoni. And when you finish that, try . . . So, Peter, at four, then. Louis, let me know how . . . I'm coming, Susan."

Louis folded the napkin, put it in his pocket, and sidled over to Peter and Alexei with a furtive look at the departing figures of Susan and Hilda. "Alexei, where you headed?" he asked.

"Tiemann Place," said Alexei.

"Walk you," said Louis.

"You should have heard my daughter go on about you," said Peter to Alexei as they walked, "after she heard your recital."

"That was . . . nice of her," Alexei replied uncertainly. Most compliments were irrelevant, but not Susan's. He would actually have liked to know just what she said.

"No being nice about it," Peter said. "She was completely snowed, as they used to say. Do they say that anymore?"

"My English idioms are not best," Alexei said.

"No," said Louis. "They don't."

"So, tell me," Peter continued. "Why'd you give up chess?"

"I still play, but usually on Internet now. I just don't compete anymore."

"You know, I was serious about what I said," Louis said with that insinuating quality to his voice that Peter so disliked. "It would be great for the film—even if you didn't win, but especially if you did."

"That would be strange," said Alexei, "if what you're saying is true."

"But that's how it works," said Louis. "Film success is all done with mirrors. I studied all about this kind of thing in business school. Kind of an interest of mine—the entertainment industry, advertising, attention, and all that. I'm not kidding."

"Well, perhaps," said Alexei, "but it's really not possible."

"Why?" said Peter, who, picking up on Alexei's heightened emotions around this subject, took the fatherly liberty of being nosy.

"Well, for one thing, I don't have a ticket and I'm broke. But assuming they would give me an appearance fee even though I've been out of this for so long . . . even so—there are reasons. You see, it's a little strange."

"Come on. Who are we going to tell?" Peter said with a paternal air both commanding and warm, to which Alexei responded almost against his will.

"It's not that you would tell," he said doubtfully. "Well, why not. You see, there's someone, someone I know well, who started gambling money on my games about ten or so years ago, when I was kind of a chess kid hotshot back in Russia. This is person who's always betting on everything, any time he can. One time, he actually offered to split winnings with me. He knows my playing and knows chess so extremely well that he's very good at guessing better than anyone else whether I'll win or lose. So I had to quit playing, because otherwise, unless I won, there was danger he would bet against me and then it would look like *I'm* betting, you see—and losing on purpose for money. And even if I won, it looked sleazy and greedy. Chess is just not a game you gamble on. Chess people would spit on gambling. It's completely unheard of.

"At first I just tried to make sure I won, and I had a long winning streak in my teens. In the meantime I pleaded and argued with this guy to stop it, and threatened him, but nothing did any good. And then the pressure to win got to me, and I lost a couple. He bet against me and won big, and a rumor about me got started. It just wasn't worth it. I wanted to stop before people got the idea I was losing for the money. So I didn't show up when I was supposed to play Boris Tarlov, because I thought I would lose to him. But, of course, everyone thought I was just being coward, which was very . . . annoying."

"I'll bet it was a little more than annoying," said Peter, wincing. "That's a rough story. Why didn't you go to the authorities and let them know? Maybe the betting was illegal."

"I really couldn't. I didn't even know what country he was betting in."

"But you could have countered the suspicion and cleared your reputation."

"No."

"Then I'm guessing this was someone close to you."

"Good guess," said Alexei. He sounded tense, and both Louis and Peter felt sorry for him.

"I'm a lawyer, you know. My business is making good guesses like that. Who? Sibling? Uncle?"

"My father. I never told anyone before."

Peter and Louis exchanged looks.

"He did this even though I was winning lots of money prizes," Alexei continued. "He was just greedy, and he always needed more money for his gambling."

"That's a shame," said Peter. "A real shame."

The three walked along in silence for a while.

"Would he still do that? Now that you're in this country?" asked Louis.

"He did, when I tried to play again here. Yes. He promised me he wouldn't, just to get me to play, but I found out he did."

"So that's the real reason? If he didn't, you'd play?" Louis persisted.

"I guess. I mean, yes, of course I would. I like chess."

"You shouldn't let this go, Alexei," said Peter. "You have to do something about it. I mean, you must be furious with him."

Alexei shrugged. "It makes no difference if I am. There's nothing I can do."

"Your mother must know," said Peter. "Can't she stop him?"

"She doesn't want to know. He even used to try to get me to cheat in chess games—signaling moves to me when I was little. I never told her, and when she heard something just recently about that, all she said was, 'Don't tell me that.'"

"I can relate to that," Louis said.

"Still, she must have known something," Peter insisted. "I know what you're thinking, Louis," he added, seeing that Louis gave him a skeptical look. Of course, Louis thought that he, Peter, had behaved exactly as Alexei's mother had. This was partly true, but Lesley had loved Louis and was never as bad as Alexei's father. Yet Peter doubted this defense as soon as he formulated it. He and Louis had to have a talk.

In the meantime, if Peter was any judge of character, Alexei had emerged from his troubled family a good kid despite it all. Not only was he richly talented, he was brave in ways that Peter wished he himself had been when he was young.

"Maybe she should have known, but she didn't. It's all over now," Alexei said. "I'm not a kid anymore." They had reached the entrance to the Frankls' building, and his face, lit by the building's lampposts, was impassive.

"Here we are," said Peter. Hands in pockets against the cold, he raised a shoulder and inclined his head to indicate the building behind him. "Can you come up for a while?"

"No, thank you very much. I have to get home. We're starting early in the morning again." His smile was friendly enough, but Peter's questions had obviously raised painful feelings. This, thought Peter as Alexei turned to go, was a young man with a few things to be unhappy about.

"Look here, wait a minute, Alexei," said Peter, obviously speaking on an impulse. "Maybe it's interfering, but I don't feel like letting this go. Someone should have put a stop to this a long time ago. It should have been your mother back then, and now it should be you. This is a hard thing to face, but you have a right to be free of your father's interference. He has no right to involve you in wrongdoing and ruin your reputation." Peter spoke to Alexei but attended to Louis's reaction.

"What about a wife, Dad? Don't people have a right to be free of interfering, immoral spouses?"

The question gave Peter the feeling he got on a boat when the deck shifted under his feet.

"You don't choose your parents. You choose your wife as an adult," said

Peter. The argument that you had a greater right to be free of your parents than your spouse sounded backward even to him, but he was still sure about what Alexei should do. "Alexei, do something about this. Look, if you tell me to, I'll go talk to him personally. Believe me, I'll know what to say, and you won't have this problem anymore. It's that simple. Just tell me to do it."

"I can't do that," said Alexei. "He's my father. I can't send strangers to threaten him and scold him."

"But you've tried the gentler ways, and they didn't work. Come on, Alexei," Peter said, kindly and urgent. He made it seem impossible to say no. Louis could see why he was so successful with juries. "It comes down to the fact that you've got to have a lawyer—that's me—a lawyer to help you make him stop. And don't worry—no one's going to injure him."

"Sometimes I've thought this way myself," said Alexei, "but I just can't—not now, anyway. Let me go home and think, and I'll call you later." In fact, Peter's paternal warmth undercut his moral qualms. Surely this good father wouldn't be telling him to act this way against his own father if that would be wrong.

"Good," said Peter. "I'll be waiting to hear from you."

"But I don't know why you would do this. It would be very unpleasant and a lot of trouble."

"Not much trouble—I don't mind," said Peter, looking again at Louis, who was listening carefully.

"Alexei, he's right about all this," Louis said. "You should let him do it."

"I think he's gonna call," Louis said after Alexei had walked off briskly, "because he knows he doesn't really owe the guy much. Mallory told me that he practically supports his parents. He's really broke, but he gives them his chess-lesson money and he's fixing people's computers day and night, giving them the money."

"What does Mallory know about him?"

"Mallory's the one who found him. He was helping her with her new computer, and the poor guy kind of fell for her, but she didn't want him."

"How do you know all this?"

"Susan told me. See, Dad, I want to marry Mallory, but I can't get her interested in me. Finally I figured out that she's a little bit stuck on this guy, Alexei, but she doesn't want to be. And you know what, I think he's a nicer person than she is. He's more everything than she is—smarter, more talented."

It was unusual for Louis to confide in Peter, and his confiding such extraordinary things was revolutionary. Again, he left Peter feeling off balance.

"But, honey," he said, as though Louis were six years old, as he was when they last had an intimate conversation, "how come you're so nice to the guy if he's standing in the way of you and Mallory?" He gestured to indicate that they should keep walking; they wouldn't be able to talk at home if Lesley was still up. They circled the block, and Louis went on with his story.

"I like him. I feel sorry for him. She wasn't very nice. Basically she told him he wasn't good enough. She needed someone with a good degree and the right connections and more money."

"That doesn't sound like Mallory to me."

"That's what she told Susan, and Susan told me. Mallory isn't proud of it, but that's the way she is. And she also wants someone brilliant and creative, whatever that means. But Mallory can't attract some great artist—intellectual, whatever—because she's just a nice, smart, pretty girl, that's all. She wants to do good things, but she's gotta have her nice co-op and hang out with the right people—all that."

"I suppose that makes sense. She's a well-meaning, liberal girl, once she's sure of her privileges. So all right. I'd accept a less than perfect daughter-in-law, if you love her despite her flaws. I've always liked Mallory."

"And look, Dad, I know I'm no paragon or anything and I've never done anything besides get decent SATs and two degrees. I mean, when it comes to my work, Mallory thinks like you. She doesn't want to be married to someone in finance. But she wants money, and I'll make plenty of money. I'd be a good husband. I'd be a good father. I'm smarter than she is. And I know what she's really like, and I love her. She's not going to do better than that, and she's capable of making a bad mistake. But she underestimates me almost as badly as she underestimates Alexei."

"Louis, I'm changing my mind again. If that's all true, leave her alone. You'll find someone else. Why does it have to be Mallory? I'm afraid my children aren't lucky in love," said Peter. "And I don't think there's anything wrong with your work. I just think it won't make you happy. I thought you could do better."

"But playing around with deals and money is fun," Louis said, "and it's not like I have any talents that are going to waste. Other than that, I just want a family, but only with Mallory."

"You're too modest. You have to understand, you're way above average. You've got brains, great coordination," said Peter. "See, that's like me, believe it or not, except my father discouraged me from doing sports."

"Maybe," Louis said. It was the first time anyone had told him he resembled his father. "Maybe I take after you a little."

"Sure, and in some personality things, too. You've got plenty of talent—all any guy needs—and you're going to branch out and discover more interests as you get older. In lots of ways you're a late bloomer."

"If Mallory marries me, I could be something."

"That's the wrong attitude. You'll be something whether or not she marries you. If she gives you a hard time, drop her. And what about Susan and this guy Chris? Does he want to marry her?"

"I hope not," said Louis. "With Chris, she's doing some sacrificial lamb routine. I'll tell you the truth, she acts like you with Mom. She looks the other way. She tolerates. She knows what hurts him and what he doesn't understand. She's into accepting his limits. You know what I mean?"

Louis looked unsmilingly into Peter's face while he was talking, and Peter thought that this unpleasant comparison of him with Susan was probably fair. He had always thought Louis was so devious, but this was straight, honest thinking and frank talk. Peter teetered emotionally between humiliation and paternal pride.

"God. I wonder if there's any way to stop her," he said.

"I don't know. And I don't know how to get Mallory to marry me. So you're right, I guess. Neither of us is lucky in love—so far. I'm not giving up yet."

"Louis, I want to talk about something else. Talk to me about your mother," said Peter, and instead of turning down 116th Street for home, the two of them headed south on Broadway and talked for nearly two more hours before they turned back toward Riverside Drive and went home to Lesley.

When Susan returned to her apartment on 114th Street, Chris was there waiting for her, sober and calm. "I know you were trying to get away from me for a while," he said, "but I couldn't stand it. I had to see you."

"It's all right," she said, accepting this confession of weakness in a motherly way. "I'm glad you're here."

"Susan, I'm sorry for what I said this morning. I know you didn't try to cut me out in favor of Alcott. Of course you'd never do that."

Susan bent her head in thought, taking off her coat and scarf.

"I don't blame you if you're still mad about it," Chris added.

"I'm not. It's just that I don't believe you really mean what you say. I think you don't care much one way or the other whether I cut you out. You care about getting backing, but not about whether I've behaved decently. You don't believe there is such a thing as decent behavior."

"Of course I do."

Susan did not believe him, but this time she chose not to argue. She had alarmed him by staying uptown, and he would say whatever was necessary to pacify her. His fear, however, was real; it softened her. Susan had come home glowing, but Chris darkened her mood. Much of the time, in fact, life with Chris was lonely, dull, and sad.

Chris watched her face intently while she thought these things. "You were having a good time, weren't you," he said. "Who was there?"

"At dinner? Alcott, Sylvie, some actors, my . . . And Alexei Mikhailov. He's actually got a big part. . . ." Susan stopped because Chris was looking at her peculiarly. Now there was no avoiding a scene, and both of them tried to conceal their inward preparations for it. Chris went to get a beer out of the refrigerator, and Susan dealt out a game of solitaire.

"You know what the solution to our problem is?" Chris said, standing at the doorway with the beer, watching her. "We need to get married. Let's get married, Susan. Your mother would love it. Your dad will come around."

Susan ignored him and thumped cards down on the table.

"I'm serious," he insisted. "I've never said that to anyone else. I don't think I'll ever say it again. Please, Susan, you don't know how miserable I've been. At the least I deserve an answer."

Susan had thought he was being sarcastic; perhaps, at first, he was. But now he meant it. She knew him, and he wouldn't stop asking until she said yes. Chris needed her, and she could help him. But, of course, she should not marry him. How could she marry a man mentally constructed the way Chris was—cool, humorless, almost amoral, with tastes and feelings so different from her own? Yet a peaceful sweet feeling came over her, and she knew she would. Of course, Susan thought, I'll marry him; I'll have to. Susan, who had always been skeptical about marriage and about her own suitability for it, was astonished that the idea of being married gave her such honeyed, warm sensations. She told Chris that she had to think about it, but what he had seen in her face made him fairly confident about the answer.

In the morning, Susan half expected Chris to back out, but he was even more determined. He insisted that they go get a license immediately, although Susan would have been content—would have preferred—to live for a while as an engaged couple. But being engaged was not enough for Chris. He knew that in Susan's mind nothing tied her to him indissolubly except marrying. And she knew that when they were married, Chris would not feel bound: she would feel tied and he would not. Yet, musing on this, she had a feeling of perfect freedom and peace. It will be out of my hands, she thought. All the weighing and struggling will be over. The moral decision will have been made, once and for all.

The following day they walked to City Hall to be married by the clerk.

"We don't need to tell anyone about this, at least for now," Chris said as they walked downtown to the Municipal Building from the Village. "This is something between you and me. I could never go through with it if we had to make a circus out of it."

"I understand," said Susan. She could not conceive of Chris in a morning coat, with a boutonniere, and flocks of bridesmaids and all that. For that matter, those things weren't really her style, either. She regretted only excluding her father, but that's probably how it had to be.

"Marriage is the most private thing anyone ever does," she said. "None of the ceremonies really respect that, do they."

"In fact, it's so private I personally can't see the point in actually going down to City Hall and asking the government to get between you and me," said Chris, looking coolly at Susan, "except I think someone like you has to do things that way."

"Someone like me? What do you mean? Chris, I thought you wanted this. Look, we don't have to—"

"Come on, Susan. This is the way it has to be. I can see that." Chris eyed her worriedly this time. He hadn't meant to spook her.

"No, I'm going home. I didn't realize you—"

But Chris held her by the arm. "Wait, Susan. Look, we can argue the whole thing philosophically some other time. Don't be so literal. Marriage is the practical thing for us. I want to marry you, I couldn't bear to lose you. So theoretically it doesn't make sense, so what? A lot of things don't. I'm not into living pure—know what I mean? Maybe Alcott Adams won't get married because he doesn't believe in it. I'm different."

Susan hesitated, then began to walk again, although she was still frowning, and Chris cajoled and caressed and, when she began to respond, joked all the way to City Hall. She felt again how desperate Chris was to hold her, how she frightened him with her schoolgirl uprightnesses and reasonings. He was fragile; he had entrusted his happiness to her. She had to be more flexible, more accommodating, or she would end by injuring him terribly. Vowing to herself that she would not do that, Susan felt transported out of ordinariness. Her familiar, comfortable melancholy lifted. She felt afloat, euphoric.

"What about rings?" she blurted out as they walked down a gleaming corridor inside the Municipal Building.

Chris hesitated. "We'll deal with that later."

"But the ceremony. I think you need rings for that."

They left the building and walked around the neighborhood until they found a shabby, narrow store between a stationer's and a deli that advertised in huge handwritten letters, "14k only $39.95!!!" They bought two plain gold bands.

Shortly thereafter Susan and Chris were married, somewhat skeptically, by the clerk, with a helpful stranger for a witness.

"You're gonna get a lot of questions if you keep that thing on," Chris said, nodding down toward Susan's ring as they walked uptown. He had already pocketed his.

"Oh!" she said, and she removed her ring, too.

They went to Chinatown for lunch, where they began to feel giggly. Even Chris chuckled a little. Then he went off to meet with a producer, and Susan went home, intending to do some work. She put the ring in the drawer of her nightstand.

CHAPTER 42

Alexei called the Frankls the morning after Peter made his surprising offer. Hardly more than a week later, Peter and Louis arranged to visit Alexei's father. A car came for them at 9:00 the following day and drove them to the shabby Brighton Beach tenement where Alexei's parents lived, in a Russian enclave. They found the entire family at home. Sophia had listened to Nikolai's end of the telephone conversation the previous evening and stayed home despite her husband's objections. If Alexei was in some kind of trouble, she must know about it.

When the buzzer sounded, she looked out the window and saw a driver in a black Lincoln sedan at the curb and two men, one old and one young, at the door to the building. Nikolai buzzed them in, smoking a cigarette nervously, then unbolted the door when they knocked. Sophia's father played the violin in the next room, unaware that they had visitors. Sophia guessed from their resemblance that they were father and son and, indeed, the older man introduced himself as Peter Frankl and the young man as "my son, Louis Frankl."

Peter and Louis saw a daybed, neatly made up in a kind of foyer, surrounded with boyish items and a computer on shelves beside the bed and inferred correctly that this had served as Alexei's room. The foyer led into a larger room that held a worn table and chairs, a sofa, and at one end, kitchen appliances.

"You have another child?" asked Peter, hearing the violin.

"My father," said Sophia with frigid politeness. The music, however—Bach, Peter noticed—stopped and an old man opened a door to the all-purpose kitchen–sitting room into which the Mikhailovs had invited the Frankls.

"Visitors, Sophia?"

"Yes, Papa. You can play. It doesn't bother anyone."

"This is where Alexei gets his talent, then," said Peter, trying to be pleasant for the sake of Alexei's mother. He had promised Alexei to do his best to spare her feelings.

"His mother, she used to sing," said Nikolai in a voice hoarse from cigarettes, and he coughed a hollow, phlegmy smoker's cough. "She studied at the St. Petersburg Conservatory, and so did Alexei until we came here."

"What is this about?" asked Sophia.

"Yes, what?" asked Papa.

"Shut up," said Nikolai. "It doesn't concern you."

"Mrs. Mikhailov, my business is with your husband. Wouldn't you rather step out for a while? It's nothing you have to worry about." Peter did not actually believe this, but he had made a promise to Alexei.

"I will stay," she answered, grim-faced and fearful. Clearly, she knew whom she was married to.

Peter saw that she would not be persuaded to leave and, with a sigh of surrender, turned to Alexei's father.

"Some years ago, Mr. Mikhailov, you began placing bets on your son's chess games, and you got substantial winnings from that."

Louis scanned the faces of Alexei's three elders: Nikolai scowled, Sophia frowned and looked at her husband, and her father shook his head and muttered something.

"Louis and I are here now at Alexei's request, because he tried to talk you out of doing that, but he couldn't. So instead he gave up chess. Now some of his friends are interested in ensuring that he has a chance to pursue chess without interference."

"But is this against law?" asked Sophia, who grew more and more frightened. "What difference it makes?"

"Your husband has surely broken the law with his betting," said Peter, "but my major concern is the damage to Alexei's reputation. People were finding out, and a few began to suspect that the two of them were colluding so that he would lose on purpose sometimes."

"I do not believe this!" Sophia cried. "Nikolai would never do such thing."

"I'm sorry, Mrs. Mikhailov, but it's true, and we are just here to see that it stops," said Peter, and he added gently, "Anyway, I wonder if it's really all that hard to believe."

"What I do or don't do is none of your business," said Nikolai.

"I'm a lawyer," said Peter, "and I've had you investigated. I know already that it would not be hard to get you in trouble for smuggling and maybe gambling, too. I would hate to do that, but you can't mistreat your son any longer. I'm just here to make a point. If Alexei chooses to play chess again, and you place a bet on the game, we will know it. Believe me, we will know it, just as we already know you're a middleman for artifacts stolen from churches near St. Petersburg. . . ." Peter, Louis, and the private investigator had had several long, helpful conversations with a man at the Marshall Club, Sergei Ivanovich Petrov, who had known Nikolai well in Petersburg.

"Nonsense. These are legitimate transactions!" shouted Nikolai, but his face was white now.

"You don't understand, Mr. Mikhailov," said Peter. "I know already. I'm not asking you to tell me anything or to agree with me about anything. I'm just telling you. It's over with bets on chess, and I'll know if you do this again and I'll have no mercy. I've written this all down"—Peter placed a thick, official-looking envelope on the table—"and you want to do everything in your power to make sure you don't hear from me again. And as for you, Mrs. Mikhailov, I'm sorry for you and your father, and so is your son. I asked your husband to meet me privately, and I had hoped to keep all this from you. But this must stop."

"Are you supposed to be his friends, then?" said Sophia. "But what are people like you compared to brilliant boy like Alexei? What can you know about helping him?"

"Sophia!" cried the old man.

"Shut up, Sophia," said Nikolai.

"Mrs. Mikhailov," said Peter mildly as he and Louis went to the door, "I have to agree with you. He's an exceptional boy in a lot of ways, and it's too bad he needs so much help because ordinary people like you and me are all too likely to let him down."

"Well," said Louis as they drove home, "did it work or not?"

"Oh, yeah," said Peter. "He's just an ordinary sleaze. She was one unpleasant human being, surprisingly. I thought she'd see it more Alexei's way. I don't get it."

"She thought we were looking down on them—on her—and that's all she cared about. But the grandfather was a good guy," said Louis. "I was watching him."

"Maybe that's why Alexei's such a good kid," said Peter. "Maybe the grandfather raised him. Poor old guy. Poor Alexei."

"Dad, the trouble with Mallory is all because *I* didn't turn out so well, you know. She thinks I'm a lowlife or something."

"Louis, she couldn't possibly," Peter protested. But he was guiltily aware that this had been his own opinion of Louis until recently. The thought came into his head that he would never have gotten himself into the mess with the Devereaux Foundation if he hadn't always felt so disappointed in Louis; he would just have leaned back and watched his son do great things.

"What are you talking about? That's what you thought, too. Mallory knows me from way back, and I made some bad moves with her. She was actually checking me out at her party, but at that point I thought I wasn't serious about her and I let her know it. I kept coming on to her, though, so she decided I was some kind of sleaze. I was sort of arrogant."

"That's not fatal. You just have to say to her, Mallory . . . and tell her . . . Look, I'm going to be talking to Mallory. She called me, actually."

"Mallory? About what?"

"About the Devereaux Foundation, I assume."

They rode in silence until they reached the Brooklyn Bridge, when Louis looked at his father out of the corner of his eye and asked with real curiosity, "Don't you think Alexei is a great guy, Dad? Compared to Chris Wylie, for example. Don't you think he's really, um, a mensch?"

"I'd say he is, yes. I like the way he goes after what he wants, pays the price, and doesn't complain. And he knows he's got all that talent, but he's not a bit inflated. Yeah, he's got a lot to him." They viewed the Manhattan skyline thoughtfully.

"Susan really likes him, doesn't she?" Peter asked Louis.

"I have an idea," said Louis, "about Alexei."

Back on Riverside Drive, Louis called Susan, and Peter called Alexei.

CHAPTER 43

On Thanksgiving Day, Alexei and Susan rang the bell at the Braithwaites' door at 7:45 P.M., the time when you should appear, Susan assured him, if you had been invited for 7:30. He was actually dressed for the occasion, in a sports coat and ironed shirt. On their way to the Braithwaites' from Alexei's apartment, she had told him how nice he looked. "You too," he said with a sidelong look at Susan, who was poignantly pretty in a tight, short black dress, with dark curls tumbling down her back. Tonight, no one would have to look twice to see that she was a very attractive young woman.

Susan knew that it was extremely odd to be going with Alexei to Thanksgiving dinner, at the home of people she had never met, when she was married to Chris. But as yet she and Chris had told no one; indeed, they hardly mentioned it to each other. Earlier, as she prepared to leave Chris's apartment, Susan's knowledge that she was behaving badly led her, paradoxically, to feel giddy anticipation and a sweet sense of cutting loose. She decided to take a moral holiday and refused to let guilt ruin the pleasures of the evening.

Chris saw that she had dressed with special care and taste and that her mood made her attractiveness obvious; he turned gloomy. He had wanted Alexei to pick her up in the Village, but Susan scoffed at this. Of course she would pick Alexei up, since he lived quite close to the Braithwaites, on Tiemann Place.

"I don't like this," Chris said. "I feel like your father sending you on a date. I'm your husband, you know." But his insisting on marital proprieties had made her laugh.

"I promised him I'd come," was her only justification.

A tall girl opened the Braithwaites' door, smiled at Alexei, and eyed Susan with friendly curiosity. She held in her arms a toddler obviously fresh from the bath, in pajamas with wet curls, who turned away from Susan with affected violence and then put out his arms to go to Alexei. A little boy came running up and tugged on Alexei's sleeve. "What is this coat?" he asked. "Will you play me one game?" Alexei first greeted Ellen, however, who stood shyly behind the others.

"This is my friend Susan Frankl," he said. "Susan, this little one hiding his face is Gilbert. This one on my coat is Stuart. This tall, pretty one is Jane, and that little pretty one is Ellen. And every one is a musician."

"Not Gilbert," said Stuart.

"Yes, he sings, don't you?" Alexei asked the child in his arms. "You sing 'Row, Row, Row Your Boat.' "

"No," said Gilbert.

"He says 'no' whatever you ask him," said Ellen, and then, remembering her instructions, asked politely, "May I please take your coats?"

A hum of voices came from the other end of the long entrance hallway, and Susan, turning shy, was glad to have Alexei hold her hand and lead her to the party.

Charles appeared with a tray of drinks just as Susan and Alexei, smiling, entered the room. Ellen and Stuart joined a crowd of children who stormed past him, followed by an old woman who took Gilbert from Alexei's arms and was, beyond any doubt, the child's grandmother.

"There you are!" Charles cried. "This is Susan?"

"Charles Braithwaite, Susan Frankl," said Alexei. "And here's Anne Braithwaite."

Anne came to greet them, her face brilliant with smiles. She stretched up on her toes to kiss Alexei and took Susan by both hands and said how glad she was that she had come. In a moment, Susan had a glass of champagne, and there were more introductions. But with so many new names, she soon lost track of them. She recognized only one face, that of the priest at the church where Alexei had given his recital. Not counting the children, she and Alexei were the youngest people present. The others—about fourteen all told—ranged in age, she guessed, from early thirties to eighties.

Everyone seemed to think she was Alexei's girlfriend. Of course, what else could anyone think? They had come in holding hands. There was a buzz of talk, laughing, more champagne. Susan, liking all of it, pushed to the back of her mind the insistent sense of being deceitful. She held Alexei's hand and resolved not to care what anyone thought; Alexei was her friend. A little moral holiday, she repeated to herself.

Among the guests—an expectable mix of friends and relatives—Alexei knew the young clergyman, a couple of musicians, and a pair who, he said, were the Braithwaites' best friends. He led Susan to these acquaintances, who showed so much welcoming interest in this young pair that Susan's qualms grew stronger and expanded to take in Alexei, too. Wasn't he rather too . . . Wasn't he assuming . . . ? She almost decided to cancel her moral holiday and confess to him that she was married to Chris and deserved none of his warmth, kindness, and attention, or anyone else's, either. The misunderstanding was so pleasant, however, that she could not resist letting it continue.

After a while, Alexei left her on her own to circulate, and soon she was deep into conversation with Victor Marx and his partner about designs for the World Trade Center site. None of them, Vic insisted, overcame the logical problem of recognizing the difference between the firemen and policemen who gave their lives in the line of duty and those whose lives were cruelly taken, or how to memorialize the murdered without aggrandizing the murderers.

Dinner was served at a large oval table that had been opened to its widest span. Even so, the children had to be seated at card tables, and the adults' chairs were jammed together. The chaos and crowding, however, encouraged intimacy.

"This is the first time I've done Thanksgiving in the evening," Anne confided to Susan. She had taken to her immediately, as both Alexei and Susan herself had noticed. This both pleased and mortified Susan, whose malaise at being present under grossly false premises intensified. Nonetheless, she was glad to see that the place cards seated her next to Alexei and near Charles Braithwaite, the priest whom everyone called Greg, and a woman whose name, Joanna Ward, Susan recognized as that of a Met mezzo.

When everyone had been served, following an elaborate ceremony of carving by Charles that was the subject of much wit and attempted wit, the Braithwaites, with no preliminaries beyond introductions, began questioning Susan about her thesis. They were obviously acquainted both with her tribulations with Ivy and with the substance of her work. In fact, she could not believe that Alexei had explained it to them so accurately or that such a subject could ever be of general interest at a dinner table; but even the priest asked something that showed he could follow. Partly, Susan saw, they were trying to make the only real stranger in the party feel that she belonged there. But partly it was also a matter of sheer interest, to which, when she perceived it, she responded with an attractive enthusiasm. When she came to the technical point on singing that she had discussed with Alexei, he obligingly swallowed his bite of food and sang what she meant, without her asking. The others found this little joint performance of theirs funny and illuminating, and Susan experienced the exhilaration of being admired and liked by a set of admirable, likable people. It all made her feel intimately bound to Alexei—as though they were a team, a pair, with stores of shared knowledge and jokes and intentions.

Charles and Anne spoke to each other about her when they were in the kitchen preparing desserts. "She's perfect. And what a beauty!" he said.

"I had no idea he would be so competent in picking out a sweetheart. But there's something wrong. She's having a good time, but she's quite upset about something and they're just a little standoffish with each other."

So accurate was Anne's sense of this that they found, when they returned to the table to serve dessert, that Susan had disappeared. After a quarter of an hour, Alexei began to look uncertain, and both he and Anne went to look for her. Anne found her standing in the hallway that led to the children's bedrooms, struggling to suppress tears.

"Oh, my God," said Anne, remembering and feeling along with Susan the terrible, bottomless grief of youth. "Susan, what's wrong? Did something happen?"

"No," said Susan. "I . . . I've lost a contact lens. I'm so sorry. This is just silly. Please forgive me."

"Where were you? Right there on the carpet? Let me turn on the light."

"No, don't bother," said Susan in a voice congested with tears. "It was a . . . a disposable, and it would be ruined by now."

"Too bad," said Anne, and seeing how upset Susan was, she added, "I'll get Alexei." But Susan begged her not to.

"Is it something about Alexei? Is that what you're crying about?"

"Oh, no!" said Susan, but Anne could tell that this was not true. I'll never again invite anyone under forty, she vowed to herself.

"You're probably thinking," Susan said tearily, "he's found some psycho and brought her into your house, but, really, I've never been like this before."

"Not at all, Susan," Anne assured her, feeling, however, as though her thoughts had been read.

"I'm so terrible," said Susan. "Everything I do is wrong."

At this mystifying outburst, Anne pulled Susan into a little room farther down the hallway, switched on a low light, and handed her a box of tissues. Susan had taken out her remaining lens and was squinting blindly.

"I'll send Alexei," Anne said, and patted Susan kindly on the shoulder as she left.

Susan saw that she was sitting on a sofa in a small untidy studio. She got up and walked about, leaning down close to examine the precarious stacks scattered here and there, which turned out to be books of music and scholarly books—studies of vocal technique, histories, composers' biographies. An upright piano stood at the opposite end of the room, and something from *Idomeneo* was open on a music stand beside it. As she was conducting this survey of the room's contents, she saw someone appear in the doorway and, by squinting, made out that it was Alexei. She was moved by the very sight of him—even as a vague blur. He was the problem—his liking her so much and being so good and accomplished and the way everything that happened between them made some sort of bond. And now he had brought her into what Susan could experience only as a miniparadise of sympathy, harmony, and goodwill. She felt a ghastly contrast between Alexei and everything here, and Chris and the secret way they were living, with its murky undercurrents and mistrust. It felt as though she were seeing her life with Chris clearly and discovering its deformities for the first time.

Alexei, looking at her, was alarmed. Her eyes were still red, her mascara smeared, and every now and then her shoulders shook with the remnants of a sob. Still, she had managed to stop crying outright—at least until Alexei sat down, put his arm around her, and asked, she thought, in the tenderest voice she had ever heard, "What's wrong?"

"I'm sorry, Alexei. I'm completely crazy. I'm embarrassing you in front of your friends," Susan said, weeping.

"I hope you don't always cry when you go out," he said, and she realized, leaning against him, that he was teasing her.

"Usually, but not always," she said, her voice cracking

He was touched by her effort to pull herself together and respond.

"I wonder just why you *are* crying. I thought you were having a good time. I liked the way you explained your ideas to those people. I wish I could talk like that, with sentences and words in order."

"It's a lovely evening. I started coming apart because it was a lovely evening, and I started thinking of Chris. . . ."

This remark stood as a barrier to further talk, but Susan's teary sniffs were all the more eloquent in the silence.

"You don't want to be with him," Alexei said hesitantly. He was obviously trying hard to be tactful.

"No."

"And he wouldn't be interested in this evening."

"No, he wouldn't be—not at all."

"I'm rather glad you say so."

"Why?"

"Because that means I would be better for you than he, even though I'm younger and poorer."

"Are you joking?"

"No. Can't you tell? The problem is you don't give me any encouragement. I would tell you things if you did. You should let me love you, Susan." He studied her face, then looked away.

They both knew, by now, that this was an authentic crisis—one of those times of real possibility and real danger that, usually, you recognized only after the fact. Alexei felt his perceptions grow slow and dreamlike—a paradoxical effect that he knew from experience meant his mind was actually speeding madly, making a frantic search for the right move when time was almost out.

Susan began to tremble and stopped leaning against Alexei. She would have to turn him away, but at the moment she lacked the strength. She was not quite prepared to give him up, and it was too late for an innocent backtracking.

"I've been so wrong," she said. "Alexei, forgive me. I can't do this. I've . . . I've made promises."

"Promises? But I think, perhaps, you shouldn't have. It's hard for someone like you to break a promise," he said in a tense voice, "but you're not his wife. You have a right to make a mistake."

Susan sprang up from the sofa, wringing her hands, and paced nervously in the four feet of open space that was all the cramped room provided.

"No, I am his wife. I'm married to him," she said. "We got married just a few days ago—secretly. No one knows." Alexei gaped at her, horror-struck. For a moment, she thought he might actually cry, but his pallor gave way to a deep flush that spread to the roots of his hair, down his neck, and under his collar.

"You couldn't have done it," he said at last. He stood up to look her in the face; the expression on his made her feel despicable.

"I did," she said.

"But why?" Alexei said accusingly, as if she had betrayed him. Of course I have, Susan thought. That's just what I've done.

"It's hard for me to tell you, Alexei, because I don't want you to despise me, and I know you will."

"You have to tell me."

"I know," said Susan. His outrage, paradoxically, calmed her—as though somehow it made things right. "It's hard to understand. Somehow, I got the idea that being married would fix things and rescue me . . . and partly, I think, I did it just . . . perversely." He waited for her to go on, but she shook her head and was quiet.

"Perversity isn't hard to understand," he said after a while. He was looking more wounded and less angry now. "You mean, you married this not-so-nice guy to avoid something you thought would be happier. People do such things."

"He asked me that night when we'd all gone to dinner after the filming. I had been having a good time . . . with you, actually. I knew something was going on between us, and I stopped it."

"No, you didn't," Alexei retorted scornfully. "After all, here you are, aren't you? *He* tried to stop it—obviously."

Susan gasped slightly, realizing that this was true. Chris had known as well as Alexei and Susan that something significant was going on between them. "It got him very upset. He's so frightened I'll leave him that I thought . . . I should help him. I didn't think about you. I'm sorry, Alexei, but there's no way to fix what I've done."

There was another long silence, and again Alexei broke it.

"Why not?" He avoided looking at her and looked instead at the window, where their reflections were visible. He sounded bitter.

"He needs me. I've gone too far. I took vows."

"Every word you just said is some kind of lie, Susan," he said, wounding her with the disgust in his voice.

"Well, at least now you know," she said, "that I'm not worth getting upset about."

Alexei relented and reached tentatively toward her hand, but she repeated, "There's really no way to fix it."

"You can't divorce him? This marriage is a complete fake anyway—just a legal absurdity, not a reality. Divorce him," said Alexei, "and go with me instead."

"Why would you want me after this? I'm sorry I've made you unhappy," she said, tears choking her voice. "Can't you see how crazy I am?"

"Well, no, I think it's just . . . um . . . just a glitch, not so hard to fix," he said, allowing a little kindness into his voice. He was strongly affected by her remorse.

"Not a fatal character flaw?"

"Not at all," he said stiffly, but he still wouldn't look at her. They sat side by side on the little sofa in silence.

"I love you, Alexei. I can tell you already know that."

He nodded, looking at his hands.

"It's hard for me to be straightforward and direct about intimate things." She grimaced and then covered her face with her hands.

"So I see."

"Not you, though."

"My problems are different—maybe worse. Look, I'm going to wait for you to divorce him, Susan. There's nothing else I can do."

For several minutes neither of them spoke, and there were no sounds but sniffs and sighs.

Of course, I'll spend years and years trying to talk her into divorcing, Alexei thought, and after all that maybe I won't get to be with her anyway. He saw those years, gloomy and contentious, stretching before him, and already began reconciling himself to them. From now on, he had not only his own considerable handicaps in life; he had just taken on Susan's madness as well. And there was nothing else to be done, because obviously the two of them were already joined together indissolubly. And I always wondered, Alexei reflected sorrowfully, how people got themselves into dreadful, absurd, and tragic situations like this one; I was always sure nothing like that would ever happen to me.

Susan shook her head vaguely, rejecting something that Alexei said or implied, she couldn't have told what. Divorce was a simple, obvious solution that, strangely, had not occurred to her until Alexei spoke. She had taken marriage vows and had learned from her father's example that divorce was not an option except in extremis. The idea that she could divorce came to her as a revelation.

A knock sounded at the door.

"Come out, you two. We're going to have some music," said Anne's voice, and this invitation to pleasure reminded Susan of her earlier feeling of being on moral holiday. Now, however, she thought that perhaps she had got this backward. That floating feeling, that sense of release, she understood now as the consciousness of acting openly, on real feelings, instead of pretended, perverted ones. Her life with Chris, that was the moral holiday—a most unpleasant one.

"No, I'll leave him," Susan announced suddenly. "I'll divorce him."

Alexei looked at her hesitantly, not yet able to suspend his compelling vision of a wretched future. How could anything so powerfully miserable, so sturdily dark, fade away so easily and effortlessly? He thought of how, in his childhood, the Soviet Union had melted away.

"Then you'll come with me?" he asked guardedly.

"Oh, yes."

"You're not making a mistake with me—like with him?"

"I'm not, but it's going to be hard to explain."

They stood to go, but were so frantic for both explanations and kisses that another ten minutes had passed, in a clumsy jumble of the two, before they left the studio.

"You were in love with Mallory just a few months ago," Susan reminded Alexei gingerly. "Maybe you still are."

"No, I never was!" he said, pulling back and looking shocked. "Where did you get that idea! I was lonely and drawn to her and interested in seeing what might develop, but she never let anything develop. I never spoke any word of love to her, I swear."

"But I think she's in love with you."

"If you say so. I don't know. I don't understand her. But, Susan, this embarrasses me because I was never in love with her and never for a moment thought I was. But I . . . I chased her a little. There were some ego things going on. . . ."

"It's all right," said Susan. They were quiet for a few moments and, again, tried to compose themselves to return to the company.

"It's nice of you to be so straight about it," Susan said as they stood to go. "You're always kind, Alexei. You help everybody."

"Not really. Susan, wait—I want you to know one more thing. I knew I was falling in love with you weeks ago, but I didn't know what to do. I didn't know what to say to you or whether I should say anything at all to you. Then your father called me, and I also had a long talk with your brother."

"What! About me?"

"Not to start with, but it ended up that way. It started that they were helping me with a problem. I'm very grateful to them, and I like them. Are you brave enough to come out now?"

Susan wiped her eyes and pushed back her hair and assumed her normal air. She hardly looked sheepish when she reappeared in the living room, where the other guests were drinking coffee and listening to the mezzo, Joanna, even though several stared, having been aware that there had been an "upset" of the sort that people under thirty were prone to. To Susan, without her lenses, their faces were blotches of warm color, which under the circumstances she didn't mind. And she behaved herself so well that by the end of the evening, even Anne had almost forgotten the incident, especially when she saw that somehow Susan and Alexei had gotten on a new footing.

"He's going to marry her," said Anne when the guests were gone.

"Did they say that?" asked Charles.

"No, but at one point she was crying in your studio and then he went in there for a long time, and when they came out she was happy."

"From there to an engagement is a bit of a stretch."

"No—not with those two. That's an unusual pair, and I think they're extremely well matched. You watch: this is going to be a couple. But Greg and Joanna were a complete flop, weren't they? She acted so superior, and he acted like a nerd—and he was so down when he went home."

Jane, listening to the discussion of Alexei and Susan, had mixed feelings. She admired Susan but had rather hoped that Alexei would wait for Jane herself to turn eighteen.

When Alexei and Susan stood on the sidewalk outside the Braithwaites' building, Susan could not decide where to go. She should, perhaps, go to Chris immediately. That would be the most honest thing to do, but Alexei strongly protested her doing that. She should stay with him or, if she didn't want to do that, go home to her father, or stay at her own place on 114th Street. There was no reason to go all the way down to the Village and spend a night of anguish. The two of them stood in front of the Braithwaites' building arguing for several minutes, before Susan finally decided to go to 114th Street and leave Chris a message that she would see him in the morning. She was so blind without her lenses, however, that Alexei wouldn't let her walk alone to 114th Street. He thought he should go up with her, too, but she insisted that she would be fine.

In the morning, Alexei was wild from the moment that Susan called to say that she was on her way to Chris's until, hours later, wearing eyeglasses, carrying suitcases, and looking ill and exhausted, she returned to her apartment, where Alexei was waiting for her on the stoop.

Chris always clung to her more when he thought he was losing her, and her declaration that she was moving out inspired frenzied resistance on his part. Then he was tearful, calmly and affectionately frank, and apologetic: he'd made a mistake insisting on keeping the marriage secret. He could see that. But, finally, when Susan was still unmoved, he was angry.

"I told you that you'd run out on me," he said as she was leaving. "Remember? You swore you wouldn't. I thought women like you were the nice type—no-talent nobodies, but nice. But you're not. You're nothing at all."

"I want to know something, Chris," Susan said. "That day when we were driving home on the Henry Hudson, did you do it on purpose?"

"What? Get some guy to slam us on purpose? How would I do that? You're crazy."

"But you were doing something, and watching me—to see how I would react."

Chris couldn't prevent half a smile from breaking through his rage. "She's so, so smart. Well, I couldn't help seeing that the moment had its dramatic potential. Is that what this is about? Susan, I'd never hurt you."

"I know you think you mean it," Susan said. She called Alexei as soon as she had turned the corner off Chris's block.

CHAPTER 44

Peter had been surprised to get the call from Mallory Holmes. She invited him to go for a cup of coffee on Broadway, and he accepted. Of course, he said to himself, it has something to do with the Devereaux Foundation. Matters there had just taken a turn—actually several turns— for the worse. Edmond had filed papers initiating proceedings against his aunt. Wanda had called and given Peter an ultimatum: three more days. "This could kill Lesley, you know," she pointed out. "I hear it's dangerous for her to be upset. You've got to behave responsibly, Peter."

Peter still felt some annoyance with Mallory for her contributions to the *Gazette* story, but in her presence he seemed only rather more sober than usual. They had arrived simultaneously at the café at about 5:00 P.M. Peter held the door for her, found her a chair, and fetched two cafés au lait, all with an ease that had elements of both fatherliness and suave date. Mallory rather admired it.

"I'm not sure you know that I resigned from the *Gazette*," Mallory began after inquiring generally about his family and more particularly about Susan, whom she said she "really had to call." She noticed that Peter had such dignity that even in the crowded café, with his knees jammed awkwardly under a tiny table, he had presence, confidence without self-importance.

Peter had not known. "Resigned? Why?"

"Because of that Kappell story last spring. It was disgraceful, but I couldn't find any way to fix things while I was on their staff. So I quit and began freelancing."

"No kidding! How are you doing?"

"All right. I wouldn't mind a regular paycheck."

Peter's annoyance quickly gave way to doubt whether Mallory deserved to give up her plum of a job and be impoverished because of the Devereaux story.

"Mallory, I'm not sure you should have—"

"I am," she said. "By the time they let me think for myself, I'd have forgotten how. So among my various gigs, I've been writing for an online magazine called *Tablet*, which you may have heard of."

"Of course. I don't read it myself, but people tell me they like it."

"They're sort of contrarian, and they love to second-guess the *Gazette*, so naturally they went for the idea of a story about your seminar and the Devereaux Foundation, which means I got a chance to try to straighten things out."

"I appreciate that."

"Anyway, in the course of interviewing people for the story, I found out things . . . things I think you should know . . ."

"Mm-hm," Peter said. He sounded noncommittal, like a doctor listening to a recital of symptoms. No doubt all lawyers sounded that way listening to clients' stories.

"For example, that Howard Kappell has known the Smith-Smythes forever, and so has your neighbor Edmond Lockhart. They're old buddies."

"No kidding," said Peter, his brows benignly high and contracted. Ideologues, he thought, probably feel an emotional affinity for other ideologues even when they have opposing ideologies.

"And before the seminar meeting last spring, Lockhart called the Smith-Smythes and told them it was his senile aunt's project, that you were a villain and had stacked the seminar with right-wingers and anti-Muslim sentiment, and how regrettable it was that his family's money came from brutal exploitation of factory workers."

"He set them up," said Peter.

"Yes," said Mallory. "He asked them to help, maybe talk to someone at Columbia. And they were glad to oblige because *they* really want to run the seminar, which they think could help them get a Nobel Prize. They probably thought this would be a great way to get you out and them in. So they called Kappell, and Kappell sees what he wants and is not too good on checking facts."

"That's quite a story."

"It's not all," Mallory said. "My source for a lot of this was—get set—Ivy Hurst. Louis—who's the one who got me going on all this—Louis had told me earlier that his mother was conniving with Lockhart. It was his idea that I should call Ivy and see what she knew. You know she left Lockhart, and she hates him now. She told me things hoping to get even with him for—well, lots of things.

"According to Ivy, your wife was constantly pushing Lockhart to get you out of the seminar and out of the foundation. Mr. Frankl, forgive me for what I'm saying—just tell me to stop if you decide you'd rather not know." But Peter wanted to hear. "Ivy said your wife convinced him to start taking drugs," Mallory continued, "antidepressants, and after that he seemed to have a personality change. He started misjudging, almost like he was manic or something. Lockhart probably would have dropped the whole thing once the initial effort failed, but your wife kept pushing him. She put him up to calling Kappell right before the second story appeared, because she wanted to bring more pressure down on you from your firm, and she dreamed up the idea of bringing legal proceedings against Lockhart's aunt—she saw a movie where that happened. I'm sorry, Mr. Frankl. I know how terrible it must be to hear me say these things."

Watching Peter's face, Mallory decided she'd told him enough, even though she knew more about Lockhart and Lesley, more that she hadn't told Louis, either. It wasn't her place. She'd enabled Peter to take steps to protect himself and his client, and that was as far as she should go.

Peter, listening to Mallory's disclosures, hardly knew whether to feel enraged, disappointed, or hopeful. On the one hand, he saw immediately that he should have guessed some of this and that his self-protective blindness when it came to Lesley had been dangerous for others. On the other hand, he could feel part of his mind looking for holes in Mallory's story so he wouldn't have to believe it—even though he knew it was true. She considerately avoided eye contact while he absorbed her intelligence. He frowned, thought, and leaned so far back in his plastic chair that Mallory feared for his safety.

"So something needs to be done," he said, "but I'm not sure where to begin. I guess I'll have to talk to Lesley. You've written something?"

"A piece about the Devereaux Foundation—the interesting things it does and its oddities and why it's so important to protect them. It's going online tonight. I get into the thinking behind the terrorism seminar and how the participants were picked, and I explain the motives behind the attacks. Howard Kappell looks as bad as he deserves to. I had a really, really good interview with Emma Devereaux and Hilda Hughes."

Mallory, like Louis, understood, and she was going to fight Peter's battle for him. Unexpectedly, this made him feel particularly powerful and deserving. Who would ever have thought that Louis and Mallory were such fighters? The whole Devereaux problem might just go away, all because Mallory had her regrets. Peter felt a surge of admiration and warmth for her. He'd known her since she was in diapers, and he'd always liked her. It was easy to see why Louis was in love with her.

"You would probably never have guessed that it was Louis who came up with the big ideas that I pursued doing this research," Mallory continued. "He's been helping me the entire time. He even had the idea that I should try to write for *Tablet*, when he found out that I knew an editor there. He's got lots of ideas. I'm not sure you know it."

"I'm beginning to know it," said Peter. Again he leaned back in his chair, contemplatively, with his arms crossed over his chest, and then proceeded to give Mallory a long, touching account of his children, her friends Louis and Susan, somewhat in the manner of a lawyer summing up the whole story for a jury—how things had gone wrong in the family, the effect of Lesley's illness on all of them, especially Louis. Louis had figured out a lot of things and overcome some big problems. He wished he could say the same about Susan.

Mallory knew that Susan was never very happy, not even now that she was living with Chris. If anything, she seemed more melancholy than ever, though she had found someone Mallory thought ideal for her. She didn't say this to Mr. Frankl, however. She had an inkling that he didn't much like Chris.

As for what Peter described as Louis's problems, and his improvement, Mallory had seen these things, too. Peter told her that he hoped she would not judge Louis by a boy's façade she may have seen in the past, erected to keep peace between two secretly warring parents, to evade his mother's control, and to conceal what he really thought and felt. Then he said he had to hurry to a meeting, and he kissed Mallory good-bye.

Mallory went home to visit her mother, for no special reason, just to say hello. Ingrid was dressing to go meet Herb at a movie, and Mallory sat cross-legged on her bed, watching her mother search in her closet and then pull on slacks and a sweater. Ingrid still had a good figure—so good that it was not easy to analyze just what it was that made it look like sixty and not thirty. Mallory soon stopped trying and instead told Ingrid every word that Peter Frankl had just said about Louis and his family. Ingrid listened attentively. What extraordinary things for a man like that to say, a self-possessed, dignified, old-fashioned man like Peter Frankl.

"This sounds authentic. Yes, he told you the way it really was, I think," said Ingrid, nodding eagerly. "My goodness, what a tangled web that family wove. And it came unraveled just because Lesley was unconscious for a few months, the way that sometimes happens because someone dies. They had expected her to die."

"You said things about Louis a couple of months ago that weren't far off this."

"Yes, and Louis has made progress, it seems, since then. Do you understand what Peter was saying to you, sweetie?"

"Yes, he was proposing on Louis's behalf. I'm not as stupid as you think I am. And I think I do want to marry him, Mother."

"I've suspected that for a long time." Ingrid was highly amused by everything. But privately she was also wondering whether Mallory would ever have reached this point without a little push like the one Peter Frankl had just given her. Mightn't she have just tilted the other way and ignored her feelings for Louis? Peter, you are sly, Ingrid thought, but she didn't really mind. She liked Louis. Her back to Mallory, applying lipstick, Ingrid could see her daughter's face glaring at her in the mirror.

"You could have resisted saying so at a time like this," Mallory said.

"But you knew I knew. So go on. What are you thinking?"

"To tell the truth," Mallory said, lying back on the bed, "I feel some of the things I did with Alexei, although nothing ever went anywhere with him. I think Louis is becoming a man like his father in certain ways. I have a real connection with him in a way I never had before with Paul or my boyfriends before Paul."

Ingrid held her tongue for once and let Mallory talk it out.

"I would never have been able to be kind to Alexei, even though I should have been, and I would have ended up hating myself and him. I wouldn't have been willing to be hard up and marginal and frustrated and put the kids in public school. I would have found it maddening to make sacrifices for his singing—I don't even like opera, and I think his obsession with it is crazy. Besides, although Alexei liked me, I was to him the way Louis was to me. Do you know what I mean?"

Ingrid shook her head no.

"He was smarter and more talented and had better taste and more strength of character. He'd been through more." Mallory sat up again and watched her mother's face in the mirror as she brushed her hair into a smooth gray ponytail.

"Ah!" said Ingrid with a nod.

"You don't have to agree with me as obviously as that, Mother, when I'm putting myself down. And Louis likes me more than Alexei did. Alexei was not in love with me so much as I was in love with him—maybe not at all, although I never really gave him a chance to be. Louis loves me. He knows me and loves me just as I am, and he always will love me. I'm more sophisticated than he is, and better educated, but you know, Mom, I truly think I'm not smarter. He's very smart."

Ingrid looked tolerant and nodded.

"Don't do that, Mother. And he's actually sweet and thoughtful and sort of . . . good. He helps, you know what I mean? Now that I'm freelancing, I feel how life could be lonely and hard. But Louis pulls with me. I don't feel alone in the world because Louis is there. And I want to make him feel the same way."

Ingrid smiled unaffectedly at this, and her eyes filled.

Mallory did not tell her last thought, that the attraction she had initially felt for Louis in those moments at her party last March, which had died so precipitately back then, lately had revived. She sat on Ingrid's bed and daydreamed. They both understood that she had chosen the lesser man, not feeling up to the challenges of life with the better one. Ingrid knew that Mallory's self-regard was wounded because of this, and even her heart, possibly, had a scratch or two. But, Ingrid thought, she'll marry Louis, and it'll be all right. Louis will handle it.

"You had better call Louis, sweetheart. Okay if I tell Daddy what you've been saying?"

"You think it will be all right with him?"

"Your father always liked Louis, from the beginning."

"No kidding," said Mallory with a pleased smile. "Dad can be really sharp, can't he."

Ingrid wished *she* had gotten some credit for being sharp, for at least not opposing an interest in Louis—for almost favoring him, if it came to that. But mothers never got the unambivalent approval from daughters that fathers got, she thought with a stoical sigh.

It occurred to Ingrid that Mallory had behaved oddly in telling her plans to her mother before she told Louis himself. Maybe a little more mother-daughter separation was in order here, but they had been far into the conversation before its ultimate conclusion began to dawn on her—on either of them. In any case, Ingrid felt more inclined to cling to her daughter for as long as she could than to move further away. It was going to be hard to watch her marry and turn into a self-reliant woman, older, savvy, well-judging—someone who would not need her and whom she could not protect. Ingrid was suddenly against the whole thing and got teary when Mallory reappeared, dressed in coat and scarf.

She kissed her mother good-bye. "I'll call," she said, and Ingrid wondered why no one said "Good-bye" or "Bye" or even "Ciao" anymore. Everyone said "I'll call." Probably no one could bear to part. Certainly that's how she felt about her rosy-cheeked Mallory, blond hair half in and half out of the scarf, as she set out in a hurry.

"Can I see you?" Mallory said into her cell phone. She hadn't waited to get home to her own apartment but called Louis from the stairwell at the Federal Express office on 116th Street, out of the bitter wind. She sniffled from the cold.

"You mean now? I'm at work," said Louis.

"When you're done. It's already past seven, you know."

"I'm working all night on a closing." Louis hesitated. "You could come down."

His voice was tight, not his usual drawl, and he sounded rushed and distracted. She could not judge what was reaction to her and what to his situation.

Louis worked in the heart of the financial district, near Broad and Wall, in a stodgy century-old building with marble floors and crystal chandeliers in the lobby. There were several uniformed security guards, and like all security guards, they talked to one another, never seemed to look at the visitors, and seemed to ignore Mallory's request to visit Louis on the twenty-third floor. Nonetheless she stood and waited, and soon enough a slender and well-built man in a tight black pullover and jeans appeared at her side.

"Mallory?" he said, smiling, easy and familiar. Sauntering gracefully, he led her to the right elevator.

"You're catching him at a good time," he said, nodding reassuringly.

"Are you a banker, too?" she asked.

"Oh, no! Please! They wear suits and ties—in the middle of the night, they still have their ties on. I'm a night-shift proofreader."

"What do you do in the daytime?" Mallory asked, smiling.

"I'm a dancer," he said. "I go from Broadway to Wall Street. Here we are. Right in here."

Mallory entered a room that contained a huge table whose perimeter was lined with neat stacks of documents that were being examined by several young men and women in suits, who clutched tattered checklists in their hands. Every one of them, male and female, in every part of the room, overtly or covertly, examined Mallory when she entered. Most were her age peers and looked enviously at the conspicuous signs of freedom she bore: loose, tousled hair, cheeks red with cold, no makeup, pea coat, and long cashmere scarf. They were making plenty of money, but Mallory was free and looked like the person they wanted to be, or have. Mallory, exuding the scent of outdoors, stood near the doorway, blond, sparkling, pretty, and quietly poised, waiting for Louis to finish telling something to a poker-faced colleague who avoided looking Mallory's way.

"What took you so long?" asked Louis with the shadow of a smile. He stepped out into the corridor with her and spoke softly.

"I got off at the wrong stop. I had to walk by the World Trade Center site. I'd never seen it before."

"You're kidding."

"No. I never wanted to. What's the point?"

"You always do that, Mallory, as though you have a right to live in a world where that didn't happen, or—"

"Look, let's analyze my shortcomings later. I want to talk to you about things."

"What's up?"

Mallory could not launch into this delicate subject as easily as that. She stood tongue-tied, and Louis pulled back and looked at her, puzzled, his arms folded over his chest.

"I know," he said, raising a finger. "You wanted to tell me that you would like to get married after all."

He looked down at her through long black lashes, and she had the same thrill in her stomach about him that she'd had at the party months ago. Her emotions were a mystery to her. Where had they come from? Where had they gone to? He had been this beautiful the whole time, and it hadn't meant a thing to her.

"Yes," she said.

Louis, who had thought of his remark as nothing more than his usual joke with Mallory, did a dramatic, unfeigned double take, which made Mallory smile. She liked to see Louis jolted out of his cynical knowingness.

"I'll be right back," he called into the conference room, and he pulled her by the hand down the hallway and into a dark room filled with the bulky shapes of copying machines.

"Oh, Mallory, Mallory, Mallory," said Louis.

CHAPTER 45

The Devereaux Foundation had called a special Saturday meeting of the board. All the members were gathered, but so far most were showing more interest in the refreshments than in the agenda. Wendell Ellery was consuming an apple tart with such enthusiasm and concentration, his eyes and his mouth childishly wide in preparation for an ample bite, that he forgot to look shrewd.

Peter had informed the board of Mallory's excellent article in *Tablet* about the Devereaux Foundation and the seminar. Only Hilda had read it on the Internet, but printouts lay on the table for everyone.

"Vindication," said Miss Devereaux, all calm and self-possession. "We are completely vindicated."

"Vimicafum!" agreed Ellery with a full mouth.

Mallory's story told the facts about the foundation, its people, and all the fine works it had made possible. She described the organization of the seminar and what careful attempts had been made to balance politics, walks of life, and personalities so as to create a rich and free environment, in which envies, statuses, ideologies, professional loyalties, and all other thought-stifling forces would be held in check. She made dark hints about people who had acted behind the scenes to discredit these good things and had better watch out.

Peter summarized all this for the group and added that he had had a conversation with Edmond Lockhart's lawyer that made him feel certain the legal proceedings against Miss Devereaux were to be dropped.

"Hear, hear," Orazio Cromwell called out, and glared at Ellery to prevent his echoing this exclamation.

It was aggravating that none of the other board members, except perhaps Hilda, seemed to feel much relief. Peter had been obliged to worry about everything all by himself. His little speech felt anticlimactic. Peter saw no need to tell them that his law partners, too, were mollified and had withdrawn their demand that he cease working for the foundation. But none of them had apologized, and Peter had not forgiven them for their disloyalty.

"All right, then," Peter continued. "Hilda, the new film looks very promising, and drafts of some papers that are going to be presented at the terrorism seminar at Columbia have arrived and they look really good, too. As for these four new small projects . . . I think they're all gems."

"I don't want to lead us astray or anything," said Orazio, glancing side to side and looking, thought Peter, as though that were exactly what he did want to do, "but Hilda, don't we need more with-it things, more garde-en-avanty things? I mean, an essay, with photographs, on decorative needlework, and this biography of a housemaid in an upstate town . . ." Orazio looked at the ceiling and held his unlit cigar between his teeth.

"Mr. Cromwell," said Miss Devereaux, "after speaking with . . . uh, with Mr. . . . I talked with . . . at the Arts Council . . ."

"We fill a niche, Orazio," said Hilda, "we play a special role. We're a foundational wild card. We don't have any fixed ideas about what we'll fund—not even any fixed ideas about funding things that are groundbreaking and revolutionary or traditional, conservative things."

Hilda spoke with such calm and self-possession that Peter hardly knew her. She looked different, too. She surely had had a haircut. Her hair was smooth and clever looking, and she had on a rose cashmere pullover and, incredibly, just a hint of rosy lipstick. She just looked nice and . . . rosy.

"It's one of the things I keep in mind when I read proposals," Hilda was saying. "You have to be open to new ideas, and also be aware of the stranglehold of old, dead ideas about newness. The people demanding innovation so often want anything but. They actually want to replay the old, easy revolutions that already happened fifty, a hundred years ago—over and over. This lets them feel superior and more advanced than thou, while actually remaining completely orthodox and censorious and rigid and in control."

". . . Lucas, at the Arts Council . . . ," said Miss Devereaux. "But, now, what was my point? . . ."

"You could justify a lot of hidebound stuff with thinking like that if you're not careful," said Peter. Hilda obviously could hold her own in an argument.

"Very true. But I'll have all of you to keep me from funding photos of babies and dogs."

"Dogmas, yes," said Miss Devereaux. "Hilda's presentation at the Arts Council. She called it 'Postmodern Dogmas.' And everyone was quite interested. Mr. Lucas said it was the most interesting thing he'd heard for a long time, but some people got very mad. He said it was a complicated idea she was explaining, one that would easily be misrepresented, and he thought her most courageous for even trying to put it across. We're finished, then, Mr. Frankl? Unless I hear an objection, the meeting is adjourned."

Peter helped Milton Steinberg carry the heavy corporate record books back to Milton's desk.

"Next meeting, we're going to vote on a new slate of officers, Milton," he said, "which will probably be the same as the old slate. So you might as well write their names into the agenda."

Milton nodded and made a note in his stenographer's pad. "Orazio Cromwell," he said, "Hilda . . . Wendell Ellery . . . Tell me, Mr. Frankl— why do so many WASPs have a last name for their first name?"

"The parents often give a child the mother's maiden name as a first name," Peter said. "Actually, in our group, not only Wendell but Orazio was named that way. 'Orazio' is Italian for 'Horace,' and his mother's maiden name was Horace. Now, actually, it doesn't work so well if you're not a WASP. For example, if my parents had done that, my name would be O'Hennessy Frankl—my mother was Della O'Hennessy."

"I have to agree, *Peter* Frankl is better," Milton said, lighting a cigarette and taking a pensive drag. "No, it doesn't work for Jews, does it. Imagine if my father had been Weinberg Steinberg."

"You and Orazio are lucky, both named after great poets," Peter added with a trace of a smile.

"Not me," said Milton. "I'm named after my grandfather."

Hilda was already out the door by the time Peter had packed his briefcase and said his good-byes. He saw the elevator door close on her face, and when he walked out onto the street, he saw her turning the corner onto Riverside Drive.

"Hilda-a-a-!" he called. He expected her to pretend not to hear and walk on, but in fact she turned to look at him.

"Coming tonight?" he asked. Mallory and Louis had invited her to their engagement party.

"Of course," she replied, even though, as they both knew, there was no "of course" about it. Hilda had not gone to a party for more than twenty-five years.

"I'll walk you home."

"I thought I'd take a walk," she said. "It's not cold."

"I'll join you." They turned south on Riverside and crossed over to the promenade. Hilda looked down, trying to read the title of a book protruding from Peter's pocket as they walked. "*The Betrothed!*" she cried.

"Louis gave it to me," said Peter. "An astonishing book—I can't put it down. I can't believe I'd never heard of it."

"I'm so glad you like it. Did Louis?" They spent ten blocks discussing the book's young lovers and the unfathomable horror of the Black Death. Hilda had a great deal to say.

"I'm going to be straight with you, Hilda," Peter said when they reached Ninety-sixth Street and the twilight was growing deep. "You're changing lately. It's nice to see. We've known each other for a long time now."

"Nine years."

"During which I've always thought you were smart and I knew it was you who kept the whole operation going. I couldn't stand the way you messed yourself up and behaved like such a neurotic. I just have to tell you that I admire the way you're speaking up and saying things that make sense."

"Thank you, Peter. If it were anybody but you, I'd die of embarrassment listening to that. How do you manage to be so tactful? That's a rare skill."

He shrugged and smiled. "And you look nice, too," he said. "So what's the deal? What's going on with you?"

"I've come out."

"Frankly, I would have thought you were out a long time ago. I knew you were gay."

"No, as straight. It turns out I'm *not* gay. Never was."

Peter couldn't help beginning to laugh. "I've never heard of anything like that," he said. "How can that be?"

"I'm going to retract what I said about your tact," said Hilda coolly, "if you're going to snicker like that."

Peter made an effort to restrain himself, but it was several seconds before he could look at Hilda with a composed face. "So when did you figure this out?" he asked, frowning so as to avoid laughing.

"This fall," she said, "just as my psychoanalysis was ending. My analyst said I was a pseudolesbian. I was always attracted to men, but that was emotionally painful and interfered with my neurotic goals. So when I was in college I convinced myself that I was gay and never was willing to rethink that until now."

"But have you ever had a boyfriend?"

"No—or girlfriend, either."

"My God, Hilda. How old are you? It's late to get into the game."

"Tact, Peter."

"I'll be your first. There. What could be more tactful?"

"Too bad you're a married man," said Hilda, "or I'd accept the offer." She looked at him with a sorrowful smile, and Peter felt unusual stirrings. Actually, he had always liked and trusted Hilda. He had even liked her silliness and whimsy, and she had a head on her shoulders. The unusual quality of the whole thing appealed to Peter: a fifty-year-old virgin, for God's sake. He realized abruptly that he was feeling attracted to Hilda. Could they nonetheless be friends? He was reminded of Rabbi Friedman's advice about finding a friend and of things he wanted to say to Lesley when he got home.

"Too bad I'm a married man, or I'd really mean it," he said.

They walked along the promenade in silence. Hilda had been aware for months that something was wrong in his marriage, although she could not decide whether this was due to an estrangement, or to the wife's illness, or to some combination of the two.

"Have you ever even held hands with a man?" Peter asked her, his face lively with unconcealed interest in her deprivations.

"No," she replied rudely.

"Okay. Why not let me be the first one to hold your hand, just to your street? Sort of in honor of what might have been—but you're not going to go unfriendly on me after this, are you?"

She shook her head and accepted his hand. They walked south to 96th Street, then north again to 114th Street, where she relinquished his hand with regret. It was very pleasant—pleasant and shatteringly ordinary—being linked that way to another human being. Peter Frankl had a strong, warm, dry hand that was somewhat larger than hers. He had squeezed hers affectionately now and then in their long walk and occasionally tugged gently to get her to come one way rather than another. She hadn't experienced that sort of physical communication since she was a schoolgirl. How strange I am. How odd my life has been, she thought. How can it ever be overcome, this mountain of oddness that I've built up! And soon I'll lose Dr. Stoller and have nothing left but peculiar memories, memories of being peculiar.

"What did you mean, in honor of what might have been?" she asked Peter.

"I mean, if I wasn't married, we could have become a number. I definitely would have wanted to."

Peter's voice was still light and amused, but from Hilda's point of view, these were serious matters. "I don't know why you would think so. Are you a very experienced man, Peter?"

"No. I have only one more person in my experience than you."

"Your wife, you mean. My goodness. How tactfully you describe the difference between us as one person rather than thousands of intimate moments."

"We could argue over which description is more relevant."

"Not really. This conversation is already totally out of control, if you ask me. I'm going to leave you here and go home."

"All right. Don't be a stranger," Peter said, and she didn't know what he meant by that.

She watched Peter turn and trudge off, trench coat flapping, eyes behind his glasses fixed on the ground, bearing a briefcase. Despite all the good news and his good-humored teasing, he did not seem much happier than she did. Yet there ought to have been a sign on his back: "Nicest Man in NYC!" Or "Closest Thing to Living Saint You'll Ever See!" The idea that Peter was unhappy was wrenching to Hilda; but if it was true, there was not a thing she could do about it.

Walking home, Peter felt guilty about holding hands with Hilda and speaking too freely. It felt disturbingly close to marital infidelity. Initially he had meant something merely friendly, a kind of joke, but he had liked holding her hand. Thinking about it, in fact, he decided it would be nice to kiss Hilda, too, and then he had to struggle to wreck a whole train of enticing thoughts that followed that one. He remembered kissing Wanda and his obsession with her that had died only when she tried to blackmail him. What explained his attraction to such a misbehaving, amoral, selfish woman? Of course, he thought, she was so sexy. Actually, this was just like Lesley—another not-so-nice sexy woman. Do I think sex has to be transgressive? he asked himself. Only bad girls turn me on? Just like any standard-issue lapsed Catholic, he thought with distaste, and for the first time he felt inclined to blame his mother for his problems. What a mess she'd made of everything, including her son. Not only was he imprisoned in a dreadful marriage, he'd never even felt free to object until now—when the world offered Hilda.

Too late for me, though, Peter concluded. He wouldn't use Lesley's betrayals to justify leaving her; she would never leave him, either. And he would not be unfaithful to her. In Peter's mind, being someone's husband or wife went all the way down to the roots of who the two of you were. Adultery, therefore, was an especially cruel kind of murder; it forced the betrayed spouse to live through her own death. He'd always been horrified watching this happening in his friends' divorces. And he was going to do this to his own children's mother? No way, he said to himself. Besides, once people did something like that, something that was cousin to murder, they got on overly familiar terms with death and that was the end of them, too. They ended up with some strange mental leprosy that ate away at them until they were gone. He'd seen that. Even if he hadn't, he knew instinctively that when you murdered, you died.

Peter found Lesley in their room, watching a movie. "I'm not coming to the party tonight," she said, her eyes fixed on the screen, which showed Judy Garland and Mickey Rooney. "I'm just not feeling up to it."

"I need to talk to you, Lesley," said Peter, switching off the movie. "It's important."

She was in a rage by the time he left. It was frightening to her, all the things he knew, and she couldn't imagine how he knew them unless Edmond had told. But what really left her trembling and furious was the arrogant way he kept saying she'd "lost any claim to certain kinds of consideration" and how different things would be. She'd see about that, she said to herself, and she'd see about Edmond, too. In the pursuit of what she regarded as her rights and interests, Lesley could be remarkably effective.

Walking to Mallory's party, Peter comforted himself that at least the children were going to be all right. Whatever his own deprivations, they would both have love and work that they cherished, and that made everything bearable. Lesley, the firm—he could put up with everything now that the children were happy.

CHAPTER 46

For weeks, Mallory had been planning to give a December holiday party. It was readily transformed into an engagement party. She wouldn't have believed, when she gave a party last spring, that she would be engaged before the year was out, let alone to Louis Frankl. She invited most of the same people, along with as many more as could fit inside her two and a half rooms. Chris, however, was not invited, and she hadn't planned on inviting Alexei either until she heard the news, first from Louis and later from Susan herself, about her and Alexei.

"I don't believe it," Mallory said when Louis told her. It was more than surprising; it was deeply unsettling, even though she was in love with Louis and had not so much as spoken with Alexei for months.

"You're the only one who liked the idea of Susan's being with Chris, Mallory," Louis said. "He was a jerk—worse than a jerk. You didn't know him."

"I know I didn't really know him," she said. "All right, so that's why she's not with Chris. But why is she with Alexei?"

"He's a great guy, that's all. I'm betting they're going to get married."

"Married! That makes even less sense to me. He's not even educated. They'll be poor. He's also four years—almost five—younger than she is."

"Nah. He's better educated than I am, and to me he seems older than Susan. She's so innocent and . . ."

"Naïve."

"Yeah, and Dad will help them out. He's so relieved Susan got rid of Chris, and he likes Alexei a lot—as much as he likes you. Besides, Alexei's got a lot of things he can do. He's this chess phenom—he can win money prizes, plus teaching, and there's acting, singing. He's no slouch, and she's not, either, and neither of them is all that interested in getting rich. Okay, Mallory, c'mon. Are you jealous or what?"

"No! Really, sweetheart, not at all. I think I'm going to be glad for both of them, because now that I think about it, I can see, sort of, how it would work for them. What I feel is more like . . . embarrassment." This was so nearly true that Mallory was able to convince herself that it was entirely true.

"I can understand that, but hardly anyone knew about it, and the ones who did," Louis added pointedly, "really don't want to think much about it. Everyone understands."

"Yes, you're right. I'd better call Susan." Mallory remembered only now that Louis, too, had reason to feel uncomfortable about her history with Alexei. Yet he seemed to have only generous feelings toward him. Louis often surprised Mallory by being large-minded, and making her feel small and limited. Having decided to marry him, she loved him more than she had known she could love anybody, except her parents. It was a revelation, a relief, to find out that she could, and it made her think better of herself— after nearly a year of having her flaws repeatedly made evident to her.

Susan and Mallory intended to continue as best friends despite the complications. Of the four of them, Mallory felt most awkward, but Alexei himself was so unembarrassed and, in a somewhat distant way, friendly that she began to think she would get the hang of it. Perhaps it shouldn't have been possible, but it was: her history with Alexei was fading from memory, erased by social necessity.

Herb and Ingrid Holmes were stationed just inside Mallory's door when Peter arrived. The crowd was so dense that it was difficult to penetrate further into the room.

"Lesley's sorry she couldn't be here. Just not up to it," Peter told them, and they nodded understandingly and made inarticulate, sympathetic noises. Originally, Lesley had said she would come even though Alexei and Susan would also be there; she was unfriendly to the point of rudeness to Alexei and called him "the gypsy." Lesley had adored Chris and in a call to offer him condolences voiced some keen criticisms of her daughter. She was less opposed to Mallory than to Alexei, but not enthusiastic. Louis could have done far, far better than some girl from the building with no money, and not even that pretty.

Peter, on the other hand, was delighted with both Mallory and Alexei. He had always liked Mallory, and now he admired her as well. As for Alexei, he told Susan, when she asked, that it was impossible not to like and respect him. "But he may never make much money or be what most people would call a success," he told her. "You'll have to invent your own kind of success. I hope that won't be a strain on you, sweetie." This speech rather anticipated the facts, because Susan and Alexei hadn't yet announced any engagement, but it left Susan in no doubt as to what her father wanted. She was staggered that he would encourage her to marry someone like Alexei, and against her mother's wishes, too.

Hilda rang Mallory's bell a few moments after Peter. She was pleased to find the older generation gathered just inside the door. Hilda had felt that she had to come since she now took such an interest in so many of the young people who would be there, and after all, these were Peter's children.

Once more, Mallory's party worked; indeed, it had something of an ecstatic mood right from the beginning. Three couples had been brought together by one party last spring, which was astonishing in itself. Several of tonight's guests hoped that last spring's magic would repeat itself. The best times for meeting someone, one guest told another, are in the spring and just before the holidays.

Mallory was invisible from where Peter stood, but he saw Louis and Susan and waved them over to his station near the doorway. They made their way with difficulty, holding glasses of wine above their heads for him, Hilda, and the Holmeses.

"Mom just didn't feel up to it," he told them, marveling at the sight of Louis receiving a kiss from Ingrid Holmes and a clap on the back from Herb. "Why not just give her a call? She'd appreciate it, I'm sure." He had left Lesley seething, silenced only by his walking out in the middle of her harangue.

Alcott and Sylvie had come up to stand on either side of Hilda, each gesturing and shouting in one of her ears, while she frowned, nodded, and looked straight ahead, trying to make sure she understood what they were saying, something about some film festival and early showings. To Mallory, taking stock of things, it looked as though Sylvie and Alcott were quarreling, with Hilda in the middle; lately Mallory had the feeling that as the work on the movie ended, Sylvie and Alcott were falling out of sympathy with each other. This saddened her, but there was little anyone could do to prevent it. Sylvie had always predicted there'd be a breakup, but could it be coming this soon? Alexei pointed out the same thing to Susan. "They just don't get along now, as though they have to have something to be involved in together. They might break up."

Susan tried to call her mother, because her father had asked her to, although Susan scarcely spoke to her lately on account of her rudeness to Alexei. Over the din of the party, she managed to determine that the housekeeper was saying that her mother had gone to visit the neighbor across the hall for a minute. "Across the hall," she told Louis gloomily. She decided not to try again, because she did not wish to know how long her mother stayed across the hall.

"What's wrong?" asked Alexei, who had also made his way to the group of elders.

"Nothing. Long story," she said. "I'll have to tell you later. Are you uncomfortable, being at this party?"

"No," he said, "not even a little bit."

Alcott, from one side of the group that now included Peter, Hilda, Sylvie, Herb, and Ingrid, was shouting for Alexei's attention. "Sorry, man," Alcott called, "but you have a conflict. I'm afraid the film festival overlaps the Berlin International."

"But you don't really need me there, do you?"

"No, he doesn't," said Sylvie. "He just has to have his hand held all the time."

Alcott ignored her. "It would help if you came, Alexei," he said.

"Well, so I'll skip the international. Who cares? There's always another tournament."

"But what about Boris Tarlov?" said Susan. She understood better than the others that Alexei's absence, once again, would give an appearance that he simply feared losing.

"You should go to Berlin," said Louis. "That'll sound great: 'Mystery Star, Chess Champ, Battles in Berlin While Indie Fans Wait with Bated Breath'—whatever that means," he added in Mallory's ear.

"I think you should go to Berlin, too," said Peter. "You know you want to play, Alexei."

Alexei was not used to receiving so much attention, especially in the form of unasked-for advice. Susan could tell that it pained him to ignore these friendly suggestions.

"Don't decide now," she said. "Sleep on it."

"Good idea," he replied, relieved to have a polite out.

Once more the younger group split away from the older one, and Peter, Hilda, Herb, and Ingrid stood shouting ineffectually at one another.

"I can't understand what anyone's saying if there's background noise," Ingrid said, but her voice was too ladylike to penetrate the din.

"What?" asked Peter, leaning toward her and cupping his ear.

"Never mind," she said.

"Susan's going with Alexei?" Herb queried in such a roar that Susan and Alexei both heard him and moved farther away to avoid overhearing the reply.

Peter smiled, and his lips could be seen to form a "Yes."

"That boy's a genius, you know," said Herb. Ingrid nodded in enthusiastic agreement. They were delighted to hear that Alexei and Susan were making a couple. Peter, the rich lawyer, could do a lot for them, whereas the Holmeses, with their limited income, couldn't help Mallory much with money. It was good to know that Alexei, who was so talented and deserving, had found someone wonderful—and even better to know that the someone wasn't Mallory. He was a remarkable young man, but they preferred, above all, to know that Mallory was safe and cared for.

Peter moved from Hilda's side to Herb's. He hadn't heard anyone say that Alexei was a genius before. Talented, he had heard, but an attribution of genius, from the Holmeses yet, was something that he wanted to hear more of.

"That's in a manner of speaking, you mean? That he's got so many talents?" Peter yelled in Herb's ear.

"No, I mean that as a singer he has genius."

Peter smiled broadly at Herb. "I haven't heard him. You really think so?"

"And charisma. You've never heard him?" Herb genuinely believed in Alexei's gifts, but relief added a certain keenness to his praise.

"I intend to, first chance I get."

Peter spent another quarter hour on this satisfying subject with the Holmeses before he announced that he had better say his good-byes soon and get back to Lesley. The idea of a son-in-law who was a first-rank musical talent raised his spirits considerably. It made it easier to think about going home. It even made it easier to think about going to the office on Monday morning.

Then Alcott was standing on a table, announcing Mallory's engagement to Louis, who grinned appealingly, almost shyly, with one arm around Mallory's shoulder, and there were shouts, cheers, toasts, and embraces. Peter kissed Mallory and hugged Louis.

"Kids, I should've been home an hour ago. I want to check on Mom, and it's past my bedtime," Peter said. He had a feeling of plenty at having to give parting embraces to so many as he left. "Hilda, ready to go? I'll walk you."

"Had any dates yet?" he asked her as soon as they stood in the dark on the sidewalk in front of Mallory's building.

"I've had dozens of invitations, but I turned them all down."

"You're too stuck on me, probably."

"Exactly. Tell me, Peter, why is it you insist on being so overpersonal with me—I'd almost call it intrusive—when I don't think you're like that in general?"

"Somehow, I seem to think you belong to me," he said. "Maybe you're the sister I never had. But let me point out, you started the whole thing by insisting you weren't gay, and no one even asked you."

"Ah!" she said.

"Why so sad, Hilda? You never used to be sad."

"Because I was successfully neurotic. It got me very far. Your street, Peter."

"I'll walk you to your door."

Peter's voice, however, was hardly audible over the siren of an ambulance that passed them just then as it careened down 116th Street, heading toward Riverside. He frowned at it.

"You're worried it's going to your building, aren't you," she said. "So go home. I'm quite used to walking home alone. Go make sure everything's all right."

"I think I will. I'll call," he said gratuitously, and gave her a quick kiss on the cheek, as though they were intimate friends. He had never done that before.

He strode anxiously down the block and, when he turned the corner, saw that the ambulance was parked in front of his own building.

"Is it Lesley?" he demanded of the doorman, whose face was drawn and anxious.

"Yes, you want to hurry up there, Mr. Frankl," he said. Peter heard something in the man's voice. But what could he possibly know? Peter felt his body trembling, although he could have sworn that he felt calm.

When he arrived at his hall, he was momentarily confused to see that it was Lockhart's door that was open and that the ambulance workers' voices were audible from inside Lockhart's apartment, not his own. Yolanda, his own housekeeper, emerged unexpectedly from Lockhart's apartment, weeping, and Peter seized her by the arm. "How is she?"

"Unconscious. She unconscious."

Wanda stepped off the elevator, but by now Peter was beyond having expectations of what should or should not be happening. They both ran into Lockhart's apartment, where in the kitchen they found Lesley, flanked by medics, lying on the floor in one of her silk robes, which flowed around her on the tiles, while Lockhart stood by, wringing his hands and moaning incoherently.

"Oh, Wanda, Wanda, my dear," he burst out when he caught sight of her. "This is too horrible." Wanda put her arms around Lockhart, and he sobbed on her shoulder.

Peter knelt beside Lesley. "My wife," he said to the medics. "How is she?"

"It's very serious, we think," said one, working rapidly as he talked, apparently preparing to move Lesley onto a stretcher. "Probably a stroke, but I'm not a doctor . . . Mr. . . . . Frankl?"

"Yes, I'm Peter Frankl. She hasn't been well since she was in an accident last spring. Take her up to Columbia Presbyterian, can you?"

"St. Luke's is better. She needs a doctor fast."

They were lifting her now, and one said, "Pulse is very weak—move it, move it." Peter, looking at her flaccid, colorless face, could not believe she would live.

At St. Luke's, he was not surprised when the doctors told him that she was dead, which was merciful, they said, for she had had a massive stroke, probably at least an hour and a half ago, that would have left her incapacitated in mind and body. The doctors muttered incoherently about the delay and immediate attention, but Peter was not sure what they were getting at.

Susan and Louis had arrived by that time, with Alexei and Mallory, and all of them stood together in the hallway just outside the cubicle where Lesley lay and listened to the doctors move quickly from the central fact of her death to the peripheral issues of the hows and whens. Each of the three Frankls could see in the faces of the others a great struggle between guilt and relief. The truth was that they had abandoned her long ago. At the time of her accident, believing that she would die, they had allowed themselves to begin altering their understanding of her—and what was that but an abandonment? Once they were willing to believe that she had distorted all their lives, and her children's very souls, out of envy, resentment, and greed, they had lost her, and that loss they had already been mourning for months.

"We had a fight," Peter told Louis and Susan, distraught and teary. "We had a big fight, but she was okay when I left." He was asking himself whether he had murdered his wife with his angry speech. For nearly forty years, he had refrained from speaking to her that way just because he thought it might destroy her. Horror began to crowd out his other emotions.

"Dad, it's not your fault," Susan said. "I called right after you showed up at Mallory's, and Yolanda told me she was at Edmond's. She was okay or she wouldn't have gone over there. Yolanda would have known if something was wrong."

"I was telling her things had to change," Peter said.

"That wasn't wrong," Alexei broke in somewhat hesitantly. Although he had strong opinions on the subject, perhaps he had no right to speak, not really being a member of the family. In the short time he had known Susan and Louis's father, Alexei had developed strong affection for him and wanted to offer him comfort.

Mallory looked sorrowfully at Louis, who, she knew, suffered as much from his recently acquired understanding of his mother's flaws as from her loss.

"The truth is, I'm the one who really made her miserable," Louis said, his voice toneless.

"Oh no, Louis, not at all," Susan protested.

How lucky I've been, Mallory thought, with my good, kind, wise parents. I did nothing to deserve them, and I'll never be half as good as they are, no matter how hard I try. This, however, was a depressing thought, and for the first time it crossed her mind that good parents could be quite a burden. She almost envied Louis his mother, who was so horrible that he could never be accused of letting her down. It was doubly puzzling, then, that he seemed to be accusing himself of exactly that. She would have to talk to her parents about this.

CHAPTER 47

Lesley's funeral was held at Riverside Chapel in a large, decorous, and ornate room filled with people. The news that she had been killed by a stroke after having struggled back to life from a coma had been devastating to her friends, and the general feeling was that Lesley was too young to die. She should have listened to the doctor, who had told her to take it easy and rest. She was actually at her neighbor's apartment helping him hang a picture, they said. And they said that there were too many tensions at home, over the kids, apparently. You would think that Peter and the kids would have pushed other concerns aside or concealed them, protected her better, controlled her better, considering that her life was at stake.

The director of Riverside Chapel stood in the doorway, looking troubled and nervous, and pointed people toward the seats. He had to look nervous, thought Peter, or it would be offputting. There were only two styles of funeral directors: the oily and the worried. Peter himself preferred the worried type, who did not inspire detestation on the part of the mourners, although there was something to be said for having a stranger to detest at such a moment, particularly when hateful relatives were in short supply, as on this occasion.

In the seats of honor, at the front of the room, there were only Lesley's sister, her elderly aunt, two cousins, and Peter and their children. Peter had no relatives at all. Judy Rostov and Lesley's old friend from Santa Fe sat with the family, on either side of Lesley's sister. Alexei and Mallory sat to Susan and Louis's left and right, respectively. These few, by some indeterminate and invisible process, were identified and directed to the proper rows, along with all those who were going to speak in honor of the deceased.

Although there were few relatives, the room was crowded, for Lesley knew many people and so did Peter. No one from across the hall—Edmond, Wanda, or Ivy—showed up. Peter would have blocked the door if they had. Mallory's parents, Herb and Ingrid, were sitting near Walter Bramford and several other lawyers from Peter's firm; Jon and Mary sat together on the opposite side of the room.

All the Devereaux people attended. Hilda was glad to have found an inconspicuous seat in the back until an exceedingly cheerful, smiling woman sat next to her and insisted on talking. Even though Hilda knew that this was no time for charades, she felt a strong temptation to begin one at each remark and question from her unwelcome neighbor. How, she asked Hilda sociably, did she know Lesley?

"A friend of the family," Hilda answered, sedate and noncommittal. "And you?" she asked, to be politely normal.

"Oh, an old friend," said the woman, smiling more broadly. "We took painting classes together, years ago. I usually don't come to funerals." An obscure little chuckle escaped her, and she inhaled in a strained way. Hilda disliked something about the woman and turned away to study the faces at the front of the room.

Rabbi Friedman managed to eulogize Lesley without ever using the word *love*, talking of her skill and energy and taste, how she was a practical, down-to-earth person with an admirable ability to enjoy herself and a great talent that would live after her. Lesley was completely recognizable in this portrait, and Friedman said just what Lesley would have liked to hear said about her.

What an artist, Peter thought, thinking the speech was done. The audience murmured and stirred restlessly, and Hilda, in the back, thought that the woman next to her snickered for some reason. But Rabbi Friedman began again, speaking of the imperfections of love. Peter had refused to look at houses in Santa Fe, and Lesley had had two shelves of his favorite books moved out of his library without even asking. (The audience laughed a little, and Hilda's cheerful neighbor rather overdid the mirthfulness.) Such failures, and deeper ones, are immortalized when someone dies, Friedman said, and we make a story out of it. We go to funerals and tell the story of the life, giving it a beginning, middle, and a satisfying ending. But we have to remember that it's not like that. All life stories end in the middle, before the failures of love can be corrected. It's lucky when the bereaved family can look back at decades of goodwill and mutual respect and civility, the way the Frankls can, for comfort for these defaults that all human beings are guilty of. Peter saw that both Susan and Louis, who were sitting next to each other between Alexei and Mallory, were teary, and the four of them were holding hands. Peter wiped tears off his own cheeks with his handkerchief. Herb and Ingrid had not been close enough to Lesley to cry, but they, too, were moved by these words.

"It was just the right thing to say to this family," said Ingrid, "almost what a psychotherapist would say." She and Herb had had a long discussion with Mallory about what a difficult time the Frankls might have with their ambivalent mourning.

"I'm just astonished at the man's sensitivity and penetration," Herb replied. "He apparently knows the family extremely well."

The speeches after this one were less memorable, but no one was long-winded except for Lesley's sister, who seemed to feel that it was her turn to be the center of attention now that Lesley was gone. Peter and his children had decided on cremation, although Peter did not relish the idea of keeping the ashes of the deceased. Louis suggested that they sprinkle them around some favorite place of Lesley's in Santa Fe, and both Peter and Susan enthusiastically endorsed this proposal. It was just Lesley's style, and Santa Fe was where she had always wanted to be.

Hilda, standing up in the back of the room, saw that the odd woman next to her was now struggling to restrain herself, giggling mischievously, incontrollably. "I can't help it," she got out with difficulty. "I should never come to funerals. They always just strike me so funny!"

As she walked out alone, Hilda asked herself whether her own little madnesses, and their perverse triumphs, were any more endearing than this woman's, which she had found most unappealing. In fact, Hilda wondered guiltily whether she, too, was not taking some improper satisfaction in the Frankls' loss, no matter how much she tried not to. Didn't she have improper feelings toward Peter? There seemed to be no way to be connected with one's fellow men and women without doing and feeling terrible things. Loneliness was unbearable, but at least it was innocent—or so Hilda had believed. Dr. Stoller always said that refusing oneself to others was not as innocent as Hilda liked to think.

CHAPTER 48

After nearly two weeks, Peter had not in the least forgiven himself for missing his wife so little. The truth was that he felt released. But, he told himself, he must have made her so unhappy. She must have sensed that she got from him only dutifulness, not real affection, which had to be the explanation for a great deal of her captiousness, her animosity. And, of course, the bottom line was that she was never really herself again after the accident. No doubt her conniving with Edmond could be chalked up largely to brain dysfunction. And no matter what Ivy said, surely Edmond was the villain in chief, and Lesley, no doubt, merely egged him on. Peter and Edmond had avoided each other since Lesley's death. Edmond no longer ran after Peter, pulling Burke on a leash, insinuating unpleasant things.

Susan helped Peter go through Lesley's things. They chose sentimental souvenirs for her sister and closest friends and packed or gave away the rest. But they left Lesley's studio untouched. Susan wandered in alone one day—for the first time since she had overheard Lesley and Edmond conspiring together. The studio, with its bare floors and strong light, seemed eerily alive. The walls were covered with Lesley's efforts, which were by no means contemptible. A large easel near the window held the painting in progress at the time of her death, and a smaller one stood near the doorway beside a file cabinet whose top drawer was slightly open. Susan, remembering Lesley's unconscious utterances, pulled open the drawer and looked in.

The drawer was filled with sketchbooks and journals, all marked with dates in Lesley's handwriting. There were mementos, ticket stubs, programs, invitations. And there was a photocopy of a letter to Henry Rostov, also in Lesley's handwriting. It was just like her mother, so superorganized and self-regarding, to save photocopies of her own letters. Susan began to read the letter, curious as to why her mother would correspond with the husband of a friend she visited all the time; and the first couple of lines left no doubt that Lesley and Henry had had an affair. The subject of the letter was whether or not to end it.

Her mother with Henry Rostov? And the three of them, Henry, Judy, and Lesley, always going places together—out to dinners and to functions—and Judy thinking she's being so nice to her friend. Did Henry come to visit her mother when her father was working or away on business trips? It was disgusting, shattering. She could not tell her father about this. He had been through too much.

Susan told Louis, however, who thought they had to tell him. "Otherwise," he told Susan, "he can't understand anything. He won't admit what she was like. He's already turning everything around, twisting things, beating himself up." And when Louis told Mallory, she told him what she had until now kept secret: that Lesley and Edmond had also been carrying on an affair.

"I had a feeling something like that was going on," Susan told Alexei. "I was worried."

Alexei agreed with Louis that they had to tell Peter everything, and this settled the question, as all of them tended to lean on Alexei when there were decisions to make; he was attached to all of them, invested in the family issues, and straight thinking. Peter had to know, and Louis was the one to tell him.

Louis found Peter in his library one Saturday afternoon and gave him a matter-of-fact recital that lasted only a few minutes but left Peter with weeks of painful thoughts. Peter put together the things that Louis told him with things he knew but had chosen to ignore until now. The affair with Henry, Peter deduced, began when he had refused to move out of Morningside Heights, when the kids were little; the one with Lockhart started when Peter began changing in ways that made Lesley feel angry and put-down. Oh, Peter knew more about the whole business than Louis or Susan did, when he let himself know that he knew it. He was forced to admit not just that he had had a marriage of extreme bad faith and dishonesty, but also that for almost forty years he had chosen to conceal it. Indeed, he had acted like a lawyer for Lesley's defense, creating a plausible argument for her innocence and goodness by distorting and selectively ignoring the realities of their marriage. He had accused himself of driving her to this by not loving her, but she had not loved him, either, and had never wanted his love. He had refused to admit what Lesley was up to because he would not have divorced or separated from her if he had. Therefore, it was easier just not to know—as Rabbi Friedman had said was the case for so many women.

At first, Peter felt no need to confront Lockhart about his affair with Lesley. But as the real motive for Ivy's campaign against Susan dawned on him, he became infuriated. "I'll take care of this," he told Louis one evening and strode across the hallway and rang Edmond Lockhart's doorbell. Wanda answered.

"Peter?" she said, brightening until she took in his expression. She didn't seem to feel any awkwardness or embarrassment about having tried to blackmail Peter just months ago.

"I expect you're surprised to see me," he said. "I have to talk to your husband." He took pleasure in reminding her of her frayed marital bonds.

"He's very, very ill," she said. "You wouldn't insist if you could see—"

"But I would, though," said Peter. "I would insist on seeing him as long as he's conscious."

"He's barely that," Wanda said with a tense sigh. "Peter, I can't allow—"

Peter walked past her into the apartment and found Lockhart lying on the sofa, reading. He did look bad, Peter thought, bad enough that he should be dying; but Peter had seen him looking this way before and he had always lived. Lockhart shoved his book under a cushion, but Peter saw that it was a popular crime novel.

"Lockhart, with all your shenanigans you've set Ivy off on a vendetta against my daughter. You're going to have to make sure she stops, or I'm going to make both of you sorry."

Lockhart looked dimly at Frankl. "I don't know what you're talking about."

"I'm talking about Ivy, and how she's trying to block Susan's degree to get even with Lesley."

Lockhart took some time to digest this information. "What proof of that do you have?"

"Susan's department wants to pass her with distinction, but Ivy is her outside reader and has been demanding she throw out two-thirds of her thesis. Ivy has felt pretty free about letting my daughter see that she hates her. Now here's the thing. You stop her or I'm going to sue you for wrongful death. I wouldn't even rule out criminal charges. I'm going to go into court and prove that you delayed getting Lesley help for more than an hour because you wanted to conceal what was going on, that you actually left her there, dying, until you finally reached Wanda, and that it was Wanda who called the ambulance—and this was somewhere from an hour to two hours after she fell. She might have lived if you'd called for help. In fact, the only reason I haven't taken you to court already is that I don't want to put my children through it. But what Ivy has done tips the balance. You fix it or I'm going to make sure you spend an impoverished old age—unless maybe Wanda and George can support you."

Lockhart seemed slow and stupid. "She won't listen to me. I won't be able to influence her—assuming even that what you say is true, which I doubt. I find it much easier to believe that your daughter is in over her head."

"Then you're in a tough spot. In the meantime, I don't want to hear you speculate about my daughter's abilities. And if I were you, and Ivy refuses, I'd just call up someone over there in that department and say you're sorry and confidentially explain the situation and point out that Ivy has a big conflict of interest and, uh, under the emotional strain, she has done the wrong thing. They'll control her if they know what's behind it. And be sure to let her know you're going to because she'll never take the chance you'd do that—she'll back off. Also, you can threaten her with my lawsuit. All kinds of stuff about her will come out. She won't like it."

"All right, Peter," Wanda said mildly. "Sure. We'll take care of it."

"Make sure it happens fast, Wanda, and make sure it's adequate and that I know about it."

"Don't worry," she said. "But how can I be sure you'll back off if we help you?"

Peter saw that she wasn't a bit angry. Yet she would never have stepped in to help unless he had been able to threaten them, and he could see that it didn't bother her in the least that Lockhart had let Lesley die on his kitchen floor. Wanda was amoral, whereas Lockhart was simply weak, crooked, and cruel. So they had belonged together after all. Just about every married couple did belong together, Peter thought. His own case had been no exception.

"You have my word, Wanda. That's enough."

"Of course it is. And Peter," she added good-naturedly, "however you may feel about other parties, there's no need for any animosity between you and me." She rather admired the way Peter had tied Edmond up. She had always liked Peter.

"Wanda, you know who you remind me of?"

"How could I guess that? I don't know anyone you know, except your children." She leaned against the doorway, her arms folded across her chest, and smiled. She was actually a little flirtatious.

"You remind me of my deceased wife."

"You're intending an unflattering comparison, I take it. I told you that living alone causes character deterioration."

But Peter had turned his back and was walking out.

He sat up for hours after this encounter. He felt confident that it had worked, but that didn't help, in the short run, to calm his anger against the Lockharts; there was little comfort in the fact that they deserved each other. He was struck again by the affinity of death to all sorts of evil: infidelity, the lust for superiority. Maybe it explained what happened to poor old Henry Rostov. Maybe, after all, Henry *had* run into the pole on purpose—a murder-suicide by a mild-mannered guy who so resented being one of life's little people that, finally, his rage offered him too much pleasure to resist. It was a good thing he didn't pilot airliners.

Peter paid a visit to Rabbi Friedman and filled him in on the parts of the story they had been missing in their earlier talks. It all took a great deal of explaining, and when Peter was finished, Friedman responded, "You know, I kept telling you that your story didn't make sense. Although your defense work was excellent, I wasn't really convinced. But I decided the wrong way: instead of concluding that your wife was much worse than you said, I concluded that she must be much better. Well, you could certainly have had a better marriage."

"So could Lesley," said Peter. "We were mismatched."

"You were mismatched, not Lesley. You could have done better, but you gave her a better life than she was likely to find without you. And guess what, if she hadn't thought so, too, she would have left you in a minute."

"I think I did right to stay, especially when the kids were growing up, but even after that."

"If she had lived, you should have divorced her—and I know you don't think so. But when the kids were little . . . I don't know. The kids had problems, but they're landing on their feet. Maybe that's because you stayed. Who knows?"

"Not me. I can't help thinking it would have been worse if I'd left, but even staying, I messed up both kids."

"The two of you did. But you finally reasserted yourself, recognized and fathered your son and stopped looking down on him, spoke out against your daughter's wretched lover, pushed a good fellow her way—that was all well done."

"Pushing the good fellow was mostly Louis's idea."

"But you helped Louis. You helped this young Russian escape from his own family villain, and that said things to your son. And I'll bet that someplace in all this you found a woman you prefer, but knowing you, you never did anything about it. Tell me, aren't I right?"

Peter didn't answer immediately and looked at Friedman quizzically. "Maybe, but how could you possibly know that?"

"An unconventional, unworldly sort of person would probably suit you, a good person, gentle and kindhearted, whimsical. Perhaps someone with ties to the arts."

"Are you a fortune-teller or something?"

"So I got this right? Hah!"

Peter had gone home to ponder the uncanny penetration of the aged little man, and Rabbi Friedman had gone to meet his wife at the bus stop at 122nd Street and begun telling her the latest news about Frankl, whose story she had always followed eagerly. They both wore long dark coats, hats, and gloves, and they kept their eyes down as they climbed the steps into the M4, alert to the dangers of a trip-and-fall. Friedman's wife was almost as aged as he but considerably more agile. She spoke with an accent, had a braid of white hair coiled at the back of her head, and wore heavy leather shoes with buckles.

Fortunately, the bus was always empty this far north, and they took seats together near the front.

"So, it's as you said, my dear," said Eli Friedman. "He is indeed interested in her."

"Are you sure he means her?" asked Margarethe Stoller. "Or maybe he's interested in more than one?"

"The man is thoroughly monogamous. And when I remarked casually that he would be interested in someone unconventional, unworldy, gentle, whimsical, and kindhearted, with ties to the arts, he thought I was reading a crystal ball. Someone he knows fits this description. How could it not be Hilda Hughes?"

"Good heavens, Eli. You might as well have instructed him to be interested in Hilda. This is hardly ethical, what we have done here. She is always accusing me of exaggerating the significance of their relationship."

"We're old now. We're entitled to have one little moral holiday, to help bring together two people who have had such deprived lives and will probably give a great deal of happiness to each other."

"They would bring themselves together without our help," said Margarethe.

"So then where's the problem if we just make sure nothing goes wrong? No big deal, my dear. It will work out nicely."

"Yes. They'll have a good life. She's a bit sad that she has no children."

"So she'll be like us. She'll find young people to interest herself in. She's already begun, and she'll have his kids, which is better than we had. Peter's children are doing very well, too. They're both going to make a good marriage, they like their work, they'll have their own children."

"Yes," she replied. "The son has picked someone he knows is doing a kind of work the father admires, and in this way he tries to win the father's approval. The daughter-in-law will have the career the father wishes the son had. Well, all right. Not the best solution, but workable."

"It's clever of you to see that," said Eli. "But the daughter's sweetheart, this young Russian boy. Him, I worry about. He really should devote himself to music, but his other talents are so marketable and his singing isn't. I'm afraid no one will understand or support him."

"Eli, I keep telling you they don't call them boys and girls anymore. Now they're men and women. But, frankly, I have the same concern. He's the only one of them with a real calling."

"Peter Frankl understands because he abandoned his calling to scholarship, which was a terrible mistake in his life. But does the daughter? That's what really matters."

"I'll talk to Hilda about it," said Dr. Stoller. "I have only a few more meetings with her, and then I'm finished with *my* calling. I would have stopped a year ago but for her. We might have been traveling all that time. And after this, we stop all the interfering and trading confidential communications. It's unethical."

"Don't worry about it. It's not unethical for a rabbi, anyway. I'm supposed to be interfering," said Eli with a reassuring air. Although Margarethe's heart was in the right place, her head was just slightly thick. Her whole life she had come to him for guidance, but she still thought she guided him.

When Hilda arrived in Dr. Stoller's office the following morning, she looked downright pulled together, but as Dr. Stoller had already commented several times on the changes in her appearance, she said nothing today.

"Now that you've achieved a love life," she said to Hilda, "let's turn a little to the work life. I want to ask you a question for once."

"For once? All you do is ask me questions lately. And I can't tell you how annoying I find your delusion that I have a love life—just because of holding Peter Frankl's hand once and agreeing that nothing would ever happen!"

"Well, and whoever said that the course of love was guaranteed to be straight and smooth!"

"Straight and smooth I never asked for. But a little sex—even just a kiss or two . . ."

"Holding hands is sex," said Dr. Stoller, with didactic certainty.

"How maddening this is. But at least you sound like a Freudian for once."

"And you don't like that as much as you thought you would. But getting back to my question—I want to ask you about the idea of a calling, when the particular work one does is felt to be necessary. One feels called upon to do it. For example, you could surely do, with equal satisfaction, other work than what you've chosen."

"Yes, I suppose you're right. I'm content with what I do, but there are other careers I might have been content with, too."

"There are people who feel called to some particular work, and if they don't do that, they are unfulfilled, guilty, existentially frustrated, so to speak."

"Of course. My young filmmaker, for one. He must make films. It makes a kind of desperate character out of him, even though he has a family waiting with open arms to catch him if he falls. Yes, he has a calling. That is actually a rare thing. What is your point? Oh, I know another one, too—Alexei Mikhailov, the one Susan Frankl is going to marry. He's like that, painfully so. I hope Susan understands what his singing means to him. I think I'll talk to her about it. *I* may even talk to him about it. Surely a little interfering is a privilege of age."

"Yes, surely so," said Dr. Stoller with a bubble of satisfaction in her voice.

"I don't know why you should be so glad that I'm interfering," said Hilda, "or what your point is."

"Quite frankly, I had hoped you would do something to help that young man, Susan's fiancé."

"But why are you so concerned about Alexei? You don't even know him."

"True, and I don't have a very good answer except that his story inspires concern, and I suspect such advice might be valuable to him and help him to avoid being misled by admiration, which he so easily gets for extraneous reasons. One doesn't know if he has in his life people who will understand and respect his interests, moral and emotional, in pursuing what may seem to others to be dying and unimportant."

"You know all about that kind of pursuit, don't you, Dr. Stoller."

"Very good point, Miss Hughes. Well, that was a little side trip, a little holiday. Let us return to your own situation."

"I think I resent being used to relay messages to other people you don't even know."

"Yet you don't sound resentful at all." And Dr. Stoller had nothing more to say that day, beyond an occasional pleasant "hm" or "Why is that?"

CHAPTER 49

Emma Devereaux invited Susan, Alexei, Peter, and Hilda, along with assorted younger Devereauxes, to an early dinner on Christmas Eve at her Riverside Drive mansion. Peter had feared that in a spirit of forgiveness, she would ask Edmond, too, and was relieved to see that he was absent. The Frankl party marveled at the totality of the Devereaux Christmas experience. There was nothing to be seen, heard, tasted, or smelled, no culinary or aesthetic detail, that was not strictly in accordance with ancient household traditions—the roast goose, the handsomely decorated tree, the wreaths and curios, the presents. The female Devereauxes all wore little pins of red and green on their collars (and all had collars); the male Devereauxes all wore sweater vests and ties. And when it was time for singing, Susan was forced to the piano bench and a battered collection of old English carols was pressed into Alexei's hands. The poor boy was deeply embarrassed by this and astonished by everything, although he concealed it well, Peter thought—with more poise than Peter would have had at twenty-five in similar circumstances.

"Now what about that construction next door, Hilda," said Miss Devereaux at the dinner table when Peter, the senior male present, had carved the goose and a maid had served everyone. "You simply must come and stay with me until it's over. It's unhealthy, living with all that noise and dust."

"Thank you, Miss Devereaux, but really, I can manage. I've been looking for a new place for weeks, but it's hard to find anything at all in the neighborhood, and I so want to stay."

"You have to stay in the neighborhood," said Susan.

"I heard good news about your thesis, Susan, their booting that horrible woman off the committee," Hilda said to change the subject, but this one was equally awkward for the Frankls, and Susan quickly changed it again.

"The film award is the really good news. Alexei is such a star—three offers to audition just last week." But mention of the auditions made Alexei look pained.

"You're going to be a famous film actor, Alexei," said Miss Devereaux in a congratulatory tone.

"No, acting is just . . . mmm . . . just . . ."

"A sideline," Peter interjected.

"Yes—sideline. Singing is what I really do," said Alexei, trying to sound informative rather than argumentative. All the interest in his acting was disquieting. How could an unemployed singer turn down film offers—especially when he was talking about getting married?

"Hilda sent me an interview with Alcott that just came out in some film magazine," Peter said. "I was supposed to give it to you, kids—forgot. Alcott says that it was Alexei winning at Berlin against Tarlov that did it. It got people paying attention to the film. Otherwise there were so many entries no one would have paid any attention to his."

"He shouldn't have said that," Alexei said, dismayed.

"But it's probably true. Remember what Louis said? I'm beginning to think Louis is always right about everything," said Peter.

Alexei laughed dismissively. "Total nonsense," he said. "But it's not a bad film, is it."

"I adored it," said Hilda, her face radiant at the memory. "Especially the singing." She, Miss Devereaux, Peter, Susan, and Anne, Charles, and Jane Braithwaite, along with friends of theirs, had all seen it two days earlier, when Alcott had previewed the film for the Devereaux Foundation, some local critics, and a dozen or so friends.

"I know you don't want to be an actor, Alexei," Susan said, "but you have to expect that people will find it exciting. And I still can't believe that you sang in the film and never told me."

"What about the waltzing? I thought I was very good at that, too. Singing is how I got the part, though. Alcott and Sylvie got an idea for changing their story after they came to my recital," Alexei explained to Miss Devereaux, who was under the impression that she and Hilda had not only discovered this young talent, but had also by that means supplied Susan with a wonderful sweetheart. She was especially proud of the latter accomplishment, and no one tried to set her straight.

"Alexei, I hope you'll stick with your singing no matter how hard it is," said Hilda, who had been gathering her courage for this speech. "It's your real calling, you know. You can't give it up. You mustn't. And, you see, it inspired Alcott to do his best work." She blushed at her own presumption in advising such a talented young man. Yet she felt sure that she was right. Dr. Stoller had been quite sure, too.

Alexei said nothing, but Hilda's words, at least for a moment, doused a fire of frustration that had burned in the back of his mind for years. No one had ever said such a thing to him before, not even Susan or her father, who always stood behind him, not even Charles Braithwaite. Everyone was always advising him to quit, warning him he was likely to fail, telling him to learn to make compromises in life. They harped on the risks of persisting and never understood the worse ones incurred in giving up. But Hilda obviously did, and fortunately, she also read the effect of her words on Alexei's face, for he responded with only a polite mutter.

"That's true," said Susan. "Alcott obviously responded to the music. The film had something—it wasn't just the Berlin business that got it the award."

"Yes, thanks—lots, please," Peter said loudly to a maid serving plum pudding and hard sauce, hoping to bring the double-edged conversation to an end. Nonetheless, he was glad about Hilda's little speech to the boy. She was right: she was trying to help Alexei avoid making the mistake in life that Peter had made.

At around 9:00, the Frankl party said its good-byes and left to visit the Braithwaites, who had called earlier to insist that Alexei and Susan come over for a glass of Christmas cheer. They wanted Hilda and Susan's father to come along, too, as they were all going to be together at dinner, and they kept repeating the promise of Christmas cheer, as though that were very witty. Hilda and Peter tried to beg off, but Susan and Alexei protested that they were expected.

"You'll really like them," said Susan, "and we're just going to stay for half an hour."

Miss Devereaux sent them into the night laden with sweets and presents. By the time they arrived at the Braithwaites', the younger children were already asleep. They were ushered in with such arch grins and undue excitement that it was obvious, at least to Susan and Alexei, that they had some happy secret. But before it could be told, there had to be introductions and congratulations about the film award, which this time were offered in such a way that no conversational dexterity was required to save Alexei's feelings. Soon Peter, Hilda, and Susan were seated on a sofa, talking with Anne and Jane and sipping glasses of the promised Christmas cheer, while Charles pulled Alexei aside and told him something startling.

"They were?" Alexei exclaimed. "Really? How can I ever thank you! I had no idea. What a big chance you took!"

"After all that rehearsing we did? I knew it would be at the least very good, and when I saw the thing I couldn't have been happier. And what did we have to lose, after all? Look, this is no guarantee of anything, you understand. But you'd better tell Susan before she bursts into tears, or before Anne loses control and tells her first." It was now a favorite joke of the Braithwaites to pretend they feared that Susan was always on the verge of tears over minor causes.

"I've got an audition," Alexei called to Susan. "Those friends Charles brought to the preview were from the Met, and they liked the movie. No doubt it was my waltzing."

"The waltzing didn't hurt," said Anne, happily watching Susan first clutch her father's arm, then Hilda's, and then leap up to embrace Alexei. "They saw that you could act and move, and that you had a little charisma."

"But, of course, most of all they liked the way you sing," said Charles, "and how you can put something across. We'll see how the rest of it goes. If you have a good audition, there are people who will find room for you there—not in every role, but they'll find something for you now and then. And once they do, then lots of things can happen."

This news merited far more than a half hour's celebration. In fact, when Susan and Alexei announced that they had to leave, Charles and Anne insisted that Peter and Hilda stay, and the four of them, in the absence of the young people, continued the party for hours. The Braithwaites assumed an attitude that was almost in loco parentis toward Alexei, which made them behave like Susan's prospective in-laws, and Hilda and Peter so willingly accepted them in that role that soon familial confidences of all sorts were being shared. It was nearly 1:00 A.M. when the Braithwaites began piling presents under the tree, and Peter and Hilda left with yet another plate of Christmas cookies, a recipe for spiced wine, and a great deal of information about Alexei.

Charles and Alexei worked diligently, Alexei's audition went well, and by the end of January he had the role of Malcolm in Verdi's *Macbeth.* The part was minor but respectable.

"No one will hear him, though," Charles pointed out. "He'll be completely drowned out."

"But he'll move well and look good, and the audience doesn't matter," Anne said. "The people who count will hear him, and there'll be parts for him. You watch." Alexei was, musically, at any rate, a pleasure to work with and to listen to; they would not overlook that. Charles was elated, almost as though he himself had been rescued.

"I've gotten one more safely into the lifeboat," Charles said to Anne when Alexei called with the good news about the results of the audition, "the one I most wanted to help and the one I least believed I could help."

"It just goes to show you—"

"Not really. This is a fluke, a weird, bizarre fluke having something to do with celebrity—with his getting irrelevant public attention, first with the chess and then that little film. It's a nice little film, but it would have been overlooked except that Alexei was a photogenic chess champion. And yes, of course, the film showed quite effectively what he could do, and he belongs in opera as much as anyone I've ever known, but they gave Alexei an audition because he already looked like a star to them."

"What I was going to say," Anne said, "was that it just goes to show you that in strange times you rely on strange means."

———————

CHAPTER 50

Peter approved of Emma's appointing the philosophical blogger Lester Maxwell as temporary chair of the seminar on international terrorism and would not hear of her attempting to get Peter reinstated.

Maxwell, who looked even younger than his twenty-two years, had put on a tie in acknowledgment of the dignity of his office. He opened the first formal meeting with a few nervous words about finding truth in such complicated matters as those the seminar had to deal with. "First," he said, "you have to value truth more than you value winning the argument. Second, you never say anything you don't really believe just so you can win a few points. Third, you bend over backwards to understand sympathetically what others are saying—you take their words in their strongest and most reasonable light. That's the whole of the law, ladies and gentlemen."

The naïveté of this inspired a general tendency to smile and cast eyes tolerantly upward and askance. The Smith-Smythes, however, were insulted. Chalmers Smythe exhaled impatiently; the corners of Teresa Smith's mouth pointed downward in obtuse angles. These juvenile ideas, said Chalmers, are ideological masks. Which is why, Teresa added, the seminar should devote itself to an epistemological examination of methods as a precondition of understanding terrorism, as they had done in the famous Text and Terrorism conference in Prague. But Martha Lovett objected. Good faith and mutual respect was all Mr. Maxwell meant, she said with teacherly authority. The group, most of whom had read the article in *Tablet* by Mallory Holmes, ignored the Smith-Smythes and looked expectantly toward Maxwell, and the meeting proceeded in an atmosphere strikingly different from that of the last one. All the crackle of importance and power was absent, replaced by the dignified ease of equality. At the meeting's end, the reaction to Maxwell's leadership was so favorable that Columbia and the Devereaux Foundation subsequently agreed to invite him to take it on permanently.

Once Lester Maxwell's appointment was announced, the Smith-Smythes' attendance began to taper off. After six months, only one or the other of them would show up at every second or third meeting. This was distressing to Orazio Cromwell, who as treasurer of the Devereaux Foundation continued to pay their stipends. Peter, however, was so happy to have them absent that he leaned on Orazio not to make a fuss. "Best not to ruffle any feathers," he said. "Remember what happened last year."

There were no more *Gazette* articles about the seminar, the Devereaux Foundation, or Peter Frankl. In fact, as the Frankls learned from Mallory, who heard it from former colleagues at the *Gazette,* Howard Kappell's misdeeds had been exposed. Some junior writers had given a senior editor Mallory's *Tablet* essay, the Smith-Smythes' article in *The London Review of Books,* and some reliable hearsay concerning Kappell's relations with them. Kappell was formally reprimanded and had not written an "Uptown, Downtown" column for weeks.

Wanda seemed to visit Edmond Lockhart nearly every day in the months after Lesley died; Edmond did not go out, as far as Peter could tell, not even to walk Burke. Nor was Ivy Hurst ever again seen in the building. When she was forced off Susan's committee, that story made the rounds, and Nancy Gettner's supporters were able to capitalize on it and undermine the credibility of Ivy's attack on Gettner's work. Few of Ivy's colleagues wanted to ally themselves with her in an attack on yet another young, vulnerable female colleague.

Sylvie and Alcott broke up for a while but reunited when they began a new film. They urged Alexei to take a part, but he had rehearsal commitments and could do nothing for several months. They ran into Chris occasionally, and Sylvie spent an evening with him once—a strange evening, she told Susan.

"He called and wanted to come over just after Alcott and I had split up. I said okay," Sylvie said. "So he came and ranted against you for two hours. He's obsessed with you. He hates you."

"But be fair, Sylvie. I wasn't exactly blame-free," said Susan.

"Wait. Then he said that *I* was the one he should have been with, and he started coming on to me—even though it's obvious you're my friend, right? And I'm wrecked because I just broke up with Alcott? And I'd as soon hop into bed with Osama bin Laden? Susan, he is truly a nasty, nutty human being."

"Well, he was obviously at his worst, but I really can't think ill of him for being interested in you."

"And *then*, Susan, I asked him to leave, and he went all cold and fishy, and when he was walking out he said—you could see him struggling to come up with some zinger—'Let's see what you write now that you're not in bed with the brains.' "

"What!"

"But, you know, for Alcott and me, there really may be some weird connection between sex and making films. Neither of us was interested when we didn't have a project in the works, and as soon as we did—wham. Maybe the sex is just an extension of the collaboration by other means. And what would be wrong with that?"

Susan had nothing to say against it, but she had her private doubts about Sylvie's analysis.

Chris's new one-act play, *Marital Pains, Criminal Pleasures,* got reviews full of awed praise. Although it was psychotically violent and sexually bizarre, the critics said, it was somehow tasteful, and whatever else you might think about Chris Wylie as a playwright, he was a brilliant, courageous psychologist of the dark places in the mind.

For months after Lesley's death, Peter and Hilda debated whether or not Henry Rostov had purposely caused his own death and, in the end, Lesley's. The motive was there: Henry could have come up with a dozen reasons to hate Lesley. And now that Peter was so aware of his own long-concealed feelings, he easily recalled seeing signs that Henry, too, hid rage against his wife; what was his affair with Lesley but an expression of it? Peter and Hilda drew pictures of the movements of the three vehicles involved in the accident and finally convinced themselves that Henry had used the craziness on the Henry Hudson to disguise murder and suicide as an accident.

"Of course, he knew that if it had been declared a suicide," Peter pointed out, "his daughters wouldn't have gotten any insurance, and they would have been devastated, too, but he'd probably been saying to himself for years, I'd like to just drive into a tree someday. So when his chance came, he instantly recognized it. He thought, Okay, that's it, and he ran into a pole and killed Lesley."

"No, he tried, but it took Edmond to finish the job," Hilda reminded him. "The separate actions of her two lovers combined to kill her, which is very strange. Mother Nature seems to have dropped her moral indifference and taken quite an interest in how this worked out."

"Hilda, that comes too close to saying Lesley deserved what happened to her," Peter said. But privately he wondered whether it was not actually the combined actions of her husband and two lovers that had killed her.

Just as Peter pressed Hilda again and again to marry him, Hilda repeatedly urged him to leave his law firm. "You hate it. You don't need all that money. Do something you really want to do."

Peter resisted because Susan and Alexei had announced that they were going to get married as soon as her divorce came through. Unlike Louis and Mallory, they'd always be poor if he didn't help them out, and the fact was that despite his large income, Peter had put away relatively little. Lesley had spent money at an astonishing rate, and he himself had insisted on supporting the children in extravagant style. Peter was particularly worried that Alexei might someday feel obliged to forsake his musical career so as to provide adequately for his children. That's just what Alexei would do, Peter thought, and the possibility horrified him.

These considerations led Peter to refuse when, about three months after Lesley's death, Emma Devereaux asked him to replace her as chair, with a salary nowhere near what partners in law firms earned. When Susan and Alexei found out that Peter had turned down Miss Devereaux's offer, they begged him to change his mind.

"Before long, I'll find a job," Susan said, "and with two of us earning we'll be fine." Peter knew that she would find a job and work hard, but musicologists were miserably underpaid.

"I'll soon be making more money," Alexei assured him privately, and Peter admired his determination, but what did Alexei know about how much it cost to raise kids?

"Dad, they're never going to take any money from you," said Louis. "Alexei couldn't stand that. Anyway, I'll have money, if anyone needs some."

Not without hand-wringing and trepidation, Peter finally announced his intention to withdraw from his firm and become chair of the Devereaux Foundation.

Mary wept at the news that Peter was leaving the firm but declined his offer of a job at the foundation.

"I'm fifty-six, Peter," she said, unself-consciously using his first name for the first time, "I'll stick it out and get my pension."

"But if you need anything, call me," Peter told her. "We'll always be able to find something for you to do with us." It was worrisome to think of her alone at the firm, without his protection. But he knew he couldn't replace her pension, and she was adamant.

"Thank you," Mary said, "but I think the one you should worry about is Jon. Mr. Bramford is too hard on him and never lets him work for anyone else—except you, of course. I don't know what'll happen now. And by the way, Mr. Bramford was quite disturbed to hear you were going."

"He'll be even more disturbed when he hears that Jon's leaving, too," said Peter, "coming to Devereaux." In fact, the Devereaux people had come up with so much for Jon to do that Peter worried he wouldn't have time for writing those awful poems of his that meant so much to him. He was to help Hilda read proposals, supervise installation of computers and an e-mail system, lift heavy things for Milton, who seemed very old lately, and even attend some board meetings. Jon might rise high at the Devereaux Foundation.

"I'm glad you're going—for your sake," said Walter Bramford with a dry laugh when Peter walked into his office that evening. "I've been telling you to get out for years."

"No, you haven't. What are you talking about?"

"Those notes I sent you."

Peter, at first, strove in vain to recollect getting notes from Walter; then his mind circled gingerly around the idea that he meant those anonymous notes and, at last, settled unwillingly on this unfathomable—and infuriating—possibility. Peter could only look with disbelief at Walter, while Walter leaned back in his chair, sober but without apparent distress, and waited.

"You're not kidding, are you," Peter said finally. "You sent them. Excuse me if I don't get the joke, but what the hell's wrong with you? Why would you do a thing like that?"

Walter's composed, relaxed face didn't fool Peter. It had the look of ease he put on in court when he was stalling for time. He was thinking as fast and hard as he could.

"If you don't even have an explanation," Peter asked, exasperated, "why'd you bother to tell me? Come on, Walter. Why'd you do it?"

With his hand, Walter motioned to Peter to be quiet. "I did it because—I think—because—I was in love with you. I was always in love with you. I knew you'd never be interested, though. Don't look at me like that. It can't be a bad thing to find out someone loves you, can it?"

Peter's legs trembled, and he sat on Walter's sofa. He had had to listen to more than his share of dramatic revelations these past few months. His tired brain struggled to understand a man's declaration of love—love that in nearly fifteen years he'd never noticed.

"I dunno, Walter. Seems like it shouldn't be a bad thing, but I just don't know," he said. Walter had sent those notes because he was in love? "Those weren't exactly love letters, you know."

"I maneuvered until I got the office next to yours so I could see a lot of you. I thought I'd kind of look after you—I did a pretty good job, didn't I?" Walter asked, looking at Peter with sad eyes ringed by dark circles. "Peter . . . didn't I? I voted for you on everything. I made sure people did your work right."

He really wanted to be told yes, he had done a good job, and Peter didn't want to hurt his feelings, but he just couldn't react yet. So he nodded, then shrugged ambiguously.

"I'm sorry if the notes upset you," Walter went on. "I really am sorry. I personally didn't even agree with what they said, but I knew *you* would. After a few years, half the time I hated you so much, I just wanted to make you squirm."

"Would it surprise you if I didn't have a clue what I ever did to make you hate me?" Peter asked.

"It wasn't just that you didn't love me. You looked down on me, and I was dying. It seemed so unfair. I'm dying, and you think I'm some subhuman and I can't help being in love with you. I started sending the notes when I found out I was positive."

Peter took several moments to think before responding. "You know, I didn't know, Walter. No one knows. I didn't even know you were gay."

"I don't relate much to being gay. In the sexual preference box, I check 'none of the above.' "

Bad faith, Peter thought. He manages not to know even though it's killing him. Bad faith hurt, and it made you go around causing hurt, too. Peter was not unsympathetic, because this was something he knew all about. Yet even though he was just as guilty of destructive self-deceit as Walter, he rated himself Walter's moral superior. Again, he sat mute while he tried to dredge up some response.

"Look, I'm sorry, Walter," he said. It was all he could come up with.

"It's okay. We're even." Walter sounded sour, and Peter knew he'd said the wrong thing.

"The drugs don't help? Those drugs?"

"I'm not doing so well on them."

"I can see that," Peter said. "But I heard they've got new ones that—"

"Look, I have no one. No family. Just don't let me die alone, okay?"

"All right," Peter said without hesitating. "I won't." It was surprisingly easy to make this promise. A year ago, he wouldn't have done it.

"You're such a bastard. You mean it, don't you," Walter said. He slumped down in his chair. "I feel rotten," he said, rubbing his face.

"I've got a car waiting downstairs. I'll drop you at home," said Peter. He wanted to act like a friend, and Walter, despite his ambivalence, evidently intended to let him. Peter saw moral courage in this. "Where do you live, anyway? Look, I know you know the score, but I have some medical friends you should talk to." He put his hand on Walter's shoulder as they walked out, as though he were Louis or Alexei. Walter had a few moral disabilities, but he also had goodnesses. Peter still couldn't help liking him, even knowing that he had sent those notes—scary notes instead of love letters. No wonder, though—he was so scared himself. Love never had much of a chance at the firm.

"Should we get married, Hilda?" Peter asked her several times each week. He and Hilda had become inseparable soon after his wife's death, and she moved in with Peter when noise and dust made her apartment uninhabitable. They worked hard undoing Lesley's décor. When they came to the den and Hilda heard the history of the photographs, she urged Peter to call his relatives and offer to bring the pictures over personally. Peter didn't know why he had never thought of doing that. He found several members of the family in Manhattan, including his niece Laurie Frankl, who was teaching at NYU, living in the Village, and remembered their telephone conversation long ago, when his father had disappeared. She was glad to hear from him, but his two surviving half-siblings, including Laurie's father, were as cool as ever.

"They're old now," Laurie told Peter and Hilda, who had arrived at her Washington Square apartment carrying a satchel of photographs, which were now spread out on her coffee table. She and Peter spent an hour combining their separate stores of knowledge about the faces in them. "Your father's remarriage was a bitter thing in their lives. My brother and I never even knew our grandfather."

"That was sad," said Peter. "He wanted to know you. He would have been proud of you."

"We sort of felt, our parents felt . . . erased. He traded us in for you, and you were even a different make."

"Of course you did," said Peter. "How else could you feel?"

"I knew you were nice back then, when you called," she said, looking kindly at Peter.

"I like having a cousin in the city," Peter told Hilda as they sat holding hands on the M5 bus, looking out the window at the wintry twilight on Riverside Drive.

"Niece," said Hilda. "We'll ask her to dinner."

"So you think we should get married?" he asked yet again, thinking that she had sounded pleasingly wifely when she corrected him that way.

"Why not just continue to live together?" she replied. "Marriage is about babies and inheritances and all that. That's not us."

"I think that's a mistake. I think marriage is about integrating an exclusive sexual union with society—a sexual union that is part of a total joining of lives—and secondarily and derivatively about babies and inheritances, which is why gay marriage is exactly right, by the way. I mean, look, God didn't create Eve because Adam wanted to have babies and ensure their inheritances. He made Eve because Adam was lonely. It says that in Genesis."

"I mistrust atheists' biblical arguments. Anyway, you're just a marriage fanatic with the most reactionary views on divorce I've ever heard of. However, I suppose I should marry you because I think you'll be happier and also because I love you."

"And you'll be happier, too," Peter said confidently, squeezing her hand.

"Impossible," said Hilda.

Dr. Stoller was the first to know of the engagement between Peter and Hilda.

"I'm going to marry the nicest man in New York City. We've got everything: love, sex, talk," Hilda told her. "The problem is, it makes you pessimistic about the young. How could kids of twenty ever manage this complicated stuff?"

"They do, though—even younger than twenty. You came to it late, but not everyone does."

"I've been stupid in life."

"Somewhat. You did the best you could, though, with what you were given."

Several other couples in 444 Riverside Drive, hearing of the marital surge in the Frankl apartment, asked Peter if he had any advice on how to influence their own children to wed. Peter told them that the trick was to set a good example. He and Hilda had the first wedding, a small home ceremony with singing by Alexei, accompanied by Susan. Rabbi Friedman did not come but wrote a note of warm congratulations saying that he regretted having to miss the wedding, as he and his wife would be in Europe. Everyone from the Devereaux Foundation attended, along with the Braithwaite family, Sylvie and Alcott, Mallory and Louis, and Herb and Ingrid Holmes.

"I'll tell you the truth," Herb said to Ingrid afterward. "I could never figure out why he was ever married to Lesley. I always really liked him."

Peter and Hilda, Herb and Ingrid, and the Braithwaites quickly established a network of quasi-familial ties, calling back and forth about arrangements for weddings and apartments. Louis and Mallory were looking for a place in the neighborhood and planning a fall wedding. Alexei and Susan expected to be free to marry by early the next year and for the time being intended to stay at 114th Street. The two young couples had not only their own relationships to sort out, but all the complicated quarrels and negotiations of a large new extended family—overextended, they sometimes grumbled.

EPILOGUE

After winning the Berlin tournament, Alexei was in demand as a chess teacher and lecturer. He had time for only a few students, but he still taught them in the library, where he continued to see Victor Marx and Cora Bledsoe regularly. Susan and Mallory, too, often worked in the library. Vic had always liked Susan, and he learned to like Mallory, too, particularly after he used the library's computers to read a few of her *Tablet* essays. Cora and Susan were good friends, but Cora never really took to Mallory, and Mallory tended to ignore Cora.

Vic knew the history of Lesley's accident and its sequelae, having gotten it in bits and pieces from the Braithwaites as well as from Alexei, Susan, and Mallory. You didn't usually hear such wild stories of envy and revenge in this neighborhood. Go two blocks over to the Henry Hudson Parkway and you'd think the world was mostly spite and hatred. But around here, people had—at least they used to have—ideas that reined that stuff in, which is not to say they got rid of it. Oh no, you never got rid of it.

But things were changing. When he talked to the younger generations, Vic noticed that his own thinking, his faith in the civilizing power of education, ideas, arts, and humane religions and creeds, seemed naïve—dated and silly. He tried to tell them that this stuff kept people faithful to their partners, driving like responsible citizens without murdering anybody, and willing to vote for something other than lower taxes. Your average poetry reader—if not your average poet—just wasn't a lane hopper, and what oboist would bother to pass someone just to go a couple of miles per hour faster?

But Vic could not convince them that a barbarous new age was dawning. "You'll see, Vic," said Susan, not stopping to think that Vic had to be at least eighty. "In music, in everything, amazing things are going to start happening. Anne thinks so, too," she insisted.

Alexei and Cora had taught Vic how to do research on the Internet using the computer in the library, and he came to admit that the Web had its place in a scholar's life. But he still made fun of Mallory's dependence on her laptop.

"I never saw anyone erase as much as you do," Victor whispered to Mallory one day at twilight, watching her struggle, for once, to edit the printout of an essay with pencil. Vic pointed to rubber bits from Mallory's erasures that nearly covered the surface of the table between them. In the library, Vic himself took notes and edited with a pen and rarely struck out anything he had written. Mallory smiled apologetically and once more rubbed out the sentence that refused to say its piece.

She had left her laptop at home because everyone was going to dinner that night at Taci, where Alexei was scheduled to sing at 9:00 P.M. They had gathered in the library to wait for Louis to join them after work. Alexei was just finishing a chess lesson. Susan was whispering with Cora about bulges in the backs of stringed instruments.

"Do me a favor," said Vic. "Here. Take this pen. Do it with this pen."

"I can't. I wouldn't have room to cross out and rewrite."

"Just do it—as a favor to me, the neighbor of the teacher of your future brother-in-law."

"I'm driving you crazy, aren't I." Mallory took the pen and sat thinking for five minutes. Then she crossed through a sentence, rewrote another one below it in the margin, and turned the page.

"Was that it? Was that the sentence you kept erasing?" Vic asked eagerly, in a forceful whisper.

"Hm? Yes. Oh, you think it was because I used a pen!"

"Of course. It forced you to think before you wrote. With pencils and with word processing, you keep putting down words and taking them away. You don't go anywhere, but you feel busy. Did you know that, word for word, nobody today writes any faster and better on a word processor than people in the nineteenth century did with their pens? They were actually faster then! See, the pen commits you. The pen is like marriage. The word processor is like living together. I can guarantee you, based on a lifetime of experience, the pen is better. You keep it."

Mallory thanked him, but she wondered how a rational mind could deny that computers were faster. Louis, who had just arrived, stood behind Mallory's chair with his hands on her shoulders to listen to the end of this debate. She smiled up at him and then over at Susan and Alexei, who had begun a game of chess at Alexei's usual table, each profiled against the window, chin in hand. But they were concentrating too deeply to have heard.

AUTHOR'S AFTERWORD

The neighborhood of Morningside Heights and most of the institutions that play a role in this book strongly resemble their real-life counterparts and in most instances bear the same names. Nonetheless, as represented here, they are fictional, and I deliberately forsook verisimilitude again and again. To give just three of many examples that might be cited, 444 Riverside Drive is an imaginary address, the real Columbia University has no chancellor, and the real Metropolitan Opera (a rather different institution from the one in this book) did not present Verdi's *Macbeth* in 2002–03. The fictional characters in this book resemble some of the kinds of people who live in the real Morningside Heights, but none is based upon, or is intended to resemble, any real person or any events in the life of one.

LOVE, WORK, CHILDREN

Cheryl Mendelson

A Reader's Guide

An Interview with Cheryl Mendelson

Random House: What was the book that most influenced your life or your career as a writer—and why?

Cheryl Mendelson: Many books have mattered enormously to my life and work. *David Copperfield* by Charles Dickens would be one of several contenders for "most influential." I first read it when I was thirteen and have reread it dozens of times since. Both the story—of a child struggling alone and unaided, against frightening obstacles, to make his way in the world—and Dickens's way of telling the story became templates in my mind, the one for living and the other for writing.

RH: What are your ten favorite books, and what makes them special to you?

CM: My list of favorites is alphabetized so as to avoid the appearance of ranking. There are easily another thirty books I like as well as these, many by some of the same authors. I like all these classics of English, German, and Russian fiction for the same reasons: because they are works of the moral imagination, their characters and societies can matter deeply to me, and the person who tells me all about these people and places, the author, is the best company in the world—someone intelligent, compassionate, passionate, and remarkably skilled in observation, description, and narration.

Austen, Jane. *Emma*
Dickens, Charles. *David Copperfield, Great Expectations*
Dostoyevsky, Fyodor. *The Brothers Karamazov, The Idiot*
Eliot, George. *Middlemarch*

Hardy, Thomas. *Jude the Obscure, The Return of the Native*
Mann, Thomas. *Buddenbrooks*
Tolstoy, Leo. *Anna Karenina*

When I read nonfiction, I favor political and social analysis, like Thomas Frank's *What's the Matter with Kansas?* or Jared Diamond's *Guns, Germs, and Steel.*

RH: What types of music do you like?

CM: I listen to lots of music, especially Bach, opera (all periods), German lieder, chamber music, and rock, old and new.

RH: If you were part of a book club, what would the group be reading, and why?

CM: I'd like to read Jared Diamond's new book, *Collapse: How Societies Choose to Fail or Succeed,* which is about how various societies have destroyed themselves through ecological and social irrationalism. I read an extract about Easter Island that was as riveting as a crime thriller. The book sounds like it's full of things we all should know. I'm also a big fan of Alexander McCall Smith, and I imagine that his new book, *Friends, Lovers, Chocolate,* would be fun to share.

RH: What are your favorite kinds of books to give—and get—as gifts?

CM: To intimate friends, I give novels. When I know people's taste less well, I try to give them something brand-new (so I can be sure they don't have it yet) on a subject that interests them—like gardening or the Civil War or French antiques. I myself love getting cookbooks and novels that some congenial person has already tried and liked.

RH: Do you have any special writing rituals? For example, what do you have on your desk when you're writing?

CM: First, I go to a stationer's and buy two notebooks, a larger hard-backed one for writing sketches, ideas, and outlines, and a smaller soft-backed one for carrying around with me, in bag or pocket, in case of sudden flashes of thought. They must be narrow-ruled, and I write entirely in pencil—unless I'm really desperate. I've usually gotten lots of material into these by the time I sit down to the desk. On the first day at the computer, my desk is pristinely neat, with a fresh notepad, sharpened pencils, and maybe even a bud vase with some actual buds. I create a new directory on my computer and update my word processor and consider, again, buying a faster printer. (I always decide not to.) This orderly state of affairs lasts for at least several hours. Then the chaos and irrationality of the process take over, and I don't reorder things until a first draft is complete—maybe a year later. All these little rituals aspire to control and order a process that is frighteningly uncontrollable, and they are completely absurd.

RH: Many writers are hardly "overnight success" stories. How long did it take for you to get where you are today? Any rejection-slip horror stories or inspirational anecdotes?

CM: I published only in academic journals in philosophy until I was in my forties, but I had been writing fiction and poetry my whole adult life—without ever once trying to publish it, and rarely letting anyone read it. I burned my first novel, page by page, in a fireplace. A couple of others got thrown into the back of file cabinets and forgotten. My style and motifs changed dramatically from the time of my twenties until 2003, when I first published fiction. When I finally decided to try to publish nonacademic things, I was surprised that each book succeeded practically immediately. This still astonishes me. I'm not sure anyone could try to imitate this, as it all happened unplanned. But it should encourage people who are hoping for a late start.

RH: Give us three "good to know" facts about you.

CM: I was born and raised (until age thirteen) in Appalachian southwestern Pennsylvania, on a dairy farm outside a little mining town—a company town, where I went to school with the miners' children. When I saw New York City as a child, I fell in love with the place and vowed to get there someday, and finally did. But I feel like an immigrant, even in this city full of people from somewhere else and even in my own small circle. My differences from the people I know here are far greater than theirs from one another, from their point of view as well as my own. (It would take a book to explain how and why.)

RH: What else would you like your readers to know?

CM: I'm a walker. I take long walks—miles and miles, with iPod, small notebook, and pencil. I play the piano. Along with the rest of my family, I am a film fanatic. We spend astonishing amounts of time researching which films we'll watch on weekends at home.

RH: What are some of your favorite films, and what makes them unforgettable to you?

CM: *The Seventh Seal* evokes a childish terror of death and uses it to expand the viewer's moral compass, to make us more compassionate, more admiring of small acts of courage, more grateful.

    Casablanca is a favorite, even though I don't esteem it enormously highly as cinematic art. What interests me about it is how contemporary this story of love and courage and sin in a world of increasing horror is. It creates a style for dealing with these things which is equal parts cool, humor, and seriousness and which does not feel even remotely dated, even though, being upwards of fifty years old, it *should* feel dated and (I hope) someday will.

    I love the *Matrix* trilogy and discovered that I can happily rewatch these films as often as my adolescent son does. What fascinates me about them is the premise that inner (psychological) events can solve outer (social and political) problems—even though it's an idea I'm deeply skeptical of. The fascination, I think, comes from a real-life sense of helplessness in the face of the things that are wrong with the world.

RH: What are you working on now?

CM: I've just finished the third novel in my Morningside Heights trilogy.

RH: What are some of the challenges involved in writing a trilogy?

CM: Aside from the obvious ones of maintaining consistency over a triply wide span of characters, scenes, and motives, there is also the fact that more time goes by and things change as time passes—not only the author and her moods and ideas, but the world too. This particularly matters when you're writing about real places, as I have been in the

Morningside Heights trilogy. The first volume was written in 2000–2001, and Random House offered to publish the book in August 2001. We shook hands and went on summer vacation, intending to get down to the work of preparing the manuscript for publication after Labor Day. In the interim, of course, came September 11. I first spoke with my editor about the novel when we were all grieving deeply, and dust clouds still hung over lower Manhattan. This tragedy profoundly affected our attitudes—and readers' too, I'm sure. Suddenly, *Morningside Heights* was about a New York that was gone.

RH: Did September 11 affect *Love, Work, Children* too?

CM: September 11 contributed a strain of darkness to *Love, Work, Children*, despite the fact that the book is a comedy and ends happily. You see this in the characters' sense of threat from the world outside the city (a reverse of the tradition that saw the city itself as the threat) and in the murderous rage that is depicted in all the book's relations—intimate, social, and political. Real New Yorkers, mourning the deaths of thousands of innocent neighbors and trying to fathom the rage that led to their murders, were stunned to hear these crimes described, with considerable satisfaction, by both radical fundamentalist Christians in the United States and Islamists abroad, as punishment for our sins. Through characters who are all given very specific and realistic histories, psychologies, and societies, *Love, Work, Children* explores the universal feelings of exclusion, inferiority, and humiliation that led to this kind of rage in so many contexts, rage with the potential to issue in murder or in cruel attempts to re-create those painful feelings in others.

RH: Are your characters based on real people? Where do you get them? Do you have favorites?

CM: I am always asked this, and I have no adequate answer. My characters are not based on real people, although occasionally (not typically) I draw on real incidents. They come into my head all by themselves, feeling very real, with complicated psychologies and life histories. When they are written up and a book is done, sometimes I see resemblances between characters and people I know, and sometimes I don't. Like many other authors, I become deeply attached to my people, miss them when I have to pay attention to other things, and mourn them when I move on. And they are like my children. I love them all, even the unlovable ones.

RH: Do any of the characters in *Love, Work, Children* reappear in the third volume of the trilogy?

CM: Yes, indeed. The Braithwaite family and Peter Frankl play prominent roles in the last book. There are also appearances by other characters from the first volume. Greg Merriweather has a central role in number three, and Morris and Merrit and Jonathan and Lily appear briefly.

Questions and Topics for Discussion

1. Why does Peter think he has to stay married to Lesley? Can you defend his thinking?

2. Some characters in the book choose meaningful work over money or status, and some make the opposite choice. How important is it to have work you believe in?

3. What do you think is Peter's biggest flaw? What does *he* think it is?

4. Do you think it's typical for siblings to be as different as Susan and Louis are? Do you know any siblings who, like them, were raised by their parents to be so different?

5. Why does Susan think she has to stay married to Chris? Is Susan weak?

6. How do you react to Alexei's unrealistic self-confidence?

7. What makes Louis a sympathetic character? What are his negative qualities?

8. Does Mallory make a bad decision when she refuses to get involved with Alexei?

9. Do Mallory's parents practice the values they preach?

10. Louis tells Mallory he wants to marry her before they have a single date. Do you think he is really in love with her at this point? Why

do you think he gets interested in Mallory at the age of thirty-two—after knowing her most of his life?

11. Why does Hilda play roles?

12. Which characters in the book are snobs? What are they snobbish about—for example, money, art, social background, or academic or professional status? Cheryl Mendelson seems to think that snobs destroy the things they're snobbish about. Do you agree?

Photo: Jerry Bauer

CHERYL MENDELSON received her PhD in philosophy from the University of Rochester and her JD from Harvard Law School. She has practiced law in New York City and taught philosophy at Purdue and Columbia universities. She is the author of *Home Comforts: The Art and Science of Keeping House* and the novel *Morningside Heights.* She lives in New York City.

A BOUT THE TYPE

This book was set in Centaur, a typeface designed by the American typographer Bruce Rogers in 1929. Centaur was a typeface that Rogers adapted from the fifteenth-century type of Nicolas Jenson and modified in 1948 for a cutting by the Monotype Corporation.